Y0-CCP-000

Book II

Gom Marsh is all grown up, but he looks years younger than he is. A police officer, he works undercover as a high school student to help fight the extreme bullying cases that school staffs can't solve. The work is heartbreaking and wearing, but lucky for Gom, there's a new man in his life. Casey Tanner, though, doesn't like to be touched. That could be a problem. Gom's still at Scarcity Sanctuary to keep up his cover, so Soldier and Dillon are always there to help. Can Casey redeem himself after a bad first impression? Hopefully so, Gom needs him.

MLR PRESS AUTHORS

Featuring a roll call of some of the best writers of gay erotica and mysteries today!

M. Jules Aedin	Maura Anderson	Victor J. Banis
Jeanne Barrack	Laura Baumbach	Alex Beecroft
Sarah Black	Ally Blue	J.P. Bowie
Michael Breyette	P.A. Brown	Brenda Bryce
Jade Buchanan	James Buchanan	Charlie Cochrane
Jamie Craig	Kirby Crow	Dick D.
Ethan Day	Diana DeRicci	Jason Edding
Angela Fiddler	Dakota Flint	S.J. Frost
Kimberly Gardner	Roland Graeme	Storm Grant
Amber Green	LB Gregg	Drewey Wayne Gunn
David Juhren	Samantha Kane	Kiernan Kelly
M. King	Matthew Lang	J.L. Langley
Josh Lanyon	Clare London	William Maltese
Gary Martine	Z.A. Maxfield	Timothy McGivney
Lloyd A. Meeker	Patric Michael	AKM Miles
Reiko Morgan	Jet Mykles	William Neale
Willa Okati	L. Picaro	Neil S. Plakcy
Jordan Castillo Price	Luisa Prieto	Rick R. Reed
A.M. Riley	George Seaton	Jardonn Smith
Caro Soles	JoAnne Soper-Cook	Richard Stevenson
Marshall Thornton	Lex Valentine	Haley Walsh
Missy Welsh	Stevie Woods	Lance Zarimba

Check out titles, both available and forthcoming, at
www.mlrpress.com

FOR
GOM'S SAKE

A Scarcity Sanctuary Book

AKM MILES

mlrpress

www.mlrpress.com

This book is a work of fiction. Names, characters, places, and incidents either are products of the author's imagination or are used fictitiously. Any resemblance to actual events or locales or persons, living or dead, is entirely coincidental.

Copyright 2011 by AKM Miles

All rights reserved, including the right of reproduction in whole or in part in any form.

Published by
MLR Press, LLC
3052 Gaines Waterport Rd.
Albion, NY 14411

Visit ManLoveRomance Press, LLC on the Internet:
www.mlrpress.com

Cover Art by Deana C. Jamroz
Editing by Kris Jacen

ISBN# 978-1-60820-315-4

Issued 2011

Thank you: Jeff, for your kind words and your stories. Jan, for your help and support. Lauren, for your valuable insights and help. Kris, for too many things to mention. Oh, and the fans who have waited, both patiently and not, for Gom to get his own story.

Thank you. ~ AKM

Dedication

To all of you who have seen this, heard about this, or lived this. Look at me putting that in the past tense. Maybe I should say see, hear, and are living this. The stories are different everywhere, but the pain is very real. I've seen acceptance and compassion getting better and it is my fervent prayer that it will continue do so and that young people will start believing that there is a way, and finding that way, to make a difference in their own lives.

CHAPTER ONE

Gom Marsh was resting in his room at Scarcity Sanctuary when he heard a soft knock at the door.

"Come in," he said, rolling over and facing the door.

Soldier stood there and Gom smiled when he saw him. Soldier always made him smile, inside and out. The man was everything to Gom, from the time he was eight years old and was a very broken child. Soldier and Dillon had, with love and compassion, put him back together. Now, at twenty-two, he still got the same warm feeling when he was with his dad. Soldier had adopted Gom and Tommy, another boy who'd been living with Dillon when Soldier first came to them. Soldier loved all the boys, but there had been something special about his feelings for he and Tommy and he took the name Marsh with pride.

"Hey, Dad. What's up?"

"Casey's back," Soldier said, with a slight frown. Gom's heart raced at the mention of Casey's name.

"Is Trick here? I didn't see him when I came in," Gom was already up and heading to the door. He'd only been lying down for a few minutes. It had been a long day and he was gearing up for the evening. He had to be back at Willington High for a ballgame.

"Trick's been in the gym for almost an hour. It's time to pull him out before he works himself to death. That boy is determined to bulk up like Randy. At least he's eating more now," Soldier said, as they walked together toward the stairs, heading down to the main floor.

Gom's heart thudded as he got closer. He didn't question it anymore. For some reason, any time he even thought about Casey Tanner, his heart rate increased and his breathing slowed. It was a strange effect, like he was trying to make himself stay calm, when there wasn't any reason to be, *not* calm. Was there?

This was only the third time he'd seen the man. Gom had been there when Casey came to ask if he could bring a kid to them who was living on the street and again when he showed up with Trick.

Both times, Gom had left the details to Soldier and Dillon and he'd quietly and avidly studied Casey Tanner. The man had this hair that Gom was dying to touch. It was long and wavy, not curly, but it was thick and lay in rolling waves down past his shoulders. Casey'd worn it down when he'd been here and Gom had been intrigued with getting his hands into it. Casey's eyes were what Gom called Husky blue, a light blue that reminded him of the eyes of a Husky dog. With that blond hair, and his obviously naturally-dark skin, the effect was stunning, to Gom at least.

Gom had also done a serious study of Casey's body. He wasn't very tall, which was a plus since Gom was a small man, too. Most men towered over him. Casey had a thin body that looked like it had been honed by hard knocks. He looked weathered, like a much older man, though Gom believed that Casey was near his age, maybe a little older. Despite his small size, Casey gave off the vibe of being able to take care of himself. His shoulders were much wider than his hips, giving him a very sexy shape. Gom could easily see himself being held in those arms and pressed against that chest.

One thing that really held his interest was Casey's hands. They were fairly large with long thin fingers. He wanted to hold hands with Casey Tanner. Just the thought of the simple gesture had him kind of freaked out. Besides, there was that mark on Casey's left hand right below the bottom knuckle of his thumb, between it and his simple black Timex watch. At first Gom had thought it was just a bit of dirt or something slashed across his hand, but it was always there, making him think it might be a birthmark or maybe a tattoo. It was a long thin line with what looked like dots or letters, but it was so small that Gom hadn't been able to make it out. *That's a goal*, he thought. Find out what that was on Casey's hand.

Casey was standing by the door, as usual, waiting for them to approach. He looked like he was two seconds from bolting, but his gaze was determined, as if he would not allow his instincts to take over. He was in control. It was clear to Gom that it was a matter of pride for Casey that he faced what came without letting his uneasiness show. He wondered what had made Casey so skittish around people.

"Hey, Casey," Gom said, smiling, wondering if Casey ever did. Smile.

"Hey. Came by to check on Trick. He doing okay?" Casey hadn't moved from the door.

Soldier went back to fixing supper for the crew that was staying here now and any of the regulars that would show up on any given night. Gom's home was a facility called Scarcity Sanctuary that Soldier and Dillon managed together. To the many boys who had been through there, it was just home. When Gom first came here, it wasn't quite the well-set-up situation it was now, but it had been a sanctuary nonetheless. There had been seven boys back then and despite coming from seven separate kinds of hell, they became a family.

Soldier and Dillon never knew when Bart, Jack, J, Randy, or even Tommy and Daniel, would stop by for a meal and to share their day's news. Four of the original ones had left the house and were living on their own. Well, Jack, Bart, and Randy shared a house a few blocks over from here and J was living with his girlfriend right now. The family was expecting to hear that they were getting married anytime. Ben was still here, in college, and helping Daniel at the shelter when he wasn't working in the theater department. The first seven stayed in close touch with each other and they heard, at one time or another, from most of the boys who'd been through here. Soldier and Dillon made a lasting impression on everyone they helped. It had to do with love, compassion, and respect; things that were new to the boys who showed up here, sometimes with overwhelming needs.

Tommy and Daniel lived in the apartment that Soldier had originally built for himself in the other section of the sanctuary.

Daniel Anderson ran the shelter that acted as a go-between with the social services system and kids who needed more than the normal foster care program provided. They were sickeningly happy and worked together in the social services area. Tommy was a counselor for troubled kids, and assisted Daniel at the shelter, often helping to set up boys who needed Soldier and Dillon's expertise in helping those boys who had especially torturous pasts.

Gom answered Casey's question, saying, "Yeah, man, Trick's doing great. He's going to school and the new start is helping. He's safe here, Casey, thanks to you. Would you like to join us for supper, maybe see how well Trick has settled in here? We'd love to have you, huh, Soldier?" Gom turned to his dad, who was moving about the kitchen setting things out for one of their favorite meals. "It smells great in here. I love when you make tacos. There's always plenty," he said, looking back toward Casey, who looked like he was ready to book.

"Nah. I gotta go. Things to do, you know?" Casey started to leave.

"Casey," Gom said, stepping closer and touching Casey's arm near his shoulder, "please stay and eat with us. We'd love to have you. We never know who's going to show up. It's not really formal here and everyone's welcome."

Casey didn't jerk away from Gom's touch. It was more that he slid out from under it in a smooth gesture. "I don't need anybody takin' care of me. I just wanted to make sure Trick was doing better is all." He seemed firm in his refusal. Just as he started to reach for the door, Trick came in from the hall and saw them.

"Casey, hey! Are you here for supper with us? Look, we're having tacos. Soldier makes the best ones ever. I'm glad to see you." Trick came over and in a surprising move, put his arms up and went to hug Casey, who stepped back quickly, leaving Trick with his arms up in an embarrassing gesture. The rejection showed clearly on Trick's face and Gom was upset. That was the first time he'd ever seen Trick even act like he was going to hug someone and it had been instinctive.

"Sorry. I'm sorry," Trick turned away. Gom was at a loss. He looked from an embarrassed and harried-looking Casey to a sad Trick to a pissed-off Soldier. Damn it! Casey's gesture had probably set Trick back considerably. Being able to make a spontaneous move like Trick had came hard for the young man and it had been met with what Gom considered callous disregard, not something he found to be a good or caring thing, especially from a man that Gom was finding interesting. He was very disappointed.

Gom looked at Casey and tried not to let his feelings show as Soldier set about trying to get them all past the small scene that had taken a toll on Trick. Gom turned from Casey, afraid his face would show how disheartened he was by Casey's move.

"Trick, help me chop the lettuce. I'll do the onions. No crying in my kitchen, huh? Gom, you're on dicing the tomatoes, and Casey, if you're staying, you can get a bowl for the shredded cheese and open the black olives. Oh, and get out the sour cream and the guacamole. Let's hop to, boys. This meat and the refried beans are almost ready. We've got tortillas, regular taco shells, and those bowl-shaped ones you like, Gom. They're ready to come out of the oven, by the way. Here, Casey, take this and grab them before they burn." Soldier handed Casey a potholder and pointed to the oven where there was a large tray of the bowl-shaped taco shells just getting brown.

Gom didn't look to see if Casey did as requested. He got his tomatoes and started dicing. It took a lot. He was a little ticked at Casey for the way he'd hurt Trick. Would it have hurt him to accept the gesture from the younger boy, especially since it wasn't something Trick did easily? Trick was seeing Tommy and making some headway in losing some of his isolationist behaviors and fears. Gom could see him really making an effort to fit in with the others at the place. There was no doubt in his mind that Soldier and Dillon, with Tommy and Daniel's help, could help Trick become another success story. He kept working with his head down.

They had big bowls of each item that went into the delicious tacos. He heard the oven door open and out of the corner of his eye he saw Casey's arm setting the shells and bowl-shaped tacos down on the trivets on the counter. He refused to smile at Soldier's clever mind. Maybe Casey had realized what a mistake he'd made and the hurt he'd caused and was trying to make up for it, even though Gom knew he wouldn't be comfortable working with them all in the kitchen. He got the impression that Casey didn't play well with others.

"Thanks, Casey. Guac's in the red bowl with the white top and sour cream's on the door. I hope you like tacos and I hope you're hungry. I've got enough meat here for the football team. Leftovers are fine, but it's all better when it's fresh. Good job on the lettuce, Trick, I like it chopped fine so it's easier to eat in the tacos. Randy and J are coming tonight. J's Beth is going out with some friends for supper so he's going to pick Randy up at the gym and be over in a few minutes. Dillon should be back in time, too, but Daniel is working late at the shelter tonight. Tommy's with him."

Gom didn't know where his other dad had been, but he was liable to show up with anything from another boy who needed them to a trunk full of food for them to help bring in. He finished with the big bowl of tomatoes and put it in line after Trick's lettuce. The door opened behind them and Dillon came in with a big smile on his face and only one bag from the grocery.

"I know that grin," Soldier said, "You've got something sweet in there."

"Brownies, ice cream, hot fudge. Anybody up for dessert?" Dillon said, walking over to Soldier, giving him a quick kiss, and opening the freezer to put the ice cream away. Gom looked to Casey and saw his eyes quickly widen then he turned away to hide his expression. Gom couldn't tell if it was disapproval or embarrassment.

"Oh, hi Casey. Good to see you again," Dillon said. "Mmm, tacos. I can't wait. You're staying for supper, aren't you?"

"I, uh, can't. I need to go. I just, he told me to, uh, help and…" Casey trailed off, ending his explanation.

"Oh no, anyone who helps, eats. Join us for supper, Casey. You don't have to worry, Trick and Ben have clean up duties tonight. Gom, show him where the plates are and you all can get the table set. I hear car doors so I bet the gang's all here. Perfect timing; I like that." Soldier just assumed his request would be met and swiveled around to turn off the stove, leaving the meaty mixture ready with a big spoon in it for dishing it up. He put the hot beans in a bowl and added it to the line on the counter, stood back, rearranging a couple of the bowls for a better order in the construction of the perfect taco.

J and Randy came in talking and Gom got two big hugs. The same was distributed to Dillon, Soldier and Trick. Ben and Niko showed up as if by magic to get in on the hugfest. They all looked at the new guy in the room.

"Hey, I'm Randy," said the tall, muscular man when he saw Casey, "and this is J. I own a gym on State Street, the Work Out. Come by any time. J here teaches at Crafton and he's missing his girlfriend tonight." Randy and J both shook Casey's hand.

"Guys, this is Casey Tanner. He brought Trick to us a couple of weeks ago. We owe him big time. He stopped to make sure Trick was doing okay and has been roped into joining us for supper. We'd better get to it while the hot stuff's still hot and the cold stuff's still cold. It's better that way. Come on, Casey, let's go wash up." Gom just acted like Casey had agreed to supper with them. He led him to a wash room off the kitchen and made short work of washing his hands, followed by each of the other men.

They were soon all seated around the table after having gone down the counter making tacos, one right after the other. Gom noticed that Casey chose the tortilla, while he and Ben liked the bowls. Everybody chose their favorites and started off with two and there was still plenty left for seconds. This was one of the few times that there were very few boys at Scarcity. Trick and Niko were the only two right now.

Randy was telling stories about some of the funny things that went on at the gym and J shared a tale about a girl fight at the elementary school where he and his girlfriend both taught. It was funny with his retelling of the names the girls were calling each other. Clearly, they'd been watching too much TV.

Casey didn't talk, but he did eat. Only when Gom got up to get a third taco, did Casey follow to do the same. Randy was on his fourth. Randy had always been a big eater. He was still making up for being hungry as a child. He'd decided to open a gym to keep in shape to support his appetite, saying if he didn't he wouldn't be able to get in the door.

"So, Casey, how'd you know to bring Trick to Scarcity? Soldier and Dillon are the best, huh, Trick?" J asked, leaving a question out there for both.

Trick, at seventeen, was a senior at Willington, having transferred there when he came to Scarcity and was doing much better at the new school. There was no truancy and no problems with classes now that he had help. He was catching up quickly. He was still prone to nightmares and was moody sometimes, but that was to be expected, considering his history.

"I'm happy here, really." Trick addressed his answer to Casey instead of J, who'd asked. "It's getting better. I never knew people could be like this, you know, being nice without expecting something back. You were right to make me come here. I had it pretty bad. I owe you. I know that." Trick's speech was the most that Gom had ever heard him say at one time.

After Casey's rejection earlier, Gom was proud of Trick for speaking his thanks so eloquently.

"Nobody owes me anything. I just wanted you to be safe. Your life was shit. Uh, sorry." Casey ducked his head.

"Not a problem. We've all been there, believe me." Randy looked around the table and then back to Casey. "None of us had it any better before coming here. We all have horror stories that we got past with Dillon and Soldier's help."

"All of you?" Casey asked and then looked surprised that he'd expressed the interest.

"Oh, yeah. Us, and so many more through the years have had their lives turned around. We won't go into it, but abuse and neglect are nothing new to any of us. It doesn't freak us out anymore. You can rest assured that you did a good thing by urging Trick to come here. Soldier worked hard at getting the paperwork all done to foster him and change his school." J nodded to Soldier and Dillon, both of whom had remained quiet, listening to the conversation around them.

"Casey, what do you do? How'd you know about Trick?" Randy asked.

"Um, I've got a couple of jobs. I work at the theater on Main and I clean a couple of offices at night to make some extra money." Casey looked down at his now empty plate.

"Oh my God, you work at the Showhouse?" That was Ben speaking up. Ben was in college, majoring in theater and English Lit. His dream was to write and direct plays. He had worked on every play the college players put on, doing everything from set design and construction to lighting and sound. He loved everything about stories, movies, and plays. It had begun as pure escape from his own life into those of the ones he saw on TV. After being escorted to a couple of plays by Soldier and Dillon, he had fallen in love with all things theater and been hooked since.

"Yeah, for about three years. You like theater?" Casey responded.

The laughter at the table at that question was quick and filled with fondness and they all looked at Ben.

"What?" Casey looked confused.

"Ben lives for the theater. He knows all the lines from all the plays, musicals, and shows that he's watched over and over. He's got the best collection of anyone I've ever seen," Gom said, proud of his foster brother.

"Uh, yeah..." Casey mumbled, "Cool."

"My brother, Tommy, used to sing songs for us when we were growing up. A lot of them were from musicals that we watched, mostly Disney then, but Dillon and then Ben got us hooked on all the old Hollywood and Broadway musicals." Gom looked fondly at both Ben and Dillon as he spoke.

"Time for dessert," Dillon spoke up. "Ben, get the ice cream, Trick grab the box of brownies, and J, if you'll heat the chocolate, we'll be good to go. Randy, Gom, and Casey, let's clear this table and get dessert bowls out. Just rinse and stack the dishes by the sink."

For some reason, Casey seemed okay with following orders and he helped clear the table. Gom noticed Soldier watching him intently. Casey didn't joke around and bump into the others like the rest of them, but he moved back and forth, and then sat quietly when everything was ready for the treat. Trick had placed a big brownie into each bowl and set them in front of everyone. Ben scooped a big blob of vanilla ice cream on top, and J followed behind, pouring hot fudge over the top. All of a sudden, Randy hopped up and went to the refrigerator and reached in, saying, "Aha!"

They all laughed when he pulled out the jar of cherries. He opened it, poured off the juice and dumped them into a bowl. He went around the table and put a cherry on top of everyone's dish.

"Perfect," he stated, when he finished. He'd put three on his treat, finishing off the contents of the cherry bowl.

For a few minutes the only sounds were hums, slurps, and soft grunts as they all enjoyed the delicious dessert. Pretty much as one they all sat back and sighed, some patting their stomachs.

"That was wonderful, Soldier. Thanks for fixing it. It's one of my favorite meals," Gom said.

"I know," said Soldier, smiling at him. Like there was anything about Gom that Soldier didn't know. The love and respect he felt for this man was bigger than anything in his life. It just filled him up.

Casey scooted back from the table and Gom figured it was time to let him go. Gom couldn't believe that Casey had stayed through dessert. He wondered where Casey lived.

"Thanks for staying for supper, Casey. I think it meant a lot to

Trick. You never said how you know him," Soldier said.

"That's his story to tell, if he wants to. I gotta go. Uh, thanks for the meal. It was really good." Casey was out the door before anyone could say anymore.

They all looked at Trick to see if he would elaborate on the story of Casey and how he came to be at Scarcity Sanctuary.

"Um, I was sort of sleeping behind the theater. It's kind of protected back there, not a lot of drunks or jerks hanging around." Trick's hands were shaking so he held them together tightly as he went on. "Casey saw me a couple of times and then I started to find little bits of food left back there, safely wrapped so I knew it was for me. He came out one time and sat down by me and asked if I wanted to go somewhere safe. I was too scared to believe him." Trick stopped, not looking at anyone. He scooted back from the table and headed for the sink. "The night he brought me here it was raining hard and I just didn't have the strength to turn down the idea of being warm…and safe. That's all."

No one believed that was all, but, too, no one asked for more details. A young man of seventeen didn't live on the street unless home was worse and they'd all been there, done that.

While Trick and Ben cleaned the kitchen Gom prepared to go to the football game at the high school. Soldier came in while he was changing clothes, grabbing a school jacket.

"Have you made any headway into finding out the source of the bullying at Willington?" Soldier asked.

"I'm getting closer. Bradley is very quiet, even withdrawn. I've seen a few kids making a wide berth around him in the halls, but haven't seen the actual aggression that was reported." Gom paused by the door, leaning on the facing and looking up to Soldier. "The guy's a little overweight, bad skin, cheap clothes; all three things that make him a target. I've heard kids call him Stink, and he does have a bit of a problem with odor. Put it together and you've got great fodder for the fools who get off on hurting someone weaker. He barely speaks in class, and then mumbles when he does. I think he'd fade into walls if he could. I can't imagine him doing or saying anything to warrant the threats and meanness that have been directed his way. He's kind of a loner."

"Keep an eye out tonight. I know things tend to happen more at events like this than during the school day. You think Bradley'll be there?" Soldier asked.

"I hope so. High school football is so not my thing." Gom laughed as he said it. He was five foot seven and weighed about one hundred and twenty pounds. He'd always been small for his age and the fact that he looked like a young teenager made his job that much easier.

Gom had majored in both criminology and social work in college. For the last year he'd been working a special program with the police department, social services, and the school systems in the surrounding counties as well as the ones nearby. He worked undercover, enrolling as a senior at the high school when there was a report of severe bullying that the school personnel felt they couldn't get a handle on. For once, Gom's small stature and young look was in the plus column, making him perfect for the job he had.

"Poor thing. Why do I get the feeling you'd rather check out what's going on at the Showhouse?" Soldier teased.

"I don't know. Why do you get that feeling?" Gom knew he couldn't hide anything from Soldier and he was interested in Casey Tanner. The man intrigued him, no doubt about it. The fact that he was drop dead gorgeous didn't hurt a thing. To top it all off, Casey wasn't that much bigger than Gom, where most twenty-two year olds towered over him and beat his weight by a good forty pounds or more.

"I'd like to know more about him," Soldier said.

"Relax. It's not like we're dating or anything. I just think it was a good thing for him to do, bringing Trick here. I don't even know how he knew about us. Can you believe he ate supper with us? I was sure he was going to leave. You're good, Soldier," Gom said, giving credit where it was due. "I know how upset you were when he didn't accept the hug from Trick. I couldn't believe Trick even offered it. It looks like Casey may have some issues of his own."

"Yeah, looks like. I didn't want to make a big deal about it, but it did hurt Trick and you know how I feel about anyone hurting any of my boys." Soldier didn't try to hide the frown Casey's action had caused. "He made an effort though, by staying for supper and trying to fit in. He's an interesting man. I'll give you that. You be careful, Gom. I can tell you're more than a little bit fascinated with Casey."

Gom blushed as he faced his dad, for the first time admitting that he was interested in another man. They all knew that Gom was gay, but they also knew that he hadn't acted on it or even been interested in anyone in particular. Gom had spent the last five years, since realizing that he was "of the persuasion" working on his schooling and helping the others. He'd never even felt the need for a relationship. Maybe that was about to change.

"I am, I admit, fascinated, that is. He's a very strange and different kind of person. He has to be a good man to have bothered to leave food for Trick and then to bring him to us. That says good things about him. I'm not going to go jump his bones or anything. You don't have to worry about me. I would like to get to know him better, though. As you say, he intrigues me."

"That's a good thing, Gom, really. I'd be happy to see you with someone, but I want to know that the someone won't hurt you. I know you're a man now and that you won't always live here. It works for now with your job, but when you move out, I want to know it's a good situation."

It might be odd that, at twenty-two, he still lived at home, but as Soldier said, it worked well with his job right now and before he'd been away at college and officer training, so he was in and out and the time he was home, he wanted to be here with his family. He would never make apologies for that.

"You're not going to like, check him out or anything, are you?" Gom asked, watching Soldier intently.

"No, I'll leave your relationship to you, if you have one with him. But I'll be watching and if he hurts you, all bets are off." Soldier smiled, to soften the threat, but Gom didn't doubt for a minute that he was serious. Instead of bothering him as it might other people, it merely warmed Gom's heart. Soldier'd always had his back, from the first night he'd met the man.

"I've got to get out of here. Football. Go team," he said in a droll voice.

"You're doing a good thing, Gom. I'm proud of you," Soldier said, touching Gom's shoulder.

"I know you are. Making you proud is one of the things that makes me very happy, you know?" Gom leaned in for a quick hug, knowing it would be there for him.

"Yeah, I know. Now, go on, Monty Marshall. I don't know how you get used to answering to that name."

"You got used to Soldier after being Keith Marsh for most of your life. You had your reasons for wanting to be Soldier and I have mine for wanting to be Monty when I'm working."

Soldier had explained that after his injuries in the war he had felt very alone and very anonymous. The fact that he was a soldier was what defined him, made him feel like he was somebody who was worthy. He'd spent the time after his many surgeries moving around Texas and checking on various properties, pretty much alone, still, and cut off from relationships. The fact that he had boogoodles of money hadn't meant squat to him at the time. It was only later that he found that it came to a useful and fulfilling purpose.

He'd found Dillon and the boys occupying one of the properties he owned and that's how they'd all met. When he introduced himself, it was as Soldier. He hadn't gone into details then about how the name had given him an identity that meant more to him that Keith Marsh did after all he'd been through in the war. None of them had cared about the whys of his name, they just loved the way he cared for them so deeply and fought for them so aggressively. He was their hero. It was as simple as that.

In Gom's case, he wanted to be someone else when he was working. He didn't want any of the unkindness and sometimes outright hatred to follow him home. He was truly amazed at the rampant amount of bullying that went on. Most of it wasn't reported because the targeted kids never told anyone, but he'd seen it so many times in the last year. He'd been in two schools already. Willington was his third.

The degree of threats that Bradley Haines was experiencing was troubling. The staff at the school hadn't been able to discover the cause of the intense level of threatening behavior Bradley was being forced to endure. Gom wondered why he continued to come to school. He was going to try again to make contact with Bradley. All of his previous attempts had been met with quiet, but firm rejection. Bradley didn't socialize.

CHAPTER TWO

When he got to Willington the noise level increased the closer he got to the stands. His eyes moved from side to side, taking in everything as he walked slowly. He spoke to a couple of teachers and several other seniors as they headed for the concessions or the bathrooms. Gom knew to check out the areas under the stands and the bathrooms for any gang or bullying activity. After looking in both places he was beginning to think that Bradley hadn't come to the game.

Seeing the school safety officer leaning against the fence watching the crowd in the bleachers, Gom decided to make another trip through the darker areas. As he neared the blackest corner at the far left under the bleachers he heard voices, loud, taunting voices. He stayed hidden but crept closer.

"You're a filthy punk. You got no business being around the rest of us. I told you to stay away from here. Are you deaf as well as stupid?" The voice, Gom knew, belonged to a senior named Tony Ramirez. He was a good looking Hispanic whose family was very well off and liked to show off. Taylor Jackson stood with him, black, very muscular and also from a wealthy family. These two were examples of money not buying happiness. They were two of the most miserable people Gom had ever seen. The other two kids were Bobby Dean and Andy Bartow, both quieter, mostly followers. Maybe they were in training.

He wondered why, if they'd told Bradley not to show at the ballgame, he had. He also wondered why they'd told him not to come. What was it to them?

"Answer me, asshole. You smell like dirty diapers most of the time and you're uglier than a mud fence. You got a big mouth, too. You been talkin' where you should o' kept your mouth shut. Why don't you tell me what you've been saying about me? I want to know and you're going to answer me or I'll have Taylor here beat it out of you."

There was no answer from Bradley. Gom didn't know if that was wise or…not.

"Shit, you make me sick. You skulk around the halls, never talking to anybody, all moody and shit. You're probably a psycho, one of those quiet ones that'll come in one day and shoot up the cafeteria. Is that you, Bradley Asshole? You got a gun at home? Got a list of baddies you want to take out during lunch one day? Why don't you just stay home with your drunk dad and your whore mom and leave us with clean air?"

The whole time that Tony was talking the four kids were circling Bradley. Every once in a while one or the other would reach out like they were going to hit Bradley, pulling back just before making contact. Just enough to make him flinch each time, keeping him in a state of fear and anxiety.

Gom was trying to think of a way to diffuse the situation when he heard Bradley say something.

"What? Speak up, queer. What did you say?" Tony got closer to Bradley, grabbing him by the shoulders and shaking him.

Gom's heart rate increased as he thought he would have to step in.

"My mom's dead and she wasn't a whore. I can't stay at home. I had to bring Missy with me. Please let me go. She's going to be scared." Bradley's voice was quiet and shaky.

"Missy? Who's Missy? Is Missy a sissy like you?" Gom hated that word after his last job at Bardstown High.

"My sister. Please let me go," Bradley was unable to hide his fear. Gom didn't know where Missy was, but this was getting out of hand.

"Why don't you bring Missy to us and maybe we'll let you go this time. How are your ribs, by the way?" Tony asked, snidely.

"They hurt, all right? And you stay away from my sister. You do whatever you have to with me, but you touch her and I *will* find a gun." Bradley's voice was suddenly more firm.

The word gun had Gom preparing for action. He stepped out

from behind the large concrete pillar that had hidden him. He walked quickly like he'd just come up.

"Bradley, hey, there you are. Missy's looking for you. She's getting a little scared, man. I told her I'd find you for her. You better come on or she's going to start crying." Gom looked at Tony and the rest of them. "Hey guys, you're missing a good game." With balls he didn't look like he had he walked right through them and took Bradley's arm and started to lead him away from the group.

"Hey, another little queer. Is this your boyfriend, Bradley baby? You all make a sweet couple. Monty is prettier than you are, but hell, anybody is." Tony started walking along with them, which was fine with Gom. They were headed toward light.

"We don't want any trouble, Tony. Come on, be cool. No problems here, okay? We need to go find his little sister." He walked faster, holding on to Bradley's arm. He looked at Bradley and said, "I thought we were going to meet at the concession stand. I looked all over for you."

"Ah, your boyfriend was missing you, Bradley. How does someone who stinks like you do even rate a date, even if it is with a queer?" Tony wasn't letting up.

Gom paused. "What makes you think I'm queer, Tony? I've never come on to you, have I? You're making assumptions based on my size and the fact that I'm what? Pretty? I thought everyone said you were good looking so does that make you queer, too?" He probably should have kept his mouth shut on that one.

"You fucking faggot! Get him, boys," Tony ordered, reaching out to swing at Gom.

Gom ducked and stepped away, pulling Bradley with him. He turned and faced the four, putting his hand out, saying, "You're also making the assumption that because I'm small I can't take care of myself, but that would be a mistake. I may not be able to take all four of you, but I guarantee I can put at least two or three of you in the hospital before this is finished if you don't back off right now."

Gom wasn't exaggerating at all. Five years ago, when he was seventeen, these boys' ages, he'd been viciously attacked and gay-bashed, left on the side of the road, literally torn up in body and spirit. When his body healed, Soldier had taught him many ways to fight, both clean and dirty. Soldier had been in the Army and knew lots of ways to hurt people. His dad didn't condone fighting unless it was in self-defense and then he expected it. He said no one was ever going to hurt one of his boys again. Gom had also had police training to add to his list of abilities in self protection. He was small, quick, and deadly if the situation called for it. It never had, but this might be the night.

"Woohoo! Listen to the little queer. You really think you can hurt any of us before we can take you out?" Tony sneered. They had gotten closer to the lights from the stadium now and Gom tried to figure out if they were close enough to run.

"I'd rather run away from you, than have to hurt you, but if you don't let us go, I'm not going to back down." It was as simple as that. As a police officer he was supposed to find a way to avoid situations like this, but it wasn't always possible and he wasn't about to blow his cover to keep from teaching these kids a lesson. He had too much more work to do to take a chance on them finding out about his program and making it impossible for him to continue.

"You make me laugh, little shit." Tony pointed to Bradley and said, "Bobby Dean, you and Andy hold on to Stinky there. Taylor, you be ready to back me up in case he gets a lick in. This little queer is due a takedown." Tony took a step toward Gom and Gom knew that he was going to swing at him.

Gom never gave him the chance. He flew into action before Tony got close enough to swing at him. Gom jumped and landed a kick to Tony's side, right below his ribs. Gom wasn't trying to break anything, just hurt him enough to let him know he meant business. Before Tony could get over the surprise of that Gom jumped back and swung low, sweeping both of Tony's legs out from under him. He landed hard and his mouth looked like a fish as he gasped for breath.

"More?" Gom asked, never taking his attention off Taylor, but posing the question to Tony.

"Taylor, damn it. Get him! He can't take you, too. Damn!" Tony was sitting up, holding his side.

Gom turned to Taylor and said, "Come on if you want to, but I *can* take you. I'm just sayin'."

Taylor looked like he wasn't sure what to do, but Tony yelled, "Taylor, Damn it! Motherfucker, kick his ass, or I'll kick yours!"

Taylor did what Soldier had told Gom to look for. He gave away his intent with his eyes and Gom was ready when Taylor came at him, bent low and head first to ram him in the stomach. Gom's knee came up just before Taylor made contact, snapping Taylor's head back. Gom stepped around him, grabbed his arm and pushed him, easily with Taylor's balance off, right down on top of Tony, who hadn't made it up yet. The two bigger kids were a tangle of arms and legs and grunts and curses.

Gom turned to the other two boys and they both, as if in a twin action, dropped Bradley's arms and held theirs up in surrender. They stepped back out of the way, eyes wide in wonder. Gom wasn't proud of having to resort to violence, and he figured he'd made things worse, but he wasn't going to get beat up, just to avoid a problem.

He looked at Bradley and they both turned and started walking away.

Tony yelled, "This isn't over, Marshall. You made a big mistake tonight. You better never be alone and you better watch your back."

Gom stopped, as did Bradley, and they turned to face Tony and his boys. "You're wrong. It is over. I don't think you're going to tell anyone that you got your ass kicked by a little queer boy like me. Trust me, if you come after me or Bradley again, there will be more than that waiting for you. You'll notice I'm not even breathing hard here. If you can't get along with people just avoid them from now on. Come on, Bradley, I hate violence. Let's go find Missy."

Gom turned again and they walked away. Shit. He'd just made an enemy. Tony would not be able to let this go. His stupid pride would demand that he get back at Gom and Bradley both for seeing his humiliation. Gom knew he was going to have a lot of paperwork after this evening's fiasco.

As they made it into the light and noise, Gom turned to Bradley.

"You okay? I'm sorry all that happened. They're even madder now, but when I got there and heard talk about guns I thought I had to step in. Promise me you won't get a gun and go after anybody, Bradley," Gom said.

"That was just talk, but they better not do anything to Missy." Bradley jerked liked he'd been prodded. "Missy! I've got to go." He started to leave and Gom touched his arm, asking,

"Can I come with you? I want them to see us together if they come out here. I don't want them to get a chance at getting you alone. We have to make our story good. Missy is your little sister, right?" Gom walked along with Bradley as he hurried away.

"Yeah, I left her with some of her friends and was going to get her a Coke and some popcorn. I saved up so she could have something at the game." Bradley was talking more than Gom had ever heard him. Adrenaline was still pumping through Gom so he figured the same was true of Bradley.

"Can I ask a question?" Gom went on before being told he couldn't. "I heard you say you couldn't stay at home and you had to bring your sister. Is something wrong at home?"

Bradley looked more scared than he had with the punks back there. Whoa! He would have to be careful here. He wished his brother, Tommy, was here. He knew how to talk to people without freaking them out.

"It's okay. Relax. I'm not anybody you need to be scared of, believe me. You don't have to answer me."

Bradley gulped. Gom actually heard it in a moment of silence as the band finished a song and the cheerleaders got ready to start a new yell.

"Where did you learn to fight like that? I wish I wasn't so scared all the time. I have to be able to take care of Missy." Bradley put his hand up to his mouth as if astonished that he'd let that much slip.

"Hey, relax, I told you. Here, come on and let's get Missy her drink and popcorn and get you settled back with her. I'll stay near until the game is over. I'll sit with you all if you'll let me, but if you're freaked out by me, I'll leave you alone."

"Alone. Hmm." That was all Bradley said as they headed for the concession stand.

"How'd *they* get you alone?" Gom asked.

"I was heading here and they just sort of surrounded me and made me walk with them. Thank God they didn't even see Missy." Bradley kept walking and they got in line.

"Yeah, that was a little scary, Tony asking you to bring her to him." Gom shuddered at the thought of Tony's depravity let loose on a young girl, who was probably as scared as Bradley was.

While they were standing there, Gom could see Bradley thinking hard on something, sighing deeply, then taking a big breath and saying,

"Thank you for what you did. I owe you. They would have hurt me again."

Gom could tell he hated saying that.

"You don't owe me anything, Bradley. They mentioned your ribs. They've hit you before I take it," he said, knowing the truth.

"Yeah, they're always slapping at me or hitting me when no one can see. I'm usually covered in bruises, not that you can tell the difference between them and the ones I get at home. Oh, God, why did I say that? Ignore that last part." Bradley looked amazed that he had revealed even more about his life to someone he barely knew.

"I wish I could, but it sounds like a bad scene to me. Is that why you have to bring Missy here, so she won't be left home with your parents? Bradley, trust me, I've been there. Really, I know where you're coming from." Gom wouldn't go into his past, but he would admit that much to try and form a bond with Bradley.

"Yeah, right."

"Hey, how'd you all get here? You need a ride home?" Gom changed the subject quickly as they got nearer to the counter.

"We live close enough to walk. I, well, I wouldn't for myself, but if you don't mind. I can't think of them waiting for us and getting their hands on Missy. I would never ask you if it wasn't for her," Bradley said, making himself clear.

"I got that, and you didn't ask. I offered. I'm hungry, how about you?" Gom said, and saw it clear as day in Bradley's eyes

But instead of just accepting, he said, "No, I just have enough for Missy's. I'm good."

"Come on, I feel like celebrating. I'll buy ours and you can get Missy's. I want Nachos. You want that or a hot dog and fries?"

"I'll take a plain hamburger, no fries. I'm too fat as it is."

Gom was just happy that he was accepting anything. It seemed that Bradley wasn't a loner so much as just alone. All of Gom's earlier attempts to talk with him had been met with cool withdrawal. Maybe this would give him a chance to get a handle on what caused the death threat spray painted on Bradley's locker. That was what had instigated his intervention into the situation.

The young woman in charge of the Safe-T program at the school was used to handling more common forms of bullying, but when it came to actual death threats, she felt like she needed more help. She'd been at the original meeting that was held last year where the police department met with the guidance/safety personnel from the surrounding schools to explain what was available to them in the way of Gom's assistance in this area.

Gom admired the way Bradley cared for his sister, but he'd like to get a better handle on what their home was like. He still questioned Bradley's statement that he had to bring his sister to the game. He tried to decide whether to tune down the interest so as not to scare Bradley or to push for more information, since they were in a nasty situation to begin with.

After getting their food orders, Gom followed Bradley up through the bleachers and nearly dropped his nachos when he saw the girl that Bradley handed the drink to. She was stunningly gorgeous, especially for such a young girl. As he stood by Bradley, she looked up at him with apprehension, and Gom was quick to make an introduction to relieve her obvious distress.

"Hey, you must be Missy. I'm Monty Marshall. I'm a new friend of Bradley's and I hope you don't mind if I sit with you for the game. I'm sort of new at Willington and don't have a lot of friends. Well, actually, none yet, but I was hoping Bradley might let me hang with him some. Is that all right with you? If not, I won't bug you all." Gom knew it sounded very weak and backward, but he was trying to ease her mind. She looked downright scared.

She looked first to Bradley and Gom saw the slightest nod of his head before she scooted over and made room for both of them to sit beside her.

Shyly, she spoke up, saying, "Hi. I'm glad to see Bradley with a friend. He's by himself too much."

Missy sounded like someone much older. He wondered how old she was. He went fishing.

"You're very pretty, Missy. I bet Bradley has a hard time keeping the guys away. What grade are you in now?" Gom asked, as he balanced the nachos on his lap and dipped one in the cheese. He crunched down and glanced at her, trying to look only mildly interested, just making conversation.

"Thank you. Evidently, I look a little too much like my mother," she said, with a small frown, then finished with, "I'm in fifth grade."

Gom almost choked on his cheesy corn chip. She looked like maybe an eighth grader at least. He coughed and said, "Wow. Bradley, my man, you're going to have a hard time in the next few years." To Gom, who was totally uninterested in the female form, Missy was pretty much developed and looked like what some of his brothers would refer to as "W-dream mat". Short for wet dream material. It was a little crude, but perfectly described a beautiful girl that made you want to dream about her and wake up satisfied. And this girl was what, ten, eleven at the most? He felt a little skanky for even thinking about it. And he wasn't even interested.

Gom looked at Bradley and saw this look on his face that pretty much said, "You have no idea!"

"Nice to meet you, Missy. Bradley agreed to let me take you both home after the game. I have a car. It's not much, but it gets me where I want to go and it's in good shape." Gom pretty much ignored what was happening on the field, since he had zero interest.

"That's nice. Thank you, uh, Monty." Missy had a soft pretty voice.

Gom let things go for a while, munching, offering some to both of them and finishing it off when they both declined. He set the trash between his feet for removal later and noticed that the half time show was just starting. When the band did the school's alma mater Gom could hear Missy singing along and he turned to her with awe again. She had a clear, sweet voice that rang with joy as she sang along, smiling.

He leaned toward Bradley and said, "Missy has a beautiful voice, too. You're going to have to keep an eye on her, huh?"

"Yeah, she's been singing since she was about three. God knows why, though. There's not much at the house that would make a person want to sing, but she's always been a happy girl, even though…" Bradley stopped and looked down, then back to Gom quickly, then shook his head a little like he couldn't believe he'd revealed so much.

Gom had that effect on people. They just wanted to talk to him. Maybe his honest care showed through and they felt safe letting their secrets and fears out to someone who wouldn't exploit them.

Gom shared, "It's okay. I know all about sucky home life, man.

Believe me. Not now, but when I was young, well, the suckiest, you know?" Gom never told anyone the extent of his horror before he went to live with Dillon at the old house with the other boys. But he didn't mind mentioning it in order to establish a rapport with someone. Whatever it took the get the kid's trust so he could help him, and now, it looked like helping them both.

"Really?" Bradley's voice held disdain, as if there was no way anyone could truly understand.

"My life turned around when I was eight. My mother died and I ended up, finally, with Dillon. Soldier came along and life was good. It took a while, but with their help, I got over all the bad stuff." Gom was talking in a low voice, not wanting to broadcast their conversation, but wanting Bradley to know there was hope. "Is it just the two of you, and your parents?"

"My mother died when Missy was a baby. I've been taking care of her since then." It was said matter-of-factly, like it was normal for an elementary school age boy to be responsible for the care of a baby.

"What about your dad?" Gom asked, quietly, knowing there was a real problem here.

"He's not…he didn't…uh, my mom's death kind of messed him up. It's okay. We deal." It sounded like Bradley didn't want to expound on the situation at home.

"I get it. So you and Missy are close. That's nice. I have lots of brothers, but I'm closest to one, Tommy. He and I both came from hell and grew up together after that with the two best dads in the world. One of them, Soldier, adopted both of us." Gom gave up a little more information, hoping for feedback.

"You have two dads? Is that weird?" Bradley didn't sound freaked out, just interested.

"Not weird at all. I knew Dillon first. He took care of a bunch of us boys in this old house. One day Soldier showed up and before long they were a couple and Soldier had enough money to build a big place for all of us. I grew up at Scarcity Sanctuary. Have you heard of it?"

Scarcity Sanctuary didn't garner a lot of media attention since Soldier was the sole form of financial security. He had enough money to keep it running probably through infinity. They didn't need to do fundraisers like some places so they didn't get a lot of notice, which is the way they wanted it. They worked with the social services system and took in boys that had too much baggage, too much trauma to deal with, to make a normal foster home a good choice.

"I think I've heard a little about it, but not much. It's kind of a home for boys, right?" Bradley asked.

"Yes, but boys that come from really bad situations who need special care and help. It's a good place. I love Dillon and Soldier more than anything on earth. And now I've told you more than I've ever divulged to anyone. How come I can talk to you so easily?" Gom was so sucking up, wanting reciprocation.

"It's okay. I'm not going to tell anybody. I kind of keep to myself a lot," Bradley said, then glanced over at Gom consideringly, then asked, "Are you gay?"

"Bradley! You can't ask him that," Missy said, obviously overhearing the question, though it had been asked quietly.

"It's okay, Missy. I am, but I don't broadcast it and I'm not in any kind of relationship or anything. Why," Gom asked Bradley, "does it bother you?"

"No, not at all. I don't look for reasons to separate people into boxes. I just wondered why those boys were teasing you. Man," Bradley's face lit for the first time ever as far as Gom remembered, "I can't believe you asked Tony Ramirez if he was queer."

"Not my smartest move, huh? Really pissed him off," Gom admitted. "You got any idea why he's after you in such a big way? What's he got against you?" Missy had turned to talk to a girl on her other side so Gom talked quietly with Bradley.

"I don't know. I honestly don't know. About three weeks ago he started picking on me, more than the regular stuff. It's gotten worse every day it seems. I'll be glad to graduate next spring and get away from all of them." Bradley's hands were shaking a little as he put his burger wrapper down with Gom's trash pile.

"Hey, I heard about what was on your locker a while ago. Do you know who did it? You think it was Tony?"

The meeting that Gom had with the Safe-T program coordinator, Laurie Summer came to mind. She'd called after "You die Stink!" appeared in dripping red paint on Bradley's locker. Bullying and taunting was one thing, bad enough in itself, but this was very serious. No longer did people think that something like that couldn't happen in their school, or their town. It happened.

"I don't know who did it. It was just there when I got to school one day. They took pictures of it and cleaned it off very quickly, but lots of kids had already seen it. So now, besides being avoided for other things, everybody thinks I'm seconds away from getting blown away, so I keep to myself. I'm even scared to have Missy with me, but I can't leave her at home. You might want to think twice about being even this close to me." Bradley looked over at Gom again and Gom could have sworn he saw hope in Bradley's eyes, hope that Gom wouldn't leave. Not a chance.

"I'm not scared. I like you, Bradley. Both you and Missy are nice. I'm not looking for anything but a friend, okay, so don't panic." Gom grinned at him, hoping to relieve his mind." Being this little and, as Tony said, pretty, makes me a target sometimes, too. I've just learned to take care of myself."

"Yeah, about that," Bradley said. "I wish I could do that, you know, feel safe. I'd like to be able to protect Missy and myself if I have to. Where'd you learn all that?"

Gom couldn't tell him where he'd learned all of it, the police department training, but he could share another secret and let him know a little more about himself. He took a deep breath and bared a little more of his soul to Bradley, feeling instinctively that Bradley wouldn't ever tell his story.

"When I was younger, I got gay-bashed. I was really badly beaten and it took a long time for me to get over it, both physically and mentally. I'd never even thought much about it, much less acted on it, but this guy's mother had a hate on for what my dads do and for gays in general and she had him and his buds beat the crap out of me. They left me on the side of the road. It was bad, man, really bad." Gom took another deep breath, forcing the pictures out of his head.

Bradley was looking at him with bug eyes. He didn't say anything for the longest time. Around them the game went on with the occasional yells or groans from the crowd. The band, the cheers from the girls down front, all of it was just background noise. It seemed like they were in a cocoon of quiet and shared pain.

"I'm really sorry that happened to you." Bradley looked sincere.

"It's over. Soldier was in the service and he knows a lot about fighting and he taught me, and has taught all the boys how to defend themselves in ways that most people don't know. He taught us to never instigate a fight, but he made sure we could handle ourselves if we couldn't avoid one." Gom sat up straighter as he continued, "I'm not scared anymore. I could see if he'd maybe be able to help show you some things, if you want. But I want to ask something in return." Gom decided to go for it and just ask some direct questions.

Bradley looked at him, again not saying anything for a few minutes.

"What do you want to know?" he finally asked, defensively.

"Why you said you had to bring your sister to the game. I thought maybe she was a cheerleader or something and she had to be here. And, this is a big one. Do you have a gun? Was it really just talk when you said if they touched your sister you'd get a gun?" Gom had to know things like that.

"I don't have a gun," Bradley admitted, "and I had to bring Missy to the game because I can't leave her home alone with my father. He's, uh, like I said, he's not right after my mom died. He's either totally withdrawn or drunk and ranting. He ignores Missy completely when he's not drinking and when he is, he doesn't ignore her enough. I watch out for her. I'm used to handling things. I've got it covered at home." Bradley's hands were fisted on his knees. He went a little further, giving Gom a sad and disturbing picture of their life. "I sleep in her room on the floor in front of the door just in case."

"Damn. That sucks, man. Are you afraid he'll hit her or, or something else?" Gom figured Bradley had gone there with his admission so he'd get as much info as he could.

"He's never hit either of us. When he's sober it's like he hates her and never even looks at her, much less speaks to her. But when he's drunk, he sometimes thinks she's my mom and the way he talks to her gives me the creeps." Bradley looked at Gom as if weighing his next words. "A few times the door has been pushed from the other side like he was going to come into her room, but I push back and he's never gotten to her."

Gom tried to keep his face straight as he listened to the horror of Bradley's life. He glanced over and saw the look on Missy's face. He and Bradley had forgotten her for the last few minutes and not known that she was listening to them. The look on her face, just for a couple of heartbeats, told Gom a different story. His first thought was, "Oh, Bradley, you just think so."

It was the look of a child who had been either sexually abused or at least, molested. She schooled her face and smiled at him as if she hadn't heard, but he'd seen it. He knew the look, knew it well. This time, *she* gave the small shake of her head, telling him not to let on that she'd heard or that Gom had figured out her secret. She clearly didn't want her brother to know that all his efforts on her behalf hadn't been totally successful. *Oh, God, what had he gotten into?*

This needed to be reported to the authorities. It couldn't be allowed to continue. It broke Gom's heart that Bradley had worked so hard to protect Missy and Gom had the feeling that somehow the father had managed to get past his defenses at some point. Bradley's attention was drawn to something down below and Gom looked back at Missy, who gazed back meaningfully and mouthed, "Please," to him. Gom knew she was begging him not to tell Bradley what he'd realized.

He knew he should report this right away. What if they went home tonight and the father got a chance to hurt her again and Gom hadn't said anything. He shrugged at her in a sort of apology. He couldn't promise not to say anything. He just couldn't, but he'd be careful in his wording to Bradley.

She deliberately turned away from them again and he said, "Bradley, I am so in awe of the way you take care of Missy. I can see why, too. She's beautiful and sweet. You take good care and be very vigilant in watching out for her. Tell me this, would you be interested in getting out of the house, both of you, and going to a foster home together? It might be safer for her and you could relax a little. As she gets older, and probably even prettier, you might have more of a problem. You don't have to answer now, but keep it in mind. I know people who can arrange it for you. You just say the word and I'll hook you up. No one should be scared in their own home."

"I don't know what my father would do if we weren't there to take care of him. I do it all, cooking, cleaning, shopping, all of it. He's not able to…" Bradley stopped himself before going on.

Gom sat there in awe again at all that this young boy was responsible for doing. No wonder he had an odor. Gom doubted that he had time to get laundry done often enough between his other duties. He didn't smell like anything other than old clothes. They were kind of wrinkled and faded.

"I'm through digging into your life, Bradley. Let's watch the game and I'll pretend I understand football. Some of my brothers played in school and I went to their games but I just couldn't get into it. I knew their numbers and watched them and cheered when everyone else did. I'm pathetic, huh? I'm only here tonight because I'm trying to make some friends." Gom laughed at himself.

"We go somewhere every night, don't we, Bradley?" Missy asked, looking at her brother with affection.

"Mmm-hmm, different places," Bradley mumbled.

"Every night?" Gom had to ask, "Where all do you go?" He didn't think they had a car.

"There's lots of places. We either go to something at my school or his or to the library or the park. That's a long walk. There are two churches close enough to walk to and they're my favorite. We sit in the back and I just wait for the songs so I can sing along with them. Nobody minds that we sneak in and out all the time. Sometimes they have things going on in the basement and there's food, too. We make a game out of it. We like it," Missy said, and Gom didn't know who she was trying to convince of that.

Bradley looked at Missy and frowned a little as if to tell her she'd told too much, but Gom figured it wasn't any worse than the stuff Bradley had revealed so she just shrugged it off. Gom silently thanked all the powers in the universe for sending him Dillon and Soldier when he needed them the most.

The game ended and they followed the crowd out, Gom dumping their trash in a bin on the way out of the stadium. He led them to his car and when they go to it, he stopped dead. The car wasn't sitting level. He went around to the side that was away from the lights of the stadium and saw that both of those tires were slashed and there were key marks down the whole side of it.

Pulling out his cell phone, he called Soldier and told him the situation. He turned to Bradley and Missy and said, "Soldier's coming to pick us up. I'm calling the police and reporting it. I don't guess we have to wonder who's responsible for this, huh? I made somebody really mad by butting in. Well, and being better at self defense than they were." Gom shrugged his shoulders.

"Wow. Can you afford to get it fixed? Tires cost a lot, don't they?" Bradley asked.

"It's okay. My dad will help me. He's good with that kind of thing," Gom said, not telling them that Soldier had more money than half the banks in town. Of course he could have paid for the repairs himself, but wasn't able to let that out. Soldier had fussed about Gom getting the older Camry when he could have afforded something better for him. But he had to keep up his cover and high school students didn't drive fancy cars around here.

Gom saw the school security officer's car driving slowly through the lot and had to wonder where he was earlier then shook it off. He'd probably been patrolling on foot at the game. Now he was keeping an eye on things in the parking area. When he got close, Gom walked over to him, waving him down, and telling him what had happened.

The officer parked near and stepped over to them, looking at Gom, acting like he didn't know him. Good man. The only people at the school who knew he was there undercover were the principal, vice-principal, guidance counselor, the Safe-T program coordinator, and this man, Officer Cane.

"You're new here, aren't you, son? You're Monty something, right?" Officer Cane asked and Gom nodded yes, adding, "Monty Marshall, sir."

Cane walked around the car, looking at the damage. "Who'd you make this mad? You got any idea who did this, or why, for that matter?"

"I can't say for sure, sir, but I had a run-in with Tony Ramirez and Taylor Jackson. Tony told me to watch my back. I think I made an enemy there." Gom tried to sound like a scared high school kid and not a police officer giving a report.

"What'd you say to him that made him this mad? That is, if it was him," Cane wanted to know.

Bradley stepped up and spoke, surprising Gom yet again, "He was helping me. Tony and his guys had me cornered under the bleachers and were threatening me and he came in and stopped them. He put Tony and Taylor both on the ground and that made Tony really mad."

"Yeah, like this one," Cane pointed to Gom, "could take out those two big guys."

"Uh, yes, sir, my dad taught me how to defend myself, since

I'm so little and all." Gom kept up the young teen routine.

Cane scratched his head and pulled out a notebook, turning so the light hit it and started writing in it. Gom turned to Bradley and Missy.

"I'm sorry, guys. Soldier will take us all home when he gets here. It won't be a problem, if you don't mind waiting. I wish you would. I'd hate for Tony to be waiting for you." Gom gave up all pretense of trying to shield Missy from what had happened. Bradley had told it himself, so Gom felt safe in putting his worries out there.

"Can we wait with him, Bradley? I don't want them to do anything more to you." And Gom knew that Bradley didn't want them to do anything to Missy, so he gave a little sigh of relief at that small victory.

In a few minutes Gom saw both a wrecker and Soldier's big old Hummer coming into the parking lot. God, Soldier loved that truck. It was fourteen years old and he kept it in mint condition. Soldier wouldn't part with it, gas guzzler that it was. It had special meaning to all of them. It was part of Scarcity Sanctuary.

Soldier was out of the big vehicle with Dillon right behind him in seconds and came over, taking in the situation quickly, and knowing he couldn't talk freely. He had to go along with Gom's cover.

"Are you okay, Monty? You're not hurt?"

"No, Dad, I'm fine. It's just the car. Soldier, Dillon, this is Officer Cane. He works at the school. He just came by and saw us here," Gom said, and then pointed to his new friends, "and this is Bradley and Missy Haines. I told them you'd take them home since I was going to until we found this mess."

Bradley stepped forward and shook both men's hands and said, "It's nice to meet you both. Monty says you all are really good people. Missy and I appreciate the ride, if it's not too much trouble."

"Not at all. It's nice to see that Monty's making some friends here. As soon as we get the car taken care of, if you all can stay out a little later, we can stop for a treat on the way. It's not a school night. I could go for pie and coffee and you all could get a sundae or something. That sound like a good thing after this bad experience?" Soldier asked, looking from Gom to the others. Missy's eyes lit so Bradley had no choice but to agree, though he tried to find a way out.

"You could just drop us off and then take Monty for a treat, sir. You don't have to spend anything on us," Bradley said.

"Now what would be the fun in that?" Soldier asked, smiling at Bradley and Missy. "We could have ice cream at home, but I like to go out sometimes for a treat. Dillon tries to make me watch what I eat, but sometimes if there's a good reason, I can get by with it. This is a good reason. So, I'm buying, soon as these guys are done. Let me go talk to them."

Like anyone would believe that Soldier had any trouble with his weight or health. He was the strongest, healthiest looking man Gom had ever known. Gom knew he was just using it as a way to let Bradley off the hook so he could accept with grace.

Gom went to stand with Bradley and Missy while Dillon talked to Officer Cane and Soldier finished up the details with the wrecker service. The three of them were quiet as they watched what all was happening. He was still going for the stunned teen act.

Gom was actually pleased he made some headway tonight, with all he'd learned from Bradley, and inadvertently, from Missy. Having heard her mention that she was going out of town this weekend, he would have to meet with Miss Summer on Monday and let her know as much as he could and see about getting some help for the Haineses. Bradley said he could handle the situation, but it worried Gom. Miss Summer had given him her cell number. Maybe he should call her. He decided she couldn't do anything from wherever she was, so it would wait until Monday.

Maybe he could get an idea of why Tony Ramirez had targeted Bradley. Tony had mentioned something about Bradley talking about him which didn't sound like Bradley. He'd been able to find out the probable source of the threat, though he still didn't know the reason. He hoped he had time to find out before Tony did something stupid.

CHAPTER THREE

Sitting in the big back seat with Bradley and Missy, Gom watched as Soldier chose to drive them to the middle of town where there was a busy ice cream shop. Amazingly enough, it was located right beside the Showhouse Theater on Main Street. Gom looked at Soldier, wondering if this was a plan on his dad's part. It didn't matter right now. He had to find out more about Bradley and Missy's situation so he'd have more to go in with for the meeting with Miss Summer on Monday.

Once they were all seated at a round table in the shop, Soldier and Dillon took their orders and left the three young people at the table.

"Bradley, Tony mentioned something about you talking about him, maybe where you shouldn't have. Does that make any sense to you?" Gom had been going over the scene below the bleachers while they drove.

"Yeah, he did, didn't he? I was so busy being scared and trying not to show it that I didn't pay too much attention. I haven't said anything about him to anybody," Bradley scratched the back of his head, looking quickly at Gom then back down. "I don't know who would go to him and talk if I did say something. I don't have any friends to talk to about him or anything else. People tend to leave me alone."

Gom had an idea, but wasn't sure how it would go over with Bradley, or Soldier for that matter. When his dads approached the table with trays of scrumptious looking ice cream concoctions, he decided to see how his plan would be accepted.

"Soldier, I was wondering if I could invite Bradley and Missy over for supper tomorrow night. I told Bradley you might teach him some of the self defense things you taught me a few years ago and Missy might like to watch some of Ben's movies. I kind of like having friends at school." Gom really worked on sounding like an unsure teenager when he knew that anyone he asked over would be welcome.

"That sounds like a great idea. I'll check with their parents and make sure it's all right when I take them home," Soldier said.

"Oh, it's just our father and he won't care, so you don't have to…"

"Now, don't start that again. We'd love to have you. We like to know that Monty is making friends at his new school. What would you all like for supper? How about a cookout?" Solider turned to Gom and said, "Did you tell them there's likely to be several showing up?" He turned back to Bradley and said, "We never know how many are going to be there for supper, so we cook for an army and if fewer show up, we enjoy the leftovers the next day. I hope you don't mind."

Bradley looked at Missy, who shrugged. "That's okay. We didn't have any plans for tomorrow night made yet, so if Missy wants to come, we'll be glad to."

Gom figured that this would save them from going to the library or somewhere else they were used to frequenting and give Bradley a chance to work with Soldier a bit. He'd fill Soldier in later on the need for it.

"Missy," Dillon spoke up, "I hope you don't mind being around so many boys and men. I'll make sure they behave. Maybe Beth will be able to come and you won't be the only female there for the meal. Maybe you could help me in the kitchen while Soldier works on the grill outside."

Missy's eyes lit up. "Oh, I would love that. Bradley does most of the cooking at home, but I'm good with dishes and setting up. I'd like to learn more."

"Wonderful. I'll check with J and see if he and Beth can join us. You'll like Beth, she's a Special Education teacher in the school where J teaches Math. Jack might be able to come and we can see if his Tiffany has the night off. Jack's a police officer and his fiancé is a dispatcher at the department. They've only been engaged for a couple of months. She's a lovely girl." Dillon's excitement was evident as he continued, "This is beginning to sound like a great idea. I'm glad you all are giving us an opportunity to have a blowout. Soon it will be getting too cold to have a backyard party. The weather is supposed to be fine tomorrow, unseasonably warm, actually. Perfect!"

Dillon loved it when he got as many of his original boys together as possible, Gom knew, and Dillon took any excuse he could find. Gom also knew that they'd all be coached on how to act around him with his current job at the school. So, little brother Ben would be acting like "Monty's" older brother. Ben loved the few times that occurred.

Missy got up from her seat and walked around the table to stand beside Soldier, who looked at her with his head tilted, waiting to see what she was going to say.

"If your name is Soldier, I bet you got these," she reached up and softly touched the scarred skin on the side of Soldier's face, "fighting for our country. May I give you a hug just to thank you?"

Gom could see tears in Dillon's eyes, surprise in Bradley's, and his own were a little moist at the sweet response from this beautiful young girl to the scars that covered the left side of Soldier's face, extended down his neck and continued under his shirt.

Soldier could only nod his head, his heart in his eyes as she put her arms around his neck and gave him a hug, whispering her thank you into his ear.

Everyone at the table was silent as they watched the scene unfold. Soldier patted her back and dipped his head, smiling at her when she pulled away.

Missy returned to her seat without mentioning the scars on Dillon's face. It was a few quiet seconds before Soldier finally broke it with his words.

"Good then," Soldier said, "I'll take you all home and explain things to your father. You'll have to get his permission."

"Oh, no, you can't…" Bradley said, hurriedly before pausing and looking unsure about how to go on. Gom could tell that he didn't want anyone to meet his father, but he also knew that Soldier would do things by his strict code of ethics. Gom wanted to be in on that meeting with Bradley and Missy's dad. He needed the information he could gather to fill out reports and maybe get things done about removing them from the environment if necessary.

Soon, the five of them were back in the big silver Hummer and headed to the address that Bradley reluctantly gave to Soldier. Gom tried to keep the chatter going to make it seem like he was unaware of the tension. In the back of his mind he was thinking about how lucky it was that he'd found Bradley under the bleachers tonight. Who knew what Tony and his crew would have done to the young man?

Gom was even luckier that the incident had freaked Bradley out enough to make him receptive to Gom's overtures. He became more talkative, Gom figured, because he was nervous and scared after the fight with Tony. It all worked in Gom's favor, getting him an "in" with Bradley and hopefully a way to find out what the reason for the death threat was, while trying to neutralize the situation before they had a tragedy at Willington High.

Gom got his mind back in the game as Soldier slowed and turned into the drive of a small house on Kenton Street. It was, as Bradley had said, fairly close to the school. As Soldier turned off the Hummer, the porch light came on and the door was pushed open quickly, slapping against the wall of the house. Soldier stepped out, as did Dillon, neither seeming to be nervous about the irate man stomping down the two steps onto the cracked sidewalk leading up the little porch. Gom, Bradley, and Missy sat for a few seconds, stunned. Then, as one, they opened the doors of the back and hurried out.

"Where in the hell have you been, Bradley Haines? You get over here right now and take what's comin' to you!" Bradley's father was so drunk he was having a hard time standing straight up. Missy stepped forward, pushing past Bradley who tried to grab her arm and stop her.

"Dad, come on, we're not really that late. Come on in and

I'll help you get settled in your chair and Bradley will fix you something to eat. How about that?" Missy tried to take her dad's arm and turn him back toward the house, but he took a step back and looked at her, raising his hand to reach toward her face.

"Lenora? Honey, come here..." Mr. Haines' voice had changed to one of completely inappropriate seduction.

Gom was afraid his eyes were wide with horror as he realized that Missy's dad was so drunk he thought that Missy was his dead wife. No wonder Bradley slept in her room!

Soldier stepped forward with his hand outstretched. "Mr. Haines, I'm Soldier, Monty's father. I wanted to come in and explain why I was bringing your children home. It's simply a matter of respect between fathers, you know? Monty's car was vandalized at the ballgame and he had promised Bradley and Missy a ride so I took them out for ice cream and brought them over. I wanted to make sure you understood that they were safe."

When Mr. Haines didn't put his hand out to shake, but tilted his head as if he didn't understand all that Soldier had said, Dillon moved up to the group and took over.

"Sir, you don't look like you feel very well. Let's get you inside and settled, huh? Bradley, you and Missy go on in and we'll help your dad inside. Monty, help them in the house, please." Gom took the directive and hustled the two Haineses into the house quickly.

He took in the front room at a glance, noticing that it was clean, but very cluttered. Bradley immediately told Missy to go to her room and put a chair in front of the door. She looked like she would argue, but he looked at her with one brow raised and she took off.

"I'm sorry, Monty. My dad's not well. Hell, my dad's drunk. I didn't want you to have to see him like that. I don't want anyone to know about him or they'll..." Bradley was whispering and he just stopped, looking around the room, avoiding Gom's eyes.

"Or they'll what, Bradley? Take you all out of here, away from him? I'm sorry, man, but I think that would be a good thing. I saw the way he looked at her and the way he was talking. I understand what you meant about it giving you the creeps. What will you do if you're not here some time and he gets to her? It's liable to happen, you know. You couldn't live with yourself, could you?" Gom felt mean pushing Bradley like that, but felt he was right, especially since he'd seen for himself that Bradley was wrong in thinking that Mr. Haines had never gotten to her. *God, what a mess!*

There was a commotion at the door and Soldier appeared, followed by Mr. Haines and then Dillon. Mr. Haines was quiet as he walked to what was obviously his chair, an old tan recliner. He more or less collapsed into it and looked around, as if not knowing what was going on in his house. Seeing Bradley, he asked,

"Where's my Lenora?"

Soldier took the bull by the horns, so to speak, and said, "If you're talking about your wife, Mr. Haines, I believe she has passed on. I'm sorry for your loss, but you need to wake up and take care of yourself and your children. Bradley and Missy have been invited to our house for a cookout tomorrow night. I hope you'll allow them to come, and you're welcome to come with them if you'd like, but you'll have to be sober to be allowed to come. I'm sorry if that sounds harsh, but I believe it's important to set a good example. I'll come by here tomorrow afternoon and see if you'll be coming with them."

Gom realized that Soldier was assuming that Mr. Haines would not veto their coming over. Like Mr. Haines was able to make a decision right now, anyway. Gom didn't want to leave them with him at all. He looked to Bradley and asked in an undertone, "Will you all be okay tonight? Will he sleep it off or will there be trouble?"

"It's okay, really, Monty." Bradley seemed quiet, ashamed.

"You'll keep watch over her tonight? I don't like to think about him and the way he talked to her." Gom would like to take them both out of there tonight and force Mr. Haines to get some form of help before he would be allowed to have guardianship of them again. They could stay at Scarcity for the night at least.

He looked at Soldier and saw that he wasn't the only one worried about the situation here.

"I've got this, you all. I've done this hundreds of times. He'll eventually fall asleep and I'll take care of Missy. I didn't want you all to see him like this," Bradley repeated, went to the door and opened it, letting them know that it was time for them to leave. Gom understood his embarrassment and tension.

Quickly, they said their goodbyes and were soon back in the Hummer and headed to Scarcity Sanctuary, home.

"Gom, it was all I could do to leave those two in that house with him. I know he's their dad and that Bradley says he's handled him before, but the way he looked at that girl and talked to her made me kind of sick." Soldier signaled the turn into their drive and Gom could see him shaking his head a little. "I understand that he's drunk and confusing her with his deceased wife, but it's not good. I'm going back tomorrow and checking to make sure that it's okay for them to come over and I'm going to talk to him. Hopefully, he'll be sober."

"Seriously," Dillon spoke from his seat beside Soldier, "that's a situation that bears watching closely."

"Uh, guys?" Gom started and as Soldier turned the key they both turned to him and he related the story Bradley had told him about sleeping in her room and how the door had been pushed a few times by his dad wanting to come in. When he said that Bradley had told him that so far their dad hadn't taken and he'd seen her face that told a different story, they both gasped. Then he told them that she was only in the fifth grade and that set them off even more.

"Oh, no, Gom! That beautiful young girl," said Dillon, his face showing his distress at the thought.

"Damn!" That was from Soldier. "What can you do for that situation, Gom? Is it too hard for you to step in and stay undercover? Maybe Dillon and I could turn him in and see about getting a foster situation set up for them that will keep them together."

"I sort of mentioned that and he immediately said they couldn't do that since he took care of his dad. I think that Bradley has been the dad in that house since their mother died. His dad seems to have gone into depression and then came the alcohol. Basically, he's raised Missy since she was a baby and has taken care of the house like a man. He's pretty amazing." Gom opened the door and headed for the house, the others following.

"I agree that it's wonderful of him, but it's gotten out of hand, Gom. If you believe that Mr. Haines has already done something to her, he'll try again. There'll come a time when Bradley can't stop him or won't be there. Since we know this, we can't just do nothing. We have to decide the best way to handle it. It's like if a teacher knows there's abuse going on, they're obligated, by law, to report it. This needs to be reported somewhere."

Gom had been thinking the same thing. "We need to talk to Bradley about how often his dad's drunken behavior happens. Should I report it to the Safe-T Program director I told you about at the school? Would it be better if the call for an investigation came from there or from an anonymous source...say, for example, you?"

"Come on in and we'll discuss it. You've landed in a mess here, haven't you, son? Between that situation and the one with the guys that you had the run-in with earlier, you need to be careful."

"I always am, Dad. I had no trouble with them tonight, thanks to you and the officer training. It sure surprised them. They thought they had a weak, little queer, their words, and were certainly surprised when I was able to handle myself." Gom moved over to fit himself into Soldier's side, knowing that he would be hugged and, frankly, he needed it. He wondered if there would ever be a time that a hug from either of his dads wouldn't be just what he needed to set his world right.

"I'm glad, son," Soldier said, providing the hug and then moving to let Dillon in on it.

§   §   §

Gom had probably only been asleep for about an hour when his door opened and Soldier was there again. "Gom, wake up. Bradley's on the phone and he sounds frantic. Here." Soldier handed the phone to Gom, who was up and reaching for it immediately. He'd never slept really deeply.

"Bradley, what's up?"

Gom listened as a nearly hysterical Bradley talked, his voice going high and then quiet, like he was scared, and then loud as he asked what to do, what to do.

It seemed that the Haineses had all been asleep when bricks and then firecrackers were thrown through their front windows, scaring them all nearly to death. Bradley was afraid to call the police, but he'd managed to find the number for Scarcity Sanctuary and got hold of Soldier.

"We'll take care of the police, okay? You get some clothes together for you and Missy… and your dad. We'll come pick you up and see about boarding up the windows after the police finish. Keep the door closed and stay away from the windows. Did you see or hear anything that could tell you who did it?"

Gom doubted it. He got the shaky answer that he'd expected and told Bradley to gather their things quickly.

He told Soldier what had happened and dialed the precinct to report the incident and to remind the officers to not respond to him as other than a teenager when they saw him.

In minutes, Gom, Soldier, and Dillon were in the Hummer and speeding back to the Haines residence. They'd left a note in case Ben, Trick, or Niko woke up and came looking for them. Gom was a little surprised that Bradley had called him instead of the police. The more he thought about it, it began to make sense. Bradley knew that Soldier had taught Gom self defense and after spending time with Soldier and Dillon earlier, he knew that they were good strong men. Bradley must have felt safe in calling them for help. It really sucked that there was always someone going through some kind of hell.

The police beat them there and they saw the lights as they

turned onto the street. Gom could see an officer talking to Bradley on the front sidewalk while Missy stood in the open doorway, her arms wrapped around her waist.

A lot of the officers knew Soldier and Dillon, both through Gom and through their work with the boys. Sometimes the police were involved in the placing of children with Daniel at the shelter and subsequently on to the Sanctuary. Gom walked right by the officers and headed for his new friends, while Soldier and Dillon stopped to talk to the officers, explaining that their son, Monty was a friend of the family at the house and had been called for support.

Gom hurried to Bradley and they headed inside the house, where police were already marking things and gathering evidence and bagging it. There were two bricks, one thrown through each front window, and the remains from the spent firecrackers.

Missy now stood between Gom and Bradley with tears still smeared across her face. She looked at Gom and in a quivering voice, said, "There were words on the bricks, Monty."

"Words? What words?" He looked at Bradley who returned a look that wavered between exasperation and uncertainty.

"'Shut up' was written on one in black magic marker and 'Faggot' was written on the other. It's funny, don't you think? I haven't said anything to anybody and I'm not gay. So *what* is this guy's problem?"

Before Gom could answer Bradley, Mr. Haines came out of what must be his bedroom. He was mumbling and it was clear that he was not too aware of what was going on.

"Bradley, what's going on here? Why are the police here?"

"I told you, Dad. Someone broke out the front windows and set off firecrackers in here." Bradley moved toward the man.

"Oh. Oh, yeah. Why, do you know? Why throw stuff at our house? What are we going to do now?" The man was maybe a little more sober, but not very capable.

Soldier and Dillon came in just in time to answer that.

"Hello, again, Mr. Haines. I met you earlier tonight. I'm Soldier, and this is Dillon. We're going to help you all board up the windows as soon as they police are finished here and then I think all three of you should come with us and spend what's left of tonight at our house. There's plenty of room there. You'll all have your own rooms and we'll figure this mess out tomorrow."

"How did you get here? Why are you here? I don't understand what's going on," Mr. Haines said, looking form Bradley to Gom and then to both men. He never once looked at Missy.

"Monty is our son and he's friend of Bradley's. Bradley called Monty for help and we called the police for him. We want you all to be safe and I don't think you should stay here tonight. If it's all right, we'll grab some boxes we brought with us and board up the windows and we can make better arrangements tomorrow. Bradley," Soldier said, looking at the young man, "did you pack up stuff for each of you?"

"Yes, sir. We're ready. Thank you for coming over. I was kind of freaked out and didn't know what to do."

"That's understandable, Bradley. This would be frightening for anyone. Monty," Soldier said, now looking at Gom, "run get the boxes and start breaking them down and we'll cover these windows. Dillon put them and some tape in the back before we came over. Let's get this done."

Before long the police left, after getting stories from Gom and Bradley on who they thought had done it based on what had happened earlier. Again, Bradley said he hadn't ever said anything about Tony to anyone. The windows were covered, belongings gathered, and they piled into the Hummer to head back to Scarcity Sanctuary.

Missy leaned on Bradley, her head on his shoulder. She'd been quiet the whole time and seemed very tired now. Mr. Haines sat quietly, as if in his own world. Gom noticed that Bradley was shivering a bit. He didn't know if it was reaction of if Bradley was just cold. He decided that it was probably a combination of the two.

Soldier, being the smart man he was, put Bradley and Missy in a room with two single beds, knowing that Missy needed her brother near in this new environment, after the trauma of the evening. Mr. Haines was in a room further away from them.

Soldier explained to them all that their rooms had locks on them and they were completely safe here. He encouraged them to sleep late in the morning and things would look better in the new day. When the newcomers were settled, Gom, Dillon, and Soldier met in the kitchen to talk quietly about the situation.

"I'm going to call Miss Summer in the morning and let her know what's going on. I don't want to wait until Monday. She needs to know what I've learned and see if she can make sense of it." Gom put his chin on his hand, his elbow on the table as he put his thoughts into words. "Personally, I can't see Bradley saying anything to anyone that would provoke this kind of response. It took me all this time to get near him and that wouldn't have happened if I hadn't showed up in time to save his butt from a beating tonight. He was so flustered he just started talking. He's probably needed a friend but felt he couldn't even think about it with his dad like he is."

"I have to say I feel for this kid. Not only does he have the home life to deal with, but this Tony character seems to have it in for him. I hope you all can get it figured out soon. Maybe with them here, Dillon and I can work on talking with Mr. Haines, once he's awake and sober, and see if he might be agreeable to seeking help. I don't mind telling him that I'll turn him in if he doesn't agree to some kind of change." Soldier never minded taking the bull by the horns if it meant making a young person's life better and they all agreed that something needed to be done in this situation.

The three of them headed for bed, tired and worried about Bradley and his problems. Gom couldn't believe that it was only early Saturday morning. So much had happened in a short amount of time. He was exhausted, both physically and mentally.

રુ રુ રુ

Gom was up early the next morning, making the call to Miss Summer that he'd talked about. After apologizing for interrupting her weekend away, he told her everything. He started with finding Bradley under the bleachers with Tony and his boys and then told her about the situation at their home. She gasped as he told her what happened with the attack during the night with the bricks' message and the firecrackers.

She told him that she would check around and see if she could put a time line together on the school information to see if she could make sense of it. She thanked him for the call and said that she would follow up on the situation with the father so Soldier wouldn't have to do it.

Gom showered, dressed, and headed down to the kitchen, getting back into the character of starving high school kid. He found his two dads working on breakfast with a quiet Mr. Haines sitting at the table staring into a cup of coffee that he cradled in his hands. Gom immediately started setting the table, knowing that the smells of bacon and French toast would have the teenagers there before long. He wondered if Bradley and Missy would wake soon.

Before he finished with the table he heard a noise at the door. Missy stood there, hesitantly watching the work going on in the kitchen.

"Is it okay to come in?" she asked, quietly.

"Of course it is, Missy. What would you like to drink with your breakfast? Monty'll get it for you," Dillon said, from the counter where he was dipping the toast in the egg mixture. Soldier was cooking bacon, lots of bacon, as he knew his boys.

"I'm not used to anyone waiting on me. Is there some way I can help?" She looked over and saw her dad at the table and said, "Good morning, Dad." He didn't respond in any way and she didn't seem to expect it.

Dillon spoke up and said, "How about you be in charge of drinks? I hear Ben, Trick, and Niko coming down now and I bet Bradley isn't far behind, huh?"

"Yes, sir. He was taking a shower when I left. He'll be right in."

"Look in the fridge and you'll find juice and milk. Soldier and I will both have another cup of coffee and you can see if your dad's cup needs to be refilled. Monty, you want juice, I take it? Yep, thought so," Dillon smiled as if at some private joke. "You probably know what Bradley would like."

"Yes, sir. He would love juice. I can just drink water."

It seemed that Missy was just like Bradley and didn't want to take from others.

Soldier turned to her and said, "Missy, I don't want to sound like a smart aleck, but I have lots of money and I enjoy sharing it with my kids and their friends. Please, don't ever feel like you shouldn't accept anything from here. Would you like some juice or maybe some hot chocolate? I know that's what Ben's going to want."

"Thank you, sir. I'm sorry. I'm just not used to being able to have just anything. I wouldn't want to take something away from anyone else."

"You don't have to worry about that here. Please, relax and enjoy the day. We'll still have our cookout tonight and you all can stay here until we get windows back in your house. I've got someone working on it. Some of us will go over and make sure that gets done. I'll take you all home after supper tonight." Soldier watched her with this quiet look that Gom recognized.

Gom knew that Soldier was worried about sending her back to that house with Mr. Haines. It felt weird that the man was sitting right there with them, but they were all feeling strange about how he acted toward her.

Even Gom saw her eyes light up at the mention of hot chocolate, so he showed her where the makings were and she made enough for both Ben and her.

What sounded like a herd of elephants turned out to be three young men who hustled into the kitchen and drew to a sudden stop.

"Dad? Uh, there's a… a girl here." Ben was quick, Gom had to give him that.

"Good eye, Ben, there is. This is Missy Haines, she's Bradley's sister and that's her father at the table. They'll be here through supper tonight at least. They had some trouble at their house last night. And you've seen girls here before. You don't have to act like it's a totally different species." Soldier kidded Ben.

"Yeah, but they were my brother's girlfriends." Ben turned to Missy, who stood, wide-eyed, watching all the boys in the room now. "I'm Ben, this is Trick, and that's Niko." Ben said, pointing to each respectively. "I guess the guy who followed us in is Bradley, huh? Sorry you had trouble, but Soldier and Dillon'll figure things out. We still having the cookout tonight?" he asked, looking at Soldier now.

"You bet. There'll be steaks for the grownups, burgers and hot dogs for the younger crowd, and all the extras that you're used to. Bradley, do you or Missy have any requests? We'll have potato salad, baked beans, slaw, chips, pickles, olives, and so on. Let's take a vote on dessert, chocolate cake, or some kind of pies?" Soldier looked around and laughed when there was a loud chorus of "Chocolate Cake!"

"Missy, would you like to assist me with the cake this afternoon? I'm always in charge of the desserts. With this many I'd say we do a German Chocolate and a Devil's Food. We've got a lot to do today, so I'd love to have the help," Dillon spoke up from where he was taking the last of a huge stack of French toast from the griddle.

Gom knew that Dillon had her figured out. She needed to feel useful. Bradley would be with them over at the house and Gom counted on talking to him about both of his situations, school and home. He wouldn't feel that his job at Willington was complete until he had things settled with the death threat and with the way the Haines kids lived, in constant fear that something would happen from the father. It was time that Bradley had a life, a life that was more age appropriate, rather than one where he was the father figure. It would take some doing, but before he called it done, Gom would see to it that they were better situated.

The large group sat down to the big breakfast and before long there was much talking and laughing and the Haines children soon warmed up and answered questions and even asked a few. Gom watched them seem to blossom in the new environment of safety and kindness. Through it all, Mr. Haines didn't speak. He took food as it was offered, even clearing his plate. He drank several cups of coffee, Missy getting up to refill it often. Gom thought that was the weirdest relationship he'd ever seen. It was like she was invisible to him and she didn't even seem to react to that at all. But, he figured, she must be so used to it that it didn't even register. To him, though, it was glaring.

CHAPTER FOUR

The cookout had been a big success with lots of good food, laughter, and warmth. Both Jack's fiancé and J's girlfriend had come with their men so with Beth and Tiffany there, Missy hadn't felt awkward with so many men around. Both women had taken Missy under their wing and the three were inseparable all evening. Gom was thankful that his brothers had found such compassionate, caring women. Tiffany was a little firecracker just like Jack had been all his life. Beth was quiet and sweet and thought that J, which was short for Johnathan James Jenkins, both hung the moon and made it shine.

Soldier, Gom, Bradley, and Mr. Haines had gone to the Haines house in the afternoon and helped clean up the mess and met the man who was installing the new windows. Dillon had stayed at home with Missy, Ben, Niko, and Trick. Gom knew that Soldier and Dillon had talked for a couple of hours to Mr. Haines in the den, but had no idea what came of it. Hopefully, he'd find out later.

Before they'd left, Ben had asked Gom if he would talk to Casey and see if Ben could come down to the theater and spend some time with him there. Ben wanted to know everything about anything to do with theater and plays and Broadway and musicals. He was excited at the thought of being able to explore the Showhouse from the inside, so to speak, and he said he hoped that Casey would show him around.

Gom wasn't even sure what Casey did there, but he said he'd see if Casey would be willing to show Ben around sometime. He warned him not to count on it, though, as Casey wasn't much into sharing. Maybe when it came to a shared love of theater it would be different. And, Gom thought, it gave him an excuse to see the man again.

It was late Saturday night. Soldier had taken the Haines family home and made sure they were locked up for the night. Gom knew that Soldier had also made good on his promise to spend some time with Bradley, showing him some basic ways to protect himself and Missy.

Gom was on his way to see if Casey was still at the theater. He knew there was a play going on right now, so Casey might still be working. He hoped so.

Parking in front of the theater, he went up to the front doors and checked them. He rattled them a little when he saw that lights were still on further inside, hoping it would be Casey working in there and not someone who would be disturbed by a late night visit. He peered in the beautiful glass doors and saw movement and then there was Casey. His heart thudded and he stepped back, now unsure. Would Ben's request look like a flimsy excuse? It was sincere, but Gom knew he wanted inside the theater for another reason entirely. He was just nervous as hell now that he was doing something proactive.

Casey unlocked the door and swept it open, asking, "Is it Trick? Did he run away?"

"No, Trick is fine. He's happy, Casey, really. Well, as much as he can be. I don't know his story yet, but he's working with Tommy. We don't pry at the house. If he wants to share something, that will be up to him. Right now, he's just a new family member, who happens to be getting help from Tommy. He seems happy with Dillon and Soldier, too. He and Ben get along great. Speaking of Ben, I'm here, uh, because Ben was hoping you'd let him come down sometime and you'd show him around. He's so into theater and you have an in here." Gom realized that he was rambling and knew it was his nerves, but he didn't know what to do about it. He was even shaking a little, tension and awkwardness warring inside him. "I don't know what all you do here, but he would love to get a chance to see it all on a bigger scale than the one at the college. This is a larger, fancier place. It's old and has such a history, too. It really is a beautiful place, huh?"

"I could do that. Come in, it's getting colder out there. Right now I'm cleaning up a little. The night janitor has already gone home after doing the heavy cleaning, and now I'm just straightening here and there. You, uh, you want to come back and hang a while?" Casey asked, looking everywhere but at Gom's eyes.

Maybe he wasn't the only one who was nervous. Gom was actually surprised at Casey's invitation.

"Sure. I have to admit I know nothing about theater except what I hear Ben talk about. What do you do here?"

"A little bit of everything," Casey answered, reaching up to tuck a strand of hair behind his ear. He had the whole of if tied back, but that one long blond curl had come loose and Gom fisted his hand to keep from reaching for it, just to touch.

"Like?" Gom asked.

"I do lighting, sometimes help with costume changes if there's no need for lighting changes for a while, some set design, some construction and painting. I help with errands when there's printing and advertisement stuff to deliver or pick up. I'm pretty much everybody's gofer here." Casey locked the door behind them and they turned to head into the theater. He continued with his list of duties, saying, "I help out whoever needs it at the time, but mostly I'm in charge of lighting for the shows. I help the set guys and even work with the props department before shows to make sure that all the props are in the right place so that no one is left looking for something they need in the middle of a play. I never know what all I'll be doing and that makes it kind of cool."

"That's a lot," Gom said, following Casey into the main theater, which was done in the old style with ornate architecture, very showy and elegant. There was a feeling of history here and Gom could see people in old limos, dressed up in forties attire coming in for shows and entertainment.

"It's a living," Casey said, shrugging. "I add to what I make here by working three nights a week at a couple of offices nearby. I clean them and that allows me to work after shows close at night. They don't care if I work at eight or one in the morning. I make enough for what I need and I'm never bored. I hate being bored."

Casey led Gom to an area that looked like an office but held a big board that Casey sat in front of and began flipping switches. Gom was treated to a light show that had him very impressed with Casey's knowledge. From spots to different colors to different mood lighting, Casey moved from one to the other seamlessly and quickly, showing that he'd been at this long enough to be comfortable with it.

"Ben would be thrilled to learn from you. I'm impressed with what you can do and I don't know anything about it." Gom watched the subdued lights in the little space shine off Casey's hair and tried to keep his mind on anything other than touching it. Casey would probably deck him if he did.

"Tell him to come around six tomorrow night or one night next week and I'll let him sit with me while I work. Actually, tell him to get here about five and I'll do a tour through the theater and introduce him around to the cast as my assistant for the night." Casey's offer had Gom smiling as he thought about how excited Ben would be. Maybe he'd been wrong in his first impressions of Casey. While Gom had thought he was quiet and reserved, almost withdrawn, he seemed willing to talk freely. Gom relaxed a little.

"That would be fantastic. I really appreciate it, man." Gom wanted to ask if Casey had much more to do tonight and if he might be interested in going for coffee or something, but he was hesitant. "I'm surprised you're being so, I don't know, willing to talk. Usually, you're very quiet."

"I don't have much to say to most people. When it's about work, it's different, easier. Here I have to be what I call 'on'," Casey put his fingers up in the quote sign when he said that, "and I become what people need me to be. Mostly, I'm pretty much by myself when I'm not working. I don't have friends away from work and that's okay. I don't have much time, anyway." Gom was trying to read Casey as he talked to see if he really was okay with having no friends or if maybe he sounded a little wistful. He figured if anybody was wishing here, it was him wishing Casey might want to be friends with him.

"Don't you ever wish there was someone to bum around with? You know, go to a movie or out to eat, a ballgame, or something. You're happy being alone on your off time?" Gom didn't think he could be that way. He'd grown up with all the boys in the home with Dillon and Soldier and wouldn't trade the bond he had with any of them for anything. Maybe Casey just didn't know how good honest affection felt.

"Never done any of that, so I don't miss it, I guess." Casey didn't sound like he missed it. He was the most alone person Gom had ever known, other than some of the boys who'd passed through Scarcity with various problems over the years. But, Casey was a fully functioning member of society, who just was so *alone*. That was the only word Gom could come up with for him. He couldn't help but wonder about Casey's life and what caused him to be so alone and happy to be that way.

"When you were at the house last night…" Gom started to say. He'd paused, thinking about how much had happened in that one night and today. It felt like it ought to be later than Saturday night.

"I'm sorry, man. I know I messed up. I felt bad." Casey looked away from Gom then back, seeming embarrassed.

"What do you mean? I was glad you stayed and ate with us. Trick really…oh, I know what you mean. Yeah, man, I had a hard time with that right at first and I know Soldier was a little ticked." Gom realized that Casey was talking about when he'd shied away from the hug that Trick had offered.

"I don't, I mean I'm not comfortable with…" Casey sighed deeply and Gom knew he was reaching for the right words.

"You don't hug?" Gom offered.

"I'm not used to people touching me. I really can't remember the last time someone did, other than an occasional handshake that I can't get out of doing," Casey said. Gom still thought Casey looked like he wished things were different. Maybe if he had someone in his life touch him in a good way, he'd be more into it. Wondering if there was a serious reason why Casey didn't like the touch of another or just had never had it was disturbing to Gom. He made himself drop that train of thought before he said something he shouldn't.

"I'm the total opposite. I love hugs and feeling loved. I have this need to touch things. I've been dying to…" Gom shut up before he admitted to wanting to touch Casey's hair. *How stupid would that have been?*

Casey glanced at him, one blond brow raised, and asked, "Do I want to know?"

"No, I'm sure you don't," Gom laughed, thinking that Casey would freak right out if Gom reached over and took that lock of hair that had fallen again and rubbed it between his fingers. He wanted to so badly. He also wanted to take Casey's hand in his and pull it closer to see what that was on it. A birthmark? A tattoo? Gom was very curious.

Casey stood up then from the chair in front of the deck with all the buttons and levers that controlled the lights for the huge theater. When he reached his feet, he was very close to Gom, who hadn't realized that Casey was getting up as he'd been looking out over the wide expanse of the main theater floor. Gom jerked when he turned back and saw that Casey was really close to him. Taking a deep breath, he gazed at Casey, wishing he had enough nerve to make a move.

Gom wasn't stupid, though. You didn't even entertain thoughts of making a move on a man until you found out if the man would be receptive. With Casey's strong dislike of being touched, Gom doubted that he'd appreciate any kind of move.

Gom stood frozen, totally sure he didn't want to make a wrong move. He was close enough to see Casey's eyes, despite the low lighting in the area.

"I love your eyes." Oh, crap, he hadn't meant to say that out loud.

"Huh? They're weird, man." Casey said, tilting his head and looking back at Gom, still not moving away as Gom expected him to do any second.

"They're Husky eyes," Gom said.

"I hate to repeat myself, but, huh?" Casey almost smiled.

"You know, the Siberian Huskies with the light blue eyes. Yours remind me of them. They're kind of cool," Gom said, then thought Casey might not appreciate the comments. "Sorry, that's probably a little too personal. I'll go now. Thanks for the lighting demonstration and for letting Ben come down. It's nice of you." Gom thought he'd better get out of there before he did something stupid and got hit for his trouble.

Frankly, he'd never been tempted to touch anyone other than family and close friends before. He was twenty-two years old and still a virgin. When he was about seventeen he'd realized that he was much more interested in boys than girls. The trauma of his early years had some bearing on the way he felt about getting close to others. He loved his family with his whole heart, but he didn't trust it to others. Being bashed, badly, when he was seventeen and still not even sure he was gay at all, had caused strong conflicts in his being comfortable dealing with his sexuality. There were just a lot of things that had contributed to his delay in exploring his needs.

For a few seconds neither of them moved. Gom wasn't about to and Casey seemed lost in thought for a moment. Gom wondered what he was thinking and why he was still standing so close. Gom took a chance and looked at Casey's eyes and found that Casey was watching him just as closely. He wanted so badly to do something, but he was as unsure of himself as he was of Casey. Gom sensed that he was caught up in a pivotal moment and he was afraid to do something wrong and screw this up. He sighed, somewhat dispiritedly.

"What?" Casey asked, his voice husky. Or was that just Gom's imagination?

"Nothing, really. I'm an idiot sometimes. Don't tell Soldier I said that. He hates it if we say bad things about ourselves." Gom felt like an idiot for not being able to follow through on what he knew he wanted, and that was to touch Casey in some way. He wanted to know if Casey would accept an overture from him.

"I'm not likely to tell on you. You seem to want something, but you're not saying what it is." Casey still hadn't moved away. If Gom moved just a bit, he would be touching the man who didn't like to be touched so he was at a loss to understand why Casey didn't just move out of the way. Was he silently asking for something from Gom?

"I'm not one to put myself out there unless I know I'm safe. I got beat up really badly when I was seventeen, for being gay, which I didn't even know I was at the time." Gom felt very brave in letting that knowledge just sit out there, waiting for a response.

"Oh, man, I'm sorry. That sucks. By the way, how old are you?" Casey asked, and Gom was delighted that Casey was showing an interest at all.

"I'm twenty-two."

"I'm surprised you still live at home, I guess. I thought you were much younger," Casey said, with that head tilt again. Gom was getting used to that motion when Casey was surprised or interested in something.

"I've always looked a lot younger than I am. Staying there works for my job, though," Gom admitted, taking another deep breath and realizing that he kept doing it because he could smell Casey since they were standing so close. He wasn't sure he'd ever responded to another man's scent before, but he certainly was finding Casey's enticing.

"I don't know what you do."

"If I tell you I have to swear you to secrecy," Gom said.

"Or you'll have to kill me?" Casey teased, smiling a little. Gom was sure of it that time.

"Nah, but I don't tell a lot of people."

"Well, I doubt you dance at a strip club or anything like that, so it can't be too bad," Casey said, moving his stance to rest his weight on the other foot, which surprisingly enough, brought him even closer to Gom.

"Seriously, if I tell you, do you promise to keep the secret?

People's safety is involved." Gom was serious and he'd never told anyone who was not part of a case what he did.

"Damn, what are you, CIA?" Casey said, brows raised. The man's face was really expressive.

"No, I'm working undercover. I'm a police officer and since I look so young I go into high schools when someone reports extreme cases of bullying, like beatings or death threats." Finally, Gom moved away a little and leaned on the door facing of the small room that held all the equipment. "I enroll as Monty Marshall and take classes, all the time trying to get close to the kids who are being targeted so I can figure out what's going on. The staff at the school knows about what I'm doing. They handle normal cases, but when it gets that serious, I come in and see if I can make a difference. And, I can't believe I told you all that. I never say anything to anyone about what I'm doing."

"I'm impressed. You're doing good things, helping people. So your real name is?" Casey paused, waiting for Gom to fill in the blank.

"Montgomery Marsh. Soldier adopted me when I was eight, me and Tommy. I've always gone by Gom because when I was little, I said that Montgomery was too big for me. When I was younger I was like, really little. Gom's a weird name, I know, but it's mine, so there you have it. I've spilled my guts more tonight than I have in years. What is it about you that loosens my tongue?" Uh-oh, Gom thought, that sounded suggestive. He hadn't meant to, but he watched Casey closely to see if he made something of it.

"Hey, I don't usually talk as much as I've done tonight either. Your secret's safe. I wouldn't want to put anyone in danger. I admire what you all do at your house. I've heard about it a couple of times, once in the paper and I heard some guys talking about it another time. I looked it up. It's good that Trick is there. That brings me right back to what started this conversation. I'm sorry about last night. I know I hurt him when I pulled back from him, but I just wasn't expecting it and well, you know." Casey looked down.

"You don't touch. I know. Yes, you really did hurt Trick that night. I've never seen him make an advance like that. It was spontaneous and you shut him right down. I'm surprised Soldier didn't come after you he was so mad at Trick being hurt. It's okay, though. Everybody is different. You stayed and that made him happy, so don't beat yourself up about it anymore," Gom said, standing straight again before saying, "I should probably get going. You have more work to do and I've got to get home. It was nice talking to you and learning a little about your work. I'll tell Ben what you said."

"You said people could be in danger. Are you? In danger, I mean," Casey was following Gom as he headed back toward the front of the theater. Gom paused and turned to Casey, pleased that Casey seemed interested in him at all.

"Not so much, really. I've been taught how to protect myself by the best there is, Soldier and officer training. I'm good. I just hope I can figure out what's going on before someone else gets seriously hurt, or worse."

"Good luck with that. I hope it works out okay. Uh, thanks for coming by. Tell Ben to come down and I'll rock his little theater world." Casey was unlocking the front door again to let Gom out. Gom got a look at Casey's left hand again and wondered what that mark was. He promised himself he was going to ask; maybe the next time he saw Casey.

"Thanks so much. Uh, come by the house sometime if you want. Trick would love it. I still don't know that much about him, but he's doing well with us. Dillon and Soldier are good at what they do." Gom knew what he was talking about.

"Uh, maybe, I don't know."

"I'd like it, too." That was about as out there as Gom had ever put himself and he was nearly vibrating with nerves as he glanced at Casey.

"Really?" Casey asked, looking at him seriously for a few seconds. Gom thought his heart would burst out of his chest as he stood there waiting for either a fist or some hope.

Finally, it occurred it him that the ball was in his court. "Mmm, yeah, I mean, if you don't like the whole big group thing maybe you'd like to do something else sometime," Gom rambled, feeling disgusted with himself for sounding like a total loser.

"Oh, well, maybe. You mean, like you and me, just us?" Casey asked.

Gom blushed, damn it. "Yeah, but you don't have to worry about me coming on to you. I just thought it might be nice to get to know you a little better. I'm sorry. I shouldn't have said anything." Gom was no longer self-conscious about anything but this. He was proud of himself in every other area of his life and that was due to Soldier and Dillon's love, direction, and support. But in this area, he was just a little lost.

"But you did, say something, I mean." Casey was looking at him, speculatively. It looked like he was thinking about his next move very carefully. Gom held his breath. All he could manage as a response was a lift of his brows in question.

Casey put him out of his misery. "I'd like to do something with you sometime, Gom. Do I need to call you Monty if we're together somewhere?"

"No, not unless I alert you to someone being near that I know from school." Gom stopped and stared for a second, then said, "Really? You'd like to maybe…you're…are you…?" Again with the loser thing! Why couldn't he just ask if it would be a date or just possible friendship?

"Relax, Gom. You look scared. I'm not going to go off on you or anything. I'm not used to the dating thing at all, so let's just say we're going to do something together and see if we like each other's company. If more develops, it's all good. Now go. I'm tired of talking. I haven't talked this much in six months and that includes working. Jesus, you're going to wear me out. I just know it." Casey gave Gom a small smile to soften the words as Gom stepped through the door and stood listening as it locked behind him. He would not turn and look back at Casey. It would just be too…oh hell; he turned back.

Casey was standing there, hands in the pockets of his worn jeans, watching Gom without any expression at all, just watching. Gom smiled a little, and got a small nod from Casey. Gom headed for the car he'd borrowed from the house.

He sat for a minute in the car, looking at the darkened front of the theater, wondering. Did that really happen? Did Casey, who never talked much at all, just spend all that time talking to him? Had he agreed to a sort of date? Did that mean Casey was gay? He hadn't been upset with the request, so he might just be. Gom started the car and headed home, his head full of Casey's words and his own thoughts and dreams and fears. Was he going to be able to do this?

When he got in, Soldier was in the kitchen with a cup of hot chocolate, sitting at the table. There was another steaming cup across from him. He looked up when Gom came through the door and said, with perfect timing,

"You want to talk about it?"

Gom leaned back against the door and looked at Soldier, his heart full.

"How do you always know?"

"We're in tune, you and I. We always have been. Your heart is heavy tonight. So, how's Casey?" Soldier kicked the chair out a little across from him and Gom left the door and moved to the table, grabbed his cup, and moved around to sit by Soldier instead of across from him. Soldier smiled at the move.

"Casey's fine. He said to tell Ben to come down at five tomorrow or one night next week and he'd give him a tour, introduce him to the cast, and let his be assistant for the night. Ben will freak out when he hears. Oh, he asked about Trick, seemed worried that he might have run away. I told him Trick was fine." Gom took a sip from the hot drink and wouldn't meet Soldier's eyes. "Casey was really nice about Ben, huh?"

"What's wrong, Gom?" Soldier's hand came out to rest on his shoulder, cupping the back of his neck. Gom laid his head over onto Soldier's wrist and sighed. He might as well tell it all. He knew he wanted to, needed to get Soldier's take on things.

"I like him, Soldier, big time. We talked a lot tonight."

"Casey talked a lot? That's new," Soldier teased.

"For real. When I left he told me to go 'cause he was tired of talking. Evidently, he talked more to me tonight than he has in the last six months. So he doesn't talk much and doesn't like to be touched. By the way, he apologized for hurting Trick last night. He knew he'd messed up, but hadn't been expecting it. Soldier, he said he couldn't remember the last time he'd been touched, except for a handshake or two. Don't you think that's sad?"

Soldier squeezed Gom's shoulder as he turned back to reach for his cup. Gom could see that he was thinking.

"Do you know why he doesn't like it? Do you think there's been some trauma there or is he just someone who is always alone and isn't used to it?" Soldier asked.

"I don't know. We didn't get that far at all. I told him about my job and we talked about the theater some. I asked him if he wanted to come to supper again sometime and he looked uncomfortable and so I got my nerve up to ask if he maybe wanted to do something together and I didn't know if he was going to hit me or ignore me or what." Gom was again very interested in his drink.

"Which did he do?" Soldier quietly asked.

"He said we could do something sometime. He didn't come out and say he was gay, but he didn't freak at the idea of hanging out, just the two of us. He said we'd just go out and see if we liked each other's company. No expectations, I guess." Gom was trying so hard not to have expectations.

"That sounds promising, son."

"I didn't think you liked him." Gom hoped he was wrong.

"I don't *dis*like him. I could have whopped him for hurting Trick last night, but I can sort of understand better now. I have nothing against him at all. I just don't want you hurt." Soldier tried to smile for Gom, but it wasn't much of one, considering the topic. "I wouldn't handle that well. I'll try not to be too much of a hovering father, but you're my Gom, and no one gets to hurt you." Soldier had never gotten over what Gom had gone through when he was seventeen. It had been really bad and Soldier felt like he'd let Gom down since he promised him years ago that nothing would ever hurt Gom again. There were just some things that Soldier couldn't control. Bless his heart for trying, though.

Gom's thoughts chased each other around his tired brain when he finally got to bed, keeping sleep at bay. He had to talk with Miss Summer tomorrow and see if that they could figure out why Tony had targeted Bradley. They needed a plan for Monday at school. Gom needed to know what kind of things to look for with Tony. Maybe she would have some ideas. He needed to check with the police and see if they'd followed up on the vandalism at the Haines house by seeing where Tony and his boys were at the time. He was afraid that things were escalating rapidly.

Before he allowed sleep to claim him, he thought about Casey Tanner. Why was he so attracted to Casey? He'd known he was gay years ago, but had not even been interested in looking for hook ups or relationships. He admitted to not being the type for a quick hook up, but the idea of sharing his body with someone else scared him badly. He was a brave man, had the training to prove it, but when it came to intimacy, he was really in a world of hurt.

Was Casey the man who would make putting his heart out there worth it? What would it be like to kiss those full lips, get close to those gorgeous eyes, really close, so he could see right into them? Would Casey ever let Gom hug him? He sighed, rubbing his hand over his face, wishing he wasn't so backward in this situation. He wanted to impress Casey, not make the man think he was still a basket case. Lord knew he used to be.

His good life with Dillon and Soldier had nearly erased the years before from his memory. Well, not really, but he didn't think about it anymore except in almost clinical terms. He'd gone through a lot of therapy and talked it out finally, then put it away.

He'd been in a good place for fourteen years. They made up for the hell of his first eight. Really, they did.

CHAPTER FIVE

Sunday had been mostly a day of rest, a much-needed one. He had made that call to Laurie Summer and had arranged to meet in her office before school started Monday morning. She was to have worked on trying to come up with possible reasons for Bradley's current situation. Gom had only been at the school a couple of weeks so he wasn't as up on the dynamics of the gangs and groups and so on. He needed to catch up. He brought in some doughnuts and coffee that Dillon had handed him as he left home.

"Wow, that's the way to make friends. I skipped breakfast so I could meet you this early. Gimme," Laurie demanded, hands reaching for the cup and the box of goodies.

Gom laughed and handed over the doughnuts and waited for the response. It came through as expected.

"Oh, God, Mmm, these are unbelievable. Where did you get them? I don't recognize them and I know doughnuts in this town, believe me." Laurie's eyes were closed in seeming ecstasy.

"My dad, Dillon, makes them. He's made them for years for special breakfasts. I like the ones with the orange glaze. Try that one," Gom said, pointing.

"Do I have to share these?" She looked up at him, unashamed of her greed, evidently.

Gom couldn't help it. He laughed again and shook his head. "No, I had mine earlier. You enjoy them."

"God, thank you. Sit down. We've got to figure this out. Are the Haines children okay? What's your take on the situation with the father? I've got a visit scheduled for later this afternoon, but your input would be helpful. They respond differently when it's an official visit, if you know what I mean."

"They're okay. I talked to Bradley late yesterday afternoon and he said his dad was sober. He sounded relieved. Miss Summer, that is the weirdest family dynamic I've ever seen. I think Bradley has raised his fifth grade sister since she was born. The father has nothing to do with her at all unless he's drunk and thinks she's the reincarnation of his dead wife and then it's just scary sick. They need to be taken out of there, but he's afraid of what will happen to his dad, who seems incapable of caring for himself. I don't even know what they live on. Not much, I'm sure."

"It's Laurie. I'll find out more information like that today. I have Bradley's file and will add to it." After downing two doughnuts and drinking half the coffee, Laurie sat back and looked at him, expectantly.

He proceeded to tell her all he'd learned about how Bradley lived, how the father acted, the actions Bradley took to make sure that Missy was never alone with her dad, and how he'd found him under the bleachers Friday night. She threw questions out as he told it and he made sure he told her everything that was said Friday night at school and again after the vandalism of their house.

"He thought it was funny that the bricks told him to shut up and called him a faggot. He said he wasn't gay and he hadn't said anything to anyone. He says he doesn't have friends. Do you know if that's true? I've only been here the two weeks, but I haven't seen him with anyone else."

"No, he's pretty much a loner, or more accurately, ostracized. I brought him in about three weeks ago and tried to see if there was anything bothering him or if there was something he needed. He was very quiet and polite and said that things were fine." She was making notes as she talked.

"Three weeks ago. When, exactly, in relation to when the words appeared on his locker?" Gom asked.

Laurie's head came up and she looked at him with a frown. "Hmm…I think the day before. Let me check the records." She moved a little, opening a drawer and digging through a thick rack of files. After looking through them she said, "Yes, it was the day before. I talked to him in the morning and the next morning, the words were on his locker. But that's all we talked about."

Gom had an idea. This was the big question. "Did you have any problems with Tony Ramirez right before or right after you talked to Bradley? Your office opens onto the hall, so anyone can see who comes out of here, right?"

If it wasn't such a serious situation, Gom would have been amused at the dawning expression on her face. He knew they were getting somewhere.

"What?"

"You hit it on the head. That same afternoon I brought Tony Ramirez in to question him about reports of him being seen with a known drug dealer. It wasn't on school property, but close enough. I only asked him about it, but he was angry. His parents are very well off and he thinks he can get by with anything because they donate money to the school for various things. The two were totally unrelated, but..." she paused and he filled in for her.

"What if he saw Bradley coming out of your office and thought that Bradley was the one who told you about the drug dealer? That would set him onto Bradley for..." Gom put his hands up in the quote gesture, "'talking where he should have kept his mouth shut'."

"Oh, my God. I bet you're right. It never occurred to me that there was any connection between the two. Okay, we've got a few minutes before people start arriving and you have to get out of here. He'll think *you* narced next." She was reaching for the phone with one hand and scribbling on a pad with the other.

"I'll be watching carefully today. I'll check in this afternoon after I know that Tony has left the building. You'll be here that late?"

"You're funny. I'm always here late. There used to not be a need for my position and now frankly, I'm not enough. We could use two more just like me to keep up with the incidents at this school." She waved him out as the person she was calling came on the line and she turned to speak to them.

※ ※ ※

Gom was sitting in the Driver's Ed class he was enrolled in and it was all he could do to keep his mouth shut. Since he drove a car to school, he'd told them he needed to take the class to take points off his license, placed there for speeding. One of the coaches from the football team taught the class, and he was likely one of the most prejudiced people Gom had ever seen. And he was a teacher! That was just wrong on so many levels. He bit his lip as the coach made another snide remark to a young man two rows over from Gom. Coach Ramsey was bent down and right in the guy's face, talking quietly.

"Well, Pretty Boy, aren't you going to answer? I asked you to bring in your papers to prove you're old enough to drive. You look like a sweet little pansy boy to me. I'm not sure you should even be in here."

Gom was stunned as there were snickers and a couple of outright laughs. Coach wasn't as quiet as he thought. Maybe he wasn't even trying to be. A few of the students had their heads down and some even had frowns on their faces. Gom wanted to say something so badly, but he knew better. He couldn't draw attention to himself.

"Answer me, Sissy! Are you sure you need to be in here?" With that, the large man pointed his finger in the boy's face. There were tears swimming in the boy's eyes, but he didn't say anything. Gom noticed his hand shaking a little. This was beyond ridiculous! How dare this teacher, this educator, treat a young person in this manner, intimidate him, ridicule him, scare him like this! This man was supposed to be a leader, setting an example. He was, all right; an example of how to be a bully.

Gom looked around to see if there was a way he could diffuse the situation.

He raised his hand and got the teacher's attention. "Uh, sir, what was the assignment again? I lost my notes. I'm sorry." He figured he would draw the man's ire toward him.

"What? Aren't you the new kid? You don't look much older than this one. Oh, yeah, you're the one with all the problems and you want to pass this to get your license cleaned up a little. Well, you're not going to do it with this attitude. Pay attention," the coach barked, and Gom could swear he could hear him mutter "you little faggot" under his breath. He looked around and saw a couple of students with wide eyes. Yep, he'd said something, all right.

How in the world could they expect to decrease the bullying and violence in the schools when it started at the top? Gom made notes during the class, but they had nothing to do with the rules of the road.

The phone on Coach Ramsey's desk rang and he headed back to the front of the room. Gom was surprised when the man looked right at him with a frown. Setting the phone back on the desk, he pointed to Gom and said, "Mr. Marshall, you're wanted in the office. Maybe you got problems other than driving, huh?"

"Yes, sir. I mean, I don't know, sir." *You're an asshole, sir.*

Gom gathered his books and hurried out of the room and toward the office. Before he got there, the school officer met him.

"You're to go to Miss Summer's office, uh, Monty," Officer Cane said.

Gom switched routes and headed there instead. When he knocked on the door, he was told to enter.

He stopped when he saw Trick sitting there in front of the desk.

"Trick, are you okay? What happened?" As far as Gom knew, Trick had not had any trouble at this school. He seemed happy here.

"Close the door, Monty." Laurie's voice was serious. Oh shit. What had Trick done?

Trick's eyes never left Gom's face and they were wide with what looked like fear. What was going on here?

He went to stand by the young boy and put his hand on Trick's shoulder and squeezed. Like he'd told Casey, Trick was family now.

"Tell me what's going on, please." Gom looked from Trick to Laurie.

The door opened and the principal and Officer Cane came in and closed the door behind them.

"Trick, will you tell us all what you saw, please? You know you're not in trouble, but this is very serious. Be sure about it," Laurie said, talking quietly.

Gom and the two other men must have seemed imposing to the young boy, but he looked at Gom when he spoke.

"I was walking through the hall, uh, I had a pass to go to the bathroom. When I walked past this guy's locker he was standing there with it open and talking to another boy. They're both seniors, I think. Anyway, I wasn't paying them much attention until I heard the name Bradley."

That got Gom's attention in a hurry. He nodded at Trick to go on.

"I slowed down but didn't look over so they wouldn't think I was listening to them. Just as I got level I cut my eyes over and saw the Hispanic guy point to a gun in his locker. He was showing it to a big black guy and laughing. He said something about no more problems. It was all I could do to keep walking slow and act like I hadn't heard anything. I went on to the bathroom, scared to death they would follow me in thinking I'd heard them. After a while, I came here. That's all. Did I do the right thing?"

Gom squeezed that shoulder again. "You absolutely did the right thing. Good job, Trick. Relax now. You're not in trouble." He turned to the officer and the principal, Mr. Hunt. "What's your procedure for this here? It's a little bit different everywhere."

"I've already called the teacher where Tony is supposed to be and he's back in class. Bradley is not in that class so we're good. I'm calling the police now and as soon as they get here, we'll escort him and the other boy, Taylor Jackson, off the premises. We'll get the gun when the officers get here. This is something I wish I could do in front of any of the students who come by, but it will be kept quiet. We don't want anyone getting ideas.

We have two people watching the locker now to make sure no one gets near it before the police arrive." Mr. Hunt told him. "Does this end your work here? Now that we know, or are pretty sure, that the reason Tony targeted Bradley was because Tony thought Bradley told Miss Summer about his meeting with the drug dealer. Is there anything else you need to do?"

"Yes, sir. I need to talk to you about another matter entirely. It's important, but it can wait until after this is dealt with properly." Gom fully intended to tell Mr. Hunt and Laurie about the crude coach and how damaging his words were in the classroom.

"Let's do this. The police should be here any minute. Trick, young man, you should consider yourself free for the rest of the day. I'm going to call your father and have him pick you up. I don't want you anywhere near when we open that locker and get that gun. I don't want Tony making the connection to you seeing him. Not that he's going to be free to do much to anyone for a while. He won't be back at this school, that's for sure. Better safe than sorry. Do you have any tests today, son?"

"No sir. I'm caught up. I don't have my books, though."

"That's okay. We'll take care of all that. Monty can bring your things home to you. Laurie, call his father and explain enough to get him here without freaking him out. Tell him to come to the south entrance to the school. That will be well away from anything going on with this."

"Sir, I think we should do the same thing with Bradley Haines. Get him out of here completely," Laurie suggested. "I just don't want any of his gang to see Bradley and try to make any kind of connection between the two events."

"He could go with Trick and my dad. Bradley and his sister stayed with us Friday night when all that happened at their house. He would be comfortable with Soldier and safe as could be," Gom said.

"Good idea. Should we call Bradley's father, too?" Mr. Hunt asked. Evidently, Laurie had already talked to him about the dad and his problems.

"If I may suggest something, I'd let Soldier and Bradley decide that. They'll have to pick up Missy, too, after school." Gom thought this was getting complicated.

"Okay, I guess you know best in this case, having dealt with the situation there."

"Yes, sir. I'd love to be in on the arrest, but I don't want him to have the chance to blow my cover. This assignment has been helpful in three situations now. I hate the need for it, but I do see that it is working. I'll be by your office this afternoon as soon as school is out."

Gom headed back out to class, acting like nothing unusual was going on. Just as he got back to the coach's classroom the bell sounded and he hurried in to gather his books. He watched closely as the boy that Coach Ramsey had harassed quietly picked up his own books and headed out. Gom moved closer to him and asked his name.

"Uh, Marty Langley. You're Monty, right. Marty and Monty. Weird, huh?" Marty asked, seeming nervous.

"I'm sorry Coach Ramsey gave you such a hard time."

They were outside the classroom now and in the middle of the flow in the hallway.

"It's okay. I'm used to it. He manages to get in at least one dig a day. As long as he's picking on me, he's letting the others have a break," Marty said, shrugging.

Gom thought that was a pretty cool attitude, but he didn't agree with it.

"Others?" he asked.

"Yeah, Coach Ramsey is an equal opportunity heckler. He hates gays, blacks, Hispanics, uh, overweight people, etc. He doesn't discriminate in his ridiculing. He's got something ugly to say about anyone who is different in any way from the perfect, the athletic, and the rich. Those he leaves alone. I'd watch it if I were you, I heard what he said about you under his breath." Marty leaned in to say more. "Once he starts on you, he doesn't let up. If he sees it gets to you, he gets worse. Never out loud to the whole class but he singles you out and takes you down."

"Geez. Is he the only one like that? Are there any others I need to look out for?" Gom asked.

"Nah, he's the worst. There are some who treat some of us differently, but he's the only one I know who comes out and says things." Marty slowed as he got to his next class.

Gom stopped beside him and asked, "Would you be willing to tell that to Miss Summer and Mr. Hunt? Can you give me some other names of people that he's picked on? It's important."

"Who are you, the bully police? I don't want to be on his list any more than I already am." Marty started to edge away, toward the classroom door.

"If we don't stand up to this, it will continue. You have a pretty good attitude about it, but what about someone who can't handle it? What if the things he says, or allows others to say, really hurts someone who isn't able to look at it like you do?" Gom saw a look pass over Marty's face.

"That hit a nerve. You know someone like that don't you?" Gom asked, putting his hand on Marty's arm to try and keep him there for another minute to get some info.

"There's this girl, Sheila. She's big, like really big, and he kept on and on at her until she dropped the class. She said he told her she wouldn't fit in a car anyway, so why bother trying to learn. He called her names and made her cry then sneered at her." Marty got this cold look in his eyes when he talked about the hazing. "She's not strong, you know? Actually, Sheila's really pretty and smarter than anyone I know. It's amazing how people don't think so just because of how she looks. She's missed a lot of days lately and I'm worried about her." Marty ducked his head before going on. "I've tried to call her, but she doesn't answer her phone."

"And you didn't think someone should be told? What's her last name?" Gom asked.

"Mason, and who do you think would listen?" Marty asked, a little aggressively. "This shit goes on all the time.

"Will you meet me after school?" Gom asked, trying to think about when he could see Marty. "How about meeting for supper somewhere? I'll buy. Can you get away from home?"

"Sure, no problem. But, what are we meeting for? I don't want to get in trouble. I don't have a car, either, so…"

"I can pick you up. As a matter of fact, we can eat at my house. My dads won't mind. Hey, can you see if Sheila would like to come, too? I'll bring a friend and we can talk about this. It's gotta stop, Marty."

Gom's mind was turning things over fast in his head. He wanted to see if Bradley and Missy could come over, not wanting Tony to have a chance to get word to his buddies to go after Bradley. He'd see if Miss Summer could join them.

"I don't know if Sheila will come out. I'll call her, though. And, did you say your dads?" Marty's look was one of curiosity.

"Yeah, I have two dads. Is that a problem?" Gom wanted to know now.

"Not at all. I think it's cool. I'll call Sheila and see if she'll come. Can you pick her up, too? She doesn't live too far from me." Marty was getting excited now.

Gom looked around. They were the only ones left in the hall. Uh-oh.

"Give me your phone number and I'll call you this afternoon and set it all up. You better get in there now." Gom got the number and left for his next class. His heart was getting lighter. He was making some headway here. Marty was a great find.

The end of the school day couldn't come fast enough for Gom. He wanted to know what was going on with Tony and he had a meeting with the principal to get through. He headed for Miss Summer's office as soon as most of the kids had left the building. He'd already heard the buzz about Tony leaving school in handcuffs. No one knew why, but they were all talking, some gleefully, some just curious. He'd also heard that Taylor had been taken in, too. Good. He wondered about the other two boys. They hadn't been in on the gun sighting, so they weren't arrested, but they would bear watching. Maybe without Tony around, they wouldn't be a problem.

When he got to Miss Summer's office, she looked worn out. She waved him in and he dropped into the chair across from her desk.

"How'd it go? You look beat." he said.

"As you would expect. He was totally pissed and ready to tear someone's head off. He made all kinds of threats and his father showed up to spew even more, but the gun was there and he had no excuses. He and Taylor both won't be back here. I'll have to go back downtown tomorrow and meet with the officers and there'll be more paperwork, but you did a good job here, Monty Marshall." She smiled slightly, rubbing her forehead.

"There's more we have to tackle. My work here isn't over," Gom said.

"Oh, Lord. What else?" Laurie sat up straight and reached for her pad and pen.

Gom proceeded to tell her about his class and the coach's comments. Laurie's eyes nearly bugged out of her head when he told her some of the comments he'd heard. Then he got to Marty's information about Sheila Mason.

"I knew she'd been absent a lot recently and have even called the house to see if she's okay. Her mother said she wasn't feeling well and she'd be back in a couple of days. She's not a problem in any way, so I left it at that. God, I hate that. Just a minute, I'm going to see if Mr. Hunt is available to meet with us here." She reached for the phone and he settled in the chair. This worked out fine for him, since he'd planned to fill Mr. Hunt in on his staff member. Two birds and all that.

Within a few minutes, Mr. Hunt came in and settled into the chair beside Gom.

"Quite a day, huh? Good job, Mr. Marsh, uh—Marshall. You said you wanted to meet with me about something." Mr. Hunt looked back and forth between Gom and Laurie.

"You've got big problems here, sir, and it's not just with the student body. It starts at a higher level." Gom went over the whole thing again for Mr. Hunt, who sat up straighter when he heard what Coach Ramsey had said to Marty, to Gom, and also to Sheila Mason. His face paled as he realized the degree of damage this one man had done at the school.

"Coach Ramsey is not on tenure here. This is only his second year. He will be terminated before the week is out. I will need statements from as many students as you can find, but this will not be a problem. It wouldn't be even if he had tenure. I would take this as far as I had to in order to get him out of this school. There is no excuse for this kind of behavior from an educator." Mr. Hunt's ire was genuine.

"I was hoping you would feel that way. I've invited Marty to my house for supper tonight and asked him to see if Sheila would come with him. I'm going to see if Bradley and Missy will stay, too. I was going to ask you to come, too, Laurie, if that's all right. If this could happen in a less stressful setting, we might get more names and information than if you called them in here. I'll need to call Soldier and Dillon, but I'm sure we can work it out. We'll keep up my Monty character. Can you come?" Gom asked, looking at Laurie.

She smiled. "What can I bring?"

"Nothing, really. But you can tell Dillon how much you liked his doughnuts," Gom teased her.

"You had doughnuts and you didn't share?" Mr. Hunt joined in the teasing.

"Hey, you weren't even here yet. It's that thing about the early bird." She gave it right back. They all chuckled and the tension in the room eased a little.

"I think Bradley will be safe now," Mr. Hunt said, standing. "This other stuff, you keep me informed on it, will you, Laurie?"

Gom liked the way they used first names when not in front of the students. It meant that the staff here liked each other and got along. Well, except for Coach Ramsey.

Unlike some of the other officers on the force, Gom found it necessary to bring his work home with him, so to speak, on occasion. Every case was different and he liked Bradley and Marty. He wanted to meet Sheila and he bet she knew of more who were treated poorly. Gom knew that teachers were required to take classes on diversity, even sensitivity training, but evidently it didn't make an impression on everyone.

To his mind, it was a sin when someone children should look up to let them down. Gom should know. He'd had examples of both sides of that coin in the extreme.

"Monty?" Laurie's voice broke into his momentary visit to the past.

"Yeah, sorry. About six tonight? You've got the address in my file, so I'll see you then. We'll just do supper with everyone then we'll go to the den for a meeting. It should work. I think we'll get a good look at some things that you need to know." Gom stood as he finished.

"Yes, I think you're right and I hate it that it takes something like this to find it out. We need to have something set up where these kids can come and let this kind of thing be known, maybe anonymously, so it can be looked into. I'm going to think about that." Laurie was again making notes on that pad.

"That's not a bad idea. There are a lot of things that might come out if the students didn't think they'd get in trouble for it." Gom was impressed with Laurie Summer. Her care for the students and her dedication to her job was evident. Would that there were more like her!

Gom drove home, anxious to talk to Soldier and Dillon about his plans and make sure it was okay. Silly. He knew they would be fine with anything that ended up helping children who were being hurt in any way. As he pulled in the parking area at Scarcity Sanctuary, his cell phone rang. Turning off the car, he pulled the phone out and answered. When he heard Casey's voice, his heart raced.

"Hey, Casey. How'd you get my number?"

"Um, hi. I called your house and Dillon gave it to me. You got plans tonight?" Casey's voice was hesitant.

"Yeah, man, sorry. I've got a big meeting at the house. There are a couple of kids at school who have been hassled by a teacher. Can you believe that? Anyway, the Safe-T coordinator will be here and we're going to see how far this goes and who else has been targeted. It sucks pretty bad," Gom said. He would never give anyone names from any of his cases, but he could talk to Casey about it in vague terms.

"Man, that does suck. I remember this guy when I was in school…" Casey trailed off.

"There's a story there, I bet. Anyway, I'm sorry about tonight." Gom wondered what Casey had in mind.

"That's no big thing. We'll get together some other night. Good luck with your meeting. You're, uh, you're doing a good thing." Casey sounded embarrassed saying that, but it meant a lot to Gom.

"So, Ben said you set a time when he could come to the theater. You were great with him. He hasn't stopped talking about it. You made him very happy and he said he would get to learn a lot. Thank you so much for that." Anyone who made one of his family members happy was wonderful in his book.

"It was good. Ben's a smart one. I told him he could come any time and I'd put him to work."

"Watch it, you'll never see the end of him," Gom teased.

"Not a problem. So, I'll call you sometime then?" Casey asked.

"Seriously? Please do." Gom was hoping to see him soon.

They said good-bye and Gom headed in to talk to his dads and set things up for tonight. He had to see if Bradley would join in the meeting. Dillon could make sure that Missy had something to do while they were talking in the den. He had calls to make and reports to fill out before the evening began.

"Soldier! Dillon! I need help tonight," he yelled as he hit the door.

In seconds both men were there, identical expressions of query on their faces. God, he loved these two men.

"I sort of invited a few people for supper. We have maybe three students and the Safe-T coordinator from school. We need to meet and discuss some very important things, away from the school formality. I offered this place as a neutral spot, comfortable but a good place for the meeting. Are Bradley and Missy still here?"

"Yes, they're here working on homework. Their dad is kind of out of things today so I'm glad they're here. I called him to tell him that I would pick up Missy with Bradley and he simply asked if Lenora was coming home. I told him that she wasn't and that Bradley and Missy would be home after supper. I want to talk to your friend from school about getting them out of there. Something could be done for him, but in the meantime, they need to be safe." Soldier's countenance was very serious as he talked and Gom could see that he was really worried about the Haines' home situation.

"That would be a good idea. You should talk to Laurie about it. Her name is Laurie Summer and she's very good at her job. She had a good idea today that she needs to follow up on. Ask her about it. Now, is there anything I need to do for supper? I asked her to be here at about six and I need to pick up this new kid named, Marty Langley, and hopefully his friend, Sheila, will join us, too."

"You take care of your business and we'll make sure supper is a success. I love a challenge," Dillon said.

"Oh, she was a mess over your doughnuts. She asked if she had to share them with anyone and the joy on her face when I told her she could have them all would have made you proud." Gom complimented his dad.

"I maybe could make a batch and send her home with some...so I'll make extra. It's only Ben, Trick, and Niko on the home front tonight, so I'll make a couple of big pots of, hmm, chili, and vegetable soup, homemade croutons to put in, cheese for the chili, and I'll come up with something for dessert. The doughnuts will be for later, maybe after your meeting, and then some for them to take home." Dillon loved cooking and seeing people enjoy his hard work.

"You're the best. Oh, Casey called and wanted to know if I could do something tonight, but I told him I had a big meeting here." Gom tried not to let disappointment show in his voice.

"You could call him and see if he'd want to come to supper again," Dillon suggested.

"Nah, I don't think he'd be into it. Plus, I don't want to make the kids uncomfortable with a lot of new people. Marty thinks the two dads thing is cool, by the way. I'd say, from the ribbing he got today, he's of the persuasion. His friend, Sheila, is overweight and takes a lot of heat for it, evidently. I hate that kids have to put up with harassment because of things like that. School's hard enough. Marty says she's smart, though. I hope she comes with him. Gotta go make some calls. See you in a bit."

Gom headed to his room and made the calls, thrilled when Marty said he'd gotten to talk to Sheila and convinced her to join them. This was good news. He worked on reports for a while, checked in with his captain and gave him a cursory report and told him the rest was coming on computer. Gom didn't go into the station, not wanting to be seen there.

It was getting near time to pick up Marty and Sheila so he headed back down. Missy was laughing when he came into the kitchen.

"Wow, it smells great in here already. You're miracle workers," Gom said, looking at the two huge pots boiling away on the stove. The scents were indeed heavenly. He hadn't realized how hungry he was until he came in here. "Hey, Missy, what are you working on?"

"I'm making two big chocolate éclair cakes for dessert. They're so simple. I can't believe it. I'm doing them all myself. Well, Mr. Dillon is telling me what to do. I hope you all like them," she said, blushing.

"I don't think there's any doubt of that. Between the two

of you, sweets are fabulous. I still remember the two cakes you all made for the cookout. Still can't decide which one was my favorite."

"I know. I like the German Chocolate, cause of the coconut and pecan frosting," she said, sighing.

"Yeah, I think that's what puts it second in my book. I like that dark chocolate taste." Gom enjoyed talking with her.

"You'll like this then, 'cause it's got dark chocolate chips melted on top."

"Mmm, I can't wait. I'll be back in a few minutes with my friends. Thank you all for getting this all set up for me," Gom said, high-fiving both dads and Missy as he went out the door.

CHAPTER SIX

As expected, supper was a huge success. So many bowls were filled and refilled until there were groans all around. Missy's cake went over very well, if the two empty dishes were any indication.

During the meal, Marty had proven to be a great source of humor and Sheila, while quieter, was sweet and very kind to Missy, making her feel part of the older group. They talked about movies and music and the kids were quite vocal about their likes and dislikes. Names like Gaga, Lambert, Bieber, Usher, even some country with Sugarland and Lady Antebellum were bandied about. It was clear that the kids were really a bit weirded out that Miss Summer was there, too, but she fit right in with them. Gom thought she was good at her job because she knew all about everything they talked about, so before long they were all sharing as equals.

Now Missy was in the kitchen with Dillon making doughnuts to send home with each guest. Dillon had taken a liking to the pretty young girl and she beamed with happiness at the attention. Soldier had been invited to join in the meeting since Monty was supposed to be a high school kid.

During the meal, Gom felt his phone vibrate and took it out to find a quick text from Casey. "Call me after your meeting. If you want to. CT"

Oh, yeah, he wanted to very much.

Miss Summer was leading the meeting in the den now and with the door closed, the students all had faces that showed their emotions. Had they been manipulated into some kind of school thing? They looked around.

"Relax, guys. I asked Monty's dad, Soldier, if we could meet here since Monty talked to me about some things that have been going on. First, let me say that I'm sorry about some of the things you've been dealing with in school. I wish I had known about them, but I understand your reluctance in talking about it.

What I want to do now, away from the school, is have a sharing session. I want to know about some of the bad things that have happened to you at school." Laurie looked around from Bradley, to Marty and Sheila, then to Gom. No one spoke up. They all looked nervous.

"Okay," she said, "I get it. I came prepared for this. I'll start." Laurie hopped up, put her feet under her in the big chair she'd chosen and made herself comfortable. In her jeans and sweatshirt, and curled up in the chair, she looked like a teenager herself. "I'm going to tell you a true story. It's about when I was your age, high school. I was overweight, not obese, but bigger than all of my friends. Every day in several of my classes, since we sat in alphabetical order, I was in front of Donnie Tibbs. Every day he picked on me. His favorite thing was calling me Fatass. 'Move, Fatass, I can't see.' 'Shut up, Fatass!' were just some of the things I heard over and over. He'd knock my books off the desk, push my chair up with his feet so it hit the one in front of me. Little things, but constant. I don't mind telling you that it hurt. I cried many a night."

Sheila spoke up. "You were big? Really? But, you're gorgeous."

"Thank you, sweetheart. That means a lot. I was big until halfway through college. I just decided that I was tired of being the biggest girl in any group. So I started eating right. I'd always known how, I just didn't want to do it. I started exercising daily and it just became the new normal for me. Eventually, I got thinner and thinner and it's stayed off. But back to my story.

"I have a little house on Tenth Street. Recently my neighbor and I worked together to rebrick my front porch. We figured out how many bricks I'd need and I went to buy them. When I got to the store, I recognized the owner as Donnie Tibbs. He kept looking at me all the time we were talking about what I needed, but he didn't say anything." She looked around and Gom knew she saw a rapt audience.

"As it happened, we hadn't planned well and I needed to go back and get a few more bricks. When I went back in Donnie came around the counter and looked at me a minute before he said, 'You look so familiar. Do I know you?'"

"What did you say?" Marty asked for them all.

"I looked him right in the eye and said, 'Yes, you know me. I'm Fatass.'"

There were cheers as the group thought he'd gotten what was coming to him. But Gom wanted to know more.

"What did he say to that?"

"He took my hand and told me he was so sorry. He said that he wasn't that person anymore and he hated the fact that he ever had been. I could tell that he was sincere, but I got my say in, too. I told him that was fine, but that he had really hurt me. That upset him. I wondered at the time, did he think it *hadn't* hurt me? Come on."

"Wow, Miss Summer, who would've thought you were ever treated like that? Is that why you do what you do?" This question came from Bradley.

"In a small way, yes. I deal with all kinds of incidents at the school, but a growing one is the bullying that has escalated in the last several years. I want to know, if you'll tell me, some of the things that have happened to you all. I'm not going to get you into any kind of trouble, but I want to know. It's my *job* to know and to do something about it. I hate that some of the things I've been hearing about have been going on and I wasn't aware of it."

Gom started, so the others would, hopefully, jump in. "I was in Coach Ramsey's class today and raised my hand to ask a question about the assignment because I'd lost my notes and he told me to pay attention and then under his breath he said, where I could hear it, 'you little faggot'. I'm sure he meant for me to hear it, but I know Marty heard it, too, and some others because I heard snickers. I had a hard time not talking back to him."

"You did a good job. I would have wanted to if I'd been there. Marty, what can you tell me? Will you tell me what he's said to you? All Monty told me was that he picked on you in class. Before anything can be done about it, I have to have documented evidence that there are several cases. I intend to do something about this, but I need your help to do it."

"I'll tell you. Frankly, I'm tired of being picked on. It's bad enough when the other kids do it, but it hurts even worse when it's a teacher." Sheila was sitting up straight in her chair. Gom thought that Marty had been right. She was a really pretty girl with beautiful long curly hair and clear skin.

"Thank you, Sheila. Tell us a little about what you've had to put up with," Laurie said.

"Coach Ramsey is the worst. I dropped his class because I just couldn't listen to him anymore. I felt so bad every time he would say things about me being too fat to do this or that. When he would say stuff the kids around me would laugh and I just wanted to die right there. It hurts." Sheila told a couple of the other comments the rude coach had said to her, well within others' hearing. "One day a guy in the back was whistling this…" With that Sheila hummed the tune that went with the words "Fatty fatty, two by four, can't get through the kitchen door." There wasn't a person there that didn't know what the tune was and that it had been meant to hurt Sheila. There was silence for a moment.

"With me, it was always about being a faggot. That's his favorite word. He likes queer, sissy, and Pretty Boy, too, but he uses faggot a lot." Marty's arms were crossed as he told some of his experiences with the coach. Gom was more and more amazed at the lengths the man had gone to in his hassling of some of the students.

To Gom's surprise, Bradley spoke next. "He always makes a point of standing by my chair at least once during a class and touching his nose and waving the air like something, no, like *I* stink. That's why Tony and the others started calling me Stink. Sometimes I run out of laundry soap and have to just wash the clothes in water or maybe other kinds of soap and we don't have a dryer so the clothes don't smell as clean as they could. I hate it for Missy, mostly. I don't care what they say about me."

Gom stole a glance at Soldier and saw that this was hard on him. Gom knew how much Soldier hated for any child to be hurt in any way.

"Okay, I appreciate what you've told me. I want you to think about friends of yours and whether there are more stories about bullying. I want you to write these things down and sign them. They will not be seen by anyone other than Mr. Hunt and myself. I have to have them, though." She looked around at the students who'd shared their stories and said, "You have to sign them, but I promise the people you tell on will never know that you talked. One thing I want to work on is finding some way for students to report cases like this without worrying about any fallout. Give me a little time as I'm still working on that one."

Marty and Sheila were whispering back and forth until they noticed that everyone else was quiet. Sheila looked up and said, "There's this girl in my class. She's very short. I mean, she's just *short*, Miss Summer. There's nothing wrong with her. But the kids pick on her all the time, calling her troll and garden gnome. She's pretty and she's sweet, but it hurts her feelings. I've even heard the bus driver tell her that if she was taller she could see the numbers on the bus better. That was one day when she walked by the bus and had to come back to get on it. The same bus driver told me if I'd exercise I wouldn't be so fat and she wanted to know if I didn't have any pride at all."

"Will you ask that girl if she'll come to me and fill out information about it? Be sure and tell her that no one will use her name. Mr. Hunt and I are serious about wanting to stop this at all levels, not just the students. It's easy to put a sign on the door that says our school has zero tolerance for drugs, alcohol, and bullying, but when it's happening with adults, how can we expect to control it with the students? Let me think about this and I'm going to come up with a way to make things better."

"Can I ask you a question, Miss Summer?" Marty asked.

"Sure, Marty."

"Why did they take Tony Ramirez to jail today? What did he do?"

"I'm sorry, but I can't tell you that, but he won't be back this year. You all can relax now, huh?" Laurie said, like she knew that he picked on a lot of people.

Gom looked at the others and there were smiles all around. He thought it was a statement about the seriousness of the situation when it made these students so happy to know that a bully would not be there to harass them anymore.

"I'm glad to hear that." Soldier entered the conversation for the first time. "I didn't like knowing that someone like that was threatening good students. What will happen to him?"

"Honestly, I'm not allowed to talk about it, but Bradley should be safe now. It's a good thing Monty was there to help him Friday night." Laurie started to get up, but Soldier asked her to stay a moment and talk with him.

"Monty, why don't you take your friends into the kitchen and see how Dillon and Missy are doing with the doughnuts? You all could probably help pack them up for everyone to take with them."

Gom figured Soldier wanted to talk to Miss Summer about the Haines family and their inappropriate family situation.

Laurie piped up with, "Are they really making doughnuts for people to take home. Like, really?" Gom had to laugh. She sounded like one of the teenagers, filled with glee at the thought of sugar and pastry.

"Go on, guys, you're not going to believe how good they are. We'll be out in a few minutes." Laurie shooed them out and closed the door behind Gom.

Work in the kitchen was going well and they were able to help pack up individual containers of the doughy treats for everyone. There was much laughter and joking as they toiled on the happy chore. There was a new lightness in the faces around him and Gom felt good about that. It looked like he might be done with his work at Willington High. The only unfinished area was Bradley and Missy's home life. He had a feeling Soldier was offering to help out with that. He'd ask him later.

After about twenty minutes, Soldier and Laurie came in and

everyone said their good-byes. Soldier said he would take Bradley and Missy home, with a quick admonition to Bradley to keep an eye out for Missy if their dad was drunk. Gom took Marty and Sheila back home and Laurie waved and tooted her horn as she told them all goodnight.

Marty and Sheila were quiet at first, but soon Marty said, "That was pretty surreal, huh? I like your dads, Monty. They're so nice and they love you so much. They were great with everybody."

"Yeah, I know. I'm lucky. I've had them since I was eight years old. They've made it their life's work to help children. Scarcity was built to help kids like me, who come from serious abusive circumstances. Some kids just don't fit into a regular foster home because of the severity of their problems. Those are the ones that come here. Regular foster homes are great for what they do, especially if it's a short term setting." Gom was thinking about Bradley when he threw in that last part.

As far as he was concerned, he would like to see Bradley and Missy in foster care and Mr. Haines in long term counseling until he could be cleared for getting them back in the home. It could not continue as it was now. He wondered how their life would improve if Bradley didn't have to do all the work at home and worry about Missy. And Lord knows, Missy's life would improve if he would recognize her as his daughter and treat her accordingly, all the time. Gom really hoped that something could be worked out, but that wasn't his place.

Sheila very sweetly thanked him for picking her up and letting her be part of the meeting. "I feel so much better about things now. I'm going to be stronger and try not to let other's comments and actions dictate how I live my life."

"Whew! Way to go, girl. I'm glad. Thanks for coming and helping out. You're going to see about having your friend talk with Miss Summer, aren't you?" Gom asked.

"I will. Do you think Miss Summer will really set something up so that students can let her know when stuff like this goes on?" Sheila asked.

"I think Miss Summer, now that she's had the idea, will follow through and before long, our school days will be better. One person can't make things perfect, but, they can make a difference. I promise you that. I've lived that one."

Before long, Gom was on his own, heading home. Sitting at a red light he remembered Casey's text. He pulled over into the parking lot of a convenience store, turned the key, and sat in silence. Relishing the feeling of expectancy rushing through him, he took out his phone and called Casey.

"Hey, Gom. Meeting over?" Casey was a man of few words sometimes.

"Yep. It went well. The problem with the threat to Bradley was taken care of today and we had a meeting tonight about some of the other bullying that is going on at the school. Can you believe that one of the biggest problems is one of the teachers?" Gom was still a little incensed about it.

"Dude, that sucks." Casey sounded just as upset as Gom felt.

"Truly. He called me a little faggot under his breath today."

"No shit? What did you do?" Casey asked.

"As student Monty Marshall, there wasn't anything I could do. As Gom Marsh, I went to the principal and the lady I'm working with and filled them in on what I'd found out. He does this to all kinds of minorities." Gom felt okay sharing just that much information, knowing that Casey wouldn't talk.

"The man needs a lesson."

Gom laughed and said, "Oh, I think he's going to get one really soon. He won't be working there for long and the students will be a lot happier and mentally stronger. He wears them down big time."

"So what are you doing now?" Casey's tone had dropped to a very husky drawl that crawled up Gom's spine.

"Is that anything like 'what are you wearing'?" Gom teased.

"No, I figure you're in the car so you're still dressed."

"How'd you know I was in my car?" Gom asked, confused.

"There are no sounds. Usually there's noise in the background at your house."

Well, that was true.

"It's quiet on my end, too. Play's over, place is clean. I'm ready to go home. Tonight isn't one of my cleaning nights at the offices so, I'm free." Casey let that comment just lay there for Gom to pick up if he wanted.

Gom definitely wanted. "I could pick you up and drive you home."

"I could walk home, but…you could pick me up and take me home." Gom laughed at Casey's words.

"I'll be there in a few minutes. You want to go for coffee or something?" Gom asked.

"I have coffee at my place, good coffee. But do you need to be drinking it when you have to get up for school tomorrow?"

"I can make it if I get to bed by midnight…or so." Gom said.

"Then I'll be waiting. Hang up, don't drive talking on the phone." Casey's words somehow warmed Gom's heart.

"I don't. I pulled over to call you and I have an ear bud. But I'll hang up and see you soon." Gom called home to tell them he wouldn't be in until late because he had plans with Casey. He swore he could hear the smile in Dillon's voice as they hung up.

When Gom pulled up in front of the Showcase, Casey was standing in the doorway, waiting for him. Gom leaned over and opened the passenger door as Casey sauntered to the car. As it slammed, with Casey next to him, Gom's heartbeat increased in anticipation. Casey looked so *good*.

"Hey. Glad to hear you got things worked out at the school. Sucks about the teacher, though." Casey said, buckling his seat belt.

"Yeah, I have to say my jaw dropped when I heard him being really hateful to this kid that I met today. He was calling him names under his breath, but others could hear and damned if some of them weren't snickering. Then when I asked him a question in an attempt to divert his attention from the other boy, he threw his hate my way. Things like that just shouldn't happen, you know?" Gom pulled out, looking to Casey for directions.

"Up two blocks, turn left, and I have an apartment in the basement of a house on Candle Street. It's got parking in front for you. Here," he said, as they neared his home, "it's the dark brick one, ten twenty-nine. Don't expect anything like where you live. I don't have much, but it's home."

"I don't expect anything, Casey. I came from hell, you know. I haven't always had all that I do now with Soldier and Dillon. Something tells me you worked for what you have. I lucked into the life I have now." Gom knew how privileged he was now, but he remembered the dark days before his life with Dillon and then with Soldier, too.

"You'd be right about that. I didn't mean anything by that, Gom. I know you had to come from something bad to be there."

"I did. Dillon and then Soldier saved me and made me whole again. I was a pretty messed up kid." Gom stopped in front of Casey's place and turned off the car. He sat for a minute, not looking at Casey.

"Are you nervous? You don't have to be scared of me. I won't do anything to you, you know." Casey sat still, too, as if realizing that Gom was at a turning point.

"I don't know how to respond to that. Maybe I want you to, uh, do something to me…maybe." Gom had to chuckle at his own inability to be sure of his desires.

"How about you come in and see my place, have some coffee, and we'll talk some? I can't believe I'm offering to talk, but I seem to just rattle on when I'm around you. It's kind of new for me," Casey admitted.

"Sounds good. I am interested in you, Casey. I think I'd like to see if we can be friends…or maybe more. I'm just not too sure of myself in this area. It embarrasses me to admit it, but

I'm pretty pathetic when it comes to this." Gom dropped his head to the steering wheel. "I'm probably going to be hopelessly awkward and say or do the wrong thing."

His head came up when he felt Casey's hand on his shoulder. "What do you have to know or say to enjoy a cup of coffee with a friend? Come on, Gom. I'm not going to jump you when we close the door. Relax. Come on, there are no expectations except conversation. Promise." Casey opened his door and got out, heading to the house, letting Gom decide whether he was coming along.

Well, Gom might be nervous, but he wasn't stupid. He liked Casey. He wanted to get to know him. He locked the car and caught up with Casey where he'd stopped at a small wrought iron gate that led to steps that went down to a door. Casey looked over at him and nodded. That was all, but Gom felt great at the slight welcoming movement.

"Who lives in the house above you?" Gom asked, as Casey unlocked the gate and they went down the steps to the door below.

"You'll laugh, man." Casey was unlocking his door as he said that, sounding embarrassed.

"Why?" Gom asked, intrigued.

"There's a sweet old couple that lives there. This used to be their son's apartment years ago." Casey was flipping on the light and motioning for Gom to come inside.

"That's cool, but not funny." Gom didn't get it.

"You'd have to see them. They're cute. I think they're both in their nineties. They've been married for over seventy years."

"That's pretty amazing. Do you see them a lot? Do you have to be really quiet down here, keep the music down and all that?" Gom teased him a little.

"No, they're both a little hard of hearing and they're two floors up. I keep trying to get them to let me move them downstairs to a bedroom there, but so far they're still going up the steps. They're in unbelievable shape."

"They sound wonderful." Gom had followed Casey into the room, just a few steps, as they talked. Now he looked around and it took a while. He had expected the place where Casey lived to be somewhat stark, kind of like the way he'd first thought Casey to be.

Casey had seemed to be someone who didn't need anyone. He didn't socialize, he avoided being around people, and he admitted to not talking much at all. Gom was truly in awe of the room as he looked around him. The walls were covered with posters from movies and plays. There was so much color.

"Oh, Case, Ben can never come here."

Casey laughed, actually laughed out loud. It was the first time Gom had ever heard that sound come from him. Of course, they hadn't spent a lot of time together, but Gom found it a nice thing, hearing Casey Tanner laugh. He looked over at Casey and grinned.

"I'm serious. It's so bright and colorful in here. Where did you get all these posters? Ben has a few in his room, but these all look like originals. Are they, or do they just look old?"

"Most of them I got on line. It's a hobby of mine, looking for them, making deals to get them, saving up for them. Do you like it?" Casey seemed to be holding his breath, waiting for approval from Gom.

"Very much. I don't know what I expected, but this kind of surprises me. I don't know why." Gom didn't want to say that he thought of Casey as a darker personality, due to his behavior in their few meetings that could only be described as standoffish. Not counting the night at the theater, Casey had always seemed to be wanting to get away.

"Want the five cent tour? It won't take long. Come on," Casey waved him forward and Gom went down a short hall to find a kitchen at the back. It was nearly full sized with all the appliances and a small table with two chairs. The refrigerator was covered with flyers for plays that looked like a collage. Gom was drawn to it to see how it was constructed. There were magnets holding all the flyers on there and as he stood for a few seconds, he realized that each magnet had been chosen to match the play. There was a microphone on the playbill for *Jersey Boys*, a witch's hat for the bill for *Wicked*, and Gom's favorite, a warthog for *The Lion King*. To Gom, the fact that Casey had searched for just the right magnet to hold each playbill showed a playful, whimsical side to him.

"You keep surprising me," Gom turned to see that Casey was leaning on the counter watching him as he took in the artwork on the kitchen appliance. "This is really cool. It shows a lot of talent, patience, and planning. Not that any of that surprises me about you; I just don't know this sort of playful, fun side to you. I like it."

"I understand. I'm not the most outgoing person. I don't get out much. I've been alone for most of my life, Gom. I didn't like it at home, so as soon as I thought I could manage to live on my own, I split."

Casey moved over to a cabinet and pulled down a couple of mugs and Gom was amused to find that one was from *Phantom of the Opera* and the other from *Miss Saigon*. The man was certainly into continuity.

"How old were you, when you left home?" Gom asked, taking the mugs as Casey handed them to him. Gom noticed that funny dark mark on below Casey's thumb and remembered his desire to find out what it was. Casey pointed to a drawer and Gom opened it to find silverware. When he got up enough nerve, he'd ask about the strange mark. Taking out spoons, he carried them to the table while Casey reached in to the freezer to get the coffee out. He was thinking that it might be easier for Casey to talk while he worked than to sit face to face and answer questions. He hadn't planned to interrogate Casey about his past, but he found himself very interested in the responses.

"I was fourteen." Casey said it like it wasn't out of the ordinary for a child to be on his own at that age.

"No way. How did you make it on your own at that age? I can't imagine how hard it must have been," Gom was freaked out thinking of all the bad things that could happen to a kid that young on his own.

"It was, but there are shelters that don't ask questions and then as I got older and learned how to take care of myself. I worked here and there, made a little, begged sometimes, found places that would hand out things from the back door, restaurants and things. There are a lot of nice people who don't mind passing a few items to someone who looks hungry." Casey stood, arms crossed, leaning on the counter, while the water ran through the coffeemaker.

"Somehow I don't think it was as easy as you make it sound," Gom said. He'd pulled one of the chairs out and sat, watching Casey.

"Oh, I'm not saying it wasn't hard. It sucked. I can remember freezing and thinking I'd never be warm again and then there were times I thought I'd never been as hot. The memories seem to be in extremes, too hot, too cold, too lonely. I've basically been alone for ten years now." Casey still didn't seem to be upset or looking for sympathy with the telling of his life's sad story. It just was what it was.

"I don't know what to say, Casey. I can't think of anything worse than being that alone for so long. I've had brothers and dads and friends since I was eight and they mean the world to me. I have this strange need to just give you a hug," Gom said, smiling, knowing he wouldn't do it. Casey didn't seem the kind who would appreciate a hug.

"Far be it from me to deny you anything you need. Feel free," Casey said, surprising Gom.

Startled, Gom said, "Really?"

Further freaking Gom out, Casey opened his arms and stood waiting.

Gom got up and walked right into those arms, wrapping his around Casey. They were about the same height, which would make Casey about five-nine like him. He stood for a few seconds afraid to move, not knowing what to do.

"I thought with hugs you were supposed to squeeze," Casey said. Gom's eyes immediately filled as he realized that Casey had never had a hug. Of course not! What was he thinking? This was the man who'd refused the spontaneous embrace from Trick saying he didn't hug. And Casey had opened his arms to Gom with what looked like ease, if not eagerness. Gom tightened his arms around Casey and hugged him like he had dreamed of doing for days. It never occurred to him that Casey would allow it, much less instigate it. After a few more seconds, he felt Casey tighten his arms a little. Gom put his head down onto Casey's shoulder and held on. He could swear he heard a shuddering sigh leave Casey's mouth as they stood there, silent.

"For someone who doesn't hug, you give great ones. I'm just sayin'." Gom pulled back, afraid to get too comfortable, though he could have stayed there for a long time. He didn't want to push Casey too far, though.

Casey cleared his throat and said, "Coffee's ready."

Gom stepped back and watched as Casey poured their drinks. His eyes widened as the side of his changed colors. As the hot water filled it, the dark cup changed and the well-known white mask appeared. He chuckled and reached for it, looking closely at the mask from the show.

"Like I said, don't ever let Ben over here. He'd never leave."

"He can come sometime. He'd get a kick out of it. How do you take yours?"

"Probably what is considered wimpy. I like it with a lot of cream and sweetener, any kind." Gom admitted.

"Me, too."

"Really? They all laugh at me and say I like a little coffee with my cream, but it's very comforting to me like that. If you can't have it like you like it, why drink it at all is what I figure." Gom laughed as he told his coffee theory.

"I agree. I don't like bitter stuff. Can't figure out how people drink it black." Casey brought sugar, sweetener, and two kinds of creamer to the table.

"Go ahead and fix it and we'll go in the living room to sit where it's more comfortable." Gom noticed that Casey watched carefully as he prepared his coffee just the way he liked it. By the same token, Gom paid attention to Casey making his, too. Casey used the yellow sweetener and he put in one more than Gom did. They used about the same amount of creamer, though Gom did use a little more than Casey. Casey put the things away and they headed back to the living room. He pointed to rooms on the way.

"Bedroom's there, bathroom there, and this is supposed to be a guest room, but I've made it a laundry room. One of the best days of my life was when I was able to get a used washer and dryer. I had to pay to get the pipes and everything done, but it was worth it. No more taking my laundry out." He pointed upstairs and said, "The DeVanes, upstairs, told me I could use theirs but I just didn't want to impose."

"You see them much? Do they get out?" Gom asked. He didn't know anyone who was ninety.

"They don't drive any more, but they have children who come often to take them to appointments and out to eat. They're pretty cool. The best thing is they leave me alone. They know they can call me if they need anything, but it's like having my own place."

Gom stood in the room, not knowing whether to go to the couch or to one of the chairs. If he went to the couch, would Casey think he wanted him to sit there, too? But if he went to a chair would he look like he didn't want to be near Casey? This dating thing was weird.

Casey stood beside him and said, "Couch. Like I said, I've never talked so much in my life, so I don't want to be yelling across the room. I know you're not scared of me. We've already hugged, right?" Casey teased.

"Good point. I'm glad you're talking to me. I want to know everything about you," Gom said.

"No, you don't." That was quick.

"I'm sorry, I didn't mean to push. I don't want to know anything you don't want to tell me. I just think you're very interesting. I'm intrigued by you and your life." Gom said, settling into the corner of the couch and bringing the coffee to his mouth. He couldn't stop the next sound, "Mmm."

"I'm glad you like it. But, I don't understand why you'd be interested in my life, or me, for that matter." Casey sat in the other corner of the couch and drank from his mug.

"I don't know how to answer that. Are you interested in me? Why am I here if you're not?" Gom was afraid he'd gone too far when Casey just looked at him for a minute.

"I guess you're right. You can probably tell I don't date a lot, huh? Not too good with the conversation thing." Casey took another drink, ducking his head.

"Casey, I've *never* dated. If you want to talk about lack of dating technique, you're talking to a master. I have no idea how to act. I just know that after you brought Trick to us, I was interested. Then when you came back to check on him, I was even more so. I took the excuse Ben gave me to come see you at the theater and enjoyed talking to you there." Gom set his mug on the small table beside the arm of the couch and rubbed his hands on his pants, nervous as hell. "I don't know how to be, what's the word, coy? I won't play games and make you wonder what's going on because I don't know how. This is the first time I've ever been on a date, ever." He was repeating himself, he thought. That was making him a great conversationalist.

"I can't believe that. You're gorgeous and you've got money and a good job and…" Casey trailed off, as he evidently thought about what he'd said. Embarrassed, he went on, "And you work undercover as a high school student so you can't go around dating men around town. What if you were seen? And what's money got to do with anything? I'm an idiot."

Gom scooted over toward the middle of the couch so he could reach Casey. He put his hand on Casey's leg where it was drawn up and patted it, saying, "You're right about all that, but that's not why I've never dated. I've never wanted to. I was pretty messed up as a kid and then when I first started to realize that I might be gay, I got bashed, like big time. So, messed up again. It took me a while to get over that one. I was lucky because I had Soldier and Dillon and especially Tommy, my brother."

"How old were you?" Casey had put his coffee down, too, and taken Gom's hand in one of his. Those long fingers felt so good against Gom's. There was a fleeting thought of asking Casey about the mark on his hand, but Gom knew this wasn't the time. Casey was waiting for a story.

Gom had to scoot closer so he wasn't reaching all the way across the couch. He wasn't sure how far he wanted to go in telling Casey about what happened. But, he'd brought it up, and Casey had told him some of his past, so Gom bit his lip and told the story.

"I was seventeen and not even sure I was gay. I just knew that I wasn't interested in girls at all. But I've always been so much smaller than others my age and, too pretty in some people's eyes it seems. Anyway, for a few weeks I'd been putting up with some mild taunts and slurs, but not enough that I felt I should tell Soldier about it. I mean, people are always being picked on, huh?" Gom looked at Casey as he talked to see if he could get a read on what Casey was thinking, but his face was stoic.

"On this day, I was walking close to home. I'd been with some friends after school and the guy driving got a call from his mother and had to hurry home so I told him to let me out since I could easily walk home. I hadn't gone a block when I heard someone behind me. I turned but didn't know them. There were three guys who jumped me and threw me down." Gom began to shake as he told the story and didn't even notice when Casey moved closer to him. "While I was there one of them grabbed my leg, pulling it out and another kicked me from behind. I thought I would die, the pain was so bad. They proceeded to beat the crap out of me, calling me faggot and queer and pervert. I don't know how long it went on, but Daniel found me. Daniel is the man who placed me in the home with Dillon to begin with."

"My God, Gom, how badly were you hurt?" Casey was suddenly very close to Gom.

"Pretty badly. They let me go home from the hospital because

I was so freaked out, and probably because Soldier is such a strong personality, but it took a while before I could move much and I was so badly bruised. It set me back quite a bit. Suddenly I was a lost child again and Soldier was the only one who could comfort me. Well, except for Tommy. Tommy used to sing to all of us when we were small and when he asked what he could do, I reverted back to the needy kid I used to be and asked him to hold me and sing to me. I was a mess, Casey." Gom looked down and saw that Casey's hand was clasping his tightly and his other hand was fisted on his knee.

"You were traumatized. I think you are incredibly brave and strong. I'm so sorry that happened to you. I wish I knew what to say. I'm so backward in cases like this." Casey looked to be very upset that he didn't know how to comfort Gom.

"It's okay. We all have our 'things' that we feel backward about. I'm over it. I ended up back in therapy for a while to get over it. Of course, Soldier and Dillon, and Tommy helped a lot. Tommy works with children who need help and he was just great with me. I even asked him about being gay and he was very good about talking to me. He's a wonderful brother." Gom smiled now, thinking of Tommy.

"I'm so glad. I haven't met him yet, but I'm already thankful to him. For some reason, I hate to think of you being so hurt. I'm sure that you've endured worse to have been in that place to begin with, but Gom, I don't understand, but it really hurts me here,'" Casey touched his chest, rubbing it roughly, "to think of you in pain. How weird is that? I don't usually invest much..." Casey paused there, clearly not knowing how to go on.

Gom filled in the word he thought Casey was searching for with. "Emotion?"

Casey raised his head and looked right into Gom's eyes for a second. "Yeah. I'm not good with that stuff."

"I think you are," Gom said, turning his hand in Casey's so that now he was the one holding on. "I think you're better than you think. You don't give yourself credit because you've lived your life alone, but you cared enough about Trick to bring him to us. You don't like the fact that I was hurt because we're becoming friends. Maybe you are a little backward in the emotion department, but it's not something that you lack, it's something that you never used. Will you tell me, sometime, not now, why you left home so young? That has to be a story. I care about what happened to you in the past, what made you what you are today."

"It's not pretty."

Gom figured now was a good time to get this next part out of the way. "Like I said, I've never been out with anyone, Casey. That translates to me being a virgin at twenty-two." *Why did he feel like he had to duck his head, as if he was apologizing?* "Frankly, I've been busy working on my career and never had any inclination to explore my sexuality other than knowing that when it happened for me it would be with a man."

"Wow. I, uh, can't say the same. I'm twenty-four and I've had sex before. I've always been safe, I can promise you that, but I've never been with anyone more than once. It was never about feelings other than getting off for me. Sorry if that makes me sound like a whore or something." Casey tried to pull his hand away from Gom with that declaration. Gom wasn't having it. He held on tightly.

"Not at all, Case. I'm not judging you. We're both individuals. Everyone's experiences are different. It's not like we have to fit some mold of how many times you're supposed to have had sex before you find the right person for you. We make our own way in the world, no matter the past or the present, but it's kind of nice that maybe we could explore this a little further and see if we could mean more to each other than just friends someday. I'm not in any hurry. I seriously want to get to know you better, and I'd love for you to spend some time with us at Scarcity. I'd like for you to be comfortable there." Gom watched Casey carefully to see if he was freaked by what he'd said. Any of it.

"I don't know. I'm not good with a lot of people. I never know what to say and if I don't talk, people think I'm rude. I don't want to mess up with your family." Casey looked as Gom had expected at the thought of being with the group at Gom's home.

"No one expects anything of you. It was all right when you ate supper with us, wasn't it? It's not like you have to entertain. There's always people who will take up the slack." Gom didn't want to sound like he was pleading, but yeah, he was.

"We'll see. Now, let's talk about the fact that if this is your first date, then I get to be your first kiss, huh?" Casey teased gently.

"Uh, Case, what if I suck?" Gom's worry was genuine.

"I don't think you're supposed to do that so much with the kissing thing. Later maybe, now that..."

"No, you did *not* just go there!" Gom said, blushing and swatting gently at Casey's shoulder.

"Hey, I'm just sayin'. I don't know that much about it myself. I've never kissed anybody, either." Casey looked serious, but Gom couldn't believe it.

"Come on, you're just saying that so I won't feel so stupid. You said you've had, you know..." Gom stopped.

"Sex. I've had sex with a few different guys over the years. It's a myth that all gay men have sex all the time. One night stands, Gom, and I didn't do the kissing thing. There was no emotion involved and I guess I always thought it was something special. Fucking is great for what it is, and I hope that if we get closer, one day..." Casey stopped this time and Gom figured it was because of his eyes and how wide they were. He was such an idiot.

"Relax, Gom. Some day. No time soon, but I really would like to end our first date with a first kiss for both of us. Is that going too fast?" Casey leaned back into his corner of the couch, giving Gom plenty of room to ease away from him if he wanted.

Gom wanted that kiss more than he'd wanted anything in a long time. He decided it was time to man up and go after what he wanted and not be such a wuss about it. He scooted again, following Casey into his corner.

Very softly, he asked, "Do you have anything against touching? Is there anything that freaks you out?"

"No. When I said I didn't hug that night at your house it was just because I was just uncomfortable and didn't know what to do. I kind of liked hugging you tonight. What about you? I know I have to be careful and go slow, but is there anything I shouldn't do?" Casey was paying such close attention to Gom's face as he asked the question.

"I won't go into what happened to me, but I'm fine with touching and holding. I wasn't sexually abused, like for sex, you know? I was... I guess you'd call it tortured and I have scars that you might see one day, but I'm fine with it all now. Unless you come at me with lit cigarettes, I'm all good." At the stunned look on Casey's face, he added, "Yeah, sorry about that, long story for another time." Wanting to get that look off Casey's face, Gom leaned closer and said, "About this kissing thing?" That took shock right into interest.

"Ye-es?" Casey asked, smiling a little. Gom decided he liked that, too. He was seeing things tonight that he'd not seen with Casey before and it made him seem like a different person, lighter, happier, more easygoing.

"I don't know if I want to just slam one on you and not have to worry about it anymore, or go for the really special first kiss thing. You know; something to remember." Gom wasn't teasing. Part of him wanted to get it over with and quit the angst and part wanted to savor and enjoy it as something very sweet and memorable.

"Can I vote?" Casey asked, in a manner that Gom could only call shy.

"Most definitely," Gom answered.

"Come here," Casey's voice had gotten huskier and Gom shivered at the way it sounded. He scooted one more time and they were sharing the same space. Casey opened his arms and drew Gom to his chest. The way they were sitting now, it was a little awkward and was going to be a bit of a stretch for a kiss. "Trust me?" Casey asked.

Gom looked up from the right side of Casey's chest and

nodded. Casey took hold of Gom's upper arms and pulled him back and then over.

"Straddle me for a minute," he said.

Gom slid his knee over and deep into the corner of the couch, putting him face to face with Casey. He took a minute to look closely at Casey's face. He'd already remarked on Casey's amazing light blue eyes, but this close they were mesmerizing. He'd love to spend a lot of time this close and looking right into those gorgeous orbs.

Since they were about the same height, with him sitting on Casey's legs and his knees digging into the couch, he was only slightly taller than Casey and very close, which he really liked. Casey's hair was pulled back with a band and Gom really wanted to touch it, had always wanted to touch it.

Gom's voice was a little husky, too, when he said, "Can I take your hair down? I've always wanted to feel it in my hands."

Casey just nodded, never taking his eyes from Gom's. Gom reached behind Casey's head and his hands brushed the back of Casey's neck and both of them shivered at the contact. Something so small, so basic, had Gom shaking with a mixture of need and nerves. He grabbed the band and carefully pulled it out. Without thinking, he put it in his pocket and then his hands were in those thick blond waves. Casey dropped his head back just a little into Gom's hands and he met the movement with caresses to Casey's scalp.

"Hey?" Casey whispered, his hands moving up Gom's back to cup his head.

Gom looked from Casey's hair to his mouth and saw that it was homing in on his own. Awkwardness fled and he leaned just that little bit to meet Casey's lips with his. They were soft and moving just a little, back and forth. Gom liked that Casey's lips weren't tight and hard, but soft and pliant as he pushed against them. Casey groaned and tilted his head, making their lips mash against each other in a totally new way and Gom liked that, too. He tried to move his lips a bit and bumped Casey's nose with his.

How goofy was he that he liked that, too? As a matter of fact, he moved so that he bumped it again. The silliness of that made him smile and this opened his mouth.

Oh. Tongue. Nice. He opened a little more and met Casey's questing tongue with his. The kiss, though, gaining strength was still slow and very sweet. It was all Gom could hope for in a first kiss, and more. He finally pulled away from Casey's mouth, his tongue dragging across Casey's bottom lip. For a second, he gazed into Casey's eyes again, then put his head onto Casey's shoulder and sighed deeply, satisfied.

"Good memory?" Casey asked, softly, right by his ear.

"Wonderful, Casey. More than I've ever imagined. I should go now. This is too perfect to mess up. Does that sound stupid?"

"Not at all. I think I understand. I felt like it was pretty special, too." Casey leaned and gave Gom another quick kiss, making Gom smile.

"See you again?" Gom didn't even make a full sentence out of it the request.

"God, I hope so. You're the one that has to go to school. Call me tomorrow after you're free and we'll talk. I have to work tomorrow night, but at least we can touch base. That okay?" Casey's hands were still moving up and down on Gom's back, slowly. Gom wanted to lay his head down on Casey's shoulder and rest a while, but knew he had to get home.

"I'll call you. Thank you for making my first date and my first kiss something really special, Casey. I mean that. If you walk me to the front door, maybe we can get another one in before I leave," Gom suggested.

With a small grunt, Casey lifted Gom off him and they stood, heading for the door. Gom laughed at how eager Casey looked. Not that he felt any less ready to repeat the experience. He didn't need his car, he could float home.

CHAPTER SEVEN

Gom was still almost levitating as he walked into the house after leaving Casey's apartment. The kiss at the front door was every bit as wonderful as the first one on the couch. He didn't think he could be any happier as he headed into the main room.

The sound of someone crying stopped him. The lights were off, but he could see his two dads on the couch. Dillon was in Soldier's arms, crying, while Soldier tried to comfort him by smoothing his hair and pressing kisses to his shoulder and neck as he shook. What in the world had happened? He hurried over.

"What happened?"

Soldier had been aware of his approach, but Dillon jumped at Gom's soft question. Gom watched him try to compose himself enough to answer. It was strange to see his dad crying like this. Both Dillon and Soldier were strong men who'd built a life together working so hard to help those who lived here. It had to be something really bad for Dillon to lose it like this. Gom's euphoria left him and he prepared himself to hear that one of his brothers had been hurt.

Dillon started to say something and then just sat in Soldier's arms, looking at Gom with the saddest eyes Gom had ever seen.

"There's been another teen suicide," Solider said, quietly, reaching up to gently wipe tears from Dillon's cheeks. He couldn't keep up with the flow, though. The sobs had stopped, but the salty sadness kept coming down Dillon's face as he just looked at Gom with such sorrow.

"Oh, no." Gom's heart broke every time they heard this news. Recently there had been so many cases in the media of young people killing themselves. He knew that both his dads took it hard whenever they heard something like that.

"This one is too damn close to home. It happened in Baiden County. A junior jumped off the top of the high school building.

The note he left was pretty clear. Gom, it will tear you apart the pain this boy went through." Soldier's eyes were bright with tears as he talked.

Soldier was the strongest man Gom had ever known, but he had a heart as big as their state and things like this really got to him, hurt him deeply.

Gom reached out to stroke Dillon's back, knowing that touch was healing.

"How did you find out?"

"Through Daniel and Tommy. Tommy was called to go over with a large group of counselors who will work with the student body of the school. They're going to be there when school starts in the morning. It's so sad, Gom. So many lives are going to be affected by this." Soldier said, his hands fisting for a moment on Dillon's back. "Now that it's too late for that poor boy."

"What did the note say?" Gom asked, almost dreading the answer.

Dillon's voice came then, low and shaky, "I can't take it anymore. The ones who made me do this know who they are. They are the ones who bullied me, the ones who outed me, and the ones who knew about it and did nothing. I'm sorry, Mom."

Gom sat stunned as the implications of that message hit him. Wow, Soldier was right when he said that so many lives would be affected. Not only the boy's family will be devastated, but what if you were one of the people mentioned in the note. That could take in countless students. How many had bullied this kid? How many were part of "outing" him? And how many, probably a much larger number here, knew about it and did nothing for whatever reason?

"Wow." Gom's quiet expression said so much.

"It's so sad, Gom. When is this going to stop? How that family must be hurting," Dillon said, resting his head back on Soldier's shoulder. Gom hadn't seen Dillon this upset, this torn up in a very long time. Of course, they'd discussed each suicide they'd heard of in the news and how horrible it was that these young people of all ages couldn't find what they needed to keep them from taking their own lives to get away from the pain.

"When did you all find this out?" Gom asked, moving to sit close to Soldier on the couch, leaning in so that he was touching both his dads, both offering and receiving comfort.

"About an hour ago. I think it happened earlier tonight," Soldier supplied the answer.

"I think I'll call Laurie. I'm sure she either knows or would want to. She might even be one of those that will be going over to help out with the students. Baiden is only two counties over. It's a lot more rural than here. From what I know, Baiden is a huge high school that incorporates all the middle schools into it. It's the only high school in that county. I haven't heard of any cases of bullying from there."

"You and I both know there's bullying everywhere and the fact that we don't hear about it is as bad as the ones we do hear about. If we know about them, something can *maybe* be done. When it's going on and no one says anything, steps up and tells, those are the ones that can end like this." Soldier had stopped rubbing Dillon's back and was just holding him now. Dillon was so much smaller than Soldier that he was still able to curl up on Soldier's lap and be comfortable. As he finished that statement, Dillon spoke quietly, "I wish there was something we could do, some way we could help." Dillon always wanted to help. Thank God.

"Let me call Laurie and see if she knows anything more. There's no way that this won't be all over the media. I can't go over there until it dies down a little. Wouldn't do for me to be seen on TV by students at schools where I've been."

Gom's phone rang before he could even take it out to call Laurie Summer.

"Hello. Officer Marsh, this is Captain Denny. I don't know if you've heard, but…" Gom's captain began, but Gom truly didn't want to hear it again.

"I've heard."

"Oh, okay, good. The school officer from that school was at the meeting last year with their counselor and wants to know if you can come in and help them find the parties that were involved in this boy's bullying."

"I wondered about that, but was afraid of being there when all the news cameras were in the school. I don't want to accidently be seen on camera because I didn't see it coming and end up losing my cover." Gom was beginning to realize how important his job was.

"Maybe you can come up with some kind of disguise that would be enough to get by, one that wouldn't be too hard to do." Officer Denny had a good idea there.

"Hmm, I know someone who might be able to help with that." Gom was thinking of both Ben and Casey. "It would have to be something easy for me to be able to do it myself."

"Well, you've done enough at Willington to be able to leave now without feeling like things are unfinished there. See about getting that disguise and show up at Baiden High in the morning. School starts there at eight. Your file will be there by the time you show up. You're to meet with Mark Sinclair, the school counselor and the officer, Hank Filer. Principal is Ms. Marcie King. The three of them will be expecting you at six-thirty. Meet in the counselor's office. The Saf-T person is new so she won't be as helpful with knowledge about the students. That school is getting ready to be hit hard from both outside and within. It's a powder keg. There will be accusations and guilt to go along with the grief this kind of thing causes. Shit, I hate this." That was a long speech for Captain Denny.

"I know what was in the note, but do you have any more information that I should know?" Gom asked.

"Yeah, let me see here. What he meant by the ones who outed him? It seems that he's been giving blow jobs to some of the jocks there to keep from getting beaten and given swirlys in the bathroom. Someone found out and put the information all over the net, several different social sites."

"When did that happen?" Gom broke in to ask.

"This was Friday morning, so he spent the day knowing that it was all out. He couldn't take it. This had evidently been going on, the bj's, for a long time."

"Damn. Okay, I'll be there and I'll come up with something. I'll tell you what when I figure it out." Gom promised.

"Gom, I want these students found and I want justice for this boy." Captain Denny was more intense about this one than any that Gom had heard before, but then they hadn't worked on a suicide case before. Gom felt pretty intense about it, too, come to think of it.

"Who, the bullies or the ones who outed him?" Gom asked.

"I want to know both, Gom. I'll talk to you about six in the morning. You'll probably be on your way there, so have your bud on. We'll pass the latest information then. Damn, we're keeping you really busy, huh?" Denny's voice gave away his exasperation.

"Yes, sir." They hung up and he looked at his dads, who'd been silent as he'd talked.

"Oh, Gom. This is going to be a hard one. What do you need from us?" Dillon asked.

"Is Ben here?" Gom asked.

"No, he's working with some friends on the set for a new play and then they were going to one of the guy's rooms to sleep and get back at it early tomorrow. What do you need?" Soldier asked.

"Help with a disguise. You heard why I need it. Hey, let me call Casey. Maybe he knows as much about makeup as he does about lighting. Cross your fingers."

"Gom?" This was Soldier.

"Yeah?" he answered, looking over.

"We love you, son, so very much."

Gom looked at the two of them and smiled from the inside out. He pushed his way onto Dillon's lap and got the best hug ever. Soldier playfully grunted under the weight of two of the people he loved most in the world. Both Dillon and Gom chuckled and eased off Soldier's legs. Dillon moved sideways and started massaging Soldier's legs and Soldier gave a yelp.

"Stop it! You know I can't take that." Soldier never could take it when Dillon grabbed his legs when they were playing, saying it was worse than tickling.

"I love you both more than I can ever say. You know that. You're the ones who have given me the strength to do what I have to do now." Gom was sincere. Without their love and guidance over the years, he would not be the man he was now.

"I'm going to call Casey."

"Hey, how was your date?" Soldier asked.

Gom blushed. He hated it, but he couldn't help it. The word date made him think kiss and that just had him glowing like a lamp in the darkened room.

"I'd say that you enjoyed yourself. I'm glad, Gom. He's a good man?" Dillon asked.

"Yeah, he really is. I'm trying to get him to come around and get to know you all. It might take a little time." Gom got up, phone in hand, touching both men on their shoulders as he walked out of the room.

When Casey answered his phone, Gom said, "Hey, it's me."

"Hey. Miss me already?" Casey asked, and Gom could tell the man was smiling.

"Well, yeah, but that's not why I called. I need your help, really badly, and in a hurry." He was sure that Casey could tell that he wasn't smiling.

"Sure. What? Where? Anything, Gom," Casey said.

"With all you do at the theater, do you know anything about makeup or disguises?" Gom asked, settling onto his bed for a moment.

"Yeah, I can do a pretty good job. What do you need?" Casey was quiet now, obviously responding to the seriousness in Gom's voice.

As quickly as possible Gom filled Casey in on what had happened and why he needed a disguise.

"I'll be there in about a half hour. I need to go by the theater for a few minutes. I'll hook you up and I'll make it easy for you to do. The fact that you're gorgeous will help." Casey sounded like he was closing his door as he talked.

"Yeah, right. You're crazy." Gom was blushing again.

"No, you're pretty." Casey said, and Gom was happy for the first time ever that he was considered pretty because Casey sounded like he liked it.

"Uh, thanks, I guess. Remember I have to be able to do this every day and it can't be too obvious," Gom directed, nervous at having to do a disguise.

"It'll be easy, I promise. Catch you in a few," Casey said, signing off.

While he waited for Casey to show up, Gom called Laurie. He found that she already knew about the situation at the other school and said that she wouldn't be going, but that the guidance counselor would be there. He knew that the guidance counselor knew about him so he should be safe with her there. They talked for a few minutes with him telling her that he was sorry he had to pull out of Willington before everything was settled. She assured him that he had done a good job and she could handle things from now on.

"Can I call you and find out how things are going for Bradley and Sheila and the rest of them?" Gom asked.

"Of course. Bradley will really miss you. I'll have to tell him something because you know he will be looking for you. You're the first friend he's had. I'd hate for him to go backwards. The threat is gone, but we still have to get the home circumstances figured out. I'll keep you informed. Thanks for all you did here. You came to help in one case and helped us with three different ones. You did a good job here, Monty Marshall."

"Thank you, Laurie Summer. I look forward to hearing from you." Gom hung up and got up to put his Willington jacket in the back of the closet and separated his clothes on the rack so that what he was going to wear tomorrow was hanging alone in the middle. He'd always done that. Well, from the time when Soldier moved in and he had more than one or two outfits from which to choose.

He heard the door, probably because he was listening for it, and hurried down to meet Casey. When he got to the kitchen he saw that Casey was carrying a case and a bag with him. Soldier and Dillon were in the kitchen. Dillon, who always cooked when there was something going on, was making sliders, small-sized cheeseburgers with all the trimmings in equally small sizes. Soldier got a pitcher of tea out and set it on the counter.

"It's decaf. You want some, Casey?" Soldier asked.

"Uh, sure. I'll just set this stuff out here, if that's okay," Casey said, laying the case on the big table and putting the bag down by his side.

Opening the case, he turned it to Gom. Whoa. The case, when it opened had three layers that had braces that let each slide out and show what was on each layer. There was makeup on the bottom, the middle layer had rows of eyelashes, dots that Gom figured were like birthmarks or something, mustaches, and his eyes squinted when he saw three rows of contact lenses that he figured were just glass, though in many different colors. The top layer held earrings, nose rings, and other piercing things that he shuddered at when he saw them.

"I can teach you how to do your make up and no one would know you. A little liner, some stuff in your hair, and I can have you looking like a Lambert clone in no time. He's good looking and is a whizz with makeup, so it would make sense that you would try to do some of the same things. Your hair's not black, but dark enough that with some gel or something you could carry it off. You can probably get by with a little bit of it, right? They don't say you can't wear stuff like that to school, do they?"

"No, I don't think so. I saw some kids who were pretty decked out at Willington. I don't know about it. I mean, I like the way Adam looks, but I don't know if I can do all that." Gom was leaning toward not.

"Second choice," Casey said, pulling the bag up, "I think the easiest thing would be for you to dye your hair and eyebrows, use some blue contacts, and no one would recognize you. You wouldn't have to do anything except put in the contacts each day. Want to find out if blonds have more fun?" Casey teased. "I'll help you. It only stays in for a few weeks. If you need it longer, we'll redo it. If not, you'll be back to your regular color before long and it won't ruin your hair. What do you think?"

Gom looked at Soldier and Dillon, eyebrows raised in question.

"You'll make a cute blond," Dillon said.

"Do the dye job. It'll be easier and I'd be afraid if you went the makeup route you'd end up being a target yourself. A good-looking, small, guy with nice makeup on, dark liner, you'd be picked on and have a whole new set of problems. The dye would be easier to carry off." Soldier was always thinking of the safety angle with any of his boys.

"I agree. I don't want you being a target, either. Come on, let's go make you a blond." Casey pulled out one of the boxes in the bag that Gom now saw was from a pharmacy.

"I'm not worried about the hair, it's the contacts. I've never worn them. If I lose one for some reason, or have trouble wearing them, there I'll be with brown eyes again." Gom got an *ew* feeling every time he thought about putting something in his eye.

"I'll show you how to do that, too. It's easy and they're really thin. They won't bother you. Come on, you need to get this done. You said you had to be there at six-thirty? Damn, that's early. This won't take long, but we've got to get you used to the contacts, too. I brought you stuff for those, too, from the pharmacy. We're all good, Gom, let's do this."

Gom and Casey headed up to Gom's bathroom and Casey put the items on the counter.

"Off with the shirt. I'll get this ready. You've got a nice deep sink so this should be easy." Casey set about getting things ready while Gom took off his shirt and put it in the hamper in the corner of the bathroom.

He heard the water come on in the sink and turned back. Casey had a hand in the sink checking the temperature, but he was looking at Gom, his eyes hooded, a slight smile on his face.

"I didn't expect to get to the half naked part quite so soon," he teased.

"Shut up, you. Come on, I guess you're my hairdresser now," Gom said, then paused as he drew level with Casey. "Really? Thanks a lot for what you're doing. Ben was not available and I thought you might be able to help." Gom leaned over and planted a quick kiss on Casey's cheek, then bent to put his head under the faucet.

In short order, he was standing again and Casey was there with a towel for his head. Gom didn't even get to see it. The weirdest part had been when Casey had to make sure his eyebrows were done, too.

"Don't look yet. Let me dry it for you, then it might not be such a shock. It's not such a bright blond, more ash blond, I think they call it, but it'll be really different from your normal color. It's going to look great, especially with the blue contacts."

"Are there any that will make me have Husky eyes like yours?" Gom asked, looking at Casey as the man moved his towel-covered hands in Gom's hair.

"Now you're being silly," Casey sounded embarrassed.

"You can tell me I'm pretty, but I can't do the same for you. I like your Husky eyes, you know. They're very expressive. Right now they say you want to kiss me again." Gom was pushing and he knew it.

"Gom! We don't have time for what you want to get started. You have to be up in just a few hours now and we still have to practice with the contacts. Oh, hell, come here, you," Casey said, dropping the towel onto the counter and taking Gom into his arms.

Gom smiled right into Casey's mouth and their kiss brought slight groans from both of them. Casey's tongue traced Gom's lips and Gom met it with his and they both sighed and tightened their arms.

"Gom! Hey, how's it going? We've got snacks down here and we need to make sure you're set to go and you need to get a little rest." Soldier's voice was outside Gom's door. He would never come in without asking first. Thank God, because besides his being shirtless, he was also hard as a rock and that would not be a good way to face his dad.

"Be right there. My hair's almost dry and we can practice with the contacts down there." Gom pulled away from an equally hard Casey and went to get another shirt, this time an old sleep shirt. They took a few moments for Casey to use the blow dryer on Gom's hair and then run his fingers through it to comb it out. Gom's cut was the same, but now his hair was glowing with a lightness that he knew would take him a while to get used to.

"Looks good. You already look different, huh?" Casey said, grabbing the mess they'd made and cleaning it up quickly. They headed back downstairs.

There were two small sliders on each plate and tea ready for them. They sat and talked for a few minutes and Soldier and Dillon kept looking at each other and then to Gom and Casey, then back at each other.

"What?" Gom finally asked.

"You do make a cute blond," Soldier said.

"Da-ad!"

"Face it, you are a pretty boy. I told you," Casey said, then realized what he'd said in front of Gom's two dads. Instead of blushing, he turned near white.

"Relax, we don't bite. Okay, Gom, wash your hands good and let him show you how to do the contacts and then you can practice a couple of times. You've got to get some rest, hon.

You're going to have a hard day, a hard few weeks, I bet. That's a really long drive. You going to drive it every day or get a place over there?" Soldier asked.

"Don't know yet. I'll have to decide that in a couple of days when I see how things go. This is the farthest I've been, so I'll see." Gom was washing his hands and getting nervous. He really didn't want to do this.

When Gom got back to the table, Casey had everything ready. He'd chosen some dark blue lenses and had some solution out ready to use somehow. You're a grown man, Gom told himself, get your shit together and act like it.

"Okay, what do I do?"

Casey took a pair of brown lenses and said, "I'll do it first and you watch. These are all brand new so no worries. Watch." Gom watched as Casey pulled down his bottom lid with his index finger and with the finger of the other hand he placed the lens onto his eye. He eased his bottom lid back and looked at Gom with one brown eye and one Husky blue one.

"Wow." Gom said, looking at Casey's odd eyes.

"Now, I want to put one in for you so you can see how much pressure to use and see that it won't hurt. Otherwise, you'll be fumbling around and it might fall or something. I know you're a little freaked out about it, but you'll do fine."

Gom took a deep breath, let it out and leaned in a little so Casey could get to his eye. They were sitting with their chairs turned and facing each other with the items on the table beside them. Their knees bumped so Gom moved one of his away so that now one of Casey's was in between his. It didn't occur to him how sort of intimate it would look until he glanced down. He didn't have time to dwell on it, because Casey was heading for him with a blue contact.

He felt Casey's finger pull his lid down and then there was a slight pressure on his eye and his lid was released. That was it? He blinked and thought it felt a little odd at first, but the more he blinked the more it felt like, well, not a big problem.

"Let me try. It's not as bad as I thought," he said to Casey.

He put the other contact in with no trouble and smiled in triumph at Casey and then his fathers.

"How do I look?" he asked.

"Like a surfer dude, man," Soldier said and they all chuckled. Gom laughed with them, then got up to go into the closest bathroom and look for himself.

Casey followed him, saying, "The hair will get a little duller as time goes by and won't be such a shock to you."

Gom turned when Casey closed the door with both of them in the bathroom.

"What...?" Gom started to ask, but got no further as Casey took his mouth quickly. Gom turned more squarely into Casey's arms and met the kiss fully. He could really get used to kissing this man. Casey was nothing like he used to think. He was sweet and kind and helpful and easy to like...a lot.

"Mmm, gotta stop. God, I like that," Gom said, pulling back and looking at Casey, who was so close and still had two odd colored eyes. Gom laughed, "You need to either put the other brown one in or take them both out. Personally, I like the blue better on you. Thank you so much for helping me out tonight. You made it much easier and quicker. I can do this for sure."

"Come on, I'll show you how to take them out, give you a case for them, and show you how to clean them. I'll also give you the other pair just like them in case of emergency." Casey evidently thought of everything.

"Wow, you are full service. I'll have to find a way to thank you."

They left the bathroom and soon Casey was gone, after being thanked by Gom again, as well as Soldier and Dillon. Dillon handed Casey a box when he left and Gom had no doubt that it held more sliders and probably something sweet. Casey had lunch for tomorrow and Gom was ready for his next case.

He got hugs from his dads and went to bed. He was so tired

he didn't even think about how much he liked kissing Casey. Much. He didn't think about it *much* before he dropped out after setting the alarm for five.

CHAPTER EIGHT

Gom's early morning meeting had been hard. Everyone was on edge and in pain. This was devastating and they knew it was going to get even more stressful. They were going to do the best they could for all the students, but it was on Gom, as Monty, and the guidance counselor, the school officer, and the new Saf-T person here. Unfortunately, the lady who'd been in that position was gone on maternity leave and the new person, Jan Stephens, was still just learning about her cases and getting to know the staff as well as the students. Gom wasn't sure she was going to have a lot of insight into the pertinent people he needed to be aware of to do his job.

"We talked a little about this last night and we wanted to get your take on it, Officer Marsh," the principal began and Gom interrupted her.

"Please, everyone, starting right now, call me Monty Marshall. It will help all of us if there are no slip ups. I'm sorry for interrupting. Go ahead, ma'am." Gom appreciated the respect they were trying to show him, but he couldn't take a chance that they would screw up later.

"You're right, I'm sorry. This is a new thing for me and I didn't think. Anyway, we wondered if it wouldn't be a good idea for you to pretend to be gay for this assignment. We feel that is a way that you could maybe meet up with some of the people that Byron Neighbors spent time with. He wasn't a problem or an unpopular student. He did okay in his classes, was bright in fact. No one knew this stuff was going on," Principal King said.

"I hate to disagree with you, but there are lots of students who knew this was going on. There's no way that a few students could do those things to that boy without others knowing or seeing it happen at one time or another. I will believe that no one said anything. It's a little too easy to ignore these things, thinking you'll be safer if you stay out of it. The feeling that 'at least they're not doing it to me' is a very strong one that keeps kids quiet, too. You have to go back to this boy's note. The ones who did the bullying, the ones who told it or outed him, and the ones who knew and did nothing. You could be talking about a lot of students there." Gom knew that they knew this, but just saying it out loud made it seem so daunting a task.

"Do you think you can do that, pose as gay and manage to get in with some of the kids who may know what was going on?" This question came from Officer Filer.

Gom wasn't about to tell these people that he was gay, but he saw the merit of his pretending for them. It would get him the right kind of attention and let him infiltrate a group that might just be willing to talk.

"No problem. I can use my size and say I was bullied at another school and came here hoping for better and now I'm scared of getting the same done to me. By the way, don't worry about me, I am very capable at taking care of myself. The fear will be an act." When Gom said that, he heard a collective sigh around the table.

"Okay, school is out here at three. We have to wait for the buses from the middle schools to get here, so shall we meet in my office every day at three-thirty to go over any information any of us have gathered, put it all together, and plan for the next day?" Mark Sinclair put that suggestion out there. As the guidance counselor, his office made sense for Gom to be seen coming in and out of.

"For the first little while that should be a good idea." Gom spoke up, adding, "After a few days we might need to ease off. If I'm seen coming out of here too often it might look funny. But here at first it will make perfect sense. I've got my schedule and the stories are in place for driver's ed and so on. Is there a theater group here? I'd like to see if there is any way I can sign up to help out there."

"Certainly, do you have skills in that area?" Mr. Sinclair asked.

"Not really. I have a brother and a friend in theater and

thought that might be something I could learn from while hoping to meet some students who can help us. Was Byron into any extracurricular activities, music, band, anything?"

"No. He spent a lot of time in the library. It seemed he was always working on something. He was quiet and I'm sorry to say one of those students that didn't make waves or act out so he got lost. No one knew he was in trouble," Mark Sinclair sounded disturbed that they'd missed the boat on this one, but Gom didn't get a feeling that the man was upset about Byron himself.

"I say again, someone knew. A lot of someones and those are going to be the students who are going to be feeling guilt and remorse, hopefully, and will need to be handled carefully. Are there any students that you think of that might have done this bullying? It shouldn't take too long for the police to find out who put the information on line, but I don't see anyone coming forward and admitting what they'd been doing." Gom was looking to the jocks, though. It was usually, for some reason, the strong, athletic ones who were most bothered by the gay ones. From what he'd seen they seemed to take it as a personal affront and set out to make the little faggots pay. Pay for what, Gom wanted to know.

"We've got some students who have been in trouble, but not for anything related to this. We're at a loss to figure out who was doing it. That's where you come in, hopefully. It's time to get to our places. The early ones will be here soon, as well as the TV cameras and the reporters and Lord give us strength." Principal King stood as she spoke and they all followed suit. This was going to be a long day.

§ § §

By the end of the week, Gom felt like he'd been put through the wringer. He was worn down, sad, and frustrated with the pain and grief that seemed to seep through the walls of the school. He'd gotten glimpses of Tommy a couple of times as well as the counselor from Willington. So far, he'd gotten nothing from any of the students he'd made tentative overtures to about Byron and what had happened. Sometimes students would be eager to talk about it and other times their eyes would fill with tears and they'd just shrug as if there was no hope anymore.

He'd been driving home every night, despite the distance, because he needed the peace, the calm, the love that was Scarcity Sanctuary. He'd talked to Casey every night. A couple of times very briefly as Casey was working at the theater, but there were times that they talked for a couple of hours even though Gom needed to get to sleep. Talking with Casey made him feel good.

Soldier and Dillon had been their usual supportive selves. He found his favorite meals each night and there were many offers of help. This was late Friday afternoon and he was just getting home. It was near suppertime and he was exhausted. He was no closer to finding any answers today than he had been earlier in the week.

Dillon was at the stove and Soldier was setting the table as he came in the door. He must have looked as dejected as he felt because they both came to him with hugs. He took and returned them, maybe even clung a little to Soldier.

"Come on in, Gom. Supper will be ready in about forty-five minutes. Why don't you go to your room and rest a few minutes? We'll call you. Stop thinking for a while and just *be* for a bit, okay? Go on now," Dillon said, smiling for Gom, as he gave him just what he needed.

Gom trudged up the stairs and opened his door. He took off his jacket and turned to put it in the closet when he saw Casey sitting in the big chair in the corner. His heart pounded in his chest.

"Are you real?" He just had to ask. There was no way that Casey was waiting for him in his room. He must be more tired than he thought.

"Want to come over here and find out?" Casey asked, archly.

"How can you be here? Shouldn't you be working? How did you get here? I didn't see your car." Casey drove an old navy Taurus. Gom would have noticed it.

"Your dads called, invited me to supper, and seemed to think you could use some company. It was Dillon that said I should wait up here and surprise you. I have several hours free. There's another lighting person that takes over if I can't be there. Doesn't happen often, but he'll cover for me tonight. Look," Casey said, opening his arms, "this is me opening myself up to rejection, something I never do, by the way."

Rejection? Was he kidding? Gom nearly skated across the floor and landed in Casey's lap. He sighed deeply when Casey's arms closed around him. They were in Gom's special chair, the one that he and Soldier used to occupy whenever Gom needed extra attention. The last time he'd shared this chair was when he was seventeen and in such awful pain. Soldier had held him and comforted him just like he'd done when Gom was young and scared.

"I can't believe you're here. And more than that, I can't believe that my *dads* called you. That's pretty awesome, huh?" Gom said. For the first time this week, he began to relax, his muscles easing a little. As if it were the most natural thing in the world, he put his head on Casey's shoulder and sank into him, seeking comfort once again.

"I gotcha, Gom. They were right. You look worn out." Casey brought one hand up to tilt Gom's face back a little, then bent to brush his lips over Gom's. Gom whimpered, just a tiny sound, then pushed forward, wanting more contact.

"Yeah, tough cop can't handle life as a teenager. Makes me sound pretty weak, huh?" He hated feeling like this, but his heart was just breaking.

"You're tough, but I'd bet you're hurting for this kid. That's taking a toll on you. Shh, rest a bit. I'm not leaving. I'm staying for supper. Yes, you got your wish there. Then, maybe we'll come back up here and make out like the teenager you're supposed to be. Rest now," Casey repeated.

How could Casey think he lacked anything in the emotion department? His caring was evident to Gom and frankly, made him feel warm all over. He was just so tired, though. He put his head down again and must have gone to sleep. Casey's warm arms and beating heart made him feel safe and good. Maybe it was just this chair. It had healing powers.

The next thing he knew, there was a knock on the door and Casey said, "Come in."

Before Gom could get up from Casey's lap, Soldier was standing in the open doorway, looking at them. Gom wondered what he was thinking as he gazed at them for a moment. Was he hurt that Casey seemed to have taken his place in this chair? Was he upset at seeing Gom in Casey's arms? He tried to scramble off Casey's lap, but Casey held onto him.

"Easy, it's all right," Casey said, relaxing his arms from Gom and letting him sit up. "Soldier, hey. Gom's been napping. Supper ready?" It's like Casey had become Gom's caretaker instead of Soldier. Gom didn't know how he felt about that, much less how Soldier felt.

"Yeah, Dillon sent me up. Feeling better, Gom? Thanks, Casey. I think that was just what Gom needed," Soldier said, smiling at the two of them. That answered that question. Evidently it was okay with Soldier, which, of course, made it okay with Gom.

"It so was, Dad. I can't believe I fell asleep like that. I feel like a kid. I'm sorry, Case." Gom felt a bit silly for reverting back to the needy child.

"What you've been working with all week is intensely draining. We could see what it was doing to you and I just had a feeling that Casey would be what you needed," Soldier said, looking at Casey now and adding, "We appreciate you arranging to be here for Gom. Supper's ready. Come on down when you're ready. It's Trick, Ben, Daniel, Tommy, and a surprise guest."

That had Gom intrigued, but he had every intention of getting a real kiss from Casey before they left the room. As soon as Soldier closed the door, Gom turned in Casey's arms and reached for that mouth. Seems Casey had the same idea because in seconds they were involved in a passionate kiss that had them both gasping for air. Casey's hands were holding Gom's head still for his lips and tongue to push into Gom's mouth over and over.

This was way more than the kisses they'd shared last time. Heat seemed to rise from all points of contact and Gom felt like he was burning up. Not that he was complaining. He loved kissing Casey Tanner. His tongue was moving against Casey's and his hands were about to reach to take Casey's hair down when he realized that they didn't have time for this. People were waiting for them downstairs.

"Mmm, stop now. Have to stop now," Gom murmured, against Casey's lips. "Don't want to stop now."

Casey pulled away and still holding Gom's head, he pulled it to his shoulder again, Gom's face in his neck. "Need to get my breath. You take it right away, Blondie."

Gom snorted a little laugh into Casey's neck and then pulled away to get up.

"To be continued?" he asked.

"Right where we left off. Count on it," Casey promised and Gom headed for his bathroom to wash up for supper. He wondered who was downstairs.

When he and Casey got to the kitchen it was filled with people, all of whom Gom was crazy about. He hoped that Casey wouldn't be too uncomfortable. Wait, he had a Ben moment when he saw a *girl* at the counter with Dillon.

"Laurie? Hey, it's good to see you," Gom said, going to her. "Laurie Summer, this is my friend, Casey Tanner. Are you here for supper with us? Yeah? Great. I've got lots of questions about what has happened this week. I need to introduce Casey to a couple of people, but we'll talk, okay?" Gom said, touching her shoulder and smiling as she went back to listening to Dillon talk about what he was doing at the stove.

Gom turned to Casey, "Come on, I want to introduce you to Tommy and Daniel." Without thinking he reached for Casey's hand to draw him over to the doorway to the main living room where his brother was standing with his partner.

"Hey, Gom," Tommy said, as he neared them, "are you doing okay? I've seen you at Baiden, but don't know how you're managing over there. It's pretty intense." Tommy reached to give Gom a hug and when he stepped back, Daniel did the same.

Daniel was the one who asked, "I get the feeling this is someone special. Hi," he said, putting his hand out for Casey to take, "I'm Daniel Anderson. Nice to meet you."

"You, too. Gom has spoken of you," Casey said, turning to Tommy. "You must be Tommy. I'm Casey Tanner. I have this weird urge to thank you for being so good to Gom all these years. Don't know where that came from." Casey looked totally freaked that those words came out of his mouth. He actually looked stunned.

Tommy was great and Gom loved him all the more for his next words, spoken quietly, and not for the whole room. "It came from your heart. Thank you. I haven't heard that much about you, but I know that you're important to Gom. That's enough for me. I'm glad you're here." Tommy shook Casey's hand and they all turned back to the kitchen when Soldier called them to the table.

Now that Gom could pay attention to something other than people, he smelled supper and his stomach growled loudly, getting a couple of chuckles from those nearby.

There were three huge bowls of spaghetti, three baskets of bread, and two big platters of meat balls. Dillon always mixed the sauce with the pasta and then the ones who wanted meat balls could add them if they wanted. There were also two gigantic bowls of salad and several bottles of dressing. The scents were amazing and before long bowls were being passed and there were clinks of silverware on dishes and thuds as bowls were replaced to the table. Trick went around the table, with Ben behind him, offering either tea or water.

Soon everyone was eating and the talking was going full force. Ben managed to sit on the other side of Casey and was grilling him about the current play in rehearsal at the theater. On Gom's other side was Laurie and he asked her about what had happened during the week.

"Tony will go before a judge next week and will probably be sent to an alternative school. Taylor is in less trouble, but will be in a pretty strict program at Willington. I'm so glad we got that figured out. It was totally unfair that Bradley was in danger," Laurie said, twirling spaghetti.

"Speaking of Bradley, I really want to know about him." Gom had worried about how Bradley and Missy were doing.

"I called him in and told him you had to move to another school and he couldn't figure out why, but I told him it was because one of your brothers went to that school and you wanted to be there to protect him. He didn't have any trouble believing that of you, so he accepted it." Laurie was amazingly adept at talking around her food. It was obvious that she was enjoying the delicious meal.

"What about the situation with their father? I hate to think of Missy in that house with him as he is. And it's just as bad for Bradley, having to do everything, including sleeping in her room to protect her." Gom couldn't stop the shudder he felt as he thought of Mr. Haines looking at Missy.

"Relax. That was priority one for me. Bradley and Missy are staying with a foster family that's in our district. They hated leaving their dad, but I can tell you Bradley looks so much better and brighter. I think he was really getting worn being responsible for all of them. Mr. Haines is still at his house, but has been told he won't see his children until he goes into a rehabilitation facility. We'll follow up on it." She looked appropriately proud of herself.

"Laurie, that's wonderful. Dad, did you hear that about Bradley and Missy?" Gom turned to look at Dillon and Soldier and neither looked surprised. Hmm, he bet either one or both of them had something to do with the Haines relocation. It didn't matter. He would sleep better knowing they were out of that home.

A hand landed on his leg and moved up slowly and Gom nearly squeaked. He turned to Casey, but he was facing Ben and they were talking about movie posters. The man was a multitasker, as he was scooping in spaghetti with the other hand. Gom reached down, took Casey's hand in his, twined their fingers, and held on. He was so happy in that moment. Casey didn't seem uncomfortable, but then he and Ben had been talking all night about theater so that must help.

Tommy was across the table from Gom and he got Gom's attention saying, "I'd like to talk to you in the study after supper. Casey can come, too. It's about Baiden. I have an idea." That sounded promising. Gom would take any kind of help he could get.

Gom thought Laurie's eyes would pop when Dillon got up to get dessert as Trick and Ben gathered dishes and rinsed them in the sink. Dillon came from the pantry carrying two large dishes of Apple Streusel pies. More enticing scents. Tommy got up to get ice cream out of the freezer and Trick brought bowls for everyone. No one turned down the scrumptious looking dessert. There were happy sighs as the dishes were soon emptied. As usual, the people around the table leaned back, rubbing full stomachs, big smiles on their faces.

Gom walked Laurie out and got a hug and a teasing, "I like you as a blond, Gom. And I really like your young man." Gom blushed, but didn't deny it. He put his hand in his pocket, touching the band from Casey's hair, pulling it, stretching it. The coated rubber band grounded him in a strange way.

After Laurie left, Tommy, Daniel, Casey, and Gom headed for the study where Tommy closed the door.

"I wouldn't usually do this in front of others, but I'm going to be giving you a couple of names on paper for you to look into at Baiden. I think we're looking at some of the football players. This comes from some comments I've heard, almost in passing. No one has stepped up and as you know, I'm not grilling people for information. I'm dealing with the high levels of grief and shock." Tommy was giving Gom his first break.

"Anything in particular?" Gom asked, looking around for Casey and finding that he and Daniel were talking quietly in a corner of the room, giving them the privacy they needed to talk.

"Just some fear from some of the students when members of the team were mentioned. I also have talked to a few students that I feel weren't surprised by what had been going on. I think they might be some of the ones who knew and did nothing like the note said." Tommy ran his hand through his hair, sighing as he continued. "I see a lot of guilt and fear. I found an anonymous note in my chair Wednesday asking if someone knew about it and didn't say anything, would they get in trouble. I'm hoping to hear more from them. Have you heard anything from the police on who put the information out there?"

"All I've heard is they're working on it. They probably have the information, but aren't ready to act on it. That's not my area of expertise so I don't know." Gom wasn't at the station so he wasn't kept up on things as much as the officers who were in and out all the time.

"I'm going to give you another name. This is a young man who is gay and scared to death. I think he knew Byron pretty well and has to know something about what was going on. He said something that resonated with me. It was about everybody having their ways of coping. I'm worried about him. I'd hate to find out that there was another young man being tormented." Tommy handed Gom a piece of paper with two names of the football players he thought Gom should check out and then another piece that had the young gay man's name on it. Gom pocketed them and thanked Tommy for his input.

"How long will you all be there working with the students?" he asked his brother.

"At least another week and then we'll look at it and decide about a lengthier stay," Tommy answered.

Tommy and Gom joined Daniel and Casey and the four of them talked for a few minutes before Gom's brother and his partner left.

"Are you doing okay with all this going on?" Gom asked Casey. After what Casey had done for him tonight, he wanted the man to be comfortable. If he wasn't, then Gom would suggest they go to Casey's apartment.

"I'm fine, Gom. It's kind of weird, but I'm not so freaked out with the people here. It's like they don't expect anything of me, so I'm good. I like seeing all the characters that make up your life, make you who you are. It's like an insight into how you came to be the Gom that has intrigued me to the point that I think about you all the time." Casey was being unusually free with his words.

"It's only fair, since I find myself thinking of you in the strangest of moments. The best thing is that when I do think of you, it makes me happy inside. I've been pretty caught up in what's going on at Baiden High and it gets pretty bad at times. There are so many young people in pain over there and it wears on me. I want to be able to help them find some closure, though that's more Tommy's job than mine, I guess. But, it's on me to help find out who was doing this to Byron and make sure they're not going to be able to do it to anyone else."

Gom was standing close to Casey and warmed inside when Casey took his hand. How long had he wanted to have someone who would simply hold his hand? The Beatles were right, he thought, *"Oh, please, say to me, you'll let me be your man…"*

"Surely, after what has happened, those boys wouldn't continue with what they've been doing? Could you do that after knowing that your actions directly, or indirectly caused a death?" Casey asked, pulling on Gom's hand so that his arm was around Casey's waist. That was pretty nice, too.

"I'm not sure that they can be charged with anything when we do establish who it was. It sounds like Byron agreed to the arrangement to keep from getting beaten up and so on. That will be up to the powers that be, a group that I don't belong to, thank God. I don't want that responsibility. It's all just so sad, Case."

"I think we need to put that away for a while and return to your room. I'll leave in a couple of hours. I told them I'd come in late and check everything out at the theater, but that won't take long. I want some alone time with you, if that's all right." Casey had turned so that they were nearly in an embrace.

"Let's go."

"Hey," Casey said, holding onto Gom so he couldn't move yet.

"Hmm?"

"I like your Tommy. He seems like a really good person. His partner's pretty cool, too." Casey said.

"That makes me very happy. You've met all of the most important people in my life and it makes me happy that you like them. If you hadn't been comfortable with them, it wouldn't be a deal breaker, but it's very important to me that you're good with them. Thanks," Gom said, leaning in for a quick kiss.

"Aht! Don't start something down here. I want to be behind a closed door with you like really soon. We're not going too far tonight, but we have some exploring to do. Interested?" Casey teased him.

"Are you kidding? Come on," This time Gom grabbed onto Casey and pulled him out of the study and headed for the stairs.

"Hey, everything go all right with Tommy?" That was Soldier, just walking in from the kitchen to the living room.

"Yes. I learned a little more. He gave me some ideas to investigate. Uh, Casey and I are going to spend some time together upstairs." It's not like he was asking permission. He was twenty-two, so why did it feel like it?

"Okay. If I don't see you when you leave, Casey, thanks for coming over. I'm glad you're in Gom's life." Well, there was nothing subtle about that.

"Uh, thank you, sir." Casey said, sounding almost like the teenager that Gom felt like at the moment.

"Soldier, son. Just Soldier. Ben and Trick went to a movie, so I think I'll grab some time with Dillon. See you all later." Soldier had a twinkle in his eye and Gom grinned as his dad went in search of his other dad for some alone time of their own.

When the door closed behind them, and Gom heard the lock click, it wasn't apprehension that had his body humming. It was desire. Okay, and a little bit of nerves, but no fear.

Like he'd told Casey, unlike Tommy, he'd never been sexually abused, so the trauma of his early years didn't spill over and affect his ability to want to be close to someone, to Casey. But when they got to certain levels, he would have some explaining to do about some of the scars he had. That was for another time.

"Bed or chair?" Gom asked.

"You'd be comfortable on the bed?" Bless Casey's heart for caring about his feelings. But…

"Yes. Come on," Gom wanted to disavow Casey of that notion right away. He really was all right with lying on the bed with Casey, even into exploring. Maybe it was knowing that they weren't going to go the full way tonight that eased his nerves, but he was sure that as their relationship developed, he would be ready for the more intimate side.

Casey chuckled as Gom took his hand and pulled, drawing him over to the bed. As they got there, Casey twisted so that he would be on the bottom and used their joined hands to pull Gom down on top of him. Gom gasped in surprise, but when Casey's arms wrapped around him, he sighed. Letting Casey take the lead, Gom was pulled more fully on top so that they were matching head to toe.

"Shoes on the bed okay?" Casey muttered.

"Right now, I could care less. I like this," Gom so did. He was looking right down into Casey's face, so close. "How can you have such beautiful eyes?" Oh, yeah, that sounded like a girl. Gom blushed.

"I don't know. How can you?" Casey teased.

"Easy answer. These are not really my eyes." Gom said, speaking of his blue contacts.

"I was talking about the pretty brown ones that match the color of your hair, when it's not dyed. I like the richness of the color in your hair and your eyes are sexy as hell."

"Really?" Gom was totally serious in his doubt. Casey's comment about his hair sort of matched his about Casey's eyes so maybe he didn't sound too bad. He'd always thought he was just average with the whole brown theme, even though he'd always been called cute and even pretty. He just didn't see it. It wasn't a lack of self-confidence. Soldier and Dillon had instilled a feeling of self-worth in all the boys they worked with in any way. But his surprise was evident to Casey.

"You know, I'm going to address that at another time. Suffice it to say, I think you're gorgeous. You turn me on in so many ways, not the least of which is the size of your…" Casey paused and when Gom's eyes started to widen, he smiled and winked before finishing, "heart." Before Gom could say anything, though who knows what he could say to that, Casey put a hand on the back of Gom's head and brought it down to his own.

Gom met Casey's lips with his, opening to allow Casey's questing tongue admittance with a pleased sigh. He became caught up in the sensation of Casey's tongue moving inside his mouth, tracing his teeth, moving against his tongue, and touching the roof of his mouth before pulling back to slide across the front of his teeth, which made the back of his lips tingle. His breath started to come faster and he moved his hips instinctively.

When Gom's cock rubbed against Casey's he echoed Casey's groan. That felt amazing. Wanting more, Gom squirmed again, brushing their groins together and felt Casey match the movement, pushing up and before long they were grinding hard. Casey rolled a little, putting Gom beside him. They broke apart for a few seconds to rearrange arms and legs into a more comfortable clench.

"Kissing's cool," Gom murmured, reaching for Casey's lips again.

"Ya think?" Casey slurred back against Gom's lips.

"Don't you?" Gom pulled back to ask. He'd hate it if Casey didn't like kissing as much as he did. Gom got worried all of a sudden that maybe kissing wasn't what Casey was interested in and that he wouldn't be able to make Casey happy.

Before he could get any further with that train of thought,

it was derailed, and competently, by Casey's mouth crushing his again. From the way that Casey was moving his lips, open and wet against Gom's, it was clearly evident that Casey liked kissing just as much. Gom settled in for more. When Casey pulled back just a little, his tongue sliding across Gom's lips, Gom sucked in a breath.

"Tongue," Casey whispered.

"Mmm?' Gom was confused.

Casey touched his tongue to Gom's lips again, but didn't come into his mouth. Gom put his tongue out, trying to entice Casey's inside. Casey touched the tip of his tongue to Gom's and instead of coming inside, he teased it, stroking and sliding, touching the tip again and again.

"Mmm," Gom hummed and Casey wrapped his lips around the tip of Gom's tongue and sucked it into his mouth, pulling on it rhythmically. Gom thought he would come in his jeans right then. It was like the muscle at the base of his tongue was directly connected to his groin. He jerked hard where their hips were glued tightly to each other. Gom couldn't get a good breath.

He pulled away from Casey's mouth and pushed his face into Casey's neck, hiding, not wanting to look at Casey and admit that he was so far gone just from kissing. Sure that he'd disappointed Casey, he took deep breaths and stayed hidden, even when Casey brought his hand up and tried to get him to look up.

"Gom?"

"Mmm?"

"You okay? Was I going too fast? I'm sorry, but God, man, just kissing you and I'm ready to blow. I've never, well, you know I've never, since you know you were my first kiss. I'd say we've graduated to the advanced class in the kiss category, huh?" Casey sounded like maybe the kiss had affected him just as much.

Gom bravely pulled his face out of Casey's neck to look at him and saw a stunned look on Casey's face. It was probably wrong of him in some way, but he was thrilled at the thought that he'd put that look there. He had no doubt that the identical look was on his face. He smiled slowly, leaning in and touching his nose to Casey's, bumping and sliding, then put his forehead against Case's. They lay there, still, breathing hard, and looking at each other's eyes, so close. Gom fell for those light blue orbs all over again when he saw the sweet, sexy, caring look in them.

"God help us when we decide we're ready for more. We're going to need asbestos sheets. I'm about to explode just from kissing you. Your hand, or God help me, your mouth on my cock and I don't know if I'll be able to stand it. Too much information?" Even Casey's eyes were smiling at him.

"Nope. I was thinking the same thing. Feels good to rub against you, and that's with clothes on. We'll certainly have to be somewhere besides here when we finally get skin to skin, and I have no doubt that it will. I really, really like you Casey. I can't tell you," Gom said, pulling his head back now to look seriously into Casey's face, "how much it meant to me that you were here tonight for me, just when I needed it. And you stayed and met Tommy and Daniel and you seemed pretty comfortable. It touched me, honestly, when I saw you here because I knew it was just for me. That's pretty heady stuff. Thank you." Gom leaned back in for another kiss, this one of gratitude and thankfulness.

"Hey, don't give me too much credit. It made me happy, too. I've never met anyone like you, or the rest of your family. They're all about helping people and doing good and being there for each other. That's a whole other world for me." Casey was honest in his response and Gom appreciated that.

CHAPTER NINE

Gom woke to a phone call from Captain Denny the next morning. He was told there'd been a break in the case and for him to log on and look for a file that was coming in for him to read.

"I've turned it on, and something is coming through now. What is this?" Gom asked, as his incoming mail brought up several emails.

"They found this on Byron Neighbor's computer. It was hidden in a file called Games so they didn't pay too much attention to it, thinking it was the name of a game. They were looking more for things that would give us an idea where his mind was in the last while. Well, this file is something you should read. It will definitely give you an idea who was hurting him, who knew, and they've also found the ones who put it out."

"I'm surprised they didn't find that out sooner," Gom suggested.

"We've known that for a while, but we've kept it under wraps. That information is in the email under 'informants'. You're not to do anything with that, but we feel you should know. Once you read the file we found, you'll understand. This is some serious stuff. How does a junior in high school get so lost that he feels some of the things he wrote in that file?"

"I'm almost afraid to read it," Gom said, his finger hesitating over the keyboard.

"Call me this afternoon and we'll talk. It's going to take you a while to process some of what you're going to read. It's intense, Marsh."

"Yes, sir. I'll check back in this afternoon."

Gom hung up and turned to the monitor. He took a deep breath and clicked on the file and when it opened and he saw the title of the missive, he had an ominous feeling. This was going to be bad. He put his hand up to the monitor and traced the words "Gateway to Hell".

Gom started reading and it felt like he was invading this kid's privacy. The file was set up like a diary and the kid was talking to the computer as if to a friend or confidant. Gom was thinking that he needed to get breakfast and talk to Dillon and Soldier, but he was in front of the computer and about to step into this young boy's private hell. Frozen in his chair, he read.

****

Why is this the way it has to be? I know I sound like a whiny weak kid, but it seems like it isn't fair. I have never hurt anyone that I can remember. There has not been a day in my life since I realized that I was gay and foolishly admitted it, that I have not been bullied in one form or another. Oh, yes, there are many forms. Of course, the worst are the painful ones, but the little snickers and pointing fingers, the whispers and snide comments hurt, too. They stay with me longer than the bruises or the totally degraded feeling I have after a turn in the bathroom.

****

How did my own personal hell start? High school. That's the only way I can answer it. When I started as a freshman, it seemed that there were boys who were on the lookout for guys who were 'queer'. There must have been something about me, well, okay; I look like the stereotypical gay guy. I'm little, blond curly hair (how girly can you get?). I have pretty features, pink lips, blue eyes, little, pointy nose. So, automatic target, huh? Go, me. From day one I was teased in both little and big ways.

I'd get bumped into in the hall which would throw me into lockers or the wall. I'd get tripped and as whoever did it walked by, they'd mutter words like 'queer', 'fag', 'homo', 'fudge-packer' (I detest that one). I don't really have friends, except for Charles. I met him in the library and we got to talking. We have two things in common. We're both gay. We both do home-

work for bullies to keep from getting beat up. The difference? He never had to give blow jobs to protect himself. Why do I?

I have a nervous stomach, which puts me in the bathroom a lot. Sucks, but that's how it is. I'd love to get through a whole day at school without having to go, but it's not possible. So, and here's the big question. How in the hell do those guys know when I'm going to the bathroom? Even if we're not in the same class they manage to find me. How do they get out of class and find which bathroom I'm in? Do they have spies that text them secretly?

Anyway, I hate swirlys. They are so very gross and painful and scary as hell. Having your head shoved into a toilet and then held under while it's flushed is just the nastiest thing I can imagine. You have to make sure your eyes are closed tight and you have to hold your breath. The fear and the grossness of it make it hard to get through. Twice this happened to me in a toilet that hadn't been flushed. Sick. Just sick. I was so afraid that I would end up with some damn disease because of the bacteria and well, just gross. It hurts when my forehead hits the bottom of the toilet and my nose gets mashed. How do you stand there and do that to somebody? A human being? And why? I promise you I never did anything to these guys. Like I would, or anyone would, come on to someone who obviously hated gays. Come on. I know not to even look at them.

In this case, 'them' is the jocks at the school.

Yes, that's who tortures me. I can't tell you how these two have made my life hell. They're big, strong, popular, and they hate gays in general, and me, in particular. And why? Because, rightly, they decided I was gay and I didn't deny it. Would It have mattered? On the defining day, one of them threw me down and once there he said since I was on my knees anyway I should suck him off. I don't know where the next words came from, but I told him I would if he'd quit bothering me. We made a deal that day. I sucked him off regularly, him and his friend, and he didn't beat me anymore. And no more swirlys! Swear *to God, it's worth it! He brought two more guys into the deal and I don't have to give them bj's but I ended up doing home-work for all four of them. Anything to keep my head out of that fucking toilet!*

****

Gom jerked, thinking now he had a place to start. Maybe he'd get some clues. The things that were done to this boy, though Gom knew it happened all over, seemed criminal to him, considered assault, at least. His heart raced and he realized it was from anger. He was furious that two boys put this kind of fear, this feeling of being helpless, into Byron Neighbors. The kid had it right. It wasn't fair. He kept reading.

****

I would love to be the cool gay guy that has friends and everyone talks to and laughs with, not at. I love music, and musicals. I would like to dress nicer than I do, but that takes more money than I've got. I would be a great gay, seriously. I would like to decorate a home, learn to cook very well, have friends over for get-togethers and all talk about things that interest us, like movies and books, clothes and fashion, TV and celebrities, music and concerts. Sigh. That sounds like a great life.

****

Everybody says it'll get better, and I'd like to believe it will. But for me? Looks pretty bleak right now. No end to the pain in sight.

****

I've never had a chance to be part of a couple, to have a gay friend that I actually did anything with, you know? It's a dream. I'm not even ready for that. But I would like to experi-ence a kiss with a guy. That would be cool. I just can't imagine how good it would feel to be close to someone like that. To know what a tender touch feels like. Why is it so wrong for me to want that? I don't get it.

****

Charles made it clear that he would not be interested in becoming anything more than study buddies, and that's okay. I don't expect that, just because we're both gay, we're going to be lovers. So, we spend a lot of time in the library. I don't know how many he's doing work for, but he's in there a lot, like me.

But I don't know any other guys who interest me, either, so, I'm kind of stuck being alone. But do I have to be alone and lonely and bullied? All of it? Really? I'm not saying that at my age, my life should be perfect. No one's is. I'm not the only one getting bullied at this school. Being so aware of it, I see it all the time. They pick on Mary because she has bad skin, Bonnie for her weight, Danny because he stutters, which, of course, only makes it worse. There are so many more. There's so much of it going on and I keep thinking about why the teachers don't see it or do anything about it if they do. I wish someone could make it stop. I just want it to stop.

A lot of kids are getting pissed about me being teacher's pet because I know all the answers to the questions in class and it's gotten to where they call on me because they know I'll get it right. I'm doing so many reports on so many subjects, researching things in History, Social Studies, and Science that I'm almost ready to take over the classes. I even caught one teacher in a mistake and when I mentioned it, she was furious, but I was right. Sri Lanka became the Democratic Socialist Republic of Sri Lanka in 1972 not 1976. I mean, you can't just give out the wrong facts and want students to remember them. So I corrected her. Didn't go over well.

****

I've thought a lot recently about the quality of my life and how long I think I can go on like this. I'm so lonely. I hate this. I hate what I'm doing as much as I hate the fact that I have *to do it to keep me safe from beatings and worse. I see other kids who go through the day and they don't have this kind of crap to deal with. Sounding whiny again, I know.*

And, since you won't tell anybody, I'll admit I've been think-ing about how nice it would be for it all to just be over, you know? I know, I know. Call someone, talk to someone, tell some-one. Who? The school Saf-T lady? She left and she just wasn't someone I could talk to. I don't know the new one at all. Oh, and the guidance counselor, Mr. Sinclair, doesn't seem to be all that crazy about gays. I thought teachers and people who worked with kids had to take classes on tolerance and diver-sity and so on. I heard him say that if people were going to go around looking and acting all gay they shouldn't be surprised at what came their way. Honest to God, I heard him. It was after school and he was talking in the break room as I went by and when I heard the word gay I stopped, surprised. He actu-ally said that. So, like I'm going to confide in him. Not. And, I must look gay, like he said, because the jocks all had it in for me without any questions asked.

****

Having met Mr. Sinclair, Gom knew exactly what Byron was talking about. Gom hadn't gotten the feeling that Sinclair was a very warm person. In talking about Byron, Sinclair had not shown anything other than a matter of fact attitude. Gom felt like a counselor in a high school should have a lot more heart, or at least be able to show that he cared about students and their feelings and needs.

****

Thinking about it more and more. What would be the big deal? Mom would be hurt for a while, but other than that, who would think it was a big deal if I checked out? The jocks will find someone else to bully.

Another reason I don't tell someone what's going on? I've been told that if I tell on them, they'll start breaking things, like arms or legs. Evidently, I'm also a chicken. So many negative things about me. Where's the positive? I'm smart. I'll give you that. But I live in fear every day. I listen to slurs every day. I feel like shit every day. Every single day. For what? So I can say this is my life? Screw it.

****

It would be doing my mother a great disservice to say I'd never known love. I know she loves me. She's not comfortable with my being gay, but she didn't kick me out or anything. We don't have a lot to say to each other anymore, but she still takes care of me, you know, feeds me, buys me clothes. It's just not the same as before. I guess love is conditional. Mom says people who kill themselves are going to hell. Little does she know, I go there every day.

****

I thought about trying to find out exactly how high the school building is. I think it would be like poetic justice if I used the school to end my life, my sick, sad, sorry life. To me, the school is my gateway to hell. It's going to that place every day that has made me feel less than human. Like my life is not important. I just feel so heavy, you know? Like there's a weight bearing down on me that makes me less and less every day, until soon I'll be nothing.

****

There it was. Gom's breathing slowed now, his heart cold. He could feel each pounding heartbeat. These entries were when Byron started thinking about taking his own life. Gom was almost afraid to read the rest, sure in his heart that he didn't want to be inside Byron's head, know those painful thoughts that led up to the final moments of his life. He shivered, dreading the words to come. Taking a deep breath and rubbing his arms, he continued reading Byron's last thoughts.

****

If I were to fail to do a report for the two main jocks, or their two friends who are also in the group now, I would be right back to the beatings and the swirlys and living in abject fear all the time. So, I'm still living in fear, I'm just working my ass off to try to make things better. So, they don't beat me, but I still get the same slurs, the names, the hate. It's the hate that's the worst. Why do so many people hate me? I don't even know them.

****

I'm just so tired of it all. Every day it's more and more of a chore to get up and go in, waiting to see who's going to trip me, put gum in my hair, stick pudding cup tops on my back, flick me on the head, and that's the mild stuff.

****

Oh my God! Someone shot me in the back of the head with a squirt gun on the bus this afternoon. When I turned there were four football players back there and all four had their hands up and were laughing at me. All so innocent! Why am I grossed out? Someone peed in the gun and I rode all the way home with urine in my hair, while there were taunts and giggles from behind me. Life sucks so damn bad.

****

I keep looking at the highest point of the building and wondering how I'd get up there.

****

I hate what I'm doing. I know, I agreed to it. But, at the time, I honestly was so happy to think of not having to endure the pain that I never considered what I'd eventually feel like. I'll even admit that when this started, I thought, you know, no big deal. I want to learn how to be good at doing this. Someday I'll make someone really happy that I'm so good at it. Just practice, right?

Lately, I've been sort of tearing up a little every time I have to hit my knees and earn my safety, so to speak. Of course, that just adds to the cause for them. Now I'm not just a slut and a whore, but I'm a crybaby, wimp, sissy as well. Whatever!. What I used to do freely, thinking I was smart to find a way out of a bad situation, is now degrading, demoralizing, and humiliating. It's like my life is worthless. I'm worthless.

****

Honestly, jumping seems to be the only way out. I imagine it will hurt bad for a little bit, but then blessed peace. I know, going to hell. Wonder if that hell will be worse than this one?

****

It's not that I want to die. I just don't want to go on living, especially like this. What's the point?

****

Peace sounds good.

****

Sometimes in class, I feel tears coming and I don't' know why. It's embarrassing. I think I'm losing my mind.

****

I wish I had at least gotten to experience a kiss, just one, to know what it feels like, you know?

****

It's pretty sad when I think that I probably won't even be missed.

****

As the sentences got shorter and the thoughts more grim, Gom's heart began to race again, knowing what was coming, wishing it had a different ending.

****

The pain of being alone right in the middle of everybody is so painful.

****

Can't they see me? Nobody sees me anymore.

****

The more I think about doing it, the calmer I get. The more peace I find in my soul.

****

Fuck me! It's all over the school. It's on the internet. Someone told it all. The day wouldn't end.

****

I hate them

****

I'm outa here

****

Gom sat, stunned, tears rolling down his face. Peripherally, he knew that the household was awakening. There was movement in the hall and he just hoped no one knocked or came in until he could get some sort of composure. He felt like he'd been shredded into pieces. He'd just read the last thoughts of the young man who couldn't find any way out of the hell he was living in. Oh, what a waste!

This kid had been smart, good-looking, witty, and full of dreams at one time. Now he was no more, and Gom felt like the world, the school officials, the teachers and counselors, his family, had all let him down to such a degree that he'd felt there was no other option but to kill himself. It was so very sad.

Gom wished he could have known him before, had a chance to talk to him, try to make him see that things would get better. And they would have. As soon as he was out of high school there wouldn't be people in his life daily who preyed on his insecurities and pushed him to his limit. It was such a shame that he'd been feeling so low before the ones who'd put his information out to the public. It had been the last straw, taking away any hope that Byron might be able to find someone or some way to keep from choosing that tragic ending.

God, so sad.

There was a knock at the door and Soldier's voice, "Gom? You up?"

Gom was up out of that chair and over to the door in seconds. He grabbed the knob, jerked it open, and looked up at Soldier. He knew there were still tears on his face.

"I love you, Dad."

That was all it took. Soldier opened his arms and Gom was enfolded in unconditional love and support. Soldier didn't have to know what had distressed Gom, he was just there. For a long moment Soldier gave what he always did, and that was just what Gom needed at the time. Somehow, he always knew. Gom shuddered and Soldier's arms tightened.

"What's happened? What can I do?" Soldier asked, quietly.

"Nothing. You did it," Gom said, pulling away, stepping back, wiping his eyes.

"What's going on, Gom? Is it work? Casey?" Soldier was in protector mode now.

"Casey? No, he's great." Gom went back to the computer, saved the file, and came back to the door. "Captain Denny called and said he was sending me a file they found on Byron's computer. It's all there, Dad. All the things they did to him, how he felt, the things he had to do in order to get by. It's all so very sad. If he could have held on, or made himself find someone to talk to and get help, it could have ended differently. He was very smart, you know? It was hard reading all that, really hard."

"God, I can't imagine. Did he name his tormentors?" Soldier asked.

"No, but I'm going to check out the ones that Tommy was talking about. I'm not going to just walk up and say 'Are you the ones who bullied Byron?' But with this new hair and eye color, I might be pretty close to how Byron looked. I'm going to put myself in their way. And I've got a real problem with someone else at the school that I need to take up with the principal." Gom was thinking of the new counselor that Byron was unable to go to because he was evidently as bigoted as the boys who harassed him daily. To Gom, this man was worse than Coach Ramsey at Willington. This Sinclair was supposed to be a person that students *could* go to for help and understanding.

"Come on down. We've kept some breakfast for you. The others have scattered. It's just Dillon and me. You can talk, or not, whichever you need." Soldier stood back and put his hand on Gom's shoulder as he stepped out of the room and they headed for the stairs.

"If it's all right, I'd like to talk about something else. I'm still processing and it's just too much now. I need perspective, just to be normal." They'd reached the kitchen and Dillon must have heard their approach, because there was hot food at his place at the table and a steaming cup of coffee.

"Thanks, Dad. It looks good," he said, looking at Dillon. Gom wasn't sure he felt like eating, but he would make the attempt. He sat and reached for the coffee, made just the way he liked it. Ah, that helped.

"I was glad that Casey came over last night," Dillon said, completely ignoring Gom's red eyes and tension. He knew when Gom needed to let something go and he was giving him an out.

"I can't believe you all called him and asked him to come. It was a nice surprise. How'd you get him to come?" Gom asked, looking back and forth between his two dads.

"Like it was a hard sell," Dillon laughed. "I kind of told him you needed him, that the week had taken a toll on you. He said he'd make arrangements and be here. That was all there was to it. There was no hesitation, which impressed me very much. He seemed to be more comfortable last night. I hope he was." That last was a statement, but Gom could hear the question.

"Yeah, I think so. I really like him. He's pretty special." Gom hoped he wasn't blushing, because all this talk of Casey had him remembering their kisses and how it felt to lie on the bed with Casey.

"You all make any plans?" Dillon asked.

"Nah, just to call. I'm going to make a call to the station. Then, oh, is there anything I can do for you all?" Gom could use some more normal activity before he got back into the Baiden High world.

Before he could say more, the phone rang. Soldier grabbed it and Gom saw him smile as he looked over at Gom and say, "Yes, he's here. Let me put him on." He held the phone out to Gom and ignored the question Gom was putting in his look.

"Hello?"

"Monty? This is Bradley Haines."

"Bradley, hi! How are you? It's good to hear from you. How's Missy? Are things better for you?" Gom didn't know if Bradley was aware that he knew about where he was living now.

He settled in at the table and listened to Bradley. Dillon cleared the table and Gom realized that he'd eaten breakfast while they'd talked to him. Soldier went into the den and Gom paid attention to Bradley. He learned that both Bradley and Missy were very happy living with the foster family that Laurie had helped to arrange for them. He was saddened to hear that their father was still at his home and not going in for help. Bradley sounded so much lighter and happier that, in turn, Gom felt much better when they finally hung up.

With his heart a little less heavy, Gom went back to his room and made some notes and sent them to Captain Denny.

He told him he would be talking to Principal King on Monday and had some ideas about how to go about finding the boys who had tortured Byron for two years and into a third. Gom wondered about summers. He thought about how Byron must have loved being away from the pressures at school and how he must have hated each new school year beginning. There was a sort of understanding of Byron coming to Gom, as he thought about how Byron must have felt helpless to find a way out of the situation he'd made for himself. Poor young man. That he would have to do those things to keep from getting beat up and Gom couldn't even think about the swirlys that Byron talked about hating and fearing so much.

While he was finishing his task, his cell phone rang. Ah, it was Casey. He almost laughed at himself when his heart raced just seeing Casey's name.

"Hey, Casey."

"Good morning. Did you sleep?" Casey asked.

"Yeah, I did. Had some nice dreams, too," Gom teased.

"Mmm, me, too. Are you doing anything tonight?" Casey asked.

"No, but aren't you working at the Showcase? When does the new show start?" Gom knew there'd been rehearsals for a while.

"Next weekend, so they're getting to the dress rehearsals with full lighting, but I'll be done by ten-thirty or so. Would you like a late date?"

Gom didn't hesitate. "Yes, I would. What are we doing?" Not that he cared. He'd just stand and watch Casey work and be happy. Hey, not a bad idea.

He asked, "Would it be all right if I came to the theater and sat with you while you worked? You wouldn't have to talk to me or anything. I'd love to see you working."

"That wouldn't be a problem, but I can't imagine you enjoying it. You sure you won't be bored?" Casey asked.

"Somehow, I don't think so. I promise not to distract you. I know this is your job and you'll have to pay attention, but I think it would be interesting to see you doing your thing." Now that Gom had brought it up, he really wanted to do it.

"Sure. Can you be here at six-thirty? Oh, I usually eat after I get off, even when it's late. Maybe you'd like to wait and have a later supper with me?"

"Maybe I would," Gom answered. Of course he would. "What about going by a deli or the grocery and eating at your place? I'll tell them here that I'll be in really late."

"They won't care?" Casey asked.

"No. I'm an adult, Casey, just playing a teenager, you know? I can stay out all night if I want to," Gom said, and then wondered if he sounded like he was inviting himself over for the whole night.

"That sounds promising. We'll have to explore that soon, yeah?" Casey asked, and Gom was grateful for Casey's answer. He'd shown interest, but hadn't gone for the obvious joke he could have made.

"Yeah, we will, soon. I'll see you tonight, at the theater, at six-thirty. Looking forward to it, Case," Gom said.

"You're the only one who's ever given me a nickname."

"Is that bad?" Gom didn't want to tick Casey off by being too familiar.

"I like it." Gom was thrilled that Casey admitted that. Surprised, but thrilled.

"Good. I didn't plan it. Just sometimes I think of you as Case. See you tonight," Gom said.

"Yeah, see you then." They hung up and Gom sat for a few minutes thinking about Casey and their plans for the evening. Was he ready to...? No, he didn't think so. He wasn't quite ready to go into all the explanations that would come up when Casey either saw or felt his scars. But he was prepared to go further than they had last night. He would make sure that he was prepared. He was inexperienced, not dumb.

After thinking about things for a while, Gom decided to call Laurie Summer, whom he'd come to consider a friend, and ask her opinion about the counselor at Baiden High. He couldn't help feeling that the man was partly responsible for what happened with Byron. If he'd been there, as he was supposed to be, and approachable, then Byron might have reached out and made an attempt at getting help. He'd said he thought about it, but overhearing Sinclair's words had turned him against the idea.

Laurie was home and listened to his story about the message they'd found, but mostly he focused on the bit about Sinclair and asked her what she thought about it. His instinct was to turn the man in as incompetent and get him out of there. Who knew if the man might also have negative thoughts about blacks, or overweight students, or Hispanics? There were any number of minorities who might feel a slight in the way he treated them, making their school experience that much worse.

"I'm having a really hard time keeping my mouth shut about these kids. I know they're in shock and it's scary and sad, but I want to ask where they were when this boy felt like he had no friends, no one to go to, talk to, ask for help. He felt so alone and isolated, despite being active in the classes. He lived with, not just the bigger cases of bullying, but with small slights every day that made him feel like he was a nonentity. Where were they then?" Gom hurt just thinking about Byron's feeling of worthlessness.

"I hear you. They are hurting now and I'd imagine a lot of them are thinking the same thing, you know? Maybe if I'd been nicer to him, talked to him, didn't laugh at others when they picked on him, etc. You're in a hard position over there. Stay strong, Gom."

"I will. It's this Mark Sinclair that I have to do something about. I can't just let it go. It's just wrong, Laurie. I can't go in and say this person is responsible for this boy's death, but an adult, and one in his line of work, should not be part of making a student feel so hopeless." Gom could feel his heart racing as he thought of how Byron must have felt after hearing the anti-gay remark from the school counselor.

"Honestly, I've met Mark Sinclair a couple of times and wasn't impressed. He's one of those with a quick joke or remark that you feel uncomfortable laughing at because it's not quite right. I can see how he wouldn't be the 'warm fuzzy' that a student in need would go to for comfort and help. I agree that you should talk to the principal about it and leave it in her hands. It sounds like the Neighbors boy was a big miss on his part and that's not acceptable. You have to be seen as accessible to the students. They have to trust you." Laurie sounded as disgusted with the situation as Gom was and her opinion mattered to him. He was definitely following through on this.

"Thank you so much, Laurie. I knew I was going to talk to Ms. King, but I value your input."

"Well, speaking of value. I like your new beau." Laurie waited for his answer to her teasing.

"I'm glad. I really like him. We've got sort of a date tonight. I'm going to watch him work and then we're going for supper," Gom said, and then remembered, "oh, Bradley called me this morning. They seem to be doing so much better at their foster home. Thank you for arranging it."

"You don't have to thank me. It's my job and a joy in this case. I was glad to get them, especially Missy, out of that house. The dad's still refusing treatment, but the children seem to have accepted that they won't be going back until he does. They're so much happier and healthier away from the stress. It's good that they're getting to see a real family and learn how it's supposed to be. We did good on that one, Gom."

Gom smiled as he replied, "We did. It feels good when you manage a change, a good change, in someone's life. I've got to go, but thanks for this. It's helped a lot."

They said good-bye and Gom gathered his things and went down to ask Dillon if he would make a dessert treat that he could take with him tonight, one that wouldn't ruin, sitting in the car for hours.

"Casey seemed to like chocolate, so I'll make a Mississippi

Mud Cake and you can take a good bit of it. It will be fine in the car. It's cold enough outside, anyway. How does that sound?" Dillon asked, looking through the cabinets.

"Delicious. I'm meeting him at six-thirty to watch him do the lighting for the dress rehearsal for the new show. After that we're going to get something to eat and go back to his apartment. I'll be back really late since we won't even eat until after eleven."

"No problem. I'll have it ready." Dillon was already gathering ingredients and setting the oven. He loved to cook and work in the kitchen. Gom knew that doing things for his boys made Dillon happier than anything. Well, anything other than Soldier. Soldier made them all happy, but he was Dillon's life and heart.

CHAPTER TEN

Gom kept his word and did his very best to keep from distracting Casey as he worked on the lighting for the dress rehearsal of "A Grand Night for Singing". The show was a collection of songs from Rodgers and Hammerstein. There wasn't a storyline, but it was a revue with songs from several movies and musicals. Casey was kept busy all night as the scene changed with each song, so the lighting was moving constantly. Gom was impressed with the ease and seamlessness that Casey managed the changes for each new number. He knew a lot of the songs from watching the shows with Ben and the others at home while they were growing up. Overall, it was a very enjoyable evening for Gom.

As the lights went down for the last number, Casey stretched and looked over at Gom.

"Were you bored out of your gourd?"

Gom denied it quickly. "Not at all. I enjoyed the songs. I even knew most of them. Ben will love this, by the way. You were a marvel with the lighting." Gom gestured to the board in front of them. "You didn't miss a trick. That was quick work on some of the changes and you didn't seem to hesitate. You're good at what you do. Thanks for letting me observe you in action. How can I help you now?"

"You can walk around if you're tired of sitting for so long. As soon as everyone leaves, I'll do a quick clean and close up. Then we can get some supper," Casey said.

"I'll help. I really don't mind. You do the technical stuff and I'll do the basics that I can't mess up in any way. Oh, and I've got dessert in the car from Dillon. Think, chocolate," Gom teased him.

"Oh, good. I'm always hungry when I get done. You sure you want to work tonight?"

"Definitely. The sooner we're done, the sooner I can kiss you again," Gom said, then almost covered his mouth when he realized he'd said the last part out loud. He was thinking it, but damn, just let it all out there, why don't ya?

"Works for me. Come on." Casey led him from the lighting booth and they got to work as they listened to the actors/singers leaving, laughing, and calling to each other.

Before long, Gom was following Casey to his apartment, parking behind him and grabbing the dessert from the back seat. They'd stopped and gotten Subway sandwiches after agreeing at the theater that neither felt like cooking or preparing anything elaborate tonight. Gom just wanted to eat and relax and talk and then he wanted to spend some time getting to know Casey's body better.

Supper was quick. They talked about the play and some of the things that Casey did besides the lights. After the easy clean up, they decided to save dessert for later. Now they stood, looking at each other expectantly. Gom was trying so hard not to be nervous. He wanted this.

"You know what's funny?" he asked Casey as they finally moved from the amusingly frozen tableau.

'What's that?'" Casey said, turning to Gom as they reached the living room.

"I've dreamed about having someone, a boyfriend, a lover, you know. But, I never felt the need to act on it. I've not felt the desire to come on to anyone or date. Does that seem weird to you?" Gom wasn't embarrassed to be a virgin, but he also didn't want to seem backward to Casey.

"Not weird. I'm thinking you were more into your life plan, getting your education, starting your program with the schools. You have a great family and your life wasn't missing anything." Casey sat on the couch and motioned for Gom to join him.

Sitting down, close to Casey, Gom agreed with him. "You're right. I didn't feel like there was anything more that I needed. I was seeing true love and devotion between my dads and then my brother and Daniel. Those relationships gave me a warm feeling and hope for the future, but no burning desire to make it happen for me. Occasionally I would wonder if there was something wrong with me."

"From what I've seen, Gom, there's nothing wrong with you. But we're not talking about your job and your home life. You're talking about something else, aren't you?" Casey's voice had lowered, deepened as he got to the crux of the conversation.

"Yeah," Gom hated that he sounded so unsure of himself.

"You know what's funny?" Casey repeated Gom's question.

"What?"

"You're thinking too hard, hon." Casey said, leaning back into the corner of the couch, stretching his legs to rest on the coffee table.

Gom couldn't keep the quick smile off his face.

"What?" Again Casey was repeating Gom's word.

"You called me hon," Gom said, tickled that tough guy Casey had used an endearment for him.

"I'm sorry."

"Oh, no. I liked it, really. I just never pictured you as the type to use words like that." Gom wished he hadn't shown his response now.

"You know what's funny?" Casey asked, a small smile on his face.

Gom chuckled at the third use of the phrase.

"What?"

Casey reached for Gom's hand and said, "I never have before, you know, used words like that."

"I like that even better." Gom couldn't help it.

"Know what else?" Casey asked, sitting up and leaning in toward Gom.

"Hmm?" Gom lost his train of thought at Casey's touch and

his nearness.

"Talking too much here," Casey murmured, right before he took Gom's lips with his. Gom moaned a sigh against Casey's mouth and settled closer. Casey's tongue came out and Gom happily opened for it as soon as he felt the soft intruder seeking entrance. Gom turned so that he was facing Casey more squarely and when Casey put both his hands on Gom's face to hold him gently for their kiss, Gom couldn't hold in his slight whimper.

Casey pulled back right away, looking puzzled. "I'm sorry. Didn't you want, I mean, don't you want to kiss me?" Casey hadn't moved far, just enough to look into Gom's eyes. "I'm kind of afraid of moving too fast and freaking you out."

"No, it's not that. Remember how I told you I used to dream about having someone?" At Casey's nod, Gom continued, "I've always thought that was one of the sexiest things, the way you were holding my face in your hands. It's like you're holding something precious and kissing with such tenderness. It's beautiful." Gom tried to duck his head, but Casey wouldn't let go of his face. "Now I sound like some high school girl or something." He really was embarrassed at how that had come out.

"Over thinking again, hon. The gesture *is* beautiful. The last part was the over thinking part. I've seen people do this in movies and so on and it feels right to hold you close and take your mouth. God, Gom, I'm not used to talking like this. I don't know if I'm saying anything right." Casey was still looking at Gom as if gauging his response.

"It means a lot to me that you go out of your comfort zone to talk to me," Gom said. He knew that Casey wasn't used to talking, especially about things like feelings.

"I feel like it's something that you need and for some reason I can't resist giving you anything I can." Casey's small shrug and rueful expression showed his understanding of Gom's needs.

"Like being there for me last night?"

"Yeah, it was like I just couldn't say no when Dillon suggested that you'd had a bad week and needed me. It wasn't even a question. You're getting to me, Gom Marsh." Casey said, leaning in again.

"Do you feel that coming right back to you, Casey Tanner?" Gom made the move this time and pushed his mouth onto Casey's.

Talking was over. Gom opened to Casey's tongue and sighed softly as he felt Casey's thumbs moving gently over his cheekbones. Casey's fingers were in his hair and Gom shivered as they moved on his scalp. Casey tilted his head, slanting his mouth over Gom's and taking the kiss much deeper. Gom responded in kind and passion took over. Gom's breathing became labored and he moved closer, wanting more contact with Casey. He lost track of time as he pressed his chest against Casey's and felt the strong heartbeat.

Finally, needing a good breath, Gom pulled his lips away, sliding them across Casey's cheek to his neck. Gom didn't want to let go, to lose the physical connection yet. He pressed his face into the space where Casey's shirt met the area below his ear. Frustrated, Gom tried to nudge the fabric out of the way so he could get to the skin that he wanted to taste. He breathed deeply and reveled in the scent of Casey.

"Problem?" Casey sounded amused at Gom's attempts to get closer to him.

"Yes, actually," Gom said, finding his nerve and going for what he wanted. "I want to feel you, taste you, and I can't. You need to take your shirt off. I mean, if you will," Gom knew what he wanted. He just wasn't sure enough of himself to be comfortable asking for it. He did it, though, he thought.

"May I make a suggestion here?" Casey said, using his hands to gently pull Gom's face out of his neck and into the light.

Gom nodded, having used all the nerve he had already.

"Come with me to the bedroom. Lie down with me where we can be comfortable and I'll take off anything you want me to, if you'll match me. If I take mine off, you take yours off, too. We'll only go as far as you feel like you can handle." Casey waited a few seconds before adding, "Ready for that?"

Again Gom resorted to nodding his assent.

"Nope. Say it. I need to know that you want to come with me and explore how we feel about each other. I don't want to push you."

"Casey," Gom said, near exasperation, "I told you that I want that." To make Casey believe him, Gom stood, reaching his hand to Casey to pull him up, indicating his willingness to go to the bedroom with him.

"Are you warm enough?" Casey asked, as they moved down the short hall to his bedroom.

"Oh, yeah, I don't think that's going to be a problem." When they got to the Casey's room, Gom wasted no time looking at the décor. He walked right to the bed and sat down, reaching to take off his shoes. As soon as that was done, he reached for the buttons on his shirt.

"Hey," Casey said, quietly, "okay if I do that?" Gom dropped his hands to his lap and sat, looking up at Casey, who'd already taken off his shirt while Gom got rid of his shoes. Casey looked down at Gom, with a sexy smirk while he started releasing the buttons from their holes. How in the world Casey could make something so mundane seem like foreplay, Gom didn't know, but by the time his shirt was open he was breathing harder and beginning to shake. He'd watched Casey's hands move down the front of his shirt and finally asked the question that had been in the back of his mind since meeting Casey.

"What's this?" he asked, touching the mark on Casey's left hand.

Casey paused, still and quiet for a few seconds and then sighed. Gom looked at Casey to see if he'd been upset by Gom's question, but he was gazing at his hand. Gom took the hand, bringing it closer to his face, looking at it closely. He could almost make out letters. It was a word. He could see that it started with an S.

"Not a very good story for this particular time. Suffice it

to say that I had a shitty childhood. My father never tired of telling me that I was nobody, would never be anybody. He usually followed up those words with his fists. Shh," Casey said, seeing the dismay on Gom's face, "relax. You've seen worse, I'm sure. But when I left home I found someone who agreed to put that word on there for me. It was one part rebellion and one part, I don't know, affirmation maybe. I put it where I would always be able to see it, know it."

Gom pulled it closer, nearly going cross-eyed trying to read the word. The letters were so tiny. He took a few seconds, looked at the length of the word and thought about what Casey had said. SOMEBODY. Casey had the word tattooed on his hand, in plain view to remind himself that he was the opposite of what his father had tried to beat into him.

Gom pulled that hand the rest of the way and kissed the spot, sighing the word, "Somebody."

"Yeah, told you it would ruin the mood," Casey said, trying to pull his hand back.

"Not at all. I've never been more into you, felt closer to you, or wanted you more." Gom smiled at the widening of Casey's eyes as he put his tongue out and drew it slowly over the word. He blew on it and then kissed it again. He felt Casey shiver and dropped the hand to put his own on Casey's jaw. Casey, who didn't like to be touched, nuzzled his cheek into Gom's hand.

Casey brought his hands up again to cup Gom's face and they leaned together, easing into a kiss that Gom wasn't sure which one of them needed more. It didn't last long, that kiss, but it was held a wealth of emotion on both sides. Casey pulled away first.

He pulled the shirt off Gom's arms and then bent to grasp the hem of his tee shirt and pulled that off, too. Dropping them onto the floor, Casey put his hands on Gom's head, smoothing his hair.

"Do you like your blond hair yet?" he asked.

"I'm still a little shocked every time I look in the mirror. I'm not used to it, so I don't expect it, but it was a good idea. Thanks for helping me with it." Gom leaned in to Casey's touch on his head.

"It still looks good. How long do you think you'll need to be there?" Casey asked, moving to sit beside Gom.

"Maybe a week. I'm getting closer to finding out what I need to know." Gom really didn't want to think about Byron and his pain and his actions right now. That just didn't belong here. "Case?" he turned to face Casey.

"I hear you. Not the time. Come here, hon." Casey stood up, put one knee on the bed, a queen size with a thick navy and white block quilt on it. He pulled the quilt away from the pillows and as Gom got up, he drew the whole thing to the foot of the bed. Gom's eyes must have given him away because Casey smiled, took his hand, and said, "Relax. We're just going to get comfortable. I want to hold you, feel you all along me."

Since that's what Gom wanted, too, he moved onto the bed quickly, eliciting a chuckle from Casey who followed and just like that, they were in each other's arms. Gom's sigh was nearly identical to Casey's.

"I'm afraid I'm going to..." Gom began.

"Shh..." Casey ended for him. He drew Gom closer and it was like coming home. Gom settled against Casey, held tightly to him, and nuzzled his face right back into Casey's neck. He touched his tongue to Casey's skin and breathed his scent. God, he wanted to inhale him completely. Gom felt his heart pounding and could feel the beat in his neck.

Casey's hands were moving over his back, tracing lines, shaping his shoulder blades, walking down his spine. Gom squirmed against Casey, loving the sensation of Casey's fingers on his skin. They were lying face to face and Gom allowed it when Casey moved to put one leg in between his, pulling his hips into closer contact with Casey's. He felt the hardness of Casey's heavy cock against his own. He could hear Casey's breathing competing with the speed of his and knew they were feeling the same needs.

Gom was puzzled when Casey pulled away for a moment, but

saw that he was grabbing some tissues from the bedside table. He didn't ask, but sank into the kiss that Casey brought to him. He greeted Casey's tongue and sucked it into his mouth. He began a rhythmic tugging that had Casey pushing his hips into Gom's in time. A little more of that and Gom was going to be embarrassed.

This time it was Casey who had to pull away for a breath. He moved and put his lips to Gom's chest. Gom gasped as Casey took his right nipple into his mouth. Oh! That was. Wow. He pushed against Casey's lips, wanting more. He felt Casey reach for his other nipple with his hand and then both sides of his chest were streaked with heat and sensation.

"Casey? Case. Oh." That was all he could say. His hips were now returning the thrusts that Casey was making and he knew he was going to come and would feel so stupid.

"Casey, please. I'm going to…oh, Casey, you have to stop." Gom was almost frantic now.

Gom gasped as Casey moved back a little, reached down, opened his jeans and reached inside to grasp his cock. A moan escaped him and he came right then, eyes wide, mouth open. He jerked and moved his hips, pushing his cock into Casey's hand, gasping. When he calmed a bit, he looked down and saw that Casey had used the tissue and was cleaning him before dropping it onto the table in a square metal dish. Gom couldn't meet Casey's eyes.

"Are you mad? Upset?" Casey asked. Gom looked up then and saw that Casey was serious.

"No. I'm embarrassed. That wasn't, I mean, you didn't even…" Gom trailed off, unable to finish his statement.

"I'm only a touch away from joining you, Gom. Will you? Touch me, I mean." Gom looked down and saw that Casey was shaking and hard in his jeans.

Gom reached out and unfastened Casey's jeans, pulling his cock out and taking the tissue that Casey handed him. He looked up from the thick cock in his hand to the face that was intently watching him. He stroked a couple of times and caught Casey's come in his hand.

Casey groaned and his breath gusted out, "Gom! God."

Gom used the tissue to clean Casey and never took his gaze from Casey's as the wet square was taken from him and placed with the other.

"Thank you. Still okay?" Casey asked him.

Gom nodded, resting his forehead against Casey's. "I feel great. You?"

"Mmm." That was all he got from Casey, who rolled his head back and forth on Gom's. "Good, really good. Still embarrassed? You shouldn't be."

"I'm okay. You're so patient with me. Thank you. I hate feeling like a backward teenager, but this is all new territory for me. I want to be enough for you." His real fear came out.

"Silly. If I was just looking for sex, don't you think I could find it pretty much anywhere around here? I want you. I want to know you. Here's that need you have for words, huh? I can handle that, for you. I'm not in a hurry. I want you, I can tell you that, and I think you want me, too. We'll take our time and do things when we feel like it. There's no timetable here, hon. We're doing what is right for us. Don't waste any more time worrying about stuff like that. Know what I want right now?" Casey asked, a teasing tone to his voice.

"Chocolate?" Gom teased back.

"Mmm, yeah, in a bit. Right now, we should put that," he pointed to Gom's soft cock, "back where it belongs and I'll do the same. Then I'd like to lie here with you for a little doze, just holding each other, getting comfortable with each other. Then, mmm, chocolate. Tell Dillon thank you for me."

That's what they did. Gom settled into Casey's arms and they rested their heads together and dozed. Gom would look over and find Casey gazing at him and he'd smile, reaching for a soft kiss. They would both close their eyes and rest for a while, then next time Gom looked over, there were those Husky eyes watching him again. Finally, he laughed and said, "You're watching me."

"I can't help it. I'm not believing I have you here in my bed, in my arms. I've thought about this a lot. It's good." Casey, for someone who professed to not talk much, was really good with words.

"Okay, time for your treat."

"That's my cue to say *you* are my treat," Casey teased.

"No, that's your cue to get off your butt and let's go eat dessert." Gom rolled to the side of the bed and then stood, reaching for Casey's hand.

Casey allowed himself to be pulled across the bed and was soon standing beside Gom. He took another long kiss before bending to retrieve their shirts and heading for the kitchen.

"Coffee or milk?"

"Ooh, if you'll heat the slice of cake, cold milk would be perfect."

When they sat down at the table to eat the delicious treat, Casey said, "You sounded upset earlier. Did something else bad happen at the school? You don't have to tell me, but if you need to talk, I'm here."

"That's sweet. No, the officers at the station found a diary of Byron's on his computer and I had to read it this morning. It started off sounding like I was reading a book about someone's life. Long passages about this and that, but it got more and more pained and distressed. The sentences got shorter and choppier as his pain grew and he saw no way out of his situation. He couldn't bring himself to talk to anyone about it and the way he rationalized what he planned was heart wrenching. It was hard to read." Gom picked at the last bit of cake on his plate, unable to finish it.

"I'm sorry," Casey said, covering Gom's hand with his. "I shouldn't have asked. It's none of my business."

"No, please. I'm not going to tell you anything confidential, but I need to be able to talk to you and you have to know what

I'm going through. Thank you for caring enough to ask. I don't think of it as being intrusive, just supportive. I think I'm going to need that. There's a situation I'm going to have to report that's going to be kind of hard, too, with one of the staff members." Gom was thinking of Mark Sinclair.

"Not another Coach like at the other place."

"No, but just as bad. This is a man who's supposed to be one that students can come to for guidance and support, but Byron overheard him making a snide remark against gays, so he certainly felt he couldn't go to him for help. That's just not acceptable." Gom knew he was getting soap-boxy, but he had such strong feelings about what was happening to young gays today.

"That doesn't sound right," Casey agreed with Gom.

Gom spoke from his heart, letting his frustration out. "What if being able to talk to this person, this particular person, was the one thing that could have turned Byron around, made him see that there was hope and that things would get better if he could just hang on? If he'd been able to talk to someone, the things he had to do to survive could have been stopped and he might have just been a high school kid, and a smart one at that. It's such a waste of a wonderful life, Case. It just breaks my heart. If he'd just been able to find someone to talk to, just gotten some help and guidance, maybe I'd be at another school where there *hadn't* been a suicide." He should just shut up about this. He was putting a damper on their night.

"I'm so proud of you and the things you do. Your job, your whole life is making a difference in the world. Kind of makes me feel, I don't know, like I don't deserve someone as good as you." Casey spoke quietly and slowly like he was voicing thoughts that he was having and that made it all seem so much more sincere. But wrong, just wrong.

"I'm not sure how to answer that. Thank you, and that's just ridiculous. I think that about covers it." Gom looked at Casey, then pointed his finger, touching Casey's chest gently, "You're making a difference in *my* life. You made a huge one in Trick's. Not everyone is a cop or a counselor, but that doesn't mean they don't contribute in a good way. I'm proud of you and the way you live your life and care for others. You have to feel like you deserve me, 'cause I'm not ready to give you up, that's for sure." Gom was clear about that.

"Well, in that case, come with me. I know you have to leave soon, but there's something I've always wanted to do, too, but I was never with anyone that I felt like it. You fit the bill perfectly." Casey stood and quickly rinsed their dessert plates and set them in the sink. He reached into a bowl and handed a peppermint candy to Gom, taking one for himself.

Gom secretly smiled. Milk-breath, yeah, not the best. He threw his wrapper away and ran the candy all over his mouth, sucking hard on it, hoping that kisses were in his immediate future. He was intrigued by Casey's words. What could he be talking about doing that he hadn't wanted to do with anyone else? As they walked into the living room, he thought about it. He remembered Casey saying he'd had nothing but one night stands before, no relationships. Hmm, he passed intrigued and sped right to anticipation.

Casey led him to the couch and sat in the middle. He looked up at Gom and using his hands at Gom's hips, turned him so that Gom was facing the couch. Pulling on Gom's hips, he indicated that he wanted Gom to straddle him, sitting on his legs. When Gom smiled and settled onto his lap, he pulled further until they were as close as possible. Gom's knees were against the back of the couch, his groin fit tightly to Casey's. Both of their bodies were showing signs of interest in the proceedings.

"I don't know what your plan is, but I like it so far," Gom teased gently.

Their positions put Gom's head just a bit higher, but he could still look right into those gorgeous light blue eyes. He waited patiently to see what Casey wanted. He liked the idea that Casey hadn't done whatever this was with anyone else and that Casey wanted to do it with him. Casey's hands moved from Gom's hips up his sides to his back and then hooked over his shoulders. Gom felt totally enveloped and liked it.

"I read something one time, a scene, where this couple just sat and looked at each other for the longest time, like they were memorizing the other's face. Occasionally they would touch each other, not sexually, but softly, as if learning about the other person. I like your face, your body, and it's not that I don't remember how you look, or feel for that matter, but I find myself thinking about this, just this. Am I freaking you out?" Casey looked embarrassed, but he didn't pull away.

"Not at all. I'm happy, comfortable being like this with you. I can't imagine it with anyone else, though."

"Yeah, see. That's what I mean. I want to be quiet and still and touch you, feel your weight on me, look into your eyes and see if I can tell if you're feeling the same things I am or not. You said earlier you thought you sounded like a high school girl. It's the talking about feelings. I know. It's something God knows I've never done before. How come with you I want to? This seems like such a, I don't know how to say it, but not a butch, macho thing, but I don't care. I want to experience this with you. Is it okay?" Gom could tell Casey was uncomfortable and was even holding his breath waiting for Gom's response.

For heaven's sake, Casey's words had gone straight to Gom's heart. He leaned and pressed his forehead to Casey's, never taking his eyes from Casey's blue gaze. "Breathe," he whispered, and smiled gently when he felt the rush of peppermint-flavored air against his mouth and chin. He moved the slightest bit and placed a soft kiss on Casey's cheek, right below the corner of his left eye. Turning his head slightly, he brushed his lashes against that spot.

"Oh," Casey breathed the word. Gom looked down and saw the little grin on Casey's face. Evidently, he was doing just what Casey had dreamed about. It felt good, right. He moved again, bumping Casey's nose and placing a soft kiss on the other cheekbone, then going for the same soft caress as before. Casey's deep breath made his stomach move against Gom's. For some reason that was another of those things that Gom felt was so intimate. Both of them were thin and they were so close that they were breathing together, their stomachs touching. He eased back to where their foreheads were just touching and their glances were caught again.

"Gom, hon…" Casey didn't say anything else, but Gom knew.

"Mmm-hmm," Gom whispered back, knowing exactly what Casey wanted to say. They sat for a long time. Gom would move his hand to the back of Casey's hair, then through it. He'd never told Casey that he still had the band he'd taken from Casey's hair once before. He was keeping it, a talisman, a memento. Gom carried it in his pocket and found himself reaching for it occasionally.

The mutual seduction continued. Casey would slide his hands up and down Gom's back, squeezing a little, just enough for Gom to feel the caress, but not disrupt the softness of the moment. First Gom, then Casey would tilt just enough to place a soft kiss on the other's mouth. The gentleness was amazing to Gom. He would never have thought Casey Tanner would get off on a scenario like this. It told him so much about his new friend, lover. Casey Tanner was his lover. What a thought. Gom suddenly needed more.

"Hold me tighter, please," he whispered.

Casey's arms immediately wrapped him up and squeezed. Oh, yes, that's just what he wanted. He tightened his arms around Casey's neck and put his face beside Casey's and held on for a few moments. He felt wonderful, rejuvenated, and so very happy that he couldn't help the laugh that burst from him.

"What in the world?" Casey asked, pulling his head back to look at him.

"Happy, I'm just plain happy. I've never felt anything like this, Casey. You're a marvel to me. You keep surprising me. Was it what you'd been thinking about?"

"It was perfect. I feel so close to you. I've never felt that before and it's good." He chuckled, suddenly, and said, "Was it good for you?"

"Don't laugh. You made me feel so very special." Gom didn't

want him making fun of what they'd shared or feeling like it wasn't important.

"That was what it was about, Gom." Casey put both hands on Gom's face in the gesture that had so touched Gom before. "Making you feel how special you are and showing you how good you make me feel. It's not just sex, though I want that more and more, but there's a connection that I feel with you that's just more than that. Your response makes me feel like you get it." His fingers moved on Gom's cheeks, smoothing the skin, then moved up to brush softly against Gom's lashes.

"Case?" It was a quiet questioning sound that Gom barely got out, so moved was he by the softness of Casey's caress.

"Mmm?" The answering sound was equally hushed as Casey's eyes moved over Gom's face, his thumbs still roving gently over brows and lashes.

"This is good."

That about said it all. Gom couldn't believe how right he felt in Casey's arms. He'd never been this close to another, close enough to see individual lashes, the intense color of Casey's eyes, how there was a darker ring of blue at the edge of his irises that got lighter toward the center. Gom could look at those eyes forever and still think they were the most beautiful things he'd ever seen.

"Hey?" Now Casey was almost whispering.

"Mmm?" Gom murmured, turning just a bit to plant a soft kiss on Casey's wrist.

"Doing anything later today? Want to meet and do something? We could..."

"Yes."

Casey grinned and rewarded Gom's quick response with a long sweet kiss. Gom could feel that both of them were hard again, but he didn't feel any great urge to do anything about it. He enjoyed the ache and the pressure as they were held tightly together, hearts beating against each other. Opening his mouth, he accepted Casey's questing tongue and met it with eagerness.

When they finally eased away from the kiss, Casey asked, "Aren't we just the goofiest gays ever?"

Gom was intrigued with Casey's question, with where it came from.

"How so?"

"Aren't we supposed to be all over each other, groping and grinding and having wild monkey sex? And what are we doing? I don't want you to think I don't want you, or…"

"Stop. I thought there wasn't a 'supposed to' with us? We do what we feel like doing, however fast or slow, whatever we want. Do you think we should…?" Now Gom was afraid that Casey thought he was too messed up to handle anything more and *he* was holding back.

"Shh. We're good. I just don't want to do anything wrong with you. I don't want you to leave. Please don't leave."

Gom couldn't believe that Casey had said that. Maybe Casey had some issues of his own to deal with.

"I have no intention of leaving. I want to see how real this is, how far we can go together. You know I've never done anything with anyone else, but I'm ready for this, Casey. Don't think I'm not. I've told you before. Sex is not a problem with me. That was not my trauma. I get the feeling you think you have to tiptoe around things with me and that's not the case. I'll tell you my sad, sordid story soon and you'll see that I'm ready for you and for making love."

Gom felt the shuddering sigh that moved through Casey. He'd been right. Despite what they'd done earlier, Casey was afraid of Gom's past causing problems for them.

"Okay. Okay, I'm sorry. I just didn't want there to be any, I mean, I didn't want to make things, you know, bad for you." Casey's sincerity was in his voice and his eyes.

"You won't. You'll make things good for me. I have no doubt. Relax. When it's time, I'm ready." Gom wanted off this subject, so he asked, "So, you want to do something later? Got something in mind?"

"Yeah. No. I can't even think when we're this close. Your eyes are pretty. They're not just brown, they're almost as dark as your pupils. Like dark chocolate. Your lashes are as long as a girl's, but don't get me wrong. You don't look like a girl, just a really pretty man," Casey teased.

"I know, heard it all my life," Gom said, pulling back just a little, Casey's hand following him, keeping the contact. "I really like your fantasy, but enough about me. Will you tell me about you? I know so little."

"What do you want to know?"

"Are you from here? Are your parents still alive? Do you have brothers and sisters? Why did you leave home so young? How bad was it, whatever it was? What all have you done in the last several years? Why are you interested in me? What is it about me that makes you like me, want to be with me?" All things that Gom had wanted to know, had wanted to ask.

"Whoa. I can't remember all those. My parents are still alive, I guess. I haven't checked. I got beat up on a regular basis by my dad and my mom didn't care enough to do anything about it. I kept thinking it would get better, but it never did, so I left." Casey's voice was flat, matter-of-fact as if telling a story about someone else. "I never had brothers or sisters, thank God. That meant I didn't have to worry about anyone else getting hurt. It was very bad. My arm was broken twice, a couple of fingers more than that. There were bruises and marks and signs that now I think teachers or counselors should have noticed and asked about, but they didn't. I didn't go to them because I'd been told what would happen if I did, and God knows I had no reason to doubt that he would follow through."

"Oh, Casey. I'm so sorry you had to go through that. That sucks. Parents aren't supposed to hurt their kids." Gom would know.

"Yeah, well, it's not an isolated case. It happens all over. Uh, other questions. I've worked at all kinds of jobs over the years, farm work, hauling in hay, planting crops, whatever was needed as I passed through. Then there was the city work, washing dishes, waiting tables, cleaning different places, but I leaned toward working in movie houses or theaters. You usually get to see the shows free that way and I learned early that other people's stories took my mind off my own." Casey dropped his hands from Gom's face to rest them on the tops of Gom's legs. "I started out in Oklahoma and worked my way here. I like Texas. It's a big enough place to get lost in if you want to, and I wanted to, believe me. I never did anything illegal, though. I promise."

"I believe you. I think you're a very honorable man, Casey."

"You say that with such sincerity. How can you know that? Don't answer that," he shook his head, "I don't need to hear it. You believe good of everyone. I don't want to ever let you down."

"You seem to think that's likely. I don't." Gom was dead certain.

"On to the good questions now. Why am I interested in you? You were there when I brought Trick to Scarcity and you caught my eye immediately. It was all I could do to talk to Soldier and Dillon about Trick and why I was bringing him there. I wanted to find out who you were and what you did. I wanted to know if you were old enough to be interested in me." Casey moved his hands now to Gom's chest, moving them slowly, pressing in over Gom's heart so Gom knew that Casey could feel his heartbeat. "God, I was so scared you weren't gay. What was it about you? I don't know. Honestly. I can't tell you. There was just something about you that drew me. I almost ran out of there." Now he looked at Gom with a rueful expression, as if ashamed of being afraid that day.

"I felt the same thing. When you came back to check on Trick that night, my heart nearly jumped out of my chest when Soldier told me you were there. I couldn't get downstairs fast enough. I had the strangest urge to run to you, but like you, I was afraid you'd deck me if I did something so obvious." Gom laughed at the memory.

"Then I nearly blew it by being so rude to Trick. I still feel bad about that. I've just not been touched much in years and then in such a bad way that I learned to avoid people." Casey ducked his head.

Gom put his hand under Casey's chin and raised his face. "It's done. Trick is fine. You made him feel good by staying and I know that wasn't easy for you. It meant a lot to him, and me. Did you feel me watching you all during that meal? I was trying not to be so noticeable about how I wanted to get to know you."

"I noticed, probably because I couldn't keep my eyes off you. Do you think your dads will have a problem with us being together? I can see how close you all are."

"The fact that they called you and asked you to come to the house Friday night tells me that they knew that you could make me feel better. That was a sure sign of approval, trust me." Gom wasn't worried about his dads.

"Good."

Gom rested his head on Casey's shoulder and felt his hands come up again and wrap around him. He sighed and settled a little. This was so nice.

"Gom?"

"Yeah?"

"Will you answer the same questions for me? Tell me what happened to you, how you grew up, and even why you like me. Turn about and all that." Casey sounded hesitant, like he was afraid of asking Gom to talk about his past, but Gom knew it was the right time. Casey had shared his pain and once it was done, he wouldn't have to think about it again. Casey would know. He kept his face hidden as he began to talk.

"My mom hated me." Gom felt the slight jerk Casey made at the words. "She did. I never knew why. I don't remember her ever holding me, you know, hugging me or kissing me. I wasn't sure what my name was. I only heard words like brat or heathen or worse. I have no idea how old I was when she started hurting me. I really don't remember a lot of it. That's probably a good thing, huh?" Gom shrugged and continued, "Sometimes there are little flashes of things, like her looking at me with such hate in her eyes and always a cigarette in her mouth, or her hand."

Casey's arms were slowly tightening. Gom didn't know if he was even aware of it.

"Go on," Casey's voice was rough.

"I guess the worst was the cigarettes. She used them on me, down there." He paused a second and shrugged. "That sounds like a kid talking, huh? She burned me on my balls and below and across the bottom of my butt cheeks. I don't know how many scars there are. Lots. I just remember how it hurt so bad and I cried and begged her not to do it and she got madder the more I cried. Finally, I stopped crying out loud. I couldn't stop the tears, but I never made a sound again."

Casey's breath hitched and he asked, "Do you know why she did it?"

"No. I never knew. I was only eight when I ended up at Scarcity. Well, it wasn't called that then. I went through the system for a bit first, but finally Daniel realized I couldn't handle a foster home with a woman and I ended up with Dillon. Soldier came later. They tell me that I was found in the bathroom, fully clothed, tied to the toilet. My mother was dead on the floor from an overdose. Evidently I had been there for days since it was the smell that brought people to the house. I was a mess, Casey. I was scared all the time. I wet the bed all the time because I couldn't stand going to the bathroom. I didn't cry out loud for a long time. I was scared of everybody except Dillon. I couldn't sleep or eat. It was not good." Gom stopped when he felt Casey reach for his shoulders and tug. He allowed it.

"My God, Gom. I don't know what to say." Casey moved one hand up to Gom's face, tracing a line from his brow down his cheek and across his lips.

"It's okay. There's only a little more. One day Soldier showed up, I saw him in the back yard and told Dillon. He was dressed in fatigues and was bald and scary looking, but Dillon went out to see who he was. When I looked out and saw them sitting on this log in the back of the yard, I figured he must be all right if Dillon was talking to him. I took him something to eat and went out there." Gom smiled at the memory.

"Brave little cuss, huh?"

"I don't know. I took him the stuff and walked right up to them. Dillon was sort of worried at first, but there was something about this man that now I know intrigued me. I wanted to be close to him. He had these horrible scars all over his face and neck. He let me touch them when I asked. I don't know where the nerve came to even ask that. I thought about how much pain he must have been in to have such big scars on him. It made me sad and I cried. That made him feel bad. For some reason, I went to him and put my head on his shoulder and the next thing I knew I was sound asleep."

"Wow." The word was quiet.

"Yeah. Casey, he sat outside all night long with me sleeping on his shoulder because Dillon told him that I never slept that good. He couldn't believe that I was sleeping finally and so comfortably on Soldier. Dillon put the rest of the kids to bed, there were seven of us. He came back out and we all three slept out there all night."

"Then what happened?" Casey was moving his hands over Gom's shoulders, chest, arms, just keeping him grounded by touch.

"Soldier left for a few days and when he came back he looked different. He was in a suit and had this big Hummer full of food and things for the house. He wanted to stay. It was the weirdest thing. I didn't understand it all at the time. I just knew I wanted him to stay. I wanted to sleep again like I had before and I could tell that Dillon really liked him, too. I didn't understand that either. I just recognized it."

"That's an amazing story. Why's his name Soldier?" Casey asked, head tilted.

"He told us that he was in the war and there was an accident that killed a lot of his friends. He was hurt, burned really badly and it took many operations and a lot of therapy to put him back together again. He spent all that time feeling like he wasn't anything but a soldier, just a soldier. That became who he was. How he thought of himself. He was a soldier and that defined him so he decided that was what he wanted to be called. We didn't care."

"His real name?"

"Keith Marsh. We went through a lot. The others finally accepted him and soon we all loved him. It seems that his family was über rich and owned like almost the whole block where that old house was that we lived in. He moved in and started buying things to make our lives better. Tommy's mother was a monster, too. She and her boyfriend were responsible for hurting him and they wanted him back to do worse. The boyfriend, Ross, came and tried to get him when they were all shopping, but Soldier protected him. Then the guy showed up here and set the house on fire." Again, Gom could feel the gasp as Casey heard that.

"Soldier and I were asleep downstairs in this old recliner that we used to sleep in sometimes. He was so good to me, Casey. Anyway, we woke up to smoke and flames and he got everyone out. Long story short, he ended up building Scarcity Sanctuary and then adopted Tommy and me. There have been many boys over the years that have come through there and he and Dillon have helped them all, but the first seven of us are still around, as you know. Those two men are home to us. They taught us how to be men with character and love and honor. I'm proud of all my brothers. They all have horrible stories but our fathers persevered with love and encouragement to where I think we are all healthy, stable men today. I guess you can figure out how the place got the name. Soldier's scars, Dillon's, from when he was gay bashed at fourteen, and all the scars, visible and not, that have gone through what is truly a sanctuary."

"I thought it might be something like that. It holds a lot of meaning for all of you, I'm sure. A lot of you decided to continue serving others in one way or another, policemen and teachers and so on. It's a testament to their parenting, I have to say, Gom, that is one hell of a story. Thank you for trusting me enough to tell me. One more question?" Casey ended with a question.

"Okay." Gom figured they might as well get it all over with now.

"You said you were bashed when you were younger. How bad was it and did they get the ones who did it?" Casey asked, and the look on his face was like he was bracing himself for more bad details.

Gom glossed over it, not letting him know how bad it really was. "There was a lady in the social services department who hated the fact that Soldier and Dillon were together and successful at helping young boys in trouble. They always took in the ones who didn't seem to fit into the normal situations the foster program provided. Ones like me and Tommy and the others. She hated anything to do with homosexuality and targeted them. She had her son and his friends beat me up."

Casey sat straighter and looked incredulous. "An adult, a woman, sent her son to beat a young man up? Did she know you?"

"Not really. She just wanted to get at Soldier and Dillon. She was crazy. Those boys had been teasing me and saying ugly things and it was almost to the point where I was going to mention it to Soldier. They caught me after school one day and beat and kicked me. They really did a number on my groin. I was bruised and unbelievably sore for weeks. It was horrible. They left me on the side of the road and Daniel found me." Gom couldn't help the shudder that went through him as he thought about that night. "I remember that I woke up and Soldier was holding me in that chair again, the one in my room. That was our chair. I felt so small and hurt again. It was like I was a kid again and only he could comfort me. I also remember Tommy sang for me again. He used to sing to all of us for years."

"Again, I just don't know what to say. I want to make it all better, but I'm helpless. Did they catch them?" Casey leaned his head forward now, putting it against Gom's chest.

"Yes. It was an accident, really. Tommy had a meeting with the lady about this boy that Daniel wanted placed at Scarcity. His name was Niko. He went in early for the meeting with her, expecting trouble from her as usual. He overheard her talking to her son about the day before. He was clever enough to tape it through the door and called the police and Soldier. They're not around here anymore. She was always saying that Soldier and Dillon were doing perverted things to all of us and how sick we all were. It was nasty and hateful."

"I'm stunned." Casey pulled back to look at Gom.

"It's funny. Tommy and I were the only two who ended up being gay. It wasn't anything to do with Soldier and Dillon. I know people are born that way, but both of our backgrounds were such that we didn't trust women much. We've grown out of that and realize it's not the gender, but you can't fight history. The trauma that was placed onto us by those who were supposed to protect and love us had left us unwilling to go looking for love. Tommy and Daniel fell in love about the time I was hurt and they are so good together."

"And you waited for me to come along, huh?" Casey asked the question softly and then waited, as if to see if he'd gone too far.

"Looks like." Gom grinned at Casey, leaning in to press his cheek to Casey's. He put his arms around Casey and sighed. "You have to be tired of me on your lap. Are your legs numb? Is your brain fried from all the ugliness that was my life before you came along?"

"Gom, you had your life back together and in good shape before I ever came along. I don't know why I feel so proud of you. But I do. I can't believe you came out of all that and you are this strong, capable, sexy, man today. I want to spend as much time with you as I can. I have so much respect for your dads, too."

Gom squirmed. Casey hadn't answered his question, but he figured Casey had to be getting tired of him on his lap. He needed to stretch his legs, so he wiggled around until he was off Casey and sitting beside him. Casey moved, grabbed Gom, and turned them so that they were lying across the length of the couch. Casey came down on top of Gom and said, "I've got you now. Kiss me and I'll let you up."

"What if I don't want up?" Gom teased.

A smile like none Gom had seen before slowly spread over Casey's face and he dipped his head, reaching for Gom's lips. Gom wrapped his arms around Casey and settled into the kiss, offering up his mouth and tongue in eager participation. Casey's tongue swirled through Gom's mouth and he felt the lean hard body all along his and felt like a real sexual being for the first time. What they'd done before had been nice, but was just experimentation.

Learning about Casey's past, and revealing his, had lightened his heart, opened him to feelings he had longed for but had always thought were unattainable in the past. Now he was beginning to believe he could have what his dads shared. Maybe one day, he and Casey would have all of it. He moaned as Casey ground down against his hips and he met the movement with one of his own that got a matching sound from Casey. It was good.

CHAPTER ELEVEN

Monday was going to be a hard day. Gom was glad he had the memories of both Saturday night and Sunday with Casey to offset the pressure of what was coming. Today he planned to meet with Principal King and discuss Byron's diary and the reference to Mark Sinclair. After that, he was going to deliberately place himself in the way of the two jocks whose names Tommy had given him. He wasn't sure they'd try anything so soon after Byron's death and with outsiders still at the school, but it was a start.

Both boys were BMOCs and went around with a sense of entitlement that Gom felt was undeserved. They acted like they'd been elected to the Big Man on Campus club as officers and others were mere underlings. Gom didn't like seeing that in kids who were this young. What would they be like when they were older? And, didn't the fact that they were harassing this young man and then he killed himself make any kind of impression on them? Did they not get it that they were the "ones who were responsible"? They certainly didn't act as if his death had any effect on their lives at all.

In the meeting with Principal King, Gom gave her the basics of what was found in the file entitled Gateway to Hell, emphasizing the bit about the counselor. He made a strong case against the counselor who, albeit unknowingly, had participated in making this young man feel like he had no one to go to for help. Despite Gom's impassioned comments, the principal could only promise to talk to Mr. Sinclair. Since there weren't any witnesses, it would be hard to prove, she argued. She did agree to put a letter in his file explaining the special circumstances and would let him know that he and his manner of speaking would be closely watched. Gom figured it was the best he could get.

As luck would have it, he got his chance with the two young men whose names Tommy had slipped him on Friday night, between fifth and sixth period classes. Gom watched as Todd Landry and Josh Marks joked and pushed each other as they headed to the bathroom on the second floor. Walking rapidly on the other side of the hall from them, he managed to get there before them. Thinking quickly, he wondered what he could do to get their attention, and not in a good way.

When Todd and Josh walked into the bathroom, Gom was attempting a pirouette in front of the mirrors over the sinks. He heard them come in, but ignored them, pretending to be unaware of them. He tried the spin again, one leg raised with his leg up and bent. Having no clue how to do the move, he knew he looked stupid. That worked fine for his plan. He heard laughter and the comments began.

"Look, Josh, a fairy. What are you doing," Todd Landry said, pointing to Gom, "little fairy?" Todd pushed Josh, who pushed him back and they headed for Gom.

Gom acted scared, stepping back and holding his hands out in front of him.

"Guys, uh, hey, I was just practicing. I want to see if I can get a part in the new play. I'm just going now," Gom tried to sidle around them. When they blocked his way, he put fear in his voice and said, "Can I, can I go?" He had backed against the wall.

"What do you think, Josh?" Todd said, looking at Marks, "Should we let the little weenie go, or should we make him pay first?" Todd laughed at the fear he seemed to think he saw on Gom's face.

"Pay? I don't have any money to pay. Can't I just go? I'm not bothering you all." Gom wanted to whip out handcuffs and throw them against the wall, read them their rights and haul them off to jail. He wasn't sure what he could charge them with, but the desire was strong.

"We'll be seeing you around. What's your name, little fairy?" Josh spoke up now.

"M-Monty Marshall. I don't want any trouble, okay?" Gom should get an award for this, he thought.

"Oh, no trouble. Like I said, we'll be seeing you. I think you're just what we need, huh, Josh?" Todd turned from Gom to Josh and snickered. "I think he'll be able to step right in, don't you think?"

Josh's eyes got a little wild and he said, "Shh. Shut up, man. Are you crazy? Watch what you say!" Josh turned to leave and Todd started to follow him, looking exasperated, but he paused turned back to Gom and leaned in quickly, pushing his chest out and lunging toward Gom. Gom actually cowered against the wall. The two walked out and Gom looked around. There were two boys at the sinks, three at the urinals and two just standing in the middle of the room, watching. Doing nothing. Jesus, just doing nothing! Gom got an inkling of how Byron must have felt.

He'd thought that the things the boys did to Byron were done in private, but why would he think that? A lot of it must have happened with an audience like this one. He made a point of looking into the eyes of each of the boys lurking in the bathroom. He was saying, "I see you. I know you saw what just happened and I saw you do nothing, say nothing. Now you live with it."

He stood and with his shoulders back, walked out of the restroom, head high. But oh, he could see how that would wear someone down, make them feel like they were worthless. Not one person spoke up or stepped in to help him while the two boys had ridiculed and threatened him. Yeah, they'd see him again, as soon as he could arrange it.

⚑ ⚑ ⚑

"So, how was your day?" Casey asked. They were in Gom's room. Casey had to be at the theater at six-thirty and had agreed to have a meal with Gom here first. Gom was planning on calling Laurie Summer again about his lack of success with the principal about Mark Sinclair, but that was later. Casey had just gotten here and when he walked in the door, asking about Gom's day, Gom turned from the window by his chair and smiled at Casey.

"Better now. I had one failure and one sick success." Gom headed over to Casey.

"That was an interesting answer, which we might explore later, but right now, let's see if I can make it a little better. I've thought about this all day." Casey opened his arms and Gom settled against him like coming home. Casey took Gom's mouth and it had an instant effect. Yeah, his day just got a whole lot better.

As far as Gom was concerned they could just stand here and kiss until they were called down for supper. He'd be even happier if it were hours instead of minutes. With arms tightening and lips opening, Gom showed Casey how glad he was to see him and just how much Casey's touch meant to him. Casey held on tightly and gave a little moan as Gom met his tongue and with a soft stroke of his own. Gom liked hearing those little noises when he did something that turned Casey on. It wasn't just the sounds that let Gom know how Casey was responding to his overtures. There were touches, both gentle and firm, that proved Casey was enjoying their embrace.

With every brush of Gom's fingers against Casey's neck or through his hair, every deep breath that caused his stomach to brush against Casey's, and every forward and backward move that caused zings of sensation to blossom from his groin, Gom stood, becoming stronger as they seemed to be trying to meld into one. Liking that idea, he pressed harder, squeezed, groped, and thrust more intensely, rejoicing in the sounds that Casey couldn't seem to help.

"Gom? Hon? You okay?" Casey pulled back to look at Gom's face, as if that would tell him what had gotten into Gom, making him go from sweet and sexy to hard and demanding.

"Yeah, I'm sorry," Gom tried to put his head down, not wanting to meet Casey's eyes, thinking he'd messed up, showing his need for a deeper connection. "Guess I got a little too aggressive, huh?"

"No such thing, Gom. You can kiss me like that anytime you want. I loved it. It just surprised me. That wasn't just a passionate hello kiss. Wanna tell me what's going on?" Casey asked, forcing Gom's head up so he could see him as he talked.

"Something happened today that made me kind of tie into Byron's feelings. I got a glimpse of what it was like for him and it must have affected me more than I thought," Gom said, wanting to close his eyes and hide the emotions that he knew lingered there. "I didn't mean to take it out on you."

"Come on, let's sit down a minute. Dillon told me as I came in that supper was at five-thirty, so we have almost an hour." Casey turned to the chair and sat, pulling Gom onto his lap, almost like last Friday's embrace. "I really like this big chair."

"It's been a good chair. This is the one that Soldier and I used when I couldn't sleep as a young kid and then later he held me in it when I was beaten and couldn't quite grasp the wheres and whys of all the pain. I like sharing it with you, too. I admit to getting the same feeling of safety and comfort when I'm in your arms here." Gom snuggled in, putting his face into Casey's neck and breathing in the scent of his lover, a smell he was coming to crave.

"I'm not going for the obvious joke about not feeling fatherly about you. I just want you to tell me what happened today. I like loving on you any way I can, but there was a feeling of desperation about that. I don't think you really felt good about yourself there for a minute and that bothers me." Casey talked softly and his hand moved over Gom's back.

He sat up, looking at Casey.

"I'm not comfortable in the role of needy guy. This case is taking a toll on me for some reason. It was just a bad day." Gom tried to lessen the intensity of the feelings he'd experienced when being treated like Byron had been every day.

"Something about your day triggered a need in you. It happens to all of us in one form or another. It could have been anger, or fear, or pain, but I think something had you feeling like you weren't enough, like you had to be more. Tell me, Gom. Why did I get that feeling?"

"I thought you didn't talk much. I thought you were tight with your feelings and aloof. Where is that guy?" Gom smiled at Casey, slowly, and continued, "I like this man who recognizes needs and wants and feelings. You're right. You hit it right on the head. I'll tell you what happened."

Gom settled back against Casey. The chair was big enough that he sat sideways, his feet pulled up beside him. He leaned on Casey and reached for his hand to join their fingers in a tight grasp. He told Casey about managing to be in the bathroom when the two boys he was targeting came in. Casey laughed when Gom told him about trying the pirouette to make the boys think he was trying out as a dancer.

"My big tough cop with the mad skills, doing ballet in the bathroom." Casey stomach moved with his chuckles and Gom pressed his hand on it, liking the movement and the lean strength.

"I think it was the fact that students that Byron at least semi-interacted with in class daily could stand by and ignore, as if they didn't see, the things that were done to him, the slights and slams, the cruel digs and vicious and continual mental and sometimes physical abuse. I can see how he felt smaller and more insignificant every day. You have to feel like you matter, like your existence has reason and power and purpose. He must have felt like he was an island, existing only to provide services and an easy target for stronger, meaner people, never getting that feeling of validation that everyone needs. How very sad."

"I feel for him, and for you, but tell me what they did to you and how you handled it," Casey requested, quietly.

Gom told him about how he cowered in fear and how the two jocks fed off that, one even implying that he would be a good stand-in for Byron, though never saying the dead classmate's name. He'd caught that Josh had enough sense to realize that was a stupid thing for Todd to say.

"I'm going to get them, Casey." It was a solid statement of fact.

"What will happen to them? If you prove that they were the ones doing things to him, what are they going to be charged with and will it stick? Hell, they're kids. Will they get off?"

"Case, it's barely been over a week since this boy took his own life because he couldn't handle what these two and their buddies were doing to him and this asshole is not even affected by it, after being named, sort of, as the reason. He had the audacity to step up and offer me the new position, so to speak. How is a teenager so ruthless, so heartless today? It's like Byron's life meant nothing, like his death meant nothing but an inconvenience to him and he was looking for a replacement. It literally makes me sick. How many other students, all over, are going through something like this and wondering why their life doesn't seem to be important enough to hang on until the end of school so that it really does get better? So that they can get away from the daily belittling and sense of hopelessness they feel. It scares me to think of it, Case. Literally breaks my heart."

Gom was physically tired after his soliloquy and Casey seemed to realize that. He tightened his arms a bit and kept that soothing rub going on Gom's back with the one hand while grasping Gom's hand tightly with the other. Gom was again feeling like he was playing the pitiful role, but Casey was so good with the support that he fell into it and took what he needed.

"You're going to make it better. Whatever happens to those two, you will have made a difference. It's who you are," Casey whispered and his voice got even lower and more intimate as he said, "It makes me so damn proud of you. Your goodness humbles me."

"Shh," Gom said, uncomfortable with the caped crusader image he got. It almost brought a smile, but he just wasn't quite there yet.

They sat, still and quiet for a few minutes and then Gom shook himself both mentally and physically and sat up, looking at Casey.

"How is it you are just what I need? You give and give and make me feel better every time." Gom leaned that little bit that put his mouth to Casey's and they shared a healing kiss. The movement of Casey's lips and tongue on and through Gom's mouth brought forth such emotion and caring that he felt was flowing both ways. This man was not just a fleeting thing for Gom. He knew his feelings for Casey were becoming deep and lasting. Inexperience had him wondering momentarily if he would get his heart broken by this beautiful man with the gorgeous blue eyes.

"You hesitated," Casey pulled away to say, "What were you thinking just then?"

"It's stupid."

"Gom, nothing you think, especially when we're kissing, is stupid. Tell me." It was a command.

Gom responded to it. "I was thinking about how much I care about you, how deeply I'm beginning to feel for you and wondering if I'm going to get hurt."

"Not if I have any say in it. I have the same thoughts, you know. Just because I've had sex before doesn't mean that I'm experienced in dealing with feelings and that's what we're all about, I think. Everything is better with you for that very reason." Casey shook his head a little and smiled at Gom, saying, "Okay. Enough of that. We have to go down to eat and I have to work tonight. Promise me something?"

"Anything."

"Be careful around those two guys. I want you to get them, but I want you to be safe. Don't take chances, please." Casey's expression was trying for stern, but he couldn't quite carry it off. It sounded more like pleading. Either way, it touched Gom.

"I promise. I'm careful and I can take care of myself. I have a plan. I want this over and I want out of there." Gom couldn't even give voice to how badly he wanted this case to be a thing of the past.

"I understand, hon. Here, quick kiss and let's go down and see if we can help a little." Casey put his hand on the side of Gom's face and turned it to him. Gom went willingly and took great joy in pressing his lips to Casey's, open and ready. For a few sweet moments Gom reveled in the calm passion they shared. Was calm passion one of those word things, he wondered, where the two meant opposite things. He didn't think so. They weren't tearing at each other, but there was certainly passion whenever they kissed.

They heard Soldier yelling for them to come to supper.

"Oops. Best laid plans and all that. Guess we won't be helping," Casey said, rubbing his thumb over Gom's wet lips.

"Not a problem. You go to work after supper and I'll help with the dishes tonight. I need to talk to Soldier and Dillon, anyway." Gom got up and put his hand out for Casey to grab. He pulled Casey up and they exited the room with content smiles on their faces.

Later that night Gom was sitting in the den with Soldier and Dillon, explaining his plan for the next day.

"You be careful, son." Soldier sounded a little like Casey there.

"Yes sir, you know I will. I don't think I'll have any trouble with it. I'm going to let Principal King and the security officer know what I'm planning. They'll make sure the cameras are working in the hall by that bathroom. I'll do my part and if it all goes as I plan, you might be getting a call from the principal. You're sure you want to do this?" Gom looked at Soldier.

"Of course. I'll always be ready to help you, Gom. It will feel good to think about getting some justice for what those two did to that poor young man, Byron. Watch your back, you hear?" Soldier looked closely at Gom as if trying to make sure he was listening and going to follow directions and take care of himself.

☙ ☙ ☙

Gom had a plan, but things didn't always fall into place. Both Todd and Josh were absent the next day. Gom decided to use his time to do a little canvassing of his own. He wanted to know how this could go on with so many people being aware of it and no one doing anything at all. Being so very aware of his mission had Gom watching closely and he was amazed at how much of the bullying went on right under the teacher's noses. He wanted so badly to shake a few of them and ask them to wake up to the epidemic of pain that was inflicted and endured in their midst. There were no safe spaces. Oh, there were signs in the halls telling where the safe spaces were and that there was ZERO tolerance for bullying.

It was nearly impossible not to be critical about the whole process. This was a school, a community of its own that had lost a student due to the ineffectiveness of said policies. Were there meetings, assemblies, groups, anything to help stop it? No. There were counselors who were dealing with the grief process, but Gom, in his newfound cynicism, felt they were dealing with shock more than grief. If this school was mourning the loss of a promising and intelligent young man, he couldn't see it.

Some of his time was taken up with assignments, but that was minimal. He talked to students, the ones he saw being taunted for whatever reason. Acne, for heaven's sakes! Like puberty was something to tease someone about. One girl was brought to tears as she tripped over a boy's foot that was stuck out as she went by. When the heavy girl hit the floor, several boys around the culprit laughed and jumped like she'd shaken the whole floor. Gom went to help her up, asking if she was okay.

"I'm fine. It's nothing new," she said, limping a little.

"It shouldn't happen at all," Gom said, looking around at the boys, who blatantly looked right back with sneers on their faces.

"Yeah, well, try being different around here. I've lost forty pounds, but do you think that matters? I might as well..."

"No. Don't let them stop you from getting healthy. Don't diet for them. They're nothing. If you feel better as you lose, keep going. As you lose more, you'll find them more interested. Then it's your time. Turn them all down, hold you head high, and go about your life, knowing that you made it through. Don't let them win." All Gom needed was a podium, he thought.

"Who are you, the self-esteem police?" She said, smiling to soften the words. "Thanks for your help."

"What's your name?" Gom asked as he picked up her books and walked with her.

"Margaret Hanover. You?"

"Monty Marshall. Are you sure you're okay? We can go to the nurse's office." Gom was noticing her wince as she walked.

"No, thanks. I've got to get to class. Nice meeting you, Monty Marshall."

Gom watched her try to hurry with her limp and all her books. What was it with people? He turned and saw the group of boys who'd deliberately hurt her, both physically and mentally.

As he walked to them he saw one taller boy look at another and he knew they were going to do something. Let them. He walked close and saw the leg come out to take him down. He rolled with it and twisted around on the way down sweeping his leg out and getting the tall one behind the knees, taking him down, too. Gom was up in seconds, looking shocked and surprised.

"What the fuck? Get him!"

Oh, shit.

Backing away, Gom raised his hands. He refused to act scared, but he did want to diffuse the situation.

"Hey, man, it was an accident. I tripped on something and must have bumped into you by mistake. I'm so sorry. I'd never hurt somebody on purpose." Gom walked off, just turned his back to them and walked away. He could hear arguing behind him, but he ignored it and turned the corner. Damn! High school was dangerous.

Keeping notes, he was truly aghast to find that during a four hour period which included classes, hall time, and lunch, he recorded eleven different forms of bullying. They ranged from name calling to pushes against the wall or lockers, teasing, to the tripping and taunting of Margaret. His surprise was partly due to the fact that so much attention was being paid to the topic of bullying right now, with the press still here, the counselors from other schools, and even more signs in the hall promising safety to students. Not once, in all the instances that he observed did an adult step in. At least six of those times there wasn't one near. So, that left five times that something could have been done to help, but wasn't.

The two jocks were absent the following day, too, so Gom kept talking to the students in his classes and taking notes from his conversations and recording the myriad ways that kids found to hurt other kids. Twice that day, he saw a teacher comment on what was happening or pull the instigator aside for a talk. Nothing was done other than that, but he recorded it as the small attempt it was.

Finally, the third day after he came up with his plan, the two boys were back in school and seemed to be ready to take up where they left off. Once when they walked by him, he heard kissing noises. When Gom turned, Todd was grasping his crotch and staring at him. Ugh! Time to get this over with. He waited for his chance and later that day, after talking to the principal and the officer, he arranged to get in their way again.

Gom headed for the bathroom where Todd and Josh had gone after him the other time. He knew the cameras were on and there was a small recording device in his jeans pocket. This was his own doing. He didn't know if it would be used or needed, but he wanted it, just in case. His heart was racing, but he'd laid the groundwork and he was ready. He'd refined his plan while waiting for the jocks to return to school.

He searched for and found Charles Knox, the boy that Byron had mentioned in the diary. Charles, who was also gay, was doing homework for jocks to keep from getting beaten or worse like Byron. Gom had wanted to know if maybe Charles would like his life back, with no fear and time to spend on his own endeavors. He found just what he was hoping for.

"What do you mean? How did you know about, I mean, who told you about what I was doing?" Charles looked a little worried at first like he might be going from the frying pan into the fire, but Gom assured him that he didn't have to do anything but stand and be a witness. If what he planned worked, Charles would not have to work for the others anymore.

Gom knew that when he stepped into the bathroom that Charles would be there at the sink. The young boy was going to stay out of the way, but watch and listen. If need be, he could run and call for help, which in this case, would be nearby in the form of Officer Filer. He wasn't aware of the recording device on Gom. He just thought that Gom was being brave by taking on the two jocks who had hassled him the other day.

He knew that Todd and Josh were headed in the same direction and he knew they would engage him again. When they came in, he wasn't doing anything overt like the first time, but he turned when he heard them. Coming from a stall and heading for the sinks, he went to one three down from where Charles was standing. Gom ran water over his hands and reached for soap. Empty. It seemed that keeping soap in high school bathrooms was a problem everywhere.

"It's the fairy dancer. Hey, what's your name, sweetie?" Todd asked, walking over to Gom.

"M-Monty. Monty Marshall," Gom answered softly.

Making it look like an accident, Gom turned quickly, his hands full of water and it flew out in a perfect arc and hit Todd full on and a little went onto Josh who was beside him as they neared Gom. Gom gasped and raised his hands to his face as if mortified that he'd gotten them wet.

"Oh, I'm so sorry!" Gom turned back to the sink, turning off the flow of water and reached for a couple of paper towels from the dispenser. He could see Todd's face in the mirror and knew he was furious. To further that feeling, Gom turned, drying his hands and when he saw how wet Todd was, he laughed.

"You little motherfucking faggot. You're going to be sorry you did that."

Before going to bed last night, Gom had looked up the term for the word connection he'd thought about earlier, calm passion, and found that the word he was thinking of was oxymoron. He used it now to push Todd a little further.

"Isn't that an oxymoron? You know, motherfucking faggot? Well, maybe not a perfect example of an oxymoron, since they should really be opposites, but well, faggots aren't really *mother*fuckers, see?" Gom was acting like he was trying to teach Todd an English lesson, while the big football player stood there fuming and making fists.

"You're stupid, too. You're a queer and you're an idiot." Todd's face was red and he took a step toward Gom.

"What do you know about queers, anyway?" Gom knew his next move would really piss the jock off.

Gom turned his back on Todd and Josh and headed for the door, giving them a wide berth.

"Hold it, fairy-boy. I know more than you think." Todd stepped over and took hold of Gom's arm. He glanced at his buddy and said, "Isn't that right, Josh?"

Josh, as before, wasn't as ready to vocalize as his buddy. Josh nodded and moved over in front of Gom so he wasn't able to get out the door. Ah, double teaming.

"Yeah, what, some of your best friends are gay, right?"Gom teased.

"You just don't stop, do you? Calling me names, throwing water on me, arguing like you're just as good," Todd was working himself up to a real fury and it fit Gom's plan perfectly. He just needed a little more information.

"Look, I'm sorry, okay? I don't, I mean, you know I can't fight you. You scare me. I don't want you to always be mad at me. Getting you wet really was a mistake. What can I do?"

"Do? What can you do?" Todd repeated.

"Yeah, so you won't be after me all the time." Gom left it at that.

While this had gone on, other students had come and gone, but several were standing around. Todd looked around at them and several left, intimidated. Charles stayed, as planned, but he moved to a stall far from where they were standing.

When it had cleared out some, Todd leaned down so that he was right in Gom's face.

"You want to be safe, is that it? That can be arranged. Maybe you want to make a deal with me." Todd waited, expectantly.

"Deal? What kind of deal? What do I have to do?" Gom asked, managing to sound fearful rather than furious.

"I won't beat your sorry ass every time I see you and you, well, in return you'll do some things for me." Todd smiled at that and Gom saw evil. Evil, in the eyes of a seventeen year old boy!

"What things?" Gom whispered.

"You know what a swirly is?" Todd leered.

Gom gasped, not having to fake it. He nodded, eyes wide for effect.

"If you don't want that to happen to you, you're going to be my bitch. I don't think you'll have a hard time doing your part. You all seem to like sucking dick." Todd sneered.

"You want me to—to, oh come on! How are you going to get away with that? There's no way you can make me do that for you. No one would agree to that!" Gom sounded outraged. Again, not hard to do.

"Oh, someone would. Someone did and now you can take over the job. Oh, and since you're so smart, I'm thinking you can start helping out with the homework, too. If I tell you I need something done, you'll do it. Otherwise, your pretty face won't be so pretty anymore. Get it?" Todd still had hold of Gom's arm and was squeezing pretty hard.

"You can't be serious. Let me get this straight. You want me to do your homework for you and then drop down to my knees and suck you off whenever you command. You're fucking crazy! There's no way. I'll tell the principal on you. I'll tell everybody."

"The hell you will, you little pussy. You wouldn't be so cool with two broken legs, huh? How would you dance then, little fairy?"

"You're going to break my legs if I-- if I don't do what you say? What are you, part of the mafia? This is high school, man. You're a real asshole, Landry. Read my lips. No. Fucking. Way."

Gom tried to pull his arm away, but couldn't. He twisted hard and finally managed it, heading for the door. He opened it and heard the two right behind him. Perfect! This would end on camera.

"Just a minute, you little shit." Todd grabbed Gom just as they cleared the door. Gom stopped, turning so that they were both visible on the camera.

"What? What do you want now?"

"Shh, shut up, stupid." Todd was speaking in a harsh whisper now. "You're not telling anybody, you hear? I'll be here tomorrow at this time and you better be ready to perform. It worked for more than two years and now you'll take over. You don't have a choice."

"You can't make me! You must be just like me if that's what you want." Gom threw at him and turned, as if to walk away.

As he'd hoped, Todd jerked him back, drew back his fist, and let fly. Gom, seeing it coming, turned his head so that he took it on the jaw and not the chin. He spun with the momentum of the hit, but didn't try to get away. He pushed at Todd with both hands, forcing him back, which made the big kid even madder. He took another swing at Gom and this time Gom moved, taking the hit on his shoulder. He went down instead of pushing the fight further. They'd drawn a crowd and he didn't want this escalating.

Luckily, Officer Filer stepped in and separated them. He held on to Todd while Gom pretended to be more hurt than he was. He got back up, cradled his jaw with his hand and leaned against the wall, still in full view of the camera.

Before long he was in the principal's office and his father was being called. Charles and a few others from the bathroom were talking to Officer Filer in another room, telling him what they'd heard. Gom had the recording, to go along with the camera's log. He was surprised to find out that Captain Denny was coming along with the officers when they came for the two boys. He'd meet privately with him and turn over what he had now and arrange to get the full report to him later. He'd have a busy afternoon.

Holding ice to his jaw and another hard pack to his shoulder, he sat, waiting for Soldier as he knew that Todd and Josh would be waiting for their parents. He told Ms. King about the notes he'd taken and promised to get them together in a report for her. The high degree of bullying still going on in her school was alarming and he noticed the mixed look of frustration and determination in her eyes as she promised that something would be done very soon.

After talking with her about consequences, and with the proof they had, he knew that Todd Landry and Josh Marks would likely be 'expelled with services'. To quote Principal King, "They will never be able to step foot on this campus again. No more football, no classes, no scholarships, no hanging with their buds from school, nothing. They can't even go to a bake sale sponsored by the cheerleaders. Being under eighteen, education will be provided, but it will be home schooling. A teacher will go to their houses and teach lessons there. It's all we can do."

"That kid has some serious problems, Ms. King. He had absolutely no qualms about offering to let me take over the activities that Byron had been doing for him. Byron's death wasn't even a blip on his radar. He was just looking for someone to take Byron's place. How sick is that? I know that Charles is talking about the ones who were making him do homework for them. At least this will make *his* life better." Gom shrugged a little as he said that.

"Yes, it's good for him. I think we need to do an assembly and have some speakers who can make an impact on these students. I'm going to make it a tribute to Byron and I'm going to make sure that the students at this school sit up and take notice. So many of us were responsible for this boy's tragic death. It must stop now. The police are already working with the students who put his information on the internet. I'm going to target both the bullies and the ones who are being hurt. Both of those groups have to stop what they're doing. The… we'll call them victims," she put her hands up and made the quote symbol, "have got to come forward, unafraid of retaliation and let us know what's happening. We've got a long way to go, but you have made a difference here." She put her hand on his shoulder as she talked.

"I hope they listen to the speakers. All those kids who saw this happening to him! I got the same thing in the two incidents that I had. Kids watched the whole thing the other time and again today and did nothing to help me. I didn't expect them to take him on, but they could have gone for help or said something. No wonder Byron felt like there was no hope. He felt totally invisible and like his life was worthless since no one seemed to care that his life was hell." Gom had hated the feeling of nothingness that he'd felt when his pain was ignored by so many boys. "What happens now?"

"After your father presses charges, this will be set in motion. Your cover will be safe and you can continue your work. It's a good thing you're doing, Monty, er, Gom. Don't ever doubt that. After this is done, we'll let it be known that your father moved you out of here."

"Yes, ma'am. I'll go back to my brown hair and brown eyes. This has been kind of weird. It was my first time using a disguise. I do feel bad about there not being anything I could do about your school counselor. That situation really bothers me. If he has those kinds of things to say about gays, how does he feel about other minorities?" Gom put his hands up and out, shrugging his shoulders in a gesture that denoted that he was not comfortable, but determined. "If he's not the kind of man kids feel like they can confide in, turn to for help, or ask for guidance, then he's not doing his job. I even know people from other schools who feel awkward around him. Ms. King, maybe it's none of my business, but I think you have a problem there. I'm just sayin'."

Gom couldn't have left without making his case again. He still felt that Mark Sinclair was partly responsible, or more so than some others, for Byron feeling he had no one to turn to for help.

"I'll look into that more closely, I promise." Ms. King looked up at a noise in the outer office and then turned to Gom.

"Something tells me this is your father."

Gom hid a smile. Soldier wasn't going to have to fake anything when he saw the marks on Gom, but it had been worth it. He stood and went to meet his dad. He dropped the ice in the trash and stepped over when Soldier came into the room.

"Who did this, Gom? Who hit you? Let me see," Soldier came over and despite the fire spitting from his eyes, his hands were tender when they probed the bruising that was beginning to show on Gom's jaw. When asked about more, Gom pulled his shirt over and showed his shoulder. Soldier's face was still and his eyes were cold.

"It's okay, Dad, really. I planned it this way. All I need you to do is make a fuss, threaten to take me out of this school, and promise to press charges against whoever did this to me. That will get the ball rolling and we will call this one done. I did what I came to do and with some counseling and teaching, maybe this will be a safer place for everyone. I'll explain it all later. Let's go. Ready to act the part of the irate parent?" Gom teased.

"Act, hell. I don't care if you *are* twenty-two. Someone hit my boy. I *am* an irate parent!" Soldier muttered that part and then he got righteous. The show he put on was picture perfect. No one had any doubt that Monty's dad was furious and determined to press charges against the two boys who threatened and hit his son.

Gom left the school that day, but he was determined to check back and see if Ms. King followed through on her plans for making things better for students there.

CHAPTER TWELVE

Gom really needed to see and spend some time with Casey. He didn't just want to see Casey, he needed to. There was no doubt in his mind that Casey would be upset with his bruises, too, but he didn't care. He had done what he felt he had to and with no cases in immediate sight, he might have time to advance things with his love life. Just the idea had Gom nearly shaking with excitement as he entered the house.

Thankfully, Soldier had prepared Dillon for Gom's appearance. Regardless, he was treated to love, concern, pampering, and his favorite foods that night. Somehow, word got around and by the time supper was over Gom had been checked out by Tommy, Daniel, Jack, Randy, J, Bart, Ben, and Niko. Dismay was voiced, anger calmed, concern displayed, and promises of backup offered. Gom was warmed by the love and care his brothers showed him.

Jack was ready to kick some ass, police officer or not. Tommy wanted to make sure he was okay with the violence part of it. Ben and Niko thought he was cool. Trick was quiet as he watched and listened. Gom wondered about Trick, his story, but quickly Gom's attention was taken up by something else. Randy, J, and Bart just wanted to make sure he was not hurt badly. At one point, Gom caught Soldier and Dillon standing together, smiling, as they watched the first seven from the original house close ranks once again. Gom was just glad both of them were finally smiling.

Gom gave them all assurances and thanked them for coming to see about him. He reminded them that he was a police officer, too, and that if he'd wanted to he could have prevented the hits. He told them it had been necessary for his case to take the two punches and that it was worth it. He got hugs and pats on the back as one by one the men left for their respective homes.

"Okay, so who called all of them?" Gom asked, arms crossed,

trying to look disapproving.

"My guess is Ben. He was upset when Soldier called and told us what happened. You know how much they all love you, Gom." Dillon was watching Gom as if to see if he was really upset.

"I know. The feeling's mutual. It was nice, really. If it's all right with you all, I'm going to call Casey." He reached for his phone, but then turned back. "You want me to help with the cleanup down here?" Gom wanted to see Casey, but he'd gladly do some chores first.

"Go on, I can tell you're dying to talk to your man. We won't wait up for you," Soldier teased as he started cleaning. Gom bet Dillon's guess that it was Ben who'd called everyone was true since he didn't stay around to clean up. He gave both his dad's a strong hug and headed to his room.

In his bathroom he checked out the bruises as he readied for a quick, but thorough shower. They were ugly, but didn't bother him. He was more interested in seeing Casey. He wanted Casey's lips on his. He wanted to feel Casey's hands on his skin again. He just wanted Casey.

Gom knew that Casey was working, but he thought he'd go down to the theater and see if he could sit with Casey and go with him to work later at the offices. So far, Casey had refused to let him help out, but since tomorrow wasn't a school day for him, maybe he'd accept some help tonight. Afterwards, he hoped to get even more special treatment at Casey's apartment.

❧ ❧ ❧

"What the *hell* happened to you?" Casey demanded, his hand reaching for Gom's face only to stop before touching.

"I closed a case," Gom said, "It's a good thing."

"Yeah, looks like it." Casey leaned in and whispered, "Hope it doesn't interfere with kissing." There was a definite glint in Casey's eyes.

"Nothing could keep me from kissing you. Simple fact." Gom was serious. Though he was glad he hadn't taken the blow to the mouth that Todd had been aiming for.

"This will be over soon, but I have to work later." Casey offered.

"And I don't have anywhere I have to be tomorrow and Soldier promised they wouldn't be looking for me to return so I was thinking maybe I could help you and then you could take me back to your place and we could see how things go from there." Gom was so ready to see how things went.

"Things?" Casey teased.

"Sex things," Gom responded.

"Gom Marsh! You devil, you, coming down here and getting me all tensed up when I have to work."

"I'm sorry. I'll…" Gom wasn't *quite* sure Casey was teasing. Surely he was.

"You'll sit right there and wait for this last act and then we will work really hard together so we can go play even harder together, with each other, alone, in my room, just us, me and you." Casey's eyes went from a mere glint to a definite glow and the words got slower, his voice got huskier toward the end.

"You get really eloquent when you get excited. And you said you didn't have a way with words." Gom loved all the ways Casey had found to mean… just them.

Casey reached out and very gently smoothed his fingers over the swelling bruise on Gom's jaw. He winced for Gom and slid his hand on around the back of Gom's neck and pulled his head in for a second and held it to his shoulder.

"I'm glad you're okay."

Gom wanted to sink right into Casey then and there, although the lighting control booth was almost dark, they weren't alone. He could wait. Barely. He made himself pull away from Casey and let the man get back to his job. Gom sat beside him and just watched as he maneuvered buttons and levers to make magic appear on the stage. Casey glanced over at him periodically and smiled, making Gom's heart speed up every time.

Gom felt like time was crawling. Casey told him that he had two offices to clean tonight and that he usually got home about one in the morning.

"Maybe with me helping, we can get that done and get home before then. Have you eaten anything? No?" Really, he thought, Casey should take better care of himself. "How about I go pick up something for you and meet you back here? You can have a quick supper before we go to the first office."

Ignoring Casey's protests that he was fine and didn't need anything, Gom gave him a swift kiss and headed out to grab Casey a sandwich and drink. While out, he decided to stop for some items from the all-night pharmacy a couple of streets over from the theater. He wanted to make love with Casey tonight. They'd not had much of a discussion yet, so Gom didn't know what Casey preferred. To his mind, he couldn't imagine Casey being much of a bottom. That was fine with him. He was fine with Casey taking him. He was looking forward to it, in fact, shivers going through his body as he thought about moving, naked, under an equally unclothed Casey.

Before long, they were at the first office, having left Gom's car at Casey's apartment. Gom had followed Casey into the small office building, noticing that it was family-owned law firm. Casey told him that the other office tonight was a travel agency. Gom thought that might be interesting, at least colorful with all the posters and ads on the walls for exotic destinations.

At first Gom just watched as Casey went about his work, but soon he moved to join him. He emptied trash cans, ran the vacuum, grabbed a rag from the cart Casey had taken from a closet and wiped down surfaces, watching Casey to make sure he was doing the right things. And they talked while they worked.

"So, you going to tell me what happened to your face? Tell me it's somebody whose ass I can go kick," Casey begged.

Gom chuckled, touched, "Sorry. High school student. I won't be going back to Baiden, unless it's to attend the assembly that the principal is planning. I'd like to see how she handles that. She mentioned making it a tribute to Byron and I'd like to be there for it." Gom paused for a minute, the hand with the dusting rag stopping the swiping motion.

"What?" Casey paused in his own dusting action to encourage Gom to express his thoughts.

"I'm thinking Tommy and Daniel might be able to help with some speakers for the assembly she's planning. Do you know," Gom said, getting back to work, "that in a four hour period I saw right at a dozen different acts of bullying from minor name calling to physical violence and threats. It was amazing to me that there was that much going on, especially in a school that was being watched pretty closely, media-wise, because of that very thing. It's ridiculous."

"Hey, I agree. Back to my original question, though. How'd you get the sore jaw, and is that all?"

Casey gathered the rags and looked around the last office, nodding, before heading back to the closet with the cart.

Gom trailed him and gave a shortened version of the event minus the names and when Casey's brows raised, Gom held his hand up and said, "Yes, I felt it was necessary and it wasn't that bad. That place will be a little safer now, for gays at least. I still can't believe that he asked me to do that, right out loud in the bathroom with people there watching and making allusions to Byron at the time, like his death was nothing but a complication to him. Honest to God, it made me sick."

Casey turned from replacing the cart and took Gom into his arms and held him a moment. "Shh, relax. You did good, Gom. Be glad you managed to stop their little reign of terror and now you can take some time for yourself. So, no school tomorrow?" Casey pulled back to look at Gom's face, a smile on his.

"No school. I worked on my reports all afternoon and sent them in. How about you?" Gom never took his eyes off Casey's.

"I don't go in until three tomorrow. Want to stay with me tonight?" Casey looked a little like he thought Gom would say no. Silly man.

"Yes."

The smile started slow on Casey's lips and soon spread to his whole face. How pretty! Gom put his arms around Casey's neck and took his mouth in a strong serious kiss of intent. They stood, holding each other tightly and Gom thought he might just fly around the room like a suddenly released balloon. He felt light-headed and breathless. Casey pushed against him and Gom felt the wall behind his back.

"Oomph! Case…" was all Gom could get out before Casey took his mouth again, rubbing his whole front against Gom's. God; that felt good!

"You feel so damn good." It was like Casey was reading his mind. Clearly, they were on the same page.

"Casey… Case… Mmm," Gom was going to try to tell Casey that they needed to finish and get over to Casey's place, but he couldn't stop kissing him. Had anything ever felt like this? Easy answer. No.

Casey was the one who finally stopped, pulling his mouth from Gom's to put it in Gom's neck. Gom took deep breaths, both to replenish what was missing and to take Casey's scent into him. As their breathing slowed, Gom held onto Casey's hips, stilling him. They were both hard, cocks pressing against each other. Gom shuddered. Yeah, they had to come down. They had another office to clean before they could finish this.

"We need to go, like right now. I don't want your first time to be on the floor and if we keep this up, that is definitely a possibility. Stop tempting me," Casey said, pulling away from Gom, laughing when he looked at Gom's face.

"Me?" Gom choked.

Casey laughed with him and drew him toward the front of the office building.

"Hurry. I want you more every minute. Are you really ready for tonight?" Casey paused a moment to look closely at Gom, waiting for his reply.

"Past ready and pushing forward into anxious. I want you, Casey."

"Come on," Casey said, "let's get this done. I want you more." Gom wasn't so sure about that.

They made quick, but thorough work of the next office and were soon heading toward Casey's home. When Casey turned the key and silence filled the space, Gom looked over at him.

"What?" Was Casey having second thoughts?

"I've told you that I'm not good with words. I can't seem to quit talking around you, but I never know if I'm going to say the wrong thing, or if something even needs to be said. I'm not comfortable in, uh, situations." Casey looked slightly embarrassed.

"You do fine, Casey. I know you've made an effort to be more open with me. What's bothering you?" Gom put his hand out and Casey took it.

"Bothered isn't the right word. I just need to say something to you, before we get inside." Casey's lips pressed together and spread into a grin. "Once we're alone I don't think I'm going to be coherent. So," he paused, looking intently at Gom and said, "this is important, Gom. It's not just sex, or playing, or messing around. You're the only man I've ever brought to my home and you're the only one I want to sleep with, all night and wake up with tomorrow. Do you get what I'm trying, probably poorly, to say?"

"I think you're saying that what we have is special. You're telling me that I'm not just going to be laid, I'm going to be loved. I mean, sort of like that." Loved? Should he have said that? Gom wanted to look away, afraid he'd presumed too much. He lowered his lashes, hiding a bit.

"That's exactly what I'm saying." Casey put one finger under Gom's chin and raised his head. "Look at me."

Gom raised his lashes and looked at Casey, feeling the importance of the moment.

"Say exactly what you're thinking right now. Don't filter it. Just say it," Casey demanded.

"I'm falling in love with you."

Well, that wasn't filtered at all, was it? Gom could feel his eyes widen as he kept looking at Casey to see his response to the words. Now Casey probably thought that Gom could only have sex if he was in love like some girl.

"Good. That's good." Casey sighed.

"That's it? That's all I get?" Gom asked, head tilting as he asked. He wasn't sure if he was teasing or dead serious.

Casey leaned in so that he said the next words against Gom's lips, "I fell for you the night you came to the theater with that lame excuse that it was for Ben. I wanted to just eat you up. I think I might just do that. You sure you're ready for this?"

Gom drew back. "What makes you keep asking me that?" He knew he sounded defensive, but couldn't help it. "I told you I want this, am ready for this, can handle this. What *is it* about me that makes you think I'm not capable of knowing my own mind?" Gom pulled away from Casey and wanted to sink right through the floorboards. Was he really picking a fight seconds away from getting what he wanted more than anything like… ever?

"I'm sorry." Casey opened his door and got out and Gom thought his heart would burst out of his chest. He'd made a mess of things. He scrambled to open his door, ready to apologize for being so sensitive and whiny.

"Come here, hon." Casey reached for him as soon as he stood up, pushing the door closed. Casey's arms were around him before he could think. "I'm sorry. It was stupid of me to make you feel that way. I know you're a grown man who can handle most anything that comes your way. I told you I mess things up with my mouth. I don't talk much around people because I always end up saying the wrong thing at the wrong time. Forgive me?" Casey was holding him, with his hands at the small of Gom's back.

"No, *I'm* sorry. I shouldn't be so bothered by the fact that everybody still feels like I need to be taken care of. I mean, it's nice, really. They all love me and want me to be safe and happy and they do believe I can take care of myself now, but it's hard for them to let go of the little, hurt, scared kid I used to be, both at eight and at seventeen." Gom shrugged within the confines of Casey's embrace. "I've worked hard to prove I'm strong and able to take care of myself. So, I'll forgive you for asking if you'll forgive me for snapping at you for it."

"Deal." Gom could feel Casey's sigh against him.

"Now will you take me in there and make love to me till I can't think of anything but you? I want to shower with you, explore your gorgeous body, kiss you till I can't breathe, and then I want you to…" Gom leaned up and whispered in Casey's ear. He was gratified when Casey jerked, looked down at him, laughed out loud, then took his hand and pulled him rapidly toward the door.

"You are something else, Gom. Come on," Casey said, opening the door and waving Gom in. "I'm going to turn the heat up a little. It's getting colder and I want you to be nice and comfortable wearing nothing at all, which is how I want you to be from now on. I'll meet you in the bathroom."

"Crap."

"Pardon?" Casey looked back at Gom in shock.

"I have to go out to the car. I need my bag and some, uh, stuff I bought when I went out tonight." Gom knew he was blushing, but he didn't care.

"I've got stuff, but by all means, get what you need. Frankly, I don't intend to let you go for a very long time so it's a good idea to be totally prepared for anything." Casey leaned in and kissed Gom quickly and said, "Go."

Gom scurried to obey. There was no other word for it. He hurried out to his car and got his things and was back in short order. He dropped his bag inside Casey's bedroom door. He put the sack from the pharmacy on the bedside table. He went back to the bag, got his shaving gear and headed to the bathroom, wanting to get that out of the way while Casey was doing whatever domestic chores that were taking him so damn long.

Gom was down to his briefs and just finishing with his razor when Casey appeared in the mirror behind him. It's a good thing he'd just put the razor down. Casey stood there, nude and proud, and with good reason.

Casey wasn't that much bigger than Gom. They were about the same size, but their shapes were different. Gom was thin, wiry, with small defined muscles. Casey had much bigger shoulders and chest for his small size. His hands were big and when Gom let his gaze fall, he realized that Casey's cock was not only large, but sexy as hell. He let his eyes feast on the big member that was pointing toward him, tilted up toward Casey's stomach. Long, thick, with a couple of veins visible, Casey's cock had a large mushroom head that was a darker, almost red color. Gom realized he was holding his breath.

"I take it you're not disappointed in the view," Casey teased, taking a step toward Gom. Gom opened his arms and they were pressed together. He soaked up the intense feelings that were being processed by every molecule of flesh that was touching Casey. He reached for his briefs and pushed them off, stepping out of them and pushing them to the corner before moving back into contact with Casey.

"Ahh, yes!" Casey muttered, against Gom's neck. Gom couldn't force a single sound from his throat. His arms tightened around Casey and he turned his head, seeking Casey's lips.

Gom felt like his world righted itself in that moment. Everything just made sense, felt good, was perfect. Opening his mouth, he sought Casey's tongue with his and breathed through his nose as their tongues moved slowly against each other. Gom pulled his tongue back into his mouth, hoping Casey's would follow. When it did, he sucked on it and felt the jolt go through Casey's body.

Casey's arms tightened around him and their groins were grinding together. The hands on his back moved down to grasp his behind, squeezing. Liking that so much, Gom matched the movement with his hands on Casey.

"Gom, you've got a perfect little bubble butt. How did I not ever notice that before?" Casey had pulled back to look at Gom with the question.

Gom couldn't help it. He snorted out a little laugh. "Gee, I don't know. It's not like I hide it or anything."

"Mmm, I like it." Casey gave said butt another caress before saying, "Will you get the water nice and warm while I shave really quickly? I like this sweet soft skin and I don't want to be scratchy on you. I'll be quick." Casey let Gom go, though it was a slow process, his hand sliding from Gom's butt to his arm and down to his hand, holding it for a second before releasing it.

Gom moved to the shower, liking the fact that it had glass doors instead of a curtain. He hated shower curtains that stuck to you while you were in there. He fiddled with the faucets, getting the water temperature just right and looked to make sure there were towels ready.

"Towels?" he asked and Casey pointed to the small closet right outside the bathroom door. Gom grabbed two and set them on the toilet lid before stepping into the shower stall. Avidly, he watched Casey put his razor down and turn to face him. He took a step back, an invitation for Casey to join him. Casey moved into the shower and closed the door firmly.

Taking Gom into his arms, Casey wrapped him up securely and they stepped under the spray together. The warm water, the slick skin, the hard cocks greeting each other eagerly had Gom totally in the land of sensation. He let the water hit his hair and he put his head back, feeling Casey's lips on his neck when he did. That felt wonderful and he moved his hands up to the back of Casey's neck, holding him there.

Gom slid his fingers through Casey's hair, something he'd really come to enjoy doing. He loved the shades of it and the thick waves felt sensuous on his hands. This had become one of his favorite things to do with Casey and Gom could tell that Case loved it, too. He caressed Casey's head and neck while Casey continued to explore his neck and shoulders with his lips. The softness of those lips mixed with the silkiness of the water made Gom shiver with desire.

"Kiss me," Casey murmured, pulling his head out of Gom's neck and moving toward his mouth. Gom met Casey's mouth and this time he thrust his tongue between Casey's lips and into his mouth, seeking and finding new ways to make Casey shiver in his arms. He moved his tongue around Casey's, then slid it over teeth and gums, touched the roof of his mouth, then slid back to caress the lips that seemed to be a little thicker with all the attention they'd garnered.

"Gom?"

"Hmm?"

Casey eased back and looked at him, water plastering his hair to his head, making his lashes spiky and his eyes heated.

"One day, we'll play in here, but right now, I want you so much. I don't want to lose it in here. I want you in my bed, in my arms. Here." Casey grabbed some body wash and put some in Gom's hand and some in his.

Without more words, they both set about washing the other in a very matter-of-fact manner that Gom wouldn't have thought they could manage. They touched, pushed, pulled, turned, bent, and reached until they were both very clean and very close to not making it to the bed, despite the way they'd tried to be quick in their ablutions.

Casey turned off the water, opened the door, grabbed the towels and passed one to Gom. They stood, facing each other, drying off, roughing up their hair to get it as dry as possible, sliding the towels over their own bodies. It hadn't started out as a sex show, but they watched each other and were soon mirroring movements until they both stood, breathing hard and yearning toward the other.

Casey took the towels and pitched them toward a hamper in the corner before taking Gom's hand and leading him toward the bed. He flipped off the overhead light and turned on the small lamp by the bed. It made a slight golden glow over the quilt. Gom went to the sack on the bedside table and opened it, dumping the contents. Two kinds of lube and two different brands of condoms spilled over the top and he tried not to be embarrassed and admit that he didn't know which was best or what he should have gotten.

Without any fuss, Casey came over, pushed one of the tubes over and one of the boxes of condoms, selecting the others. Gom nodded slightly and opened the box, taking a few out and dropping them on the table. When he turned, he saw that Casey had pulled the cover and sheet back and the bed looked beyond inviting. It looked like heaven to Gom. He turned to Casey, feeling the smile that took over his face. Finally.

Casey opened his arms and Gom stepped into them. He put his head to Casey's shoulder, turning his face in so that his nose was nudging Casey's neck. He pressed his hard cock against Casey's, his hand moving up and down Casey's back. He was about to make love with Casey Tanner. His heart soared.

Casey bent his head so that his cheek met Gom's and moved tenderly, nuzzling against him.

"You'll tell me if I do something you don't like?" Casey's voice was hesitant, as if very aware of not implying that Gom wasn't ready for this, but still needing to make sure he was.

"And I'll tell you if you do something I *do* like. Relax, Case." This time Gom just thought it was sweet of Casey to be thinking so much about him.

Deciding they'd never get anywhere if he didn't take over, Gom pulled away a bit, grabbed Casey's hand, turned and fell backwards onto the bed, pulling Casey down with him. Surprised, Casey grunted as he landed half on Gom. Gom could see Casey trying to make sure he hadn't hurt him, so Gom made sure Casey knew he was fine. He wrapped his arms around Casey's shoulders and pushed, twisting, so that now Casey was on his back and Gom was leaning over him, a triumphant smile on his face.

"Don't worry, I'll be careful with you," he teased, moving his head down to press his lips to Casey's. Casey's mouth opened immediately, his arms coming up to firmly enclose Gom in a tight embrace. Gom was suddenly greedy, wanting to do and feel everything at once. He put his hand to Casey's chest and held it there, wanting to feel Casey's heart thudding. His lips moved softly against Casey's mouth when he did feel that hard rhythmic beating that he thought might be pounding as hard as his own.

Gom's action got the response he wanted. He didn't think Casey was thinking about anything but what they were doing. That's just the way Gom wanted it. He eased over a little more, so that he was nearly completely lying on top of Casey. Squirming, he moved until he finally had what he considered the perfect position. His cock was rocking gently against Casey's, each leaving spots of pre-come on the other. Gom gasped at the absolute joy he felt as Casey's hands moved over him. He looked down into those unbelievable blue eyes and thought he'd never forget this moment. For just a second or two, he felt himself getting a little misty-eyed, watching the emotions clearly in Casey's eyes.

"Gom? Hon?"

Gom just shook his head, the moment passing as he bent to trace Casey's lips with his tongue, loving the taste as Casey touched the tip of his tongue to Gom's. They teased back and forth for a bit before Gom pushed further into Casey's mouth, thrusting now. Feeling Casey's hands cup his buttocks, he pressed down harder and began to grind against Casey's groin, his breath coming hard as he pushed them both to the limit.

Gom knew he surprised Casey again when he moved back, putting his hands on the bed beside Casey. He moved his legs up on either side of Casey and sat now on Casey's thighs, his cock brushing Casey's as he leaned forward. Casey gazed up at him, letting him take the lead and do whatever he wanted. Gom was a little surprised at himself. He just knew that he wanted to let Casey know that he wasn't some shrinking violet who was afraid of intimacy or passion. He watched Casey's face to see how he felt about what Gom was doing. Casey's eyes blazed with passion and something else that Gom chose to believe was equal to the feeling in his own heart.

"What do you want, hon? Anything, just do something before I melt or cry or come without you. I'm dying for you." Casey's hands were on Gom as he watched to see what Gom was going to do. One hand was clutching Gom's leg and the other was gently caressing the bruise on his shoulder, his face a study in desire and tenderness.

Gom leaned forward again, pressing their cocks harder together, enjoying both the feeling and the sounds Casey couldn't seem to keep in. Just before he reached Casey's mouth, Gom reached down and took both cocks into his hand.

"Give me your hand," he whispered. Casey complied and they both were moving seamlessly as one, increasing the pleasure and they each seemed to know just when to slow and then stop, glancing down at their joined efforts before letting go and reaching for each other. Gom eased down so that his chest was nearly resting on Casey's. He pressed his lips to Casey's right nipple and the bud hardened in his mouth. Casey gasped, his hand touching the back of Gom's head, holding him there. Gom gave lots of attention to his prize before moving to do the same to the left side. The whole time Casey was making the sexiest little noises, grateful, happy noises that pushed Gom to please him more.

Sliding up a little, Gom trailed his lips and tongue up to Casey's neck, licking the bumps of his collarbone and then up to his right ear.

"I know how you felt that day," he whispered.

"Mmm?" Casey was beginning to shudder as he moaned his question.

"I want to just eat you up. As a matter of fact..." Gom started and then paused, smiling down at Casey's uncertain countenance. Gom took his courage in hand and suggested, "Sixty-nine?"

The brightness of Casey's eyes was his answer. Swiftly, he pulled away, turning and maneuvering until he was facing his goal and he could feel Casey's hands moving over him. Now Gom was shuddering as Casey took his balls and smoothed his hand over them, cradling them, feeling them. Casey paused, his hand still for a few seconds and Gom's heart nearly stopped.

God, he'd forgotten. He had literally forgotten about the ugly scars and ridges that covered his testicles and beyond. He would have moved away, but Casey's other hand held him in place. Those fingers moved again, caressing tenderly, blessing with the gift of acceptance and gentle care. Some of the area was still tender and responded to Casey's touch. The scarring left some the area deadened to feeling. That had never bothered him before, but now he couldn't help resenting the fact that he didn't have the full effect of Casey's touch.

The moment was over and Gom sighed as Casey took his cock and drew it unerringly toward his mouth. When Casey's lips touched the tip, then slid down over the head, Gom gasped.

Taking a deep breath, Gom managed to say, "Casey. God, that feels good."

Casey's only response was to tighten his hand around the base of Gom's cock and to push his hips upwards making his cock brush against Gom's chin. Gom wasted no time in grasping it in his hand and bringing it to his lips to copy Casey's actions. He touched the large head with his lips and then slid them down, going as far as he could without choking and ruining the whole thing.

Moving his head up and down a few times he made sure the length that he could reach was wet. Releasing it now, he moved his head so that he could lick from the base to the tip, moving his hand so that the hard cock was covered completely with his kisses and licking motions. He leaned a little further, taking each of Casey's balls in his mouth to roll them and suck on them, delighting in the jerks and moans that caused.

Desire and a healthy dose of curiosity had him moving even further, using his hands to push Casey's legs apart enough for him to reach his hole with not only his finger, but his questing tongue. He didn't hesitate, touching his tongue to the soft tissue then moving it back and forth, his fingers holding Casey spread for him.

"Jesus, Gom! What are you—ahh!" Gom took all that to mean that Casey liked his attempts. He kept it up for a little longer before moving back to Casey's cock. He took the weeping head back into his mouth and sucked hard. His reward was immediate. Casey groaned deeply and tried to pull out of Gom's mouth, but Gom wasn't having it.

"Gom, oh Gom, hon. Jesus." Gom moved back just enough to let the come hit his lips, chin, and cheeks. He tasted it while he gripped Casey tightly, milking him until he was limp. He licked again, cleaning Casey and patting him gently as he rested his head on Casey's thigh.

Gom couldn't believe it. He'd made Casey come first. Now he realized just how much he needed to do the same. He moved his hips a little to remind Casey that he'd been left sort of, well, hanging. Casey reached to pat his hip as if to say sorry and then took Gom back into his mouth, sucking hard and moving his tongue around the tip, pressing into the slit. Gom jerked and when Casey added in some rolling and squeezing on his balls, Gom felt his orgasm hit.

"Case, I'm…" Gom got no further in his warning. His whole body shook as he spurted into Casey's mouth. Casey held his hips in a tight grasp so he wouldn't push too hard, but he took all that Gom had, swallowing and moaning. Gom was gasping and rubbing his cheek on Casey's thigh as he felt like he'd been totally emptied.

"Come up here, hon. I've got to look at you. I can't believe you just did that." Casey pulled on him, making his desire to have Gom in his arms clear.

"Me? I'm not the only one," Gom said, smiling down at Casey as he crawled up to meet his eyes.

"You were the first. Gom, no one's ever done that to, for me. My God, and you're a virgin." Casey pulled Gom close and held him still for a long slow kiss that meshed their tastes and had Gom squirming.

"So, I did good, huh? No more worries about me?"

Casey laughed. "None. Where did you learn about that?"

"Rimming?" Gom raised his brows and couldn't help the

smug expression. "I've never done anything before, but I can read. Did you know that there are gay romance books that have sex in them, really good sex? I've learned a lot. There are stories about cops, lawyers, soldiers, doctors, mmm, and cowboys. I like those a lot. I've always known that I would want to do that only with someone that I cared greatly about. I've read about things I would never do, or wouldn't be comfortable doing, but there's a long list of things I *want* to do with you."

"God help me. You surprise me over and over. You're the sexiest thing I've ever seen, felt, touched, or tasted. I want you to do all those things to me, whatever they are." Casey looked at Gom closely and said, "You tired? Want to sleep a while?"

"Mmm, maybe. Why? What do you have in mind?" Gom looked right back, smiling.

Casey reached up to smooth his fingers over the swollen bruise on Gom's jaw and then pulled his head down so he could kiss the abused area.

"I want to hold you, sleep for a while, and then I'm going to make love to you right here in our bed."

Gom moved his head so that Casey's hand was caressing his cheek and said, "Our bed."

CHAPTER THIRTEEN

Gom lay very still when he woke up the next morning. It was very early and he didn't want to wake Casey. That's not right. He wanted to wake Casey, but he felt that Casey needed the sleep. He was afraid to move at all, not knowing how soundly Casey slept. A smile spread on his lips, though, as he thought about last night. Gom wasn't a virgin anymore. He didn't think he could have been any happier right then. He was lucky, he knew. Not everyone had a first experience as wonderful as his had been. Maybe something had aligned in the universe and decided that Gom was due a good experience where his abused body was concerned.

Casey may have a reputation as being cold and quiet and brooding, a shell, so to speak, but Gom knew it all hid a soft gooey center. Casey had taken such care with him when they'd both awakened from a short nap. Gom was sure that his eyes had spoken of the same anticipation and eagerness that he'd seen in Casey's. Gom felt that they had seemed to flow toward each other in slow motion, both knowing what was about to happen and both wanting it.

Patience wasn't something that Gom would have expected from Casey, but it's what he got. Taking his time, Casey silently invited Gom to go on a trek of discovery with him. They both, in the soft golden light, took the time to touch each other slowly and tenderly. That wasn't to say that Gom's heart wasn't pounding out of his chest and his breathing didn't hitch and stutter as his hands moved over Casey's exciting body. But, the reverence that Casey showed as he moved his hands and his mouth over Gom's body was nothing short of inspirational.

Through Casey's meticulous attention to detail, Gom found that there was an area just below his right shoulder blade that when touched, grazed gently, made him shiver in ecstasy. The first time it happened he thought it was nothing special, but when

Casey came back to it over and over and got the same response, Gom wiggled and gasped.

"Who knew you had an erogenous zone under your shoulder blade? Not one of the usual spots, but hey, I'm glad I found it," Casey said, smiling at Gom. "I'll be able to touch you there in public and no one will know that I'm turning you on, making you blush, mm-hmm, just like that. I love that you do that." Casey's fingers were softly stroking the spot, now sensitive.

"I'm still looking for yours. Do you have any places that make you shiver and blush?" Gom asked.

"Not telling. The discovery is half the fun. You'll just have to make a careful examination in an attempt to find mine, if I have any, that is." Casey went back to moving his hands over Gom's skin and Gom was delightfully determined to ferret out any such areas on Casey's body. It wasn't a task that he took lightly. Determined to discover a way he could elicit the same responses from Casey, Gom was very thorough.

Having reached Casey's feet without being able to make the same claim as Casey, he almost gave up. But, that wasn't his way. He started over, at the top of Casey's head and success was nearly immediate. When his lips were sliding across the base of Casey's neck below his hair, Casey shivered and Gom heard a small gasp. You'd have thought he'd found gold. He chuckled and touched his tongue to the spot and Casey groaned. Gom was elated.

"Aha! You were right, it was more fun to find it myself." Gom brought his hand up and smoothed Casey's hair out of the way before pressing his mouth right over the spot and torturing Casey in the best possible way.

"Stop. God, Gom, I'm gonna freak out. That's so damn hot," Casey turned and Gom allowed him to escape. It's not like he couldn't return any time he wanted to, now that he'd made his tasty discovery. "That's a smug smile. Proud of yourself, huh?"

"Mmmhmm," Gom replied, wanting to laugh from pure happiness.

Casey had finished turning over and pulled Gom into his

arms. Gom wiggled and squirmed, enjoying the touch of as much of Casey's bare skin as he could get to against his own.

"Why do I get the feeling you're having a really good time? You're like a new puppy. Just can't be still, moving and touching and just all happy, happy." Casey looked at Gom with fond amusement.

"You had a puppy?" Gom asked, settling finally with his arms and legs entwined with Casey's, their torsos together. He liked feeling his and Casey's stomachs moving together as they breathed. His hands were moving over Casey's back, buttocks, and hips.

"No, never. I, uh, sometimes I go to the pet store or the humane society and watch them. The humane society needs help all the time and they let me play with the little ones sometimes. They need someone to hold them and love on them, kind of like babies in the hospital that don't have anybody. People need to go in and hold them, rock them, and feed them." Casey finished his speech and suddenly looked like he'd eaten something awful.

Gom was beginning to understand Casey. He knew right away that Casey felt like he'd talked too much, revealed too much about himself. And he was coming to realize that Casey wasn't comfortable doing that. Gom thought he was getting better at it, though.

"That's cool. I'd love to go with you sometime. We had these two wonderful dogs when I was growing up. We haven't replaced them, but they meant so much to all of us while we had them. Soldier took me to pick them out right after he came to stay with us. It was one of the best days I remember." Gom was trying to reciprocate with his own story. He decided to lighten it up. "I named one of them Pee Wiggles."

It did the trick. Casey chuckled and said, "Pee Wiggles?"

"Yep. Soon as they let me hold him he pee'd on me and wiggled constantly 'cause he was so happy. I named him on the spot." He bent closer to Casey to softly admit, "I loved him because he wasn't the only one who pee'd when he wasn't supposed to. I thought I'd found my soul mate."

"I'm glad you had them. I think it's great, what Dillon and Soldier did, and still do. You were part of the first group there, right?" Casey lay, with his head on the pillow, looking at Gom as he talked with him. His hand was moving softly through Gom's hair and over his brows and cheeks. Gom didn't know if Casey even knew what he was doing as they conversed. But Gom liked it, a lot.

Caresses. If asked, Casey might not say that he was one who enjoyed the gentle caresses he was bestowing, but Gom loved it and began to do the same. He brought one of his hands up and took Casey's, pulled it down to his mouth, kissed it gently before letting it go. Gom put his hand on Casey's neck and slid it up through those golden waves. As he caressed Casey, he answered his question.

"Yes. We all had such horrible problems, such awful memories of things we had lived through. Dillon was a lifesaver and we loved him. When Soldier showed up, it was like our life turned around. We were a family. We had stuff now, lots of stuff, but it was the feeling of peace and love and honest caring that we soaked up like sponges. These were things none of us were used to and it took a while for us to believe that this new happiness wasn't going to be taken away from us. Soldier made us believe. He's amazing." Gom shook his head, and said, "I probably am killing the moment, huh? Shouldn't be talking about my dad so much while I'm in bed with my lover."

"No, you should be talking about anything you want. Tell me more. What did he do to make you all believe?" Casey really did look like he wanted to know, so Gom thought about it and answered.

"He seemed to know just what each of us needed and he set about providing that thing. It might have been teaching Tommy to defend himself so he'd never feel like a victim again, or allowing Jack to be angry, but to learn to understand it. He made sure that Bart got the counseling and training he needed to talk again. He and Dillon made sure we all felt like a family, but that each of us got just what we needed to become healthy and happy." Gom was sure his love and respect was evident in his voice and words, but he made no excuses. He loved Soldier. Period.

"What about you? What did he do for you, other than the obvious?" Casey asked, his hand still moving in those sweet touches.

"He loved me. He made me feel safe enough to sleep, something I hadn't done in a while before he came. He made me feel special. Dillon did, too. He was there first, but something about Soldier when he came just, I don't know, he saved me, brought me out of a deep ugly place. I don't know how to explain it. It wasn't what my mother *did* to me, it was just that it could happen, such evil. Through Dillon and Soldier's love and care I learned what love was and that I deserved it. We all did." Gom looked at Casey and said, "You do, too."

Casey looked right back at him, as if taking in the words, accepting them.

"Think they're going to accept me as your guy?" Casey asked, very seriously.

"I think they already have. They more or less gave you a stamp of approval when they let me know they wouldn't be looking for me to return last night. I made my choice. I chose you and I couldn't be happier. Well, maybe I could…" Gom left the statement open-ended on purpose.

"Oh, yeah? Like maybe if I did this?" Casey pushed and Gom was on his back, Casey rising over him, looking down.

Gom smiled up at him and tipped his chin up in an invitation that Casey accepted immediately. Casey's mouth covered Gom's and his tongue searched and found its counterpart. Gom nearly went up in flames as Casey kissed him with a passion that grew as Gom participated fully.

Gom's mind was reeling with one thought, "At last!" Talking with Casey was wonderful and he loved getting to know him, but he wanted what was about to happen.

Casey's cock was pressing against Gom's hip and. Gom moved

enough to make room beside his own and they were then rocking together. Sensations poured in, intense and increasingly strong.

When Casey moved his mouth to Gom's neck, Gom managed, "Oh, good Lord. Case."

"Shh, hon, I'm going to take good care of you. You'd tell me if there was something…"

"Shh, *hon*. There's nothing. Scars, old ones that affect nothing. We're good to go." When Gom saw the look of surprise on Casey's face, he grinned, leaning to kiss him quickly. "Yes, I knew what you were thinking. She burned me with cigarettes, a long, long time ago. There's a good bit of scarring, but it doesn't cause me any problem. There's some loss of feeling on the scars, but not completely. Your touch felt good."

Gom had a horrible thought. "Unless it turns…"

Casey pulled up and glared down at Gom. "Don't you *even* go there. Every single thing about you turns me *on*. Everything you've ever gone through, survived, and learned from has made you the person that we already agreed I've fallen for." Casey's forehead was now pressed to Gom's as if he wanted to be as close as possible when saying these last words, so Gom would be forced to pay attention.

"Okay. Good. Okay." Gom wanted this conversation to be over to never be visited again.

"Now, it might be a little easier, maybe less painful, on your knees, but I really feel like you'd enjoy the experience more if we were face to face. Knowing you, I think the eye contact will make it better for you."

"You're right. I want to see you. If you go slow, I can handle it. I know it's not always great the first time or so, but I want you so much, Casey. Make love to me, with me. If you need something from me, for God's sake, tell me. I want to make you happy, too. Please."

"For God's sake," Casey repeated, then paused and said, "For Gom's sake. The next hour or so is strictly for Gom's sake."

"What does that mean?" Gom asked.

"You're my whole world right now. Everything is for you."

"No, that's not what I want. It's us, both of us. I don't want this to be one-sided, Case."

"Relax, hon. It'll be good for both of us, but this is your first time is all I meant and I want it to be something you remember forever. Mine sucked. Maybe I'll consider this my first time, too. The first time I've ever made love to someone as opposed to having sex just to get off. It's going to be different for me because of you, so for Gom's sake, I have to make this good. Besides, for Casey's sake just doesn't have the same ring to it."

Gom smiled, as he was supposed to and just looked at Casey for a moment. There was a lot to take in from those last comments. Casey's first time had been bad, but he considered this to be making love. Gom knew that Casey's words, as well as his actions, would be what made this memorable.

Casey was wrong about himself. He really was good with words. Or maybe, as he'd said, he was just better when he was with Gom. That thought made Gom warm from the inside out.

No matter how good the words were, the time for them was over. Gom pulled Casey's head back down to his and kissed him, hard, pointedly. He wrapped his arms around Casey's shoulders and spread his legs to wrap them around Casey's. Still kissing, Gom's lips spread in a smile against Casey's mouth. He had his man bound up tight, right where he wanted him.

Casey got the idea. In a nod to Gom's earlier movements, Casey moved over the top of Gom, touching him in as many places as possible. Gom laughed as Casey did the eager puppy routine. He hadn't expected to have such fun. He'd pretty much run the gamut of feelings tonight and it wasn't over. Thank God.

"I can't believe how happy you make me," he said to Casey, who'd stopped his squirming and was pulling back to sit on his knees between Gom's legs. The lamp on the bedside table was still on, so Gom felt like he was pretty much on display. For some reason, the look in Casey's eyes kept him from being self-conscious. He began to shiver a little, not with cold or fear, but excitement.

Casey took a few minutes to run his hands over Gom's body. Gom didn't take his eyes from Casey as he gave himself up to whatever Casey wanted. From Gom's shoulders to his chest and down to his stomach, Casey's hands left small shudders and warm pink skin behind. Gom could feel the heat of blood rushing to his skin as Casey continued the caresses, fingers grazing the area on his lower belly, tender and sensitive. Gom shook harder.

Casey looked up from his tactile tour and grinned, clearly knowing what his tender touches were doing.

"You're driving me crazy on purpose," Gom said. There wasn't any question there.

"Mmm-hmm. Feels good, doesn't it? I've never done this, you know. With no one else have I ever taken this much time, done any kind of exploring and preparation. It's not just for you. I like it, the freedom to touch you all over and know that you want it from me. It makes me unbelievably high to know that I'm making you feel so good."

"M-making me pretty high, too." Gom couldn't reach Casey, so he pushed himself up awkwardly, now meeting Casey's mouth in another mashing kiss, less technique and more passion.

Casey leaned, pushing Gom slowly back to the bed and continued where he left off before Gom spoke up. Now his hands caressed Gom's cock, threading through the lush brown hair surrounding it. Gom thought he would embarrass himself by coming right then. Casey bent to touch his lips to the tip of Gom's cock, licking and teasing the slit.

Gom shouted and bucked his hips.

"Easy, hon. It's okay, I want you to come for me. Come on." Casey slid his lips down Gom's cock and then back up, sucking hard as one hand went to Gom's balls, smoothing and rolling them. Gom had feeling there, in between the worst scars. It was odd, feeling the pressure on the inside of his balls, but not so much on the skin over them. Casey's movements increased and

Gom did as Casey had requested.

"Case!" That was all he could articulate. Gom came off the bed again and nearly bumped heads as Casey brought his up to watch the come spouting from Gom's cock, held firmly in his hand. Gom shuddered and gasped as he sat, his forehead now pressed to Casey's as they watched Casey's hand slide up and down as Gom covered it with sticky come. Gom was breathing deeply as he calmed a little, bringing his arms up to Casey's shoulders and dropping his head to Casey's neck. He brushed his lips against the skin there and sighed as Casey put his other hand up to slide through his hair.

"Lie back. I want you so much."

Gom moved back immediately, watching as Casey reached for one of the condoms. He ripped it open and moved closer as he covered his hard cock. Gom got the lube and put some on his fingers before reaching to slather it over the now sheathed cock that was jutting from the blond curls at Casey's groin. Casey groaned as Gom couldn't help stroking and squeezing as he made sure Casey was covered with slick. Casey eased back from Gom's touch, holding out his hand for the lube.

Covering his fingers he bent to spread Gom further, moving to pull Gom's cheeks back so he could put his wet fingers to Gom's opening. Gom sucked in his breath at the sensation of the cool lube and the warm finger. Reaching down, he put his hands under his knees and pulled his legs back, making it easier for Casey and making Gom feel like he was both strong and vulnerable at the same time. It took a lot of courage to open himself like that, especially knowing that he was scarred and ugly down there, but this was Casey and Gom was in love.

Again, the look in Casey's eyes told Gom he had done the right thing, letting Casey know that he was ready for this.

So. Damn. Ready.

Casey's finger moved around the tight ring guarding Gom's hole and then eased in slowly. In the next few seconds, Case moved in and out, around and around, stretching and loosening

Gom to take the second finger Casey introduced. Sucking in a breath, Gom knew to expect the burning, but the discomfort was more than he'd expected. Ouch.

"You okay?" Casey asked, pausing.

"Mmm-hmm. Don't stop." There was no way in hell that he wanted Casey to stop now. He knew, he'd read and studied, and he knew this was going to hurt. No matter how much Casey tried to prepare him, he was going to be putting a large cock into a small opening. The stretching would help, but come on.

Casey got more lube and slowly moved those two fingers, curling them until they touched Gom's prostate, making sensations zing through him. Yes! That felt so good. Casey moved in and out, each time touching, teasing that spot so that Gom was stimulated constantly.

"Can you take one more?" Casey whispered, watching Gom's face closely. Gom nodded. He could, couldn't he?

Casey looked at him for another few seconds, as if trying to gauge from Gom's face if he really could.

Gom was worried. In all the books he'd read, this part didn't take this long. People just made love. They touched and pleased each other and stretched and then, without pain, the deed was done. Some books did a better job than others in describing the action and the best ones were able to show in words the depths of feeling that was part of the act of lovemaking. He nodded again at Casey.

More lube and Casey added another finger and as he pushed, Gom couldn't help pulling away a little. The sting was intense, the pain surprising. Casey stopped immediately. It wasn't a mild discomfort. It was damn painful.

"It's okay, shh." Casey could evidently see the look of dismay and disappointment on Gom's face.

Gom's eyes filled and he pleaded, "Please don't stop, Case. I'm okay. I was just surprised."

"I could tell it was hurting you, Gom."

"Have you, uh, had any other virgins? Am I your first? I feel so stupid. I don't want you to stop, Casey. Just tell me what to do. I'm not some kid, Case. I just play one in my job. This isn't something I'm playing at here. I want this. Don't make me beg, okay?" Gom knew he sounded like the kid he professed not to be, but he wanted Casey to finish this.

"Okay. Okay, Gom. I don't mean to make you feel like that. I just hate hurting you, and no, I've never had a virgin before. I've never had to hurt someone like this. It's hard."

Gom had leg his legs go and now he reached up with both hands to grasp Casey's face. He looked right into Casey's light blue eyes and said, clearly, "Do it. For God's Sake, Casey. Just do it."

To Casey's credit, he only hesitated a couple of seconds before leaning down and kissing Gom's lips.

"I love you, hon. I know you're a grown man, even if you do look like a cute little twink."

To Gom, that said it all. Casey loved him and he *was* a grown man. Very deliberately, Gom reached down and grabbed his legs again, pulling them up. Casey pressed his lips together in a tight grin and reached for more lube.

"Maybe you should turn…"

"No, this way." Gom figured that was direct enough. Maybe it lacked a little romance, but enough was enough.

Casey eased back in with two fingers, stroking them, spreading them. Gom began to rock against them so that they were forced in further. It didn't hurt so he nodded his head. "Go on, another one."

With every ounce of strength in him, he managed to not flinch or change expression as Casey pushed another finger in to join the other two. Casey held them still for a bit while Gom adjusted. It got better. The hard sting, the feeling of being pulled too tightly was strong, but Gom kept his eyes steady on Casey's and nodded again.

Casey moved slowly and it got easier. Brushing Gom's gland helped, too, as streaks of pleasure flew through him. He began to concentrate on those flashes and soon the pain eased and he could get a good breath again.

"Now, Casey."

"You're not…"

"Shh. I am. Please, trust me." For that's what it boiled down to for Gom. Casey trusting him enough to know that Gom could handle whatever came next if he said he was ready.

Casey was no fool. He slipped his fingers out and added more lube to his cock before pressing the head at Gom's hole. Gom smiled up at Casey, his heart in his throat and probably mirrored in his eyes. Casey pushed and Gom bore down. He'd read somewhere that it would help and it did. Casey, at the least the tip of Casey's cock, was inside him. It wasn't comfortable, but it wasn't excruciating, either.

"Yes, Casey. 'S good. I want more. It's okay, really." Gom was tired of feeling like he'd ruined this whole thing by being a wuss. "Come on."

Casey could evidently tell how Gom felt because he moved Gom's hands from his knees and took hold of them himself, pulling them just a little wider. He eased a little further inside Gom and when Gom didn't even wince, he pushed until he was seated all the way inside. Gom heard the sigh from Casey and he used his free hands to reach for Casey. Casey leaned and Gom stroked his hand from Casey's neck down to his stomach, before moving them to the bed sheets to hold on.

The intense sensation he felt as Casey slid out slowly until just the tip was still inside him had Gom gasping. He brought his hips up, inviting Casey to come back in again. Casey did and they set up a slow but steady rhythm. Casey still watched Gom closely, but Gom was sure he saw nothing but passion and happiness on his face now. It wasn't all pleasure. There were streaks of pain as Gom was stretched more than he'd thought possible, but the joy outweighed the discomfort now and it got better.

It wasn't long before they were moving together and the pain was the farthest thing from Gom's mind. He could not believe how much sensation was centered in that small area that was being stimulated perfectly now by Casey's cock. His whole body was shuddering. His breathing was labored and his mind was blown. So this is what it's all about. All the other things they had done were wonderful, but this is what the books were talking about.

Gom could feel Casey start to increase his speed and the depth of his thrusts. Gom brought his hips up each time Casey plunged in, making the feeling that much stronger. Casey's breath was coming harder and Gom knew he was about to explode. He curled up and reached down for his cock and began to slide his hand back and forth. It was so tender from before and with just a few pulls, he was losing it again. He felt Casey thrust one last time, harder than before and he felt the warmth of Case's come filling the condom. He squeezed his sphincter and heard Casey gasp. Gom repeated the action and Casey gave another couple of thrusts before collapsing onto Gom. He released Gom's legs and lay between them, mashing an accepting Gom.

Gom could feel Casey's softening cock sliding out of him and he noticed that Casey reached down to secure the condom as he pulled the rest of the way free. Gom watched as Casey tied it and dropped it onto the table.

Casey eased off Gom, letting him get a full breath. Pulling Gom into his side, he looked closely at him and grinned.

"Was it all you hoped for?" he asked.

"Oh, yeah." Gom 's heart was still pounding and he didn't know it if was exertion or emotion. He felt such a swell of feeling for Casey right then and wished he knew how to express it without sounding too sappy or whatever. "It was intense, Casey. I don't even have the words to tell you. I'm just sorry I almost messed the whole thing up before." Gom was embarrassed now and trying to hide it.

"Shh, Gom. Come here." Casey pulled Gom into his arms and nuzzled his face into Gom's neck. "It wasn't just you. I should have trusted you to know what you could take. I didn't mean to make you feel like…"

"Shh, Case. Done. Over. Wonderful. I only remember how good it felt when you were inside me, making love to me." Gom felt his eyes get wide, one brow going up. "You told me you loved me."

"Caught that, did you? Yeah, I was wondering if I was going to hear it back."

"You know I love you. You have to know it. You're the only one, Casey, the only one I could picture myself doing that with. It's so, so big. It's so… I don't know how to say it, but it's so personal, so intense. I'm overusing that word, but you were inside me. It was an incredible feeling, both physically and mentally."

They'd cuddled for a while, hands roaming, lips touching softly, and Gom thought he was so happy he might just never leave. Casey had gotten up and brought a warm wet cloth from the bathroom to clean him gently, patting him dry and kissing him gently. Gom felt very well cared for and loved.

He turned, deciding that it was time for Casey to wake up. Gom needed kisses. As he moved, he gasped as he felt more than a little discomfort.

"Easy, hon. You'll be a little sore for a while, not long. Still think it was worth it?"

Gom got all the way turned over, only wincing once and saw that Casey was looking at him, trepidation clear on his features. What, did he expect Gom to say that because it had been a bit, well, more than a bit painful, that he was done with Casey?

"It was worth everything, Casey. Relax." Gom settled into the open arms that Casey provided and snuggled down, his head resting on Casey's shoulder. "I knew there would be pain involved and I'll admit I was surprised by how much it did hurt at first, but you were very good to me. It ended up being a wonderful feeling, and before you ask, I'm not just saying that. I can see your expression."

"No, you can't," Casey teased, since Gom was pretty much looking at the morning hard on Casey was sporting, not his face.

"I can see it in my mind. Give me some time to heal a little and I'll be ready for you again. Do you, I mean, do you ever, you know…?"

"Are you asking if I would let you make love to me, take my ass?" Casey sounded like he was teasing again.

"Yes." Gom wasn't.

"Yes, I would. I've done it a couple of times and wasn't crazy about it, frankly. With you, hmm, I've been thinking about it and I want you to do it, Gom. That's if you want to, I mean."

"We are being so polite and hesitant, aren't we? I thought we were past all the awkwardness with each other. Right now, I just want to hold you, maybe get rid of these." Gom pointed to his and Casey's hard cocks and rubbed his face against Casey's shoulder. "A shower, some food, and I'm ready for anything. Do you have something here or should we go out to breakfast? God, I could use some Cracker Barrel blueberry pancakes right about now. How about you?" Gom laughed as Casey's stomach growled and moved his hand over the flat surface.

"Mmm, their French toast and hash brown casserole. Join me in the shower and we'll take care of our mutual problems in a good way. I'll take you to breakfast. I have to go in later this afternoon. What are you going to do?"

Gom raised his head and dropped a kiss onto Casey's chin as he answered. "I want to check with Laurie and see how Bradley's doing and then I want to get a report from the captain about what's going to happen with the two boys we charged yesterday. Plus, I want to put a call in to the principal, Ms. King, and see if she's going to have the assembly program she promised and when she's shooting for with it."

Casey rolled out of bed and put his hand out to pull Gom up and out with him. Gom moved into Casey's side and they headed to the bathroom together. As they went through their early morning rituals, Gom paid attention and thought to himself that this was what his parents had. Doing the mundane, everyday things together, which made the tasks less of a chore and more a chance to build a bond. They both brushed their teeth, standing at the sink and smiling goofily at each other. Gom spit, wiped his mouth, and turned to push into Casey, who'd stood waiting for him to finish.

Casey's arms closed around him and he squirmed closer, his mouth open and inviting. Casey wrapped Gom up in those strong arms and cradled him against the firm chest. Gom licked Casey's lips and met his tongue, his hands coming up to hold Casey's face gently. Their cocks were bumping and leaking on each other as Casey plundered Gom's mouth, his arms tightening. One hand moved down his back and very tenderly caressed Gom's ass, moving over the cheeks, teasing the crack, and patting along the bottom of his cheeks. His fingers traced the line of circular scars that covered the area closest to where his buttocks joined his legs.

Gom didn't say anything, but he wondered what Casey was thinking as he continued to smooth his fingers over them.

"I'll never understand how someone could do something like this to a child. You know I care nothing about you having scars, other than the fact that I hate that you had to go through that. I love you, Gom. I just can't get my head around how a mother could hurt her kid like that. I hate that your life was so unhappy." Casey was shaking just a little as he talked and caressed Gom.

"Hey, it was all a long time ago. It doesn't hurt me anymore. Dillon and Soldier banished those horrible memories and replaced them with love and acceptance. Besides, you couldn't have been much happier if you left home at fourteen." Gom pulled away so he could look up at Casey and read his expression. He had to admit he wanted to know more about Casey's life.

"I was abused and hurt, yes, but not tortured Gom. I was ignored for the most part, and then was a scapegoat for when my parents got tired of fighting with each other. They both blamed me for how unhappy they were, neither having wanted me to begin with. When I told them I was gay, I thought they wouldn't care since they didn't seem to care about much that I did. Both of them." Casey paused and gave one of those smiles that didn't really reach his eyes. "I think it's the first time I ever heard them agree on anything. They both told me if I ever said that again, they would make me sorry. There was such coldness in their eyes, Gom."

"That's so awful, Casey. Was there no one to help you, love you?"

"Nah. They'd never been loving. Ha! They were pretty unfeeling as parents, barely doing the minimum to get by without social services coming in. Sometimes, people at school wondered about why I wore the same clothes several days in a row, or why I was always hungry. They were gone a lot and I fended for myself. They drank, went to bars, came in plastered and basically ignored the fact that they had a child. If they weren't drunk, they were fighting, yelling, throwing things, always such ugly things. Boy, they sure agreed on that one thing. They treated me like a leper after I told them I thought I liked boys instead of girls. Hell, I wasn't even sure. And why, I've wondered since, did I feel the need to share it with them? It wasn't a week before I'd decided to leave."

"God, Case; that sucks. So, you never had any, I mean, no hugs, no kisses, no…" Gom made sure there was no pity in his voice, but God, he hated thinking of Casey growing up that way.

"No nothing, hon. No birthdays, no vacations, no cookies and milk. It was a bare existence and I hated it. I wasn't stupid. I saw other kids and how they were treated, how happy they were. I used to think there was something so wrong with me, so horrible about me that made them that way toward me. Then when I realized that I was different in that way, too, I thought that must be it. That was what was wrong with me, why they'd never wanted me. It was a long time before I realized that it was them, not me."

"No, it wasn't you. Soldier and Dillon say that some people just should never be parents. You deserve so much more. You're right, it was them, not you."

"Thanks, Gom. Now, enough with the soul-baring. I know, I

started it, but I couldn't help it." Casey's fingers went back to the row of scars on Gom's bottom. "I love your ass." Casey turned them, putting Gom so he faced the sink and then pushed his shoulder, bending him over. Gom was confused. Casey didn't leave him wondering long. He dropped to his knees behind Gom and with his hands on either side of Gom's hips, he bent his head and kissed Gom's scars. Casey started on the left side and kissed each circle of pain, blessing it and making it a small round spot that was now loved. Gom gasped when he felt Casey's lips on the first one. By the time Casey'd moved across and kissed each of them, ending on the right side of Gom's hip, Gom's eyes were filled with tears. Looking into the mirror over the sink, he watched them slide down his face as Casey gave him one final kiss on each cheek before standing.

Gom didn't even try to hide his face from Casey as his face joined Gom's in the mirror. Gom was in shock. He couldn't believe that Casey had just done that. It was such a simple act, but he was deeply touched by the gesture. Casey's arms wrapped him up from behind, his face coming level with Gom's as he looked into Gom's eyes in the mirror.

"Do you get it? I love every inch of you, every scar, every freckle, and every hair. We were made to find each other and be together. I need you, Gom. I've never, ever, felt like this before. I've never told anyone about my life, never really cared about theirs. You are *so* special to me."

Gom brought his hands up to wipe his tears away and let a slow smile spread across his face. He saw what that did to Casey's face. He saw the lightness come into his eyes and a matching smile appear on his lips. Good Lord, the man was gorgeous.

Gom pushed his butt back, moving Casey out of the way so he could turn. He hopped up so his bottom was now on the sink and his legs went around Casey, as did his arms.

"I love you, Casey Tanner, so damn much." They kissed for a long time, holding tightly to each other. Gom finally came up for air, laughing in sheer joy.

"Come on. Shower, wet, slick fun, food, and then let's meet

the day. I can handle anything with you in my life."

CHAPTER FOURTEEN

Gom spent the entire drive home thinking about Casey and their night together. As he parked and turned off the car, he thought about Soldier and Dillon. In no way was he concerned about facing them after spending the night with his lover. He knew they'd be happy for him. His thoughts were about the love and affection he'd grown up with in this house. Through their love for each other, his dads had given all their children an example of how a relationship based on deep emotion can enrich and ensure a good life.

They had never done anything overt in front of their kids, but the affection, the deep abiding love was evident in the way they looked at each other and the subtle touches they shared. Gom was grateful that he'd had a chance to know what true love looked like so he could recognize it when he felt it.

He got out and headed in. Both of the father figures in his life were in the kitchen when he got there. It was a little after lunch and they were cleaning up and Gom couldn't help the chuckle when he saw how they both tried to look nonchalant when he walked in.

"Go ahead and laugh. You come in here, obviously in love, and find amusement at our expense." Soldier dropped the pan he was holding and came over to Gom with open arms. Gom stepped into them and wrapped his dad in his arms.

"Hi, Dad."

"Hey, what about me?" Dillon said, pushing his way into the affection fest.

Gom laughed out loud and opened his arm to add Dillon into the hug.

"You all are so funny. Thank you for your support."

"That's all we get?" Dillon asked, easing out of the embrace and crossing his arms.

"What more do you want?" Gom teased.

"Well, you can relax. We're not looking for details here. Actually, the smile that hasn't left your face since you stepped in and the constant glow in those eyes are enough for me. We both knew how you felt about Casey. It's clear you've found that those feelings are returned. It's good, Gom."

Soldier had pulled away, too, to look closely as Gom answered, "Yeah, it's good, the best."

Dillon went to the refrigerator and opened the door, pulling out the orange juice and getting three glasses.

"Sit down and talk to us. Tell us anything you want to. We already know you love him and now we can relax because if he didn't love you, you wouldn't have that glow about you. Just tell us a little about him. We want to love him, too."

That was it. That's how they were. If Casey made Gom happy then Soldier and Dillon wanted to know and love him, as well. That's the kind of men he'd had as role models. God, he wished the Bradleys and the Byrons of this world could have known this kind of acceptance and love. Their lives would have been so very different. They'd have had the strength from within to handle the situations they were faced with and known that someone had their backs. His face must have shown what he was thinking.

"Where'd you go, Gom?" Soldier asked. Usually, it was Dillon who was quick to catch the small things like a changed expression or sad eyes. Gom smiled for his dad.

"I was just thinking how much you all love me and what that has meant to me over the years. I wish every young boy could have known the kind of care and acceptance that you all have shown all of us. How their lives would have been so different if they'd had someone to talk to like I did." Gom had never been shy about letting his dads know how much he loved them and what they meant to him.

"You're thinking about Byron, aren't you?" Dillon asked, handing him his glass.

"Yeah, him and Bradley. Bradley's not gay, and the threat to him had nothing to do with anything like that, but his life at home was horrible, no love or caring. It's a wonder that he's as good a young man as he truly is. That speaks of an inner strength, but being good isn't being happy. I hate how so many kids today are so damned unhappy, desperate even because no one was there to show them it was okay to feel whatever they needed to, to be whatever they had to be."

"We know how you feel. We see it over and over, have seen it all along. But our work, and your and Tommy's jobs bring it all home to us every day so we're closer to it than most people. We just have to work harder and reach more young people." Dillon's voice was strong as he spoke of his desire to do more when he'd already done so much.

"It's never enough, is it? You all have helped so many of us over the years, but there are so many that we hear about and think, what if we'd had a chance to be there for them, help them? It must tear you all up every time you become aware of another case, a suicide, a news story about a teen being bullied to the point that it *makes* the news." Gom knew both men's hearts and was sure that they felt every story deep in their souls. He could not love them more.

"We had to come to the realization years ago that we can only help those we can reach. It does hurt to hear about so many young lives ruined or lost, but we have to focus on the ones we can reach and help. It took us a while to get to that point, and still we have trouble coping with the sad news at times. We don't have to know the child personally for our hearts to break when we hear about their pain. Do we wish we'd known about Byron earlier, had a chance to talk to him, help him? Of course, but you are in the same position." Dillon looked intently at Gom as he continued. "You can't beat yourself up, take on the responsibility of what if. You will make a difference in so many lives, Gom, and you have to let that be enough or you'll make yourself crazy. Work as hard as you can, allow yourself to have a life, too, and you'll be the best Gom there is. It's enough, son." Dillon covered Gom's hand on the table and Gom turned his to clasp Dillon's.

Gom wished he felt the same way. It was never enough. He thought about all the kids he'd seen.

"You know, I was thinking…" He stopped, getting his thoughts in order. He looked at Soldier and Dillon and told them what had been eating at him.

"These kids, a lot of them, are like ghosts. They feel invisible and to a large extent, they are. They're not the loud kids, the mean ones, the troublemakers. Often they're not the prom queens, the jocks, or the academic leaders who get all the attention and accolades. They don't *get* attention. They end up feeling invisible. Sometimes, they purposefully fly below the radar trying to be unnoticed, or they're just forgotten because they sort of blend in with the woodwork. They don't have the self-confidence to demand that they be seen or heard. They just float through and every new instance of being ignored or glanced over for whatever reason compounds their feeling of worthlessness. These kids are lost in the middle between the super good and the super bad, and they are the ones who need help, support, and encouragement. But all too often, they're ghosts. Just…ghosts."

"You're absolutely right. It's up to the adults to get a clue about that and not forget the quiet ones, the lost ones. Teachers, staff, and counselors need to become more aware of these kids being the ones who need help before they feel, like Byron, that it's hopeless." Dillon, soft-hearted, soft-spoken Dillon nailed it, of course. Soldier, put his arm around Dillon and did his part next, drawing them back to happier thoughts.

"Okay, you two, another topic. We want to know about Casey. He's a good man, strong enough to handle what you do and how you'll need him sometimes when it gets bad?" Soldier asked. That made sense. Soldier was the one that provided the strength around here so he would consider that an important trait.

"Yes, he's very good and strong. He lets me talk about as much as I can on the cases and he empathizes and understands my need to vent and then he's there to make me feel better. He's good to me, Dad."

"That's all I need to hear." Soldier's shoulders eased as some of his worries were lessened.

"What about his place? Is it nice?" Dillon asked.

Gom told them about Casey's basement apartment and how Ben would love it with all the movie posters and memorabilia. They suggested that he invite Casey over for supper, but he told them Casey was working that night. When he admitted that Casey was off the next night the invitation moved to then and he said he'd talk to Casey.

"Can we have breakfast for supper?" Gom didn't often ask for particular meals as he liked everything that Dillon made, but he and Casey hadn't made it to Cracker Barrel as they'd discussed and Dillon's pancakes and French toast were just as good.

"Sure. It's been a long time since we did that. I know blueberry pancakes and bacon for you. What does he like?"

"French toast. That would be cool. I'm going to make some calls and um, I'll probably help Casey again tonight after he's done at the theater. It makes his cleaning work shorter and we'll want to go back to his place afterwards." Gom wasn't asking permission, just letting them know his plans. It was only polite as he was still living with them.

"That's cool. You'll be here for supper or you going down there early?" Soldier asked, getting up and taking the three empty glasses to the sink.

"Would it be okay if I, I mean…" Gom stopped and Dillon filled in the blanks.

"Would you like to take Casey some supper for when he gets a break?" Dillon had always been there to make things easier for him. The man just knew what was needed and provided it.

"That would be cool." Gom watched as Dillon started writing on a note on the refrigerator.

"We're having burgers and fries tonight so that should travel well. Since they're home fries, they should heat up well, too. I'll put all the trimmings in a separate container so you all can make your sandwiches later. That way they won't get soggy. I'll take care of you all, and I won't forget something for dessert. Let's see, he liked the brownies that night he came by to check on Trick, so I'll make a couple of batches, cut them really big, and send two along with you. That work?" Dillon asked, smiling at the look on Gom's face. "I guess that works."

"You're the best. I'll talk to Casey about supper tomorrow night. He asked if I thought you all would accept him into my life. I told him you already had. I love you for it, though, I really do." Gom stood and went to both of them for quick hugs before going up to his room to make some calls to the station, the school to find out if there were any plans for the assembly and then to Laurie Summer, whom he'd come to really like working and talking with.

It was no surprise to find that both boys' parents had shown up with high-priced lawyers, but they would not be getting off or back in school. Too bad about their football scholarships and careers. Laurie had a few minutes between sessions with students and they talked about the case, as much as he could, and she said she wanted to come to the assembly as a tribute to Byron. She wanted to see what the principal came up with in the way of speakers and education for the students.

Gom had talked to Tommy and suggested that if he knew of any powerful voices in the area he should tell Ms. King so she could contact them. He thought Tommy's idea of showing some of the videos that were being made by celebrities who were standing up and saying how wrong bullying was and how they "gave a damn" would be helpful.

Let's face it, he thought; if these kids didn't have it in their own hearts to be kind to others just because it was right, maybe they would be swayed by their favorite singer or actor suggesting that it would be cool to do so. Anything that worked, Gom thought. Anything that worked. It still tore at him that so many students were aware of what was happening to Byron and then to him in the bathroom that day, and never said a word or tried to help in any way. Totally blew his mind.

Ms. King said she was setting the assembly date for the following Friday, attendance mandatory, and parents were strongly encouraged to attend and sit with their children. That would go over well, but she had a point. It came from the home. If these kids had parents who were more aware, like his, then they wouldn't be going through this. He said he would be attending with his family and bringing a couple of friends if that was all right. She said they were welcome and thanked him again for his part in solving the case.

ℛ   ℛ   ℛ

Gom had wondered if last night could be improved upon, but he shouldn't have questioned it. The more time he spent with Casey, the more comfortable they became with each other and he reveled in the feeling of togetherness.

He arrived at the theater about a half hour before Casey was done working, taking the brownies in with him. Casey's eyes lit up when Gom appeared and that made Gom feel wonderful. He handed over the brownies and Casey's stomach growled. Gom sat down in the chair beside Casey, the one he was beginning to consider his, and watched as Casey opened the container. They shared the treat as the show wound down and Casey had a few minutes of frantic work with the final lighting processes. Gom stayed out of his way and watched Casey's expertise, as always impressed with the speed of his hands over the board as he lit one section of the stage after the other, always spot on.

Despite Casey's professing to not like talking, they did just that as they cleaned the offices as quickly as they could and still be thorough. They talked about Gom's brothers, Casey's job, and Casey accepted the invitation to supper the next night. Gom told him about the assembly program and Casey surprised him by asking if Gom wanted him to go to it with him. Gom was touched that Casey offered and told him it would mean a lot. His heart was warmed.

When they got to the apartment Gom asked if Casey wanted supper right away. Casey laughed as he took Gom's hand, drawing him into the kitchen. He took the container from Gom and put it into the refrigerator, turning to take Gom into his arms.

"I take it we'll be eating later," Gom said, unable to keep the smile from his face. It wasn't there long, though, since Casey kissed it right into oblivion. Gom opened to Casey's questing tongue and met it with his. He wrapped his arms around Casey's neck, pulling him as close as possible. Casey's hands met on Gom's back and slid down to his hips, drawing Gom's hips into delicious contact with his. Gom pushed in loving how hard they both were and how the anticipation of imminent lovemaking had his breath hitching and his body beginning to shudder.

"You okay?" Casey pulled away to ask.

"Excited, happy, horny," Gom said and blushed when Casey laughed again. "What?" he asked.

"Nothing, hon. It's just exactly how I feel, but you're always so willing to say things out loud. I've got to get better with that. I don't ever want you to think I'm not crazy about you, or that I don't want you just as much because I'm too chicken to say things. You're so brave." Casey ducked his head and rested it on Gom's shoulder.

Gom was stunned. He rubbed his cheek on Casey's head and whispered, "In no way do I find you lacking, Casey. I love the way you talk to me, the way you talk *for* me. I can't tell you how much I feel for you."

"Yes, you can. Tell me how much you care for me." Casey's head was up now, looking closely at Gom, waiting for his response.

Gom looked back at Casey, wondering what he was asking for. Did he want Gom to admit he was in love? He'd said last night that he was falling in love with Casey and Casey had said he had fallen for Gom early on, but he didn't mind saying it straight out.

"I love you, Casey Tanner. No doubts, no fears, no hesitation. I love you." Gom felt so good saying it aloud and seeing the joy in Casey's eyes at the words.

"Ah, Gom. You have no idea how much that means to me. I

was beginning to think I would never know what love was. I've never had it in my life at all, you know that. I was afraid I was too lacking, or would be unable to feel normal emotions, love and caring. You came along and the fear is gone. I know what love feels like. It's holding you, knowing you, spending time, and touching you. Your smile makes me melt inside. That's really girly sounding, huh?" In line with his no fear statements, Casey had not taken his eyes from Gom's through his whole speech.

Gom was unbelievably touched by Casey's words. For someone with his background with a lack of love and affection growing up, Casey's saying that Gom's smile made him melt had Gom near tears, just thinking about what it took to say something like that. Before Gom lost it completely, he pulled Casey to him and took his mouth with joyful intent.

He began walking, trying not to take his lips from Casey's. He'd seen this in movies and read about it books, but it was harder than it sounded. When they bumped into the door facing into the hall, Casey pulled away, grinning at Gom as he took Gom's hand and pulled him quickly to the bedroom.

Gom started removing Casey's clothes and with Casey following suit, they were soon pressed together, sighing in mutual delight.

"Are you sore, Gom? Were you okay today? I should have asked earlier." Casey smoothed his hands down Gom's back, slowing as he reached Gom's butt, caressing in smooth strokes. Gom pushed back into those tender touches, loving Casey for his concern. He made himself answer honestly.

"A little tender, but nothing I couldn't handle. I'm fine, really. The slight discomfort was worth it. Last night meant so much to me, Casey." Gom squirmed to get closer to Casey, doing that thing where he wanted as much of his skin touching Casey's as possible. Casey laughed again and that joyful laugh made Gom so happy.

"My little puppy. You tickle me when you do that," Casey admitted.

"Want to touch as much of you as I can," Gom said, chuckling, too. Laughing wasn't something Gom expected from lovemaking and he found that he loved it.

Casey eased them down to the bed, reaching for the drawer. Gom watched and noticed that there were a couple of towels on the nightstand. Casey must have put them there this morning, getting ready for the night. He liked knowing that Casey had planned for this.

Casey turned to him and Gom gave himself up to touch and taste, tenderness and love. He kissed and caressed along with Casey until they were once again straining to reach completion. Casey had reached down between them and was clasping their cocks together, his hand lubed and slick. Gom gasped and surged against Casey, knowing that he wasn't going to last very long at all. It didn't matter since Casey was right with him. They came within seconds of each other, Gom shooting first, holding Casey tightly as he jerked and shot streams of come against their stomachs. Casey followed and dropped his head to Gom's shoulder as he settled after splashing his own come to join Gom's.

"If you do your happy puppy thing now, we'll end up stuck together by morning," Casey mumbled.

"Mmm," Gom managed, able to manage a small grin at the vivid image in his mind.

Casey eventually reached for one of the towels and cleaned them up, sliding up to pull them together again after he dropped it back on the table. Gom planted kisses all over Casey's face and neck, light ones, quick ones, sliding ones that ended in small nibbles. He noticed that Casey moved slightly as Gom left his tiny kisses on him, giving Gom new areas to touch. Gom realized that Casey was unconsciously begging for more of the tenderness Gom was bestowing.

Gom set about covering Casey's whole body with his lips, tongue, and teeth. All the touches were gentle and loving and he watched as Casey's body soaked up the sensations as if he'd never been touched this way. Gom knew that he hadn't. From what Casey had told him about his encounters in the past, softness and loving touches had nothing to do with them, but Casey seemed to crave them now. Gom didn't stop until he was at Casey's toes, at which point he took hold of Casey's feet and pulled and turned, indicating that he wanted Casey to turn over for him.

Casey did as requested and Gom continued his quiet easy adoration of Casey's body, showing him how much Gom loved him in those soothing, loving movements that required nothing from Casey but acceptance. Actually, Gom figured it took a lot for Casey to lie still for his ministrations. The emotions and caring in the attention Gom was paying him was clear as Gom worked his way up to Casey's shoulders, ending with his lips and tongue teasing that spot at the back of Casey's neck. He watched the goose bumps and shivers take Casey.

Gom moved to lie on top of Casey, putting his face beside Casey's on the pillow, essentially enclosing him in an embrace that spoke of affection as well as love, something he thought Casey needed just as much.

"Gom." The whisper was barely there, but Gom heard it.

"Mmm?" he answered.

"I love you."

There was only one answer to that and Gom quietly repeated the three words.

Casey turned and Gom settled into the open arms waiting for him. Casey's kiss was sweet, soft, to go along with the caresses from Gom. They sighed and Gom fell asleep with his head on Casey's shoulder, wrapped tightly in his lover's arms.

ⵣ ⵣ ⵣ

Supper the next night was fun and Gom was happy to see Casey opening up to his dads and talking animatedly with Ben about plays. Gom told Ben about Casey's apartment and Ben got an invitation, which sent him over the moon. Trick was thrilled to see Casey again and they spent some time in Trick's room with Casey doing a good job of being impressed with Trick's things and complimenting him on how well he was doing in school.

The meal was delicious, of course, and they all settled with decaf coffee in the den as they talked about everything from school to work to sports to music. They didn't all agree on favorites, but that was fine. Gom caught both Soldier and Dillon at different times studying Casey and noticing how he would touch Gom as they sat beside each other on the couch. Casey had his arm across the back with his hand on Gom's other shoulder. Added to that, he would reach over with his opposite hand to touch Gom's leg or even his stomach at one point in a fleeting touch. Gom wasn't even sure Casey was aware of it, but it meant the world to Gom.

Casey was becoming a toucher, clearly craving that connection, and Gom was thrilled Casey felt safe enough to take what he needed from him, especially in front of his family. Gom thought if it was pointed out, Casey would freak out. Gom settled closer to Casey, being one who had always felt the need for closeness. It made the evening more than special to Gom.

Soldier and Dillon were both planning to attend the assembly at the school and looked surprised when Gom said that Casey was coming with him. He told them that Laurie was going to be there, too. Of course, Tommy and Daniel would be present. They were going to be quite an entourage. Talk continued for a few minutes about what might happen during the event, but none had any idea what all was going to occur.

"I just hope it has some kind of impact on those students." Gom knew his expression was glum, but he couldn't help the way he felt.

"I think you were more hurt by the ones who ignored what was happening to you than by Todd hitting you." Dillon understood.

"You're right. I can't get over it. I need to let it go."

Casey surprised Gom by hitting the nail on the head. "I think that their apathy and lack of compassion were as much a part of Byron's feeling of hopelessness as what the two jocks were doing to him. Not excusing *them*, but admittedly he agreed to the arrangement with them, clearly as a way to get by without being hurt. The hurt came from everyone else who perpetuated his sense of invisibility."

Gom just looked at Casey and noticed that Soldier and Dillon were doing the same. Gom hadn't divulged any of the confidential parts of the case to anyone, but a lot had been in the media, garnered from different sources. Casey had clued in to how Gom felt and what happened to Byron to make the statement that perfectly explained Gom's feelings.

Gom looked from Casey to his dads and knew his expression said, "See, he gets me."

Casey, noticing all the looks going back and forth got nervous, evidently, because he said, "I'm sorry. Maybe I shouldn't have said any of that."

Gom, ignoring the presence of his dads, turned to Casey and wrapped his arms around him. Casey looked stunned at the PDA, but didn't move away from Gom. He circled Gom's waist with his arms and watched closely

"You should never refrain from saying anything in front of me or my family. The strange looks were because you got it so right, Case. There were things in Byron's diary that I never told anyone, but without knowing all that, you figured out what tore him apart and recognized that it is what bothered me the most, too. Don't ever say you're not good with words. You slay me, in a good way." Wanting so badly to kiss Casey, Gom looked over and saw that both Soldier and Dillon had disappeared.

Gom took Casey's face in his hands and drew it forward so he could bestow the kiss he was dying to give Casey. Casey tightened his arms and they shared a kiss that spoke of love and understanding. Casey's insight into how Gom, and Byron for that matter, felt at the school, showed that he'd been paying attention and working to comprehend and empathize with Gom. Casey was showing a deep level of caring and support. He'd obviously spent time thinking about what Gom had gone through and how he'd felt. Oh, he was so in love with this man.

"You kissed me in front of your dads." Casey sounded stunned.

"Nah, they left. They probably knew I was going to have to kiss you and they're very good with the privacy thing. They don't kiss in front of us that much, though none of us doubt the passion they feel for each other. I saw them dancing together late one night when I was young, but they've never done anything that could be construed as," Gom put his fingers up in the quote symbol, "'unhealthy' for young people to be around. They're careful that way, but we've all grown up knowing how deeply they feel about each other. It was a good house to grow up in." Gom put his head on Casey's shoulder, soaking up his own version of that love.

"That's obvious. The degree of love they feel for each other and for all of you is evident in everything they do. I'm not jealous because I never had that, but I am glad I'm getting to see what it can be like." Casey's voice rumbled beside Gom's head and he tightened his arms around Casey.

"I'll be glad to share them with you. I have a feeling you won their hearts even more tonight."

They sat, holding each other for a good little while. Gom was comfortable in a way he'd never been before. He didn't feel the need to talk or kiss Casey or fill the silence with anything at all. Maybe he and Casey were merging their personalities and he would be able to calm down and enjoy being quiet with Casey and Casey would become more verbally responsive with Gom.

Eventually, Casey moved a little and Gom pulled back to look at him.

"You staying here tonight or you want to come home with me? I don't go in to work until three tomorrow night," Casey looked hesitant, as if after seeing all the love and caring in this house, Gom wouldn't want to leave it for his.

"Hmmm… my bed or *our* bed? What do *you* think?" Gom teased.

"Mmm, good point."

CHAPTER FIFTEEN

The gymnasium didn't look anything like it had before. The lighting was subdued and there were flowers in large pots, all white, set about. Each pot sat on a large square of what looked like plastic. Gom was sitting beside Casey, next to Dillon and Soldier. Laurie was in front of them, beside Tommy and Daniel. They sat in the middle of the bleachers about three rows up. The people on the dais were all wearing white choir robes, which Gom thought was a little strange. Even Ms. King had on a long flowing white gown. As Gom looked over the group, he began to grin.

"What?" Casey whispered.

"Looks like a pretty diverse group," Gom said, pointing subtly at the people in front of them.

Casey looked across the row and nodded. He said, "Got their point across without hitting anyone over the head with it. Clever."

Gom put his hand down beside his leg and Casey took it with his, threading their fingers together. Glancing around, he noticed a woman in black on the front row of the bleachers, her head down. She was pale and her eyes, when she looked up for a moment, were red. Gom figured her for Byron's mother. His heart bled a little for the pain she must be experiencing.

On the small stage that had been set up in front of the bleachers there were seven people. Ms. King, one of the black janitors that Gom remembered, an Asian man, tall and thin, and a short, overweight man who was going bald. There was a lady with long gray hair with two braids hanging down in the front sitting beside another who was beautiful, elegant, with upswept hair and pearls. The person on the end was in a wheelchair, one of the newer racing ones, it looked like. He looked to be very strong in his upper body. He had no lower body. Gom wondered how he'd lost his legs, or if he'd ever had them. He, too, was in a robe.

There was a large screen on the back wall and Gom had noticed a projector at the top of the bleachers when they were seated. He and Tommy had gone through a lot of videos and looked at sites on the computer that dealt with issues related to bullying. Gom hoped that some of them were scheduled for viewing today.

Right at ten, when it was set to begin, music began softly. Gom recognized it immediately as Katy Perry's "Firework". The lights got even dimmer and he, along with everyone else, craned his neck to see what was going to happen. From either side of the back of the gym he could see several people walking in. These people stopped, each in front of a flowerpot. As one, they bent and Gom could just make out that their arms were moving back and forth. Casey squeezed his hand and he tightened his. The mystery and sort of edginess of the events happening in the near dark were intriguing.

Next he noticed that all but one of the people on stage stood and, altogether, drew off their robes. The man beside the one in the wheelchair helped him draw his off. Gom could see the people in the back marching out.

The lights slowly brightened until what had happened became clear. There were gasps from the audience as everyone saw that what had once been all white was now a rainbow of color. The flower pots had been sprayed with paint, each one a different color, and as the people had marched out, they'd drawn the flowers together so that they made a beautiful and colorful arrangement.

So, too, were the people on stage now dressed in different colors. The gray-haired lady had on a tie-dyed dress that looked like it was from the sixties. The woman beside her had on a beautiful red suit that looked like it probably had a designer's name on it. The Asian man had on a navy suit and the large man beside him was wearing beige. The man in the wheelchair had on Army fatigues which sort of answered Gom's earlier question. The janitor was wearing his uniform which was green and Ms. King wore a gold-colored pantsuit.

"What do you think?" began Ms. King, "Do we look better now? Not quite as dull as before with everyone the same. I'd hate looking like everybody else. That's what our program is about today. Everyone is not the same. If we were, life would be dreary, uninteresting. As I look at you all I see every color in the rainbow and all sizes and shapes and that's how it should be. Right?" She got nods and mumbles of agreement.

"Let me start by saying that this assembly is too long in coming. No, let me correct myself. It is too *late* in coming. We are honoring a young man who went to this school. He didn't cause trouble, but that is all he knew. Without divulging anything from his diary, I will just tell you that he titled it 'Gateway to Hell'. Can you imagine how that makes me feel? How it should make you feel? The one place where a young person should be happy, healthy, free, excited, where he should be learning and preparing for a future, bright with hope and knowledge. Byron Neighbors killed himself right here because he could not take the degree of bullying he had known for almost two and a half years."

She paused, looking up at the audience, meeting eyes here and there, letting her words sink in.

"I've failed, we've failed, as a school, as a society, and as a community. We have a program planned, but before it starts, let me promise you this. Even though our signs says," her voice got louder for the next four words, "**ZERO TOLERANCE FOR BULLYING**, that's ridiculous. Someone working for me brought it to my attention that in a short period of time there were eleven instances of bullying noted. How short a period of time?" She paused again for effect. "Four hours. In four hours eleven different students were hurt, made to feel less in one way or another. That is just not acceptable. I didn't just take this person's report. I put on a disguise and went undercover, so to speak, and made my own notes. I'm almost too sick to tell you my findings. I spent a whole day walking these halls as a new janitor."

There were gasps and wide eyes as she waited for that to sink in, too. On the screen behind her appeared a picture of her in a green uniform like the other janitors, but she must have worn padding as she was very large, had thick glasses and you could see a couple of moles on her forehead and one tooth was blacked out.

Good Lord, Gom thought. She must have been laughed at all day. He knew how these kids could be.

"If you're wondering, and I hope you are, I'll tell you about my day. In seven hours, I saw and heard forty-three cases of bullying. These ranged from name-calling and teasing to tripping people and knocking their books out of their hands. Maybe I saw so much because my job that day and the way I looked made it easier to ignore me as someone unimportant and go right on with whatever mean things were planned. I listened to some of the worst language I've ever heard in my life and it was coming from *my* students. Kids who call me Ms. King, and show me respect every day. Oh, by the way, six of those forty-three cases of bullying were directed at me. Don't panic," she raised her arm and pointed her finger all along the bleachers, "I'm not going to do anything to the ones who called me names, or the one who tried to trip me. It's partly my fault."

Gom was as stunned as everyone else in the audience. He thought nearly all the people in the room were holding their breath.

"As a district, we've failed. But at this school, the fault is mine. Do not," she stopped, leaned into the microphone and said very loudly, "*Do not*, for one minute think that I haven't learned my lesson. I will carry with me to my dying day the blame for Byron Neighbors death. But it stops here, now, today. If you can't handle being at a school where people, all people, are treated with respect, then you can leave. Yes, parents, I'm talking to you. These are your children who are doing this. I will suspend anyone that I find touching another person in a negative way. Like it or not. I will put into detention any student that I find out has been calling names or teasing someone. That's for a first offense. Repeat it and you will face suspension. Any form of bullying will be dealt with. There are two students who will never step foot in this school again...three if you count Byron. That is over. All I can do is change the future."

Ms. King reached down in the podium and took out a bottle of water, opened it, and drank. Putting it back, she said, "I will also take action against any teacher or staff member who does not respond to and report bullying. I'm going to need help. I have to know when it happens, who is involved, and it has to be taken care of immediately. Yes, I want tattletales. Bring 'em on. Programs and plans will be explained as they take effect. Don't worry. I'm not saying everyone has to wear pastel colors and talk softly. I just want the hate and the fear and the ugliness to stop. And. It. Will." Those last three words were spoken with strong emphasis.

Gom and Casey, everyone really, was mesmerized. Those were some powerful words.

"We have some speakers today and there are some surprises, too." Ms. King looked around and said, "You didn't think I was going to talk the whole time, did you?" That got a few chuckles. She sat and the two ladies got up. Both put on head mikes and stood facing the audience.

Elegant lady said, "Stereotypes. Think about that for a second. Okay, time's up. Which of us is older? I am. Sally and I were in the same class, but I was held back one year. Which of us is richer? She is. She's a scientist. I'm married to a banker."

Now Sally spoke up to say, "Which of us is smarter? I am. I have an IQ of 145."

Before Sally could go on, the other woman spoke up and said, "I didn't even go to college."

Sally smiled at her and said, "Crystal was a cheerleader and homecoming queen. Everyone loved her. Which one of us is happier?"

They answered the same time, "I am."

The point was made.

Next the janitor and the Asian man stood up and took the mikes. After settling them on their heads, the Asian man said,

"Differences. Think about us for a second. Who would garner the most respect? Evidence shows that I would; dressed as I am in my Armani suit and Ferragamo shoes. Is this right? No, my name is Tommy Sang. I went to prison when I was twenty-two for armed robbery. I got out six years ago. Since then, I've gotten very rich working on computer gaming programs. But Thomas here," he pointed to the janitor, who stood quietly, "was in Desert Storm. He saved the lives of nine men in his troop when a bomb went off in their barracks. He carried men out two at a time, going back into the burning building again and again until it was completely engulfed. Don't make judgments. I'll always be richer, but I'll never be as good as this man." The janitor, still quiet, sat when Tommy did.

Next the overweight man and the one in the wheelchair headed for the front of the stage. The big man spoke first. "Bullies. You all aren't the newest best thing, you know. I was one, just like you. I teased and taunted and called names. I pushed and shoved and laughed at others. I thought I was a big shot. I was a punk. I used to be a good-looking hunk. Don't laugh, I was. I have kidney disease and the medicines I take cause me to be bloated and uncomfortable. I get it now. People look at me differently and even make fun of me. Me, Mr. Cool. I was an idiot." With that he turned to the man in the wheelchair. "This is Dan Rawlins. I used to tease him because he was uncoordinated and couldn't do sports without making a fool of himself. My words, not necessarily the truth. He went on to join the service and became one of the guys who handle the bombs. He was in the Special Forces and was decorated for his service and in Iraq he lost his legs. He went to war, fighting so idiots like me had the right to go around making fun of others. Where is the justice in that? By the way, Dan is also a gold medalist in the Paralympic Games. He'll be going to London next year for the next Olympics. Good luck to you and your team, Dan."

Dan spoke up, "Thanks, Bobby." Dan turned to the crowd. "I've been bullied all my life. Bobby was right. I was so uncoordinated I couldn't walk and chew gum at the same time. The service took care of that. Now I still can't walk. I still get called names and it still hurts. All I can say to you is to please think about what you say to others. You have no idea the effect it has on them. I'm stronger now and I can let it go. People your age haven't had time to build up enough strength to know how to not take those hurtful words inside themselves. Please, stop it." With that he took off his mike and rolled back to his place.

For a few seconds there was no movement on the stage. The crowd got a little restive wondering what was going to happen next. They'd been given a lot to think about. Gom was impressed with the program so far. Music started again and the lights got dim again. The screen lit up and there followed several of the videos and programs that he and Tommy had discussed. Famous actors, musicians, and other celebrities came on from the "Give a Damn Campaign", followed by still more in the "It Gets Better" program of videos. Gom sat, enthralled, though he'd seen most of them. One of the videos listed several stars who were gay. All were prominent in their field. He wanted to turn and seek out some of the students and see if they were paying attention, taking any of it in.

Not all of the small scenes were talking about gays, which Gom was thankful for. There were so many different types of bullying going on here.

Glancing at his watch, he saw that there were about twenty minutes left. The program had said an hour. He wondered what was next.

As the last video ended and the screen went black, Ronnie Daniels came on and said, "Hello, Baiden High." There were a few squeals from the crowd. Ronnie Daniels was one of the biggest country stars around and he was from Texas. "I'm sorry to hear about your loss. It saddens me to hear that the young man felt he had no one to turn to for help. Being different is not a bad thing. It's just a different thing. If you'll listen, I'd like to sing a song for you. It's from a" he put his fingers up, "'different' singer, but the words touched me and I'd like to do it for you. And I'd like to dedicate it to Byron Neighbors' memory."

With that, he strummed his guitar and the camera pulled back to show him sitting beside another man. The man smiled into Ronnie's eyes and winked. Whoa! Ronnie Daniels was gay? What do you know? Go, Ronnie. He looked happy.

Ronnie started singing, "Aftermath." It was from Adam Lambert's album and was reportedly one of Adam's favorite songs. The words were powerful and the message was clear. He sang about being true to yourself and not letting others pull you down and know that you're not alone. Gom was glad to hear it sung here. Troubled kids need to know that they aren't alone and that it would get better and that people gave a damn. If they could just hold on, find help, don't give up. All the things that were being said today in so many ways. Don't judge people for being different, don't make assumptions based on looks or perceived notions, and going back to the basic rule. Do unto others.

When the screen went black after the last note, Ms. King stood. "I hope you paid attention. Starting the minute this program is over life at this school will be different. If you can't get through your days without hurting others in any form, you will be dealing with me. To my teachers, staff, and students, I love you all. Make me proud." She paused, took a deep breath and said, "And I humbly apologize for the fact that this starts now instead of long before now. Before a beautiful young man felt so hopeless, fearful, lost, and alone that he couldn't go on. There are going to be programs put in place for students, or anyone, since it doesn't seem to be just the kids who are being treated unfairly, to seek help if they are being hassled in any form. You want to talk about a safe space? Baiden High is going to be a safe learning environment, starting right now. Thank you."

She turned from the podium to complete silence. Gom and his whole group stood and began applauding. Soon, the whole gymnasium was filled with thunderous applause and everyone was standing. He looked around and saw that there were more than a few tears. The students were stamping their feet and making a huge noise. He'd bet that those who'd been bullied were making most of that noise. How they must feel right now!

Gom looked at Casey, who smiled at him and then patted him on the back, showing his support in the knowledge that Gom was responsible for some of this. His hand met Soldier's as it came around Gom's shoulder for a hug. Casey and Soldier looked at each other and grinned in joint understanding.

As they were walking out, Gom thought about taking Casey's hand, worried about reaction, but then after thinking about it, he reached out and grabbed hold. Casey held on and though he didn't look over, he did grin. He knew what Gom was feeling, Gom had no doubt.

"Uh, Monty?" said a voice behind him. They all stopped and Gom turned to face the student. It was one who usually followed Todd and Josh, but didn't say much. This should be interesting, he thought.

"I'm sorry, really. If you want me to turn myself in to Ms. King, I will." There were actually tears in the kid's eyes. He looked down at Gom's hand, still held in Casey's.

"Is this your guy?"

Gom just nodded.

The student, Gom thought his name was Walsh, looked at Casey and then at Soldier and Dillon who now flanked both men. He simply said, "I'm sorry."

"I don't want you to do anything," Gom said, "except change. Be better than before. Learn something from Byron's death and today's program. Take care, man."

Gom reached to shake the kid's hand and after a few seconds, the boy took it and then turned away to disappear into the crowd.

"One down, how many hundred to go?" Soldier asked. "Let's go to lunch. I'm treating everyone at Jason's. You, too, Laurie. You have to get a lunch time."

Jason's was a very nice restaurant and suddenly Gom was hungry. He turned to Casey who nodded just as his stomach growled.

Casey looked up at Soldier and Dillon. "We didn't eat

breakfast. We were…"

"You don't have to finish that," Dillon teased.

Casey tilted his head and laughed. "We were nervous about the program, or Gom was, and I was nervous for him, with him." Casey turned to Gom and said, in front of everyone in their group, "And yeah, I'm your guy."

⚥ ⚥ ⚥

A week later Gom was a student again, this time in another neighboring county high school. He'd been called in when a note was found on the floor. It read, simply, "Faggot, you will die before the year is over. Your kind is poison. Careful what you eat!"

The problem came because no one knew who had gotten the note. It was found on the floor, near the principal's office. Actually, it had been stuck to the floor with tape so it wouldn't be swept away. Someone would have to handle it. After discussing it with the staff, the principal had called Captain Denny and asked if Gom could come and help them find both who received it and who had written it. They could hardly ask.

So Monty Marshall enrolled and began his next assignment. It was hard and disheartening, but Gom came home every day to, either the love and support from everyone at Scarcity Sanctuary, or the love and support from Casey Tanner. Most of his belongings had been moved to Casey's and they spent every night together. His home with Soldier and Dillon was still his base for his job, but now his life was with Casey, too.

Yesterday Casey had mentioned that the guy who owned the cleaning service was going to retire and had offered to sell out to Casey. When Gom asked him if that's what he wanted to do, Casey had thought long and hard before answering.

"Yes. It would mean less actual cleaning and more office work as there are several people working for him now. I would oversee and fill in if need be, but I'd be able to spend more time with you or at the theater. It would mean more money and someday we could move to a nicer place."

"I'm happy here, but Casey, we can move anytime you want to. I've got more money than I'll ever use. Basically, I live off my salary, but I've got a trust fund, we all do, that's huge and can be used however we want. How would you feel about a trip to New York to see a few plays and do the tourist thing?" Gom asked. It was something he'd been thinking about lately.

Casey's face lit up and the smile that appeared was Gom's answer. But Casey was Casey.

"I don't want to feel like I'm…"

"Do not go there. If it's mine, it's yours. We're not married, but we're together. If you ever want to leave me, you can, but I feel like I'm home. So everything is ours as far as I'm concerned. Don't ever think of us as anything other than equal. Got it?" Gom's voice was firm.

Casey just looked at him, his heart in his eyes. "Are you real?"

"Wanna feel me and see?" Gom teased. "Of course, I'm real."

"Leave you? Wait a minute, did you say if I want to leave you? Get over here. It would take a crowbar to get me away from you."

"Mmm, good." Gom took Casey's face in his hands and kissed him, soft and slow, building to heated passion. Casey started shuffling them toward the bedroom.

ጸ ጸ ጸ

The staff had tried to make note of any student who was no longer eating lunch at school. Of course that was hard as high school students didn't follow routines as a rule. The guidance counselor had been paying close attention to anyone who seemed nervous or scared. Nothing they had done or thought of had brought them any closer to finding either person.

For the first few days he went to classes and tried to listen to different conversations and see who stood out as being a hater. At lunch one day he said to the people around him that at the school he'd been at before a lot of people got into trouble for picking on queers. A couple of students ducked their heads, but one snorted in contempt and Gom had a starting place. He made himself look at the boy who'd made the rude noise and smile as if in approval.

The guy grinned back at Gom as if they were best buds and Gom felt hope that he'd find a trail now. As he took his tray back he saw the guy beside him dumping his and pitching it toward the window instead of setting it down like Gom did. The boy's tray slid across the top of the others and into the cafeteria worker behind the open window.

"Oops, my bad," the boy said, laughing. Gom was not amused. He wanted to ask the lady behind the window if she was okay since the tray hit her arm, but couldn't break from his character.

"So, what happened at your other school?" the kid asked, walking away with Gom.

"Oh, it was all over the news," Gom hedged.

"No way, dude. The kid who offed himself? Suh-weet. Took care of it himself, saving someone else the trouble."

No way, dude, Gom thought. It couldn't be this easy.

"You got a bunch of 'em here?" Gom asked.

"Some. Damn Faggots." Gom didn't have to be looking at his face to get the sneer on it.

"You let them get by with stuff?" Gom asked.

"You're awful nosy for a new kid," the guy said, suddenly and frustratingly showing some intellect.

"'S 'cuse me. You just seemed to feel the same way I do. Later." Gom walked off, not looking back but feeling like the kid watched him until he walked through the cafeteria doors. His heart was pounding and he stopped a few seconds to take a few deep breaths. He moved on a little and waited for the guy to come out. When he did, Gom asked the girl standing next to him what the boy's name was.

Her eyes got big and she said, "That's Mack Beard. If you're new here, you need to stay clear of him and his buddies. They hate everybody and they're mean, really mean." She walked off quickly.

So there was a group of them. There always seemed to be. In most of the cases he'd worked there were at least two and sometimes up to five people who hung together and harassed other students. There was usually a leader and the others followed along, feeding off the anger, minions of hate. What a mess!

Gom went through that day and the next waiting to see if he could make contact in some way with the group. To his distress, nothing happened. No one came up to him to confess to doing mean and hateful things to gays in the school. Damn. He was going to have to do something to draw their attention.

His chance came, interestingly enough, in the cafeteria. Gom had been given a list of the students who were out at school so when he saw Jason Hilyer sitting alone at a table he thought he'd found the perfect opportunity. According to the counselor, Kelli Young, Jason was a strong young man, not likely to crack under pressure. He was glad he could work his plan on someone who could handle it.

Gom used a deeper, scornful voice to say, "Yo, fag. This table taken?" Gom sat down close to Jason and scooted against him until the boy fell onto the floor. "Oops, clumsy much?" Gom laughed, dying inside at the look of pain on Jason's face. He applauded inside as the boy stood up and looked down at Gom and said, "Nah, just sometimes." Jason took his milk off his plate and turned it over, pouring it over Gom's plate. It splattered on the table and Gom's shirt. It was all Gom could do not to smile, laugh out loud and say "Way to go!"

Jason, looked Gom in the eye and said, "Oops." He picked up his tray and walked to the window, setting the tray down and speaking to the lady on the other side, thanking her. Gom would make a point of apologizing to Jason later.

As he headed for the door he was bumped, hard from the side. He stumbled and was pushed from the back into someone else. He felt like a pinball, all of a sudden. He heard laughter and turned to find Mack and his friends sneering at him.

"Dude, skunked by a fag. You lose!" It was the guy from the other day. Gom turned, looking angry to see him standing with two other boys. Gom wondered which one was the alpha, which the followers.

"Fuckin' faggot," Gom muttered, honestly hating the words as he said them.

The boy to the left of Mack looked Gom up and down and at some unseen signal all three boys turned and left. As they went out the door the boy looked back at Gom.

Gom wondered what the look was about. Maybe Mack had told him that Gom was asking too many questions earlier in the week. Either way, he figured he was about to find out one way or another. The day passed with nothing happening and he got home feeling frustrated.

Soldier knew immediately something was up and asked all the right questions. Gom told him all about what had happened and his feelings about the three boys.

"If I know you, Gom, saying that to this Jason kid is what has you so upset." Dillon was pretty smart, too.

"Yeah. I wanted to give him a high five when he dumped the milk over my tray. He's not as weak as some and not at all likely to be the one who got the note. Jason would take it right to the principal with a demand for justice. I like the guy."

Gom's phone rang with Casey's ringtone and he grinned as he took it out of his pocket. Soldier and Dillon both scattered as he said, "Hey, Case."

"Hi, hon. How was your day?" Casey asked.

"Sucked, but it's getting better. I'll tell you what I can when I see you, which will be when?" Gom asked.

"Good news. There is nothing going on at the theater for the next week. I have a break. Wanna go somewhere this weekend?" There was such hope in Casey's voice that Gom knew the Big Apple was what he had in mind.

"Hmm, I had actually had a longer stay than a weekend in mind, but we could do several little trips. Why don't you check out what plays are on and see if you can get us tickets for a couple. I'll arrange a couple of nice dinner reservations. Other than that, we'll play it by ear. Maybe just stay in our rooms and make love. Perhaps we'll have one nice dinner out, and a few deli meals in the room. I'm getting into this idea."

"I can't wait, Gom. I'll see you tonight. What do you want to do for supper?"

"Supper?" Gom had to get his mind off of the two of them spending time in New York.

Dillon walked by and said, in passing, "Pizza night. Sundaes for dessert. He's invited."

"Case, Dillon says…"

"I heard him. Sounds good. I'll be there. Ask him if he needs anything." Casey was beginning to fit in here with Gom's family and nothing made him happier.

"Dillon, you need anything for tonight?" Gom turned to his dad.

"Actually, I do. Randy's coming and I don't have any cherries. You know he has to have them or his sundae is not complete. If he doesn't mind…?" Dillon waited.

"Tell him no problem. I'll stop on my way over. See you soon, hon."

"You found him, didn't you?" Dillon asked as Gom put his phone back in his pocket.

"I did, Dillon. He's my Soldier. He makes me feel so much. I can't imagine being with anyone else. He lights me up inside." Gom knew he sounded goofy.

"Then you're right. You've found your Soldier. I'm so happy for you."

The man in question came in and said, "I heard my name. And why are you happy for Gom? Although, if you are, I am, too."

"He's happy because Casey does for me what you do for him and that makes him happy." Gom explained the previous conversation.

"Wow." Soldier drew Gom to him and gave him a hug. Clearly he was touched by the statement.

After the hug, Gom explained about the weekend trip they were planning. Soldier and Dillon jumped in and said they'd be glad to make reservations for them at the Manhattan at Times Square Hotel and suggested they go to a bar and grill called Gotham for a nice meal out. Gom was so looking forward to the weekend.

Supper was great and the feeling of family was wonderful. Casey had been accepted and he seemed so much more comfortable with everyone. Everything in his home life was going great. If he could just get something figured out at school things would be perfect.

Gom and Casey headed home where Gom had what he needed for school the next day. He pulled up right behind Casey and got out, meeting Case on the walkway that led to the steps to Casey's apartment. As soon as the door closed behind them, Casey wrapped his arms around Gom. That was so what Gom had been waiting for and he met Casey's lips eagerly. Casey's hands moved down Gom's back and Gom felt them sliding down into this back pockets, gripping his behind. He moved his butt back into those hands.

Casey pulled away and before Gom could complain, he pulled his hand out of Gom's pocket and held up a folded note. There was a question in his eyes.

"What's this? You writing me notes? How'd you know I'd find it?" Casey teased.

Gom said, "I didn't even know it was there." He was completely baffled.

Casey handed it over.

"What the hell?" he asked, stunned as he took the paper, unfolded it and read the words.

"Meet us before school under the f_ball bleachers if

you're up for some fun with a fag."

"What is it? Gom, are you okay? You're white as a ghost," Casey said, locking the door and pulling Gom into his arms.

Gom turned the paper to Casey and watched his face as Casey read the words.

"Shit. That's creepy. How'd it get there if you didn't even know it? Damn. What are you going to do?"

Gom thought for a second and said, "I don't know how. Wait," he thought back to earlier in the day, "I bet it was in the cafeteria when they bumped into me. They kind of pushed me from one of them to the other for a bit. I wondered what that was all about. Somebody's got skills because I never felt them putting it there. I'm calling Captain Denny. I want that place covered and I'm going to show up like I'm up for whatever they've got planned. I'll make sure whoever they're after isn't hurt…if I can. I'll let the police take me in with the others, but I'll branch off after we get to interviews. I'll see if I can find out anything during the scene about the threat. If I'm lucky this weekend will be a celebration for two reasons." Gom was calming down. He went toward the couch.

"Two reasons?" Casey asked, head tilted as he followed Gom.

"Well, yeah. Time with you is the first one. I can't wait to be away from everyone and have an adventure with you. We're going to have a ball." Gom pulled Casey down onto the couch beside him and settled into the arm Casey put around him. He dialed his commanding officer.

He explained what had happened today at school and what he'd just found in his pocket. He didn't see any reason to explain that it was Casey who'd found the note during a heated embrace. He had no doubt that the three boys who'd stopped him today were the ones who put it there. He'd really made no contact with anyone else.

Casey got up and headed for the bedroom while Gom finished his call with the captain. When he closed his phone and got up, he went through the bedroom door and saw that Casey had turned the bed down and way lying across it, his underwear still on. Gom's surprise must have shown on his face because Casey chuckled, holding out a hand to him.

"Tonight, I'm going to hold you until you fall asleep. You have a hard morning ahead and you need to be alert and ready for whatever happens. We don't have to make love every night to show how we feel. Right now, you need to relax and sleep well. I want to do that for you. Come here, hon."

Gom felt such love for Casey, his man of few words, who always seemed to find the right ones. He shucked his clothes quickly and settled in with Casey. Snuggling into Casey's side, reveling in the feel of his skin on Casey's, Gom sighed deeply.

"Don't start that happy puppy thing or my good intentions will go out the window," Casey ordered.

Gom laughed, his breath hot on Casey's neck. Casey turned and kissed his forehead, letting his lips trail down his cheek to his mouth. Gom opened for him and they shared a kiss like none other. It was like Casey was trying to keep it simple, not push for anything deeper. What it did, was touch Gom's heart and make the kiss one that filled him with a glow and a sweet feeling. He finally drew away and settled against Casey's shoulder, slid his arm over Casey's stomach and felt Casey's over his back, grasping his hip.

Gom murmured, "Is it this easy?"

Casey's voice rumbled in his chest, "Is what easy, hon?"

"Love. Finding the one, falling in love, finding out they feel the same way, and then feeling such intense happiness. I thought there was supposed to be such angst and heartbreak involved in the whole process. It's what I expected, anyway. All the movies and songs make it seem so impossibly hard." Gom was afraid it had all happened so quickly and was so good that it surely would be taken away somehow.

It was a while before Casey answered, but he spoke, finally, his hand smoothing over Gom's back.

"Maybe the powers in the universe decided that your life to date has seen enough pain and heartache, starting early on. You've dealt with a lot and now you face ugliness and hate daily in your work, too. It's time for Gom to have something good without any angst, as you call it. Don't question it. You deserve it. Go to sleep, hon. I love you, heartbreak free." Casey turned to kiss Gom's head.

"Heartbreak free," Gom sighed. He tightened his hold on Casey and smiled into sleep.

The next morning Gom woke to the smell of bacon and eggs cooking. Casey had gotten up early to fix him breakfast. How sweet. He dressed hurriedly and went in just as Casey put plates on the table and turned to pour coffee. Gom needed to get Casey into the whole orange juice thing. He had to have it often or he went into withdrawal like others did with caffeine. Orange juice, besides tasting delicious, made him feel good inside. It was something that had been important to him since he was eight and Soldier had showed up with it and thrilled the boys at Dillon's house. Since then, Soldier'd kept them all supplied with it steadily.

With a strong hug and a long kiss for strength, Gom headed for school, early. He parked and headed for the football bleachers. Not knowing what to expect had him nervous and worried. There wasn't time for nerves since he heard voices as soon as he got under the edge of the bleachers. Why did these guys always choose that location to do their dirty work? He felt a small bit of déjà vu from when he'd found the guys hassling Bradley.

He came upon the three boys from yesterday, Mack and his friends. The guy who had looked at him for so long was standing back a little and watching as the other two pushed a young man around, back and forth, roughly. Gom's first instinct was to rescue the kid. Not possible yet.

"There you are. 'Bout time," Mack said, with a sneer, right before putting his fist against the victim's shoulder and pushing him back toward the other boy who was working with him to intimidate and humiliate the young man Gom was there to help. Hopefully.

"This little faggot didn't follow directions. He needs a lesson." The guy who was watching filled him in.

"What was he supposed to do?" Gom asked.

"Die." The guy answered Gom's question without hesitation and with complete seriousness. It was all Gom could do not to gasp and roll his eyes.

He looked at the boy and wondered if he was the one who'd gotten the note. The poor young man was still being pushed back and forth between the other two. Gom wanted this over.

"So, what's the plan?" He stepped forward, placing himself between Mack and the boy. The ring leader stepped over and leaned down to whisper something in Mack's ear. Mack nodded and looked at Gom.

"John thinks you need to prove your good intentions, your desire to join us in getting rid of this poison that is infiltrating our lives." The venom in the words was chilling and Gom's heart raced when he heard the word poison, the same word used in the note.

"So, what? You told him to just die and he didn't? We've got a plan, I take it?" Gom asked, looking at the guy Mack had called John.

"He was warned."

That was enough as far as Gom was concerned. He pushed for a little more.

"What do you want me to do? Let's get this over with," he said, looking at John.

John smirked and pulled out a switchblade, flicking the button and extending the blade. Gom forced himself not to react as he reached for it.

"How far am I going in this demonstration of my good intentions toward the group?" He wanted to pat himself on the back for sounding so menacing and eager to take part in this farce.

"I want his pretty face scarred and a solid cut somewhere like his stomach or back." Gom just looked at the hatred in John's face for a second. He had to remind himself that this was a high school student. The kid was every bit as evil as a hardened criminal! Knives and threats and talking about death like it was *nothing!*

Chills ran down his spine as he turned to face the young kid whose eyes were huge in his ashen face.

Gom put the knife down by his leg and walked right up to the guy he was supposed to disfigure and then stab. Jesus.

"Let him go," Gom said to Mack and the other guy, whose name he'd not gotten yet. "I'll take over from here. Watch and learn, boys." The two moved away and went to stand beside John.

Gom went behind the kid and put his arm around his neck from behind. He growled something ugly, he didn't even know what, to cover the sound of the blade going back into the knife handle. He pushed the knife hard against the guy's back, causing him to jump and yell. Gom made it hurt, but it was just his hand and the end of the closed knife.

There were shouts and suddenly the five of them were surrounded by policemen. The knife was taken from him and he was cuffed before he could say anything. Thank you, God, was all he could think of, anyway. There was yelling and cussing and Mack and John tried to pull away from the officers, but that didn't work. Gom's relief was so strong he had to work hard at seeming to be pissed at being stopped from his mission. He struggled some to make it look good. They were all put into different cars and taken from the area. Gom told his officers to make sure and find out for sure that the kid was the one who'd received the note. He felt sure he was, but if that was the case, he was done here.

New York and being alone with Casey was looking better all the time.

He was hidden at the station and fed information as it came through. The boy's name was Tim Dodd and he was, indeed, the one who'd gotten the note and left it to be found. It also came out, from Mack and the other follower, that it was John who had written the threat.

Gom felt like his job was doing good things, but they were hard-won victories. He needed to see goodness. He wanted supper with his whole family and he *needed* Casey.

When he finally left the building he was surprised to see Casey waiting for him. His heart soared. He was shocked, but he didn't question his good fortune. Gom had come out the rear of the building so was shocked to see his love standing there, leaning on the hood of the car, legs and arms crossed, smile right there for him.

"I don't know how you knew to be here, but I haven't been so happy to see someone since I was eight and Soldier came back after disappearing for a few days. I thought he was gone for good and when he came back it was like Christmas." Gom was babbling, but he was so freaked out. Casey opened his arms and Gom walked into them, hiding his face in Casey's neck, breathing deep.

"I'm so proud of you, hon. You saved a boy's life today. From what the principal told Soldier, that boy was destined to die and you managed to turn things around. I love you so much. You're a hero, Gom."

"Right now, I'm just glad it's over and so damned happy that you're here." He tightened his arms around Casey and held on.

"Soldier and Dillon say we're to come for supper with the whole family at six tonight. Until then, you're mine." Casey slid his arms down to pull Gom even closer, making Gom want.

"Take me home and make love to me. I can't think of anything I need more, well, except dinner and the family, but that's for later. Now, it's you and me. Take me home, Casey."

"You got it, hon." Casey let him go and they got into the car, heading for home.

They hurried inside and Gom headed straight for the bedroom and then the shower, Casey following. For some reason neither felt the need to talk. Gom soaked up the care that Casey was showing him as he bathed and shampooed Gom slowly and gently, then himself very quickly. Stepping out, Casey drew Gom to him and with a big navy towel, he dried Gom, taking great care with him.

Gom thought about feeling bad about seeming so needy with Casey, but he was enjoying the attention and frankly, he did need it. He was just thrilled that Casey was so clued in to him that he realized it and provided it. He made a promise to return the favor when they got to New York. He would blow Casey's mind. Right now, he needed for Casey to make long sweet love to him. He had to counteract the violence and hatred of the morning with love and joy. Casey was perfect for the job.

Casey drew Gom to the bed and eased him down, following closely. Casey covered Gom from head to toe, pressing him down into the bed, grounding him in skin and sensation. Gom would have wiggled if he could, knowing that Casey would laugh with him. Gom put his arms around Casey and hugged him hard, loving the strength in the embrace.

"You seem to know just what I need. That means so much to me. I love you, Casey." Gom was getting emotional and didn't want to go there. He moved his hips upwards, nudging Casey's and got the response he was hoping for.

Casey chuckled, his face beside Gom's on the pillow. "I love you, too, hon, more every day. That surprises me, you know? I thought you just loved someone. I wasn't aware that it could grow and get bigger and be just more than anything I'd ever imagined." With that, Casey had evidently talked all he could handle and he moved his head over to take Gom's lips with his.

Gom brought his arms up to wrap around Casey's neck, holding him there, letting him in, allowing Casey to sink into him, literally and figuratively. Casey was taking him over and he gave himself up to the experience. Casey started slowly, pushing his tongue inside, teasing, questing, taking, but always softly. Gom let go and accepted Casey's successful efforts at making the rest of the world go far, far away. He became lost to sensation and sweet desire.

"God, Casey, you make me feel so good, so loved. Don't stop, okay?"

Casey pulled his head up and looked at Gom, smiling gently. His look said it all and Gom sighed, smiling back.

"You ready for some 'Gom's sake'?" he teased, referring to their words while making love the first time.

"Mmm, for *Casey's* sake, too." Being with Casey was more than Gom had ever dreamed. His heart filled with love for this man. Gom pushed on Casey's shoulder, following the push until he was on top of Casey, moving against him, earning that grin. He bent down so he was closer to Casey's mouth and he sighed at the next words.

"For *our* sake," Casey whispered the words, his lips soft against Gom's lips.

His man, his beautiful man who didn't talk much, didn't like to be touched. Ha! Gom didn't think he could possibly be happier. He set about proving that very thing to Casey, no words needed.

ABOUT THE AUTHOR

AKM Miles loves to read M/M. She loves to write. She loves characters. A good story line is great, she figures, but if you don't care anything about the characters, why would you care what happens to them? That's pretty much why and how she writes.

She loves, absolutely loves, to hear from readers. She's quite tickled when the emails she gets all say something along the lines of… "When is Daniel going to get a story?" or "I'm still waiting for Gom's story?" "What about Randy, that Brack and Austin helped. Will he get a story, too?" and "You are going to write one about Mark and Wade, aren't you?"

That shows that people love the characters in AKM's books and that's why she writes. She loves it when readers love her guys. Often called for being too mushy or romantic or sweet and told that guys don't talk like that, she replies, "Actually, yes, they do." Her motto is ***love is love*** and she believes that guys do feel deeply and care deeply and if they're happy people, they don't mind sharing that love. It's a good thing.

Keep up with AKM by checking out her website at www. akmmiles.com. There are many ways to reach her, though. To talk, use the email (she loves to hear from readers) akmmiles@yahoo.com

To look, use the following:
http://bookworld.editme.com/akmmileshomepage
http://www.facebook.com/akm.miles
http://www.goodreads.com/author/show/2869347.AKM_Miles

Trademarks Acknowledgment

The author acknowledges the trademark status and trademark owners of the following wordmarks mentioned in this work of fiction:

Armani: Giorgio Armani S.P.A.

Cracker Barrel: CBOCS Properties, Inc.

Ferragamo: S-Fer International Inc.

Gotham: Gotham Bar & Grill

Jersey Boys: Marshall Brickman and Rick Elise

Manhattan at Times Square Hotel: The Manhattan at Times Square Hotel

Miss Saigon: Claude-Michel Schönberg and Alain Boublil

Subway: Doctor's Associates Inc.

Taurus: Ford Motor Company

The Lion King: Disney Enterprises, Inc.

The Phantom of the Opera: Andrew Lloyd Weber

Timex: Timex Group USA

Wicked: Winnie Holzman and Stephen Schwartz (based on book by Gregory Maguire)

THE TREVOR PROJECT

The Trevor Project operates the only nationwide, around-the-clock crisis and suicide prevention helpline for lesbian, gay, bisexual, transgender and questioning youth. Every day, The Trevor Project saves lives though its free and confidential helpline, its website and its educational services. If you or a friend are feeling lost or alone call The Trevor Helpline. If you or a friend are feeling lost, alone, confused or in crisis, please call The Trevor Helpline. You'll be able to speak confidentially with a trained counselor 24/7.

The Trevor Helpline: 866-488-7386
On the Web: http://www.thetrevorproject.org/

THE GLBT NATIONAL HELP CENTER

The GLBT National Help Center is a nonprofit, tax-exempt organization that is dedicated to meeting the needs of the gay, lesbian, bisexual and transgender community and those questioning their sexual orientation and gender identity. It is an outgrowth of the Gay & Lesbian National Hotline, which began in 1996 and now is a primary program of The GLBT National Help Center. It offers several different programs including two national hotlines that help members of the GLBT community talk about the important issues that they are facing in their lives. It helps end the isolation that many people feel, by providing a safe environment on the phone or via the internet to discuss issues that people can't talk about anywhere else. The GLBT National Help Center also helps other organizations build the infrastructure they need to provide strong support to our community at the local level.

National Hotline: 1-888-THE-GLNH (1-888-843-4564)
National Youth Talkline 1-800-246-PRIDE (1-800-246-7743)
On the Web: http://www.glnh.org/
e-mail: info@glbtnationalhelpcenter.org

If you're a GLBT and questioning student heading off to university, should know that there are resources on campus for you. Here's just a sample:

US Local GLBT college campus organizations
        http://dv-8.com/resources/us/local/campus.html
GLBT Scholarship Resources
        http://tinyurl.com/6fx9v6
Syracuse University
        http://lgbt.syr.edu/
Texas A&M
        http://glbt.tamu.edu/
Tulane University
        http://www.oma.tulane.edu/LGBT/Default.htm
University of Alaska
        http://www.uaf.edu/agla/
University of California, Davis
        http://lgbtrc.ucdavis.edu/
University of California, San Francisco
        http://lgbt.ucsf.edu/
University of Colorado
        http://www.colorado.edu/glbtrc/
University of Florida
        http://www.dso.ufl.edu/multicultural/lgbt/
University of Hawai'i, Mānoa
        http://manoa.hawaii.edu/lgbt/
University of Utah
        http://www.sa.utah.edu/lgbt/
University of Virginia
        http://www.virginia.edu/deanofstudents/lgbt/
Vanderbilt University
        http://www.vanderbilt.edu/lgbtqi/

Stimulate yourself.
READ.

www.manloveromance.com

THE HOTTEST M/M EROTIC AUTHORS & WEBSITES ON THE NET

CPSIA information can be obtained at www.ICGtesting.com

224047LV00001B/15/P

9 781608 203154